THE COMING

In Those Days the Sun will be Darkened

BORTOLAZZO
Publishing

A Last Days Trilogy

THE COMING

In Those Days the Sun Will Be Darkened

PAUL BORTOLAZZO

~ Author of *'Til Eternity*

"...IN THOSE DAYS,

after that tribulation, the sun will be darkened, and the moon will not give its light; the stars of heaven will fall, and the powers in the heavens will be shaken. Then they will see the Son of Man coming in the clouds with great power and glory. And then He will send His angels, and gather together His elect from the four winds, from the farthest part of earth to the farthest part of heaven."
Mark 13:24–27

DEDICATION

This novel is dedicated to Christians who will overcome the accuser of the brethren by the blood of the Lamb and the word of their testimony.

How will the days of the Great Tribulation (Satan's wrath against the saints) be shortened? Our Blessed Hope will do this by gathering up believers before the wrath of God is poured out on this Christ-rejecting world.

After the sun, moon, and stars lose their light, the Son of Man will come with His angels, and they will gather the dead in Christ from heaven.

Then overcomers alive on earth will be caught up together with them in the clouds.

Amen and Amen!

TABLE OF CONTENTS

First Seal : The White Horse

"Now I saw when the Lamb opened one of the seals...And I looked, and behold, a white horse. He who sat on it had a bow, and a crown was given to him, and he went out conquering and to conquer."
Revelation 6:1-2

It was just after midnight when Pastor Mark Bishop fell to his knees behind his cherry wood desk. He had heard from the Holy Spirit before in his cramped study, but tonight was different. The burden pressing upon him was urgent, like the birth pangs before the delivery of a baby.

"Holy Spirit, what do you want me to do?"

Mark shuddered when he saw a vision of a scarlet beast. This grotesque animal had seven heads and ten horns.[1]

"Is this from the Book of Revelation?" he gasped. "Doesn't this hideous creature represent Satan's kingdom in the last days?"

Instantly the border of Israel appeared in his mind. Invading her were armies from Iraq, Pakistan, Lebanon, Iran, Jordan, Syria, Turkey, Egypt, Libya, and Ethiopia. These ten horns were following a world leader.[2] The Abomination of Desolation was written across his forehead.[3]

Continuing to pray, Mark saw many faces trapped in a valley of decision. This vision was for the body of Christ. It was all part of God's plan. Any moment now, a heavenly event will trigger a sequence of events affecting the lives of every man, woman, and child on earth. Waiting on the Holy Spirit into the early morning hours, the young pastor prayed for the interpretation of the faces in the valley of decision, the ten nations attacking Jerusalem, and the identity of their leader, the Abomination of Desolation.

God the Father sat upon His Throne with a scroll in His right hand. [4] The outside of the scroll was sealed with seven seals. It was time.

A strong angel cried out, "...Who is worthy to open the scroll and loose its seals?" [5]

In the midst of the heavenly host stood the Lamb of God, looking as if He had been slain. A rainbow was on His head. His hair was white like snow. His eyes were like fire, His feet like fine brass. [6]

Receiving the scroll from His Father, Jesus opened the first seal.

One of the four living creatures before the throne thundered, "'...Come and see.'" [7]

A rider on a white horse appeared with a large bow. A crown was given to him. [8] Angels instinctively stepped back from the evil exuding from this mysterious rider. He was smiling as he looked toward earth.

A warrior angel announced, "Woe, woe, woe, the rider of the white horse is coming to conquer those on earth. Satan will soon persecute the saints of the Most High by giving his power, his throne, and his authority to one man." [9]

A nervous Mark Bishop hadn't eaten in three days. Lying on the sanctuary floor of his church, he pleaded, "Holy Spirit, I don't understand what's happening to me. The vision You gave me is still fresh in my mind. The invasion of Israel by surrounding Muslim nations is clear enough. It's coming and no one is going to stop it. I get that much. It's the identity of this world leader called the Abomination of Desolation that's troubling."

Bowing his head he returned to prayer. It was near ten in the evening when the Holy Spirit gave the young pastor the interpretation of the vision.

"Listen carefully, My child, the events you saw in your vision are coming. The faces in the valley of decision represent billions of people. Each person will be given an opportunity to choose who they will follow. From Satan's scarlet beast kingdom, having seven heads and ten horns, a world leader is emerging. He is going to deceive many believers by proclaiming Jesus is the Christ." [10]

Mark lay perfectly still. These words were not audible but were directed to his spirit. He knew this was a divine visitation.

"Satan will eventually give his power to American President, Joshua Kayin. For those who overcome the accuser of the brethren by the blood of the Lamb and the word of their testimony, they shall call Kayin the Abomination of Desolation." [11]

Before Mark could answer, a holy fear gripped his heart.

"Holy Spirit, how is this possible? President Kayin is the world's champion against Islamic terrorism. He was the one who proposed the roadmap of peace for Israel. He goes to church and regularly quotes the Bible. How can he be the Antichrist?" [12]

Two nights later, thousands of Jews and Palestinians were ecstatically celebrating side by side. Every major news agency was filming this historic event.

"Good evening, this is Natalie Roberts reporting to you live from Jerusalem. Just moments ago, on October 8th, the most holy day of the year for Jewish people, Yom Kippur, began. With the sun setting, Israel's Prime Minister, Avi Rosen, signed the Jerusalem Peace Accord with the Palestinian Authority and the Middle East Federation. This Federation consists of Iraq, Pakistan, Lebanon, Iran, Jordan, Syria, Turkey, Egypt, Libya, and Ethiopia. This treaty is an answer to prayer for Jews and Arabs alike." [13]

The Israeli Prime Minister was joyfully shaking hands with the President of the United States as photographers took a picture that most thought would never happen. Leaders from around the world were applauding his diplomacy. This man of peace had skillfully stopped the bloody fighting in the Middle East. In a decisive move which ended the killing, Joshua Kayin convinced the sworn enemies of Israel to allow the Jewish people to rebuild their Temple atop Mount Moriah. In exchange for peace, over two million refugees were granted permission to safely return to their own Palestinian state. To the shock of many Jews, an eastern portion of Jerusalem has been set aside for a Palestinian capital.

Israeli Prime Minister, Avi Rosen, gratefully announced, "Peace has finally come to the land of Abraham, Isaac, and Jacob. God has sent President Kayin to help us stop this needless killing. Now we can rebuild our Temple so our High Priest may once again offer atonement for our sins."

Many celebrations were underway. At one treaty signing party, a jubilant Israeli soldier reflected, "Think of it, a covenant of peace with people who have fought for over two thousand years. I wonder why it took so long for such a simple, yet convincing treaty."

Indeed, this day was historic. It would impact two worlds, the spiritual and the physical. Events were unfolding that would soon shake the reality of Christian and non-Christian.

She could hear her girls laughing in the living room. Julie Bishop was in the kitchen preparing Hope and Lindsey's favorite breakfast. Dressed in faded blue jeans, a yellow t-shirt, white Reeboks, her long brown hair was pulled back. Curls fell along her face, framing her sparkling blue eyes and always ready smile.

Mark was in his study praying over the Jerusalem Peace Accord, a covenant guarantying the end of the Muslim Jihad against the Jewish people.

"I don't understand Holy Spirit. Didn't I see the Antichrist and his ten nations invading Jerusalem? As Christians, aren't we to pray for the peace of Jerusalem?" [14]

Sensing there had to be more to his vision, he returned to prayer. It wouldn't take long. Under deep conviction, he froze.

"Beware; the 70th week of Daniel has begun. The first seal of the heavenly scroll has been opened. The rider of the white horse is coming to conquer. This day I have called you to be a Watchman to the body of Christ. [15] To those who have ears to hear, you must proclaim the events warning of the coming of the Son of Man." [16]

Pastor Mark Bishop had just been given the most powerful end time prophecy any believer could ever receive. Even so, his doubts seemed so overwhelming.

"Holy Spirit, I'm asking You to teach me. [17] Only You have the power to show me these events in the Word of God."

Miraculously, the Spirit of God led Mark to I Corinthians 15:50-52, I Thessalonians 4:13-17, II Thessalonians 2:1-4, Matthew 24:3-31, Revelation 6:1-17, and 7:9-14. Minutes turned into hours as he studied these passages. Like pieces of a puzzle, the events were falling into place. Sitting amidst his Bibles, lexicons, and concordances, the pastor whispered, "How did I ever miss this? It's the gathering of believers to heaven out of the Great Tribulation." [18]

"That's not true," hissed the spirit of Doubt. "The church is long gone before the Great Tribulation begins."

"No one knows that," pressed Unbelief. Trying to gain a stronghold, the demon threatened, "If you teach this new revelation, your denomination, your pastor friends, even your own family won't believe you. Why risk your reputation over the timing of the coming of the Lord?" [19]

After commanding these demonic spirits to leave in Jesus' name, Mark felt a comforting peace. The events warning the elect had always been there.

"How can I be sure?" he candidly asked.

The reply in his mind was from the Holy Spirit.

"Before this month is over, I will send you another Watchman. His name is Stephen. He will need your prayers as well as your encouragement. Remember, My child, you will not be held responsible for those who refuse to heed what the Spirit is saying. There are divine appointments awaiting you. Many believers will be saved as you proclaim the truth of His coming. Fear not what man can do but honor Jesus by obedience to His Word."

Demons clawed and spit at each other for a better view of the rider of the magnificent white horse. Gazing upon the two world leaders Satan looked pleased. American President Joshua Kayin and Israeli Prime Minister Avi Rosen were intently watching the Pope address the United Nations via satellite.

"For such a time as this, God has brought together the sons of Abraham. As His children we all worship the same God. I firmly believe the Jerusalem Peace Accord is the result of constructive dialogue between the leaders of Judaism, Islam, and Christianity. The only way for us to ever achieve a lasting world peace is to work together in eliminating religious intolerance. The future of humanity is at stake as we reject all forms of violence between the nations."

"Peace comes with a price," whispered the spirit of Death.

The Jerusalem Peace Accord would usher in a false peace, an agreement Isaiah called a covenant of death to the Jewish people. [20] Another holocaust will soon take place after a massive Gentile army invades Jerusalem. [21] All because the world refused to recognize the intentions of the rider on a white horse. [22]

THE SIGN OF YOUR COMING

"...What will be the sign of your coming..."
Matthew 24:3

From the dark hallway, she could see him praying in his study. He looked anxious, almost pale. This time she wanted to help, at least try. Mark could barely hear her knock.

"You ok, hon?"

"It's hard to talk about, much less believe."

"Can you share it with me?"

Handing him a hot cup of coffee they sat together on their small couch.

"Julie, do you remember Professor Wynn? I had him for Eschatology in my senior year at Bible College."

"You mean Mr. Excitement? No one got as wound up as Wynnie when he taught on the rapture. He once lost his voice shouting, 'No man knows the day or the hour.'" [1]

"Did you believe him?"

"You mean about Jesus coming at any moment?"

"Wynnie called it imminence. He stressed there are no events left to be fulfilled before the rapture. Jesus will secretly catch up His elect just before the Antichrist appears on the world scene."

"To be honest, it's way too controversial. Winning souls should be our focus. Jesus will come when He wants to."

"This past year I've regretted not teaching more on His second coming. Our denomination's rapture position is written in stone. Every year I have to agree to teach it. Their dogmatic interpretation has always bothered me."

"Even when you were in college?"

"I'm afraid so."

"What about now?"

"Recently I met some pastors who believe the Blessed Hope will deliver the saints from the persecution of the Beast. In II Thessalonians 2:3, Paul warns believers not to be deceived by those teaching the day of the Lord comes before the Man of Sin reveals himself." [2]

"So you're having doubts?"

"Most of these ministers were forced to resign."

He was already feeling the responsibility of being a Watchman. It felt like a giant weight upon his shoulders.

"Julie, when was the last time you had a vision?"

"It's been a while."

"Last Monday night I was interceding for the Jewish people. While praying I saw a vision of Israel's border. The armies of ten Muslim nations were invading an unsuspecting Jerusalem." [3]

"Did the Holy Spirit give you the interpretation?"

"Yes, this invasion of Jerusalem is in our future. It's going to take place in the middle of Daniel's 70th week prophecy." [4]

"It's been awhile since I studied Daniel. How about a quick review, hon?"

"I've never taught the prophecy of Daniel 9:24-27 at our church."

After taking a sip of hot coffee, she smiled and asked, "Why not start with me?"

Her encouragement was something he never took for granted. Even on their wedding day, Mark knew he was marrying a giant in the faith.

"Ok, sweet one, I'll try. In 539 B.C. the angel Gabriel prophesied to Daniel two critical events. The first was the exact day the Messiah would be killed. [5] The second is the exact day Jesus will return and forgive Israel of their sins." [6]

"Now I remember. Since Israel refused to repent, the Jewish people have to suffer seventy weeks of Gentile domination. [7] One week equals seven years. Gabriel predicted Israel would reject their Messiah after sixty-nine weeks (69 x 7 = 483 years)."

"You nailed it, Julie."

"Didn't this Gentile domination begin when the Jewish people were given permission to rebuild Jerusalem?"

"The seventy weeks began in 445 B.C."

"And when was Jesus was cut off?"

"Jesus Christ was crucified in 32 A.D. Exactly 483 years from the decree by King Artaxerxes to rebuild Jerusalem." [8]

"What an awesome prophecy," marveled Julie. "So there is still a seven-year period left before the Messiah can physically return and save a remnant from Israel."

"It's called the 70th week of Daniel."

"Doesn't this seven year period begin when an evil leader confirms a false peace between Israel and her enemies?" [9]

"It just happened."

"You can't mean the Jerusalem Peace Accord?"

"It appears so."

"Are you saying President Kayin is the Antichrist?"

"I believe this is from the Holy Spirit. Now that it has been confirmed, I'm going to share it tomorrow morning from the pulpit."

This pastor from Bethany Assembly didn't have much time to prepare. He wasn't fully grasping the consequences of such a warning, not yet.

"Father, Julie and I come before You as Watchmen to the body of Christ. Our prayer is for You to open their ears. They need to hear Your voice. Let them search Your Word and prepare for the spiritual warfare that's coming." Raising his hands high, he cried out, "Give my family a passion for you, Lord. Empower us to speak forth this end time warning under the anointing of the Holy Spirit."

Choir members were enjoying coffee and donuts in the activity center when the Bishops arrived. Lindy and Allie Hart, sisters in their early twenties, greeted Hope and Lindsey. Even though several parishioners were surrounding Mark, no one except Julie could discern the intense struggle raging within his spirit. His sermon this morning was only forty minutes long, but it would forever change the lives of the Bishop family.

The young pastor carefully scanned the audience, a body of believers he had known for only a year. There was a buzz of excitement in the air due to Israel's peace agreement with the Palestinians. Those interested in Bible prophecy were praying for Mark to preach on the dramatic changes in the Middle East. After several worship songs and the reading of announcements, he was ready to address his congregation.

"Welcome, saints. This morning I'd like to share a powerful message from the Holy Spirit concerning our future called, *The Sign of Your Coming.* Let's turn to Matthew 24:3."

The rustling of pages was a sound he loved to hear.

"Tuesday night before His crucifixion, our Lord sat with Peter, John, James, and Andrew atop the Mount of Olives. 10 A few days earlier He shared His death, burial, and resurrection with His twelve disciples. 'Behold, we are going up to Jerusalem, and the Son of Man will be betrayed to the chief priests and to the scribes. They will condemn Him to death and deliver Him to the Gentiles to mock and to scourge and to crucify. And the third day He will rise again.' 11 For some of His disciples, like Thomas, it was hard to believe."

"Hallelujah," praised a senior saint. "C'mon, Pastor, let the Holy Ghost lead you."

"With the death of their Savior about to transpire right before their eyes, the disciples had one question burning in their hearts. They asked, "'What will be the sign of Your coming and of the end of the age?'" 12 Church, the disciples weren't asking for an exact date of when Jesus would return. They wanted to know the sign that would warn of His coming. Jesus answers by exhorting believers to be ready by watching for a specific sequence of events. 13 After these events take place, every eye will see the Son of Man coming in the glory of His Father for His saints."

"What events?" blurted out a deacon sitting in the first row.

"Jesus said, 'when you see all these things, know that it is near at the doors.' 14 What things is Jesus talking about? Saints, I stand before you this morning as a Watchman with a warning for the body of Christ. 15 Now how many of us are watching for the events which will signal His coming is right at the door?"

Scanning an audience of over two hundred, the pastor's heart sank. Only a few knew what he was talking about. How could this be, Mark silently pondered. Some of the members of Bethany Assembly had known Jesus as their Savior for over forty years. How could he make them see?

"At this time I would like to share a pearl I experienced last Monday night. When I say pearl, what I really mean is a special moment I had with the Holy Spirit. I'm talking about a divine visitation that was very precious to me and my family."

Several members who had brought guests looked uneasy. Peeking toward their friends, they just smiled. Others, who didn't believe in the gifts of the Holy Spirit, silently prayed for their inexperienced pastor not to embarrass himself.

"In the past, I have shared some pretty wonderful pearls with friends who basically could care less. Surely, we have all experienced the deep pain of opening ourselves up to friends, only to have our precious pearls trampled on as if they meant nothing."

Billy B whispered to himself, "Something's not right. Father, may You use Mark to inspire us to become overcomers for Jesus."

The well-liked deacon signaled to some young adults to begin interceding.

"This past week I received a powerful vision from God. The first image in my mind was an ugly scarlet beast. It had seven heads and ten horns. Then I saw Israel being invaded by the armies of ten Arab nations. Suddenly a deep valley, called the valley of decision, appeared. It was filled with many faces. For three days I fasted and prayed for the interpretation of this vision. Thursday night I received the answer."

"He's at it again," grunted a senior saint. "God's talking to him again."

Pausing for a sip of water, Mark couldn't help noticing the youth group sitting on the very edge of their seats. To his left sat the choir who really only listened when the worship leader was talking. The head usher just sighed and shook his head in disgust at the young preacher's emotionalism.

"The interpretation came with such conviction; I just knew it was from God."

His congregation didn't look happy. Mark had faced this intimidation before but this time it was different. God had given him an opportunity to preach on the coming of the Lord. It was now or never. Suddenly, three events flashed in his mind. In the past, Mark chose to compromise in order to keep his job. The major tithers of his first church threatened to leave if he continued to teach so much on holiness. Later, the Holy Spirit moved in prophetic words inspiring several young adults to enter the full-time ministry. The church board immediately expressed their opposition to such emotional antics. After the Bishops arrived at Bethany Assembly, the worship leader refused to tarry for the presence of the Holy Spirit, insisting the parishioners favored a more strict set of hymns. In all three instances, Mark surrendered to the spirit of Control. When the Bishops accepted their first pastorate, Satan knew the damage they could do to his kingdom. The spirits of Lust, Greed, and Pride, stepped forward for the coveted assignment. Satan knew better. The devil already had thousands of pastors hooked on pornography through the Internet. To his delight, a fashionable prophet had just made wealth his top priority. The enemy was especially proud of a Bible teacher from Tulsa, Oklahoma. Recently this highly esteemed leader lost his ministry after being corrupted by the approval of man.

"Imagine," mocked the spirit of Religion, "believers having a form of godliness but denying its power." 16

Several were begging to attack the Bishops but to no avail. In this case a specific demon would be picked by the devil himself. This foul spirit would oppose God's anointing in church services, intercession for lost souls, prayer for the baptism of the Holy Spirit, healing for the sick, and deliverance for those being tormented by demons. 17

The spirit of Control boldly stepped before Satan's throne. Once the command was given, this filthy demon was filled with the overwhelming desire to control Mark Bishop, his family, and the members of his church.

IF YOU WILL NOT WATCH

"...Therefore if you will not watch, I will come upon you as a thief, and you will not know what hour I will come upon you."
Revelation 3:3

What could he do? He had a family to support. They were dependent upon him. Standing motionless behind the large wooden pulpit, his head bowed, he could hear nervous whispers throughout the sanctuary.

Seated in the first row a popular Sunday school teacher named Harriet Jones gently asked, "Pastor, are you okay?"

In his mind, Mark heard, "The Lord is my helper; I will not fear. What can man do to me?" 1

Lifting his head up, he bravely asked, "How many of us believe Jesus Christ has a prophetic plan for the overthrow of Satan? That's right. Jesus is coming back to deliver believers from the wrath to come before taking back spiritual and physical rule of this earth." 2

The sporadic cheers revealed the spiritual division among the membership. Even so, the boldness bottled up within Mark by the spirit of Control was breaking forth.

"The interpretation of the vision I received from God is sobering. The final seven years (70th week) before the Messiah physically returns to earth began yesterday with the signing of the Jerusalem Peace Accord. In Revelation 13:1, John describes Satan's end time beast kingdom having seven heads and ten horns. Last night, ten Muslim nations (horns) signed for peace with Israel! The faces I saw in the valley of decision represent billions of people who will be given the opportunity to follow Jesus Christ or the Antichrist."

An irritated Harriet Jones hastily interrupted, "No one knows the identity of the Antichrist."

"Please listen to me! In the Book of Revelation, John saw a heavenly scroll sealed on the outside with seven seals. 3 This scroll contains the wrath of God. When the seals are opened, the scroll will unravel and God's wrath will be poured out upon the wicked."

"What does that have to do with us?" shouted the head usher.

"The first seal of the scroll has been opened by Jesus." 4

"How can you be sure, Pastor?" challenged a choir member.

"The rider of the white horse is coming to conquer those who dwell on the earth."

The youth group erupted out of their chairs. For the young people, the cheers were electrifying. But for most of the members, it was downright embarrassing. Seated in the back row, Deacon Dwayne Pressley wasn't happy with such sensationalism.

Turning around to see if anybody was listening, Harriet interrupted again.

"Pastor Bishop, I don't understand what you're trying to teach us this morning. Are you saying the seven year tribulation period has begun? How is that possible? The rapture must come before the Antichrist appears. Everyone I know believes this."

Without any hesitation, Mark boldly shared, "Harriet, the answer to your question isn't what you're expecting. The 70th week of Daniel began yesterday when ten Muslim nations from the Middle East Federation signed for peace with Israel."

An eerie silence swept over the congregation.

From the ceiling, the spirit of Lying snickered, "They won't believe you."

"In Daniel 9:27, an evil world leader confirms a seven year covenant with Israel. In the middle of this covenant he breaks the peace by invading Jerusalem with armies from Muslim nations. This is when the Abomination of Desolation defiles the Jewish Temple. 5 This is what I saw in my vision."

"What Temple?" snapped someone from the second row.

"The Middle East Federation has given the Jewish people permission to rebuild their Temple just north of the Al Aqsa mosque."

"Some of these Muslim nations are already having doubts about supporting this Jerusalem Peace Accord."

"All ten horns will eventually give their power to the Beast." 6

"Let's be realistic, Pastor," interrupted a retired minister. "Look at how many times preachers have falsely predicted the arrival of the Antichrist. No one really knows."

"I understand what you're saying. The apostle Paul warns us not to be deceived by those who teach the saints will not face the Man of Sin. 7 His true identity won't be revealed until he breaks the peace with Israel by invading Jerusalem in the middle of the 70th week. This is when he will exalt himself above God."

Beads of perspiration were already dripping from his forehead.

"I know for most of you this is a shocking revelation. Please don't tune me out. The most critical truth revealed to me this past week involves the events which will warn us of the coming of the Lord. Jesus wants us to be ready by watching for the opening of the first six seals of the heavenly scroll."

"So what if we don't?" scoffed Harriet. "God is always with us."

"For those who refuse to repent and watch, Jesus promises to come like a thief." 8

A youth leader raised his hand.

"Pastor Mark, are you saying we are supposed to watch for the four horsemen in the Book of Revelation?"

"Yes, the rider of the white horse has come. In the next three and a half years we are going to see the red horse of war, the black horse of famine, and the pale horse of persecution. The pale horse will initiate the Great Tribulation in the middle of the 70th week. 9 This is when Satan gives the Beast authority over the nations. Now why is the devil going to give his power to one man?"

After an awkward silence, it was obvious that no one was willing to reply. Perched on the back pew, the spirit of Fear was laughing at those hopelessly paralyzed.

"The Beast is going to war against the saints who refuse to worship him, his image, or to receive his mark." 10

Mark could easily sense waves of disapproval after mentioning the mark of the beast.

"Hey, Dwayne," chuckled a visitor in the direction of the deacon. "When did your pastor begin believing Jesus couldn't come at any moment?"

Seated on the back pew were two retired missionaries.

"What do you make of this?"

"It's really confusing. He lost me a long time ago."

"Saints, let's be watching. Jesus, Paul, Peter, and John warn believers who see these events not to be deceived. We have relentlessly been taught that the next event on God's prophetic calendar is the rapture of the church. We've been led to believe the body of Christ will be taken to heaven before the Great Tribulation begins. This is not what Jesus taught."

Sensing the warfare, several teenagers bowed their heads and began interceding for their pastor.

"In Matthew 24:21-22, Jesus is warning believers who will face the persecution from the Beast during the Great Tribulation. I challenge everyone here today let us overcome this evil world leader by the blood of the Lamb and the word of our testimony." 11

Frank Donnelly, a well respected deacon and close friend of the Bishop family sincerely asked, "Pastor, as born again believers, aren't we already overcomers?"

The reaction engulfed the sanctuary as the older saints sat with their arms tightly folded across their chests. Sporting an attitude much like the Pharisees in Jesus' day, they thought of themselves as more mature than their inexperienced pastor.

An excited freshman from Lakeview High named Drew Henley stood.

"Pastor, is the Great Tribulation the wrath of Satan against the saints or is it the wrath of God against the wicked?"

Ned, Drew's twin brother then asked, "Pastor Mark, are you saying the coming of the Son of Man is the rapture of the saints?"

Hurrying down the aisle Dwayne Pressley raised his hands.

"Church, Pastor can't possibly answer all your questions this morning. So everybody take out a piece of paper, write down your questions, and I will gather..."

For a brief moment, Mark saw what he was up against. He knew he would never be able to be a faithful Watchman if he continued to yield to the manipulation of man.

"Excuse me, Dwayne; I'm not quite finished yet."

The surprised deacon smiled and sat down on the front pew.

"Obviously, we all have questions concerning our Lord's coming for His saints. With this in mind, the Holy Spirit is leading me to focus on God's prophetic timetable of end time events. This also includes intercession, end time evangelism, and spiritual warfare."

"Hey Pastor," interrupted Drew, "who do you think the Antichrist is?"

Looking into their eyes, Mark dreaded their reaction to his next statement.

"I believe the Antichrist is our President, Joshua Kayin."

An alarmed mother sprang to her feet and insisted, "Pastor, isn't it a bit dangerous to over-react like this; especially over a so called vision from God?"

Pastor Mark never hesitated.

"This isn't blind faith. Ask yourself, how prepared will you be when the mark of the beast becomes law during the Great Tribulation?" 12

"Is this some sort of playacting skit?" smirked a deacon's wife to her husband.

"The only way to be ready is to watch for the events Jesus gave us. 13 Let's pray."

The demons of Control, Fear, and Compromise were already sowing their lies. God's truth had been proclaimed. Now the spirits of darkness would attempt to deceive.

In the church foyer, Mark was greeting those leaving. Julie was praying when their eyes met. She had been there in the past, when the spirit of Control overwhelmed her husband. The discouragement for not standing for the truth had affected the man she loved in a devastating manner. When they were first married, Mark loved God and was led by the Holy Spirit. Standing for righteousness was something he always enjoyed. It was different now. After two years of pastoring, the constant battles had caused him to grow weary. His desire for revival and holiness had been replaced with prayers for unity and tolerance.

As she took his hand, Julie could see the Lord had performed a supernatural miracle. The spark of God was back in his eyes; the fear of man was gone. Tears flowed down her cheeks as they embraced.

Do I Seek To Please Men

"For do I now persuade men, or God? Or do I seek to please men?
For if I still pleased men, I would not be a bondservant of Christ."
Galatians 1:10

While Pastor Bishop greeted members of the church, the Board met in the activity center. The four deacons looked perplexed, not knowing which direction their meeting would take. Frank Donnelly was the first to speak.

"I would like to say how proud I am of Pastor for taking such a courageous stand on what the Holy Spirit has shown him. This type of preaching will put the fire of evangelism back in our church."

The naive deacon was not prepared for the reply.

"But is it biblical?" scolded a skeptical Dwayne.

Dwayne Pressley was in his mid-fifties, married, and had two daughters. The short, slightly graying CEO of his own consulting firm, trusted no one, especially those in leadership. Hovering above the deacon, the spirit of Control was hoping to tighten its grip before the pastor arrived.

"We need to stick to the Scriptures, not to some vision supposedly coming from God. Looking back, I feel like we might have jumped the gun last year when we voted Mark in as our pastor. You can only allow these spiritual gifts to go so far and then you begin to turn people off."

"I'm afraid Dwayne's right," affirmed Kevin, the youngest member of the board.

Kevin Collins was an officer in the Air Force, in his early thirties, and just recently married. Elected to the Church Board a year ago,

Kevin always went by the book and most of the time he didn't see eye-to-eye with his pastor, especially on spiritual issues.

"In my opinion, our Pastor crossed the line by broadcasting the Holy Spirit told him our President is the Antichrist. As Board members we cannot allow such..."

The officer was finishing his rebuke when Mark pushed through the double swinging doors leading from the sanctuary. He took a seat at the head of the kitchen table. Two deacons were seated on each side, each pleading silently for some sort of justification on what just happened.

Ever since receiving the interpretation of the vision on Thursday night, Mark had fervently prayed for this very moment. He knew the strengths and weaknesses of each deacon. Some had been on the Board for years, while others seemed uncomfortable in their new role of leadership. The real issue before them was not one of experience or intelligence, but whether these men had the spiritual ears to hear what the Holy Spirit was saying to the body of Christ. They needed spiritual discernment, a gift that comes through prayerful intercession. Pastor Mark knew Dwayne Pressley and Kevin Collins didn't believe in visions, especially like the one he described this morning.

Standing to his feet and with a soulful stare, Dwayne shared, "I've got some bad news for you, Pastor. Your interpretation of this vision has a lot of people shook up. Honestly, I'm very concerned about what this will do to our youth group. Last month, when Pastor Lance was out of town to visit family, I was able to show a film on the rapture. After seeing this excellent movie on the last days, I believe a lot of the questions our kids had were answered. Quite frankly, your new interpretation concerning the timing of Christ's return can only bring confusion. Billy B, what do you think?"

Billy B was a quiet man who drove a heavy duty rig for a living. He was not the kind of person who would interrupt or dogmatically push his opinions on anyone. Recently, the single, stocky trucker had just finished teaching a class on the Book of Revelation to the college and career group. As a young boy growing up, he attended the Bethany Baptist Fellowship. He was taught the most literal interpretation of Christ's gathering of the saints was a secret at any moment rapture. But the more questions the young adults at Bethany

Assembly asked, the more doubts he was having about the timing of the rapture. With all eyes upon him, the trucker nervously cleared his throat.

"I believe our young people will be okay if the truth of His Word is taught through the witness of the Holy Spirit. After teaching the Book of Revelation, I must say I've got some serious doubts about a secret catching up before the Great Tribulation erupts. What I mean is, huh, aren't we supposed to be looking for the glorious appearing of our great God and Savior, Jesus Christ?" 1

"So what's your point?" pressed a restless Dwayne.

"Well don't you think that would be pretty hard to do if the scriptures didn't tell us what to look for? Didn't Jesus warn believers to watch for the events taking place before His coming? But instead of understanding the eternal consequences of these events, most just say no one knows, cause of all the fussing and arguing."

Immediately, a heated dispute erupted between Kevin and Frank.

"What we need is a study of the events warning us the coming of the Son of Man is near. I'm talking about a study with meaningful debate. Pastor, do you..."

"Sounds like a plan," interrupted an impatient Kevin. "The problem is we need answers today. The Glovers told my wife they're going to leave our church if Pastor can't scripturally prove the Antichrist comes before the rapture. I have to agree. God speaks to me through His Word, not by emotional impressions supposedly coming from Him. Trust me; when the Beast and his false prophet show up in Jerusalem, the church will be long gone."

An awkward silence settled over the meeting while the young pastor carefully weighed his next words.

In his mind Mark heard, "'For do I now persuade men, or God? Or do I seek to please men? For if I still pleased men I would not be a bondservant of Christ.'" 2

"Gentlemen, let's open our Bibles to I Thessalonians 4:15-17. Paul is teaching believers about the coming of the Lord. Verse 17 is about the catching up of the saints from the wrath to come. Catching up in Latin is translated rapture. Someday Jesus will descend from heaven in the clouds, with a loud shout, with the voice of an archangel, with the trumpet of God. Alive believers will be caught up together with Old and New Testament saints who have died. Together, this vast multitude will receive their resurrection bodies for eternity. On the same day the saints are delivered, God will pour out His wrath on a Christ-rejecting world." 3

"Pastor Mark, does the wrath of God have a name?"

"Yes, Frank, it's called the day of the Lord. Peter warned us this day would come like a thief in the night and the earth will be burned up. 4 Paul wrote, 'But you, brethren, are not in darkness, so that this Day should overtake you as a thief.'" 5

"So when does the day of the Lord begin?"

"His wrath will begin when the seventh seal is opened and the heavenly scroll unravels. When you compare scripture with scripture, the events taking place before the coming of the Son of Man fit together perfectly."

Kevin condescendingly added, "This is just your interpretation."

"I'm sorry," interrupted Dwayne, "but I'm not seeing this. Famous prophecy teachers Arthur Lawrence, Gene Lloyd, and Tom Bray, all teach Jesus can come at any moment. C'mon, Pastor, if the Antichrist comes first, then we would be looking for him and not our Blessed Hope."

"The Thessalonians were confused too. Especially when false teachers taught that they had missed His coming and entered the day of the Lord. Paul wrote, 'Now brethren, concerning the coming of our Lord Jesus Christ and our gathering together to Him, we ask you ... Let no one deceive you by any means; for that Day will not come unless the falling away comes first, and the man of sin is revealed, the son of perdition.'" 6

Shaking his head, Kevin Collins couldn't believe the Board was wasting so much time on such a non-issue.

"If the Antichrist comes before the rapture, then Jesus can't come at any moment. Are you saying His imminent return is a lie?"

"This past week has been a whirlwind for my family. After putting the events together, there seems to be an obvious pattern."

"How so, Pastor?" asked a curious Billy B.

"It was late Monday night when I had the vision of the valley of decision. After three days of fasting, I received the interpretation late Thursday night. Deep down in my spirit, I knew this was from God. Even so, I still struggled with the magnitude of the message. It wasn't until yesterday morning that my doubts disappeared."

"What doubts?" sighed a cynical Dwayne.

"The Antichrist has to broker a false peace with Israel before the Son of Man can come back and gather us to heaven. Yesterday the entire world watched as the Jerusalem Peace Accord was signed."

"No man knows the day or the hour."

Mark quickly glanced up at the ceiling before answering.

"The misinterpretation of Matthew 24:36 is going to have eternal consequences for many believers. This is why the Holy Spirit has promised to send us another Watchman who will speak the truth concerning the coming of the Son of Man."

"Is this really from God?" challenged an annoyed Kevin. "And where do you get this Watchmen stuff from anyway?"

Mark knew it was time to seek the Holy Spirit for His leading.

"Brothers, let's pray for spiritual discernment over the events which will soon transpire."

As they bowed their heads to pray, the spirits of Control, Compromise, and Fear huddled together in the far corner of the activity center.

"This time the preacher didn't give in," hissed Fear. "His past failures aren't affecting his decisions anymore."

Control and Compromise weren't listening. They were already plotting their next attack against the saints from Bethany Assembly.

A WATCHMAN

*"Son of man, I have made you a watchman...therefore hear a word
from My mouth, and give them warning from me."*
Ezekiel 3:17

Four days later, a couple from Santa Barbara, California, arrived on a
rainy Thursday afternoon. The evangelist and his wife seemed to fit
right in as they were introduced to the Bethany Ministers Seminar
Committee. Several of the most prominent churches in Bethany were
represented. The Committee was led by the charismatic pastor from
Bethany Baptist, the Reverend John Ryals.

Earlier in the summer, members of the Committee voted to
schedule an evangelist for their annual Fall Bible Prophecy Seminar.
The topic: The Rapture of the Church. 1

It was late afternoon as the Committee gathered at the hotel
where the Corbins were staying. The seminar would be held at the
adjoining Robert E. Lee Conference Center. There was a sense of
excitement of how God had divinely inspired this event.

"Reverend and Sister Corbin, I would like for you to meet Pastor
J. W. Brown from Bethany Presbyterian. J.W. has been a close friend
of my family for many years."

"Greetings, my brother in Christ," smiled Pastor Brown. "It's His
will you and your pretty wife can join us for such a time as this."

"Like I told my congregation last night," added Pastor Ryals, "we
need to get back to the Bible and stop playing around with all these
new teachings. My great grand pappy used to ride the circuit trails and
preach how Jesus could come at any moment. There was no
confusion or debate; it was just simple faith," chuckled the rotund
pastor. "God said it; I believe it; that settles it."

"Thank you," beamed Stephen. "This is my wife, Michelle. This is our first time preaching in the great state of Alabama."

A line quickly formed to the evangelist's left as Chairman Ryals introduced the rest of the Committee.

"I would like you to meet Pastor Elmer Dyer from Eastside United Methodist Church, Pastor Allen Colson from Calvary Community, Pastor Louis Cooper from Lakeview Assembly of God, Pastor Floyd Stanton from Shepherd of the Hills Lutheran Church, and Deacon Dwayne Pressley from Bethany Assembly."

Dwayne just recently met with Pastor Ryals over the confusion dividing Bethany Assembly. When the displeased deacon asked for counsel on how to biblically handle the problem, Pastor Ryals cautioned him to go slow and allow God time to reveal the truth. This was not the type of counsel Dwayne was hoping to receive. He had to continually fight the urge to convince the lay leadership to vote Pastor Bishop out and seize control of the church.

"It's so nice to meet you all. Michelle and I believe it is God's desire to bring revival to your city this week."

"You're certainly an answer to our prayers," offered a hopeful Pastor Ryals. "Tomorrow morning we'll have some prayer and a review of our three night seminar. Let's meet here at ten o'clock."

"Thank you for such a wonderful reception," shared Michelle, a petite strawberry blonde with a charming smile.

After exiting the hall, the couple from California thanked the Lord for such an open door of ministry.

The deacon lingered while the other pastors emptied out of the hotel lobby.

"Brother Corbin, may I have a word with you? It's such a divine appointment for you to come and teach our young people. You have no way of knowing, but there are pastors in Bethany who are teaching our President is the Antichrist. I know God is going to use you to refute such heresy."

Michelle was silently rebuking the spirit of Control when Stephen asked, "Thanks for the encouragement, Dwayne. Say, what is your pastor's name?"

"Uh, well, his name is Mark Bishop."

Not waiting for a reply the distracted deacon made a hasty retreat out of the lobby.

The next morning, Hope and Lindsey Bishop were getting ready for school. Playfully racing down the stairs, they were excited about completing their assignment. Julie had promised her girls a surprise for memorizing fifty verses from the Book of Revelation. Dark clouds were hovering overhead.

"Mom and Dad must be planning a trip to the lake for us," predicted an eager Lindsey.

"It's going to be awesome," added Hope as the phone rang. "Hello... sure, let me see if he's available."

Jogging down the hall, the slender teenager respected her father more than anyone else in the world. Peeking into his study, she could see his unshaven face and disheveled reddish brown hair. He had just finished praying.

"It's for you, Daddy."

"Thanks, Hope. This is Pastor Bishop. May I help you?"

"Good morning, Pastor, I'm Reverend Corbin. I've been invited to speak at the Prophecy Seminar this weekend."

"Why of course, I've heard the announcements on the radio. Julie and I are looking forward to it."

"That sounds great. The Seminar begins tonight at seven. Michelle and I would really like to pray with you and your wife to touch the lives of those attending."

"It would be a pleasure. So what are you teaching on tonight?"

"My message is, 'The Coming of the Son of Man: One Taken, One Left.'" 2

"Ah, yes, Matthew 24:40. What exactly has the Holy Spirit revealed to you concerning His coming?"

"Before the Son of Man can come back and gather His elect, many saints will be overcome by the Beast. Actually, I was called to be a Watchman over a year ago."

Mark paused before asking his next question.

"Reverend Corbin is your first name..."

"Please call me, Stephen. So can you and Julie meet us in the Conference Center tonight at five?"

"It would be a pleasure."

"Excellent my brother, we need to be prayed up, the beginning of sorrows has begun. God bless you."

Mark froze while listening to the dial tone.

"It's God! It's God! The Holy Spirit has sent His Watchman just like He said!"

The Spirit of Control detested such praise. Immediately this foul spirit decided to persuade other demons to join forces in order to deceive those attending tonight's seminar.

It was a little before ten in the morning. Just as the couple entered the Robert E. Lee Conference Center, Committee Chairman John Ryals waved for the Corbins to join him at the head table. Pastor Louis Cooper of Lakeview Assembly of God opened with a short prayer. Pastor J. W. Brown of Bethany Presbyterian read the minutes of their last meeting and shared the Seminar schedule for the next three nights. Chairman Ryals then stood to express his approval.

"God is good. Isn't it a joy to see Baptists, Methodists, Presbyterians, Lutherans, and Pentecostals coming together under the banner of Christ? The Bible says, 'Salvation is found in no one else, for there is no other name under heaven given to men by which we must be saved.'" 3

A chorus of amens echoed through the hall.

"Tonight," bellowed the distinguished orator, "believers from all over our state will be visiting our great city to hear one thing; Jesus could come at any moment. The scriptures exhort us to be watching for our Blessed Hope. 4 At the age of twelve, my Momma used to say to me, "Johnny, you'd better get saved because Jesus could split the eastern sky at any moment and the saints will be caught up. You don't want to be left behind, do you?"

"Not me," hollered a jovial Dwayne Pressley.

"I thank God for ministers who teach the truth concerning the rapture of the saints. I got saved because someone cared enough to tell me the truth, no matter what it cost. Tonight, we need to be ready to answer any questions our young people might have. They deserve the plain truth."

Their smiles clearly motivated John to continue.

"It's so encouraging to see different denominations represented here today. Even though we differ on doctrinal views such as communion, worship, even baptism, we can all agree the most critical doctrine inspiring Christians today is the imminent return of our Lord Jesus Christ."

The utter emotion from his voice demanded a response. Rising to their feet, the Committee members offered a standing ovation.

Dwayne Pressley noticed the evangelist and his wife weren't clapping. It appeared the Corbins were reflecting on what had just been said. The deacon didn't have a good feeling about this blonde, blue eyed, preacher from California. There was something about him he couldn't put his finger on. An inner voice kept telling Dwayne this polished evangelist had come to confuse the churches.

Pastor Floyd Stanton of Shepherd of the Hills Lutheran Church stood and announced, "There will be six out-of-town buses arriving at five o'clock. We have twenty volunteers ready to feed these kids, compliments of Max's Barbecue."

Seated in the first row, Max Larson waved and smiled.

"That's all I've got to say, Pastor Cooper."

The Reverend Louis Cooper leads the largest Pentecostal fellowship in Bethany. Just recently, during an all night prayer meeting, two members of his church were supernaturally healed, one of Aids, and the other of cancer. Both would be testifying on the second night of the seminar.

"My brothers in Christ, I want to thank you all..."

"Excuse me, Louis, may I speak?"

Pastor Cooper glanced over at the Chairman. John Ryals didn't like interruptions. Reluctantly he waved his hand.

Pastor Elmer Dyer pioneered the Eastside United Methodist Church twenty-five years ago. The community looked upon his faithfulness as a shining example of what Bethany stood for. Slowly shaking his head, the Methodist pastor did not look happy.

"This morning I come to you with a heavy heart. What I am about to share isn't pretty. As some of you may already know, Pastor Mark Bishop of Bethany Assembly prophesied last Sunday morning the seven year tribulation period has commenced. He is predicting the Jerusalem Peace Accord is a covenant of death for the Jewish people. Furthermore, Mark actually believes the President of the United States is the Antichrist."

Their disgust said it all. Over the years, every pastor here had to deal with hyped-up teachers predicting everything from the exact date of the rapture to the end of the world.

"Now, you all know Mark and I are good friends. When his family moved to Bethany, our church was the first to make Julie and the girls feel welcomed. We have found him to be friendly, hardworking, and faithful to his family. He is a servant who unites with other pastors in order to reach our city for Christ. But someone has to publicly draw the line when it comes to personal prophecy on end time events."

"Tell the truth," shouted Dwayne.

"First of all, the Word never says the Antichrist comes from America. Second, we can't be living inside the tribulation period because our Lord will never pour out His wrath on the church. And finally, if Christians have to first face the Antichrist, then the imminent return of our Lord Jesus Christ would be impossible. Of course, we all know that couldn't be true because the apostle Paul taught that Jesus could return at any moment."

Most were trying to grasp how such a wonderful pastor could be so deceived.

"Now I know how persuasive Mark can be. To be perfectly honest, so can the Mormons, the Jehovah Witness's and the Seventh Day Adventists. My brothers, we need to understand the consequences involving this type of false teaching. When Pastor Bishop warns believers not to take the mark of the beast, I, as a minister of the gospel must strongly object. My God never motivates His children through fear. Any pastor who teaches the bride of Christ will be persecuted by the Man of Sin should be publicly rebuked. We cannot allow such scare tactics to frighten our children. Our God is a God of love, not wrath."

It was close to five when Mark arrived at the hotel. Julie decided to stay home with Lindsey who was running a high fever. Michelle Corbin felt led to intercede from their hotel room while Stephen and Mark met in a small office at the Conference Center. Mark was kneeling in prayer as Stephen paced the room praising God for the opportunity to teach the truth. Each had been used in spiritual warfare before, but tonight was especially hard. More and more demons were arriving by the minute. Both men of God were struggling with heaviness in their spirit.

While the Watchmen prayed, six buses pulled into the parking lot. Most headed for the tables loaded with Max's popular barbecue pork sandwiches. In less than two hours, a spiritual battle would burst forth, an invisible warfare having eternal consequences.

By the time the worship team finished its second song, every seat was taken. It was obvious the younger crowd was far more interested in end-time prophecy than the senior saints. For most, this would be their first time hearing an in-depth teaching on the coming of the Lord.

"No man knows the day or the hour," yelled a boy.

"But the women do." hollered three girls seated behind him.

Their infectious laughter spread quickly. For some this was just a time to get away from the folks. For others, it was an opportunity to meet new friends. There was a third group. These were youth who had come to meet God. Despite their young age, these intercessors could sense something heavy was about to go down. It was a diverse group coming to hear the truth about the coming of the Lord.

The Watchman could feel his Savior's love for these children. The end of the age was so much closer than the world could ever imagine. This was a rare opportunity to preach the truth to so many open hearts. For someone who loved God, it was an opportunity of a lifetime.

From the pulpit, Pastor Ryals announced, "Let's welcome from Santa Barbara, California, Reverend Stephen Corbin."

Most expressed their appreciation by standing and cheering. Outside the hotel, Mark Bishop was meeting with deacons Billy B and Frank Donnelly.

"Are you ready, guys?"

"Amen," smiled Billy B, "what has the Lord shown you?"

"We need to do a prayer walk around the Conference Center."

The demons of Control, Compromise, and Fear had not anticipated such an attack. As soon as these foul spirits heard the blood of Jesus being declared, they planted the last of their lies before being forced to depart.

The Beginning of Sorrows

"For nation will rise against nation, and kingdom against kingdom. And there will be famines, pestilences, and earthquakes in various places. All these are the beginning of sorrows."
Matthew 24:7-8

The peace of God radiated from his smile as the Watchman adjusted his microphone.

"Thank you all for such warm hospitality. Michelle and I are very excited to be here. So what cities are ya'll from?"

The Committee beamed with approval as cheers came from kids representing Huntsville, Birmingham, Mobile, Auburn, even Alabama's state capitol, Montgomery.

While looking over his audience, the middle aged evangelist calmly closed his notebook. He wouldn't need his notes tonight. He was very familiar with the spiritual warfare raging within this packed out hall. God's desire was a simple message of truth.

"This evening, I feel led by the Holy Spirit to begin a three night series entitled, *'The Coming of the Son of Man: One Taken, One Left.'* Saints, there is coming a day when God will blow His final trumpet and our Blessed Hope will send forth His angels to gather His elect from the farthest part of heaven and earth." 1

The crowd roared for the time when they would see their Savior. But not everyone was smiling. Amidst all the fun, the hugs, and high fives, sat several angry Committee members with their arms crossed.

"Jesus taught two men will be in the field: the one will be taken and the other left. Two women will be grinding together; the one will be taken and the other left. 2 Church, this passage is describing the glorious gathering of believers to heaven. The Son of Man will deliver His saints while those left behind will experience the day of the Lord. Just like in the days of Noah and Lot; deliverance then wrath."

The eruption of praise was a real rush for many who had just become Christians. For a small group of senior saints, the response was so loud they had to cover their ears.

"This is the message of the hour for the body of Christ. There is coming a day when our Blessed Hope will descend from heaven and all those who follow Him will be caught up. But before the elect are delivered, our Jesus warns us to watch for six events. First, there will be many teachers who will come saying Jesus is the Christ and will deceive many. From these shall emerge a world leader coming to conqueror the nations. The next event will be wars and rumors of wars. Because of these wars, famines will spread throughout the world. In Matthew 24:8, Jesus calls these events the beginning of sorrows. 3 These three events are more fully described by John in Revelation 6:1-5. The apostle sees the Lamb of God opening the first three seals of the heavenly scroll."

The Corbin's knew Bethany was no ordinary city. There was a lot more involved than what could be physically seen. Who would have ever dreamed this quaint farming town would become such a demonic stronghold in these last days.

"The opening of the fourth seal will initiate the days of the Great Tribulation. Our Lord warns Christians who experience it, 'For then there will be Great Tribulation, such as not been since the beginning of the world until this time, no, nor ever shall be.' 4 This will be the worst persecution ever for the body of Christ. During this period, believers will be hated by all nations. 5 The persecution will become so intense many Christians will betray and hate one another. Brother will betray brother. There will be children who will rebel against their parents and have them put to death. The increase of wickedness will be so overwhelming that many believers will allow their love for Christ to grow cold." 6

The evangelist could hear the whispering. An undercurrent of division was forming. Those open to demonic attacks would soon receive an all out assault.

"Jesus warns believers to flee when they see the Abomination of Desolation invading Jerusalem with his armies. The Man of Sin will announce his intentions from the Temple on Mount Moriah. 7 This specific event will initiate the Great Tribulation."

The Committee was vainly trying to control themselves. This wasn't the type of message they wanted to hear.

"Jesus promises the elect experiencing the Great Tribulation, 'Unless those days were shortened, no flesh would be saved; but for the elect's sake those days will be shortened.' 8 I ask you, how will our Lord fulfill His promise to shorten the persecution of the elect during the Great Tribulation?" Glancing toward the angry Committee, Stephen prayed under his breath, "Allow them to see it, Lord."

The passionate evangelist smiled at those nodding their heads. "That's right the persecution will be cut short by the catching up of the elect. Those who endure to the end of the age will be physically saved. 9 Does anyone get a witness?"

The thundering amens were painful to the Committee.

"In Matthew 24:4-29, the elect are exhorted to watch for these events. In verse 33, Jesus clearly shares, 'When you see all these things know that it is near—at the doors.' 10 Now what things is our Lord talking about?"

Confused faces were a familiar sight in the Corbin's ministry. For years, most pastors rejected the events warning believers of the coming of the Lord. Now, in God's timing, the truth would be revealed to those with ears to hear. Suddenly interpretations were coming from every direction.

Raising his hands, Stephen shouted, "Jesus warned believers who see the arrival of the Antichrist, the wars, the famines, the persecution, and the martyrdom of the elect, that His coming is right at the door. Our Lord prophesied, immediately after the tribulation of these first five seals, the sixth seal on the scroll in heaven will be opened. The sun will be darkened, the moon will not give its light, and the universe will become pitch black." 11

"You mean these heavenly disturbances come right before the rapture of the church?" shouted someone from the first row.

"This is what Jesus taught."

"If that's true, then what is the sign of His coming?"

A teenager from Bethany Assembly stood and read, "'For as the lightening comes from the east and flashes to the west, so also will the coming of the Son of Man be.'" 12

"That's it, my brother," encouraged the Watchman. "Our Lord gave us a perfect description of His coming for His elect when He said, 'Then the sign (like lightning) of the Son of Man will appear in heaven, and then all the tribes of the earth will mourn, and they will see the Son of Man coming on the clouds of heaven with power and great glory. 13 And then He will send His angels, and gather together

His elect from the four winds, from the farthest part of earth to the farthest part of heaven.'" 14

The evangelist wanted to continue but the applause forced him to pause. Through all the demonic attacks, the Holy Spirit was still convicting. Stephen could sense their spiritual hunger, a hunger crying out for the truth.

"Now listen up everybody. We all need to understand this important truth. In I Thessalonians 4:15-17, Paul wrote of Jesus' coming in the clouds to catch up His saints. Now check it out. The apostle doesn't say how the saints would be caught up to heaven."

"I know, Brother Corbin," squealed a teenage girl. "I believe the Holy Spirit just showed me. In Matthew 24:31, angels gather the elect to heaven."

"I see it," affirmed an excited Sunday school teacher. "Jesus taught, 'For the Son of Man will come in the glory of His Father with His angels, and then He will reward each according to his works.' 15 Isn't this the rapture followed by the judgment seat of Christ?"

"Glory to God." praised Stephen. "The upward gathering by angels at the coming of the Son of Man is the resurrection of believers into heaven." 16

The members from the Seminar Committee were livid. To them, this stranger from California was manipulating their kids by distorting the Word of God.

"Okay, let's have a quick review. Is everyone still with me?"

The roar could be heard a block away. The Watchman smiled before asking for quiet. He paused while choosing his next words.

"First, angels will gather believers out of the Great Tribulation to heaven. After the body of Christ is delivered, the day of the Lord will be poured out on the wicked. Our Lord uses the destruction of Sodom and Gomorrah by fire as an example of His wrath."

"You've got the body of Christ being persecuted by the Beast during the Great Tribulation," Pastor Elmer Dyer anxiously blurted out. That's not possible; God will never pour His wrath out on His bride. Believers inherit salvation, never God's wrath." 17

The disdain for the Watchman could be seen on the faces of the entire Committee.

"Pastor Dyer, in Revelation 5:1, John saw a scroll in heaven sealed with seven seals. When all seven seals are opened, the scroll will unravel and God's wrath will be poured out on a Christ rejecting world. The events of the seven seals are not God's wrath, but represent the rebellion of man and the wrath of Satan." 18

"May I speak?" interrupted J. W. Brown, senior pastor from Bethany Presbyterian Church. "Mr. Corbin, you're making a fatal error when you teach the seals are not God's wrath. In Revelation 6:17, John clearly sees the wrath of the Lamb coming after the sixth seal is opened. The people of the earth are hiding from the face of Him who sits on the Throne and from the wrath of the Lamb. 19 Think about it, if the sixth seal is God's wrath, then the other five seals must also be His wrath. After all, it's Jesus who opens each of the seven seals during the tribulation period."

Amidst the cheers, a youth pastor nudged one of his kids, "I told you Pastor Brown was a preaching machine. Can't you just feel the Holy Ghost?"

"Pastor, is it true that only the Lord will be exalted during the day of the Lord?"

"Isaiah 2:11 says so."

"So you believe the seven year tribulation period represents the day of the Lord?"

"Yes sir. After the rapture, God will pour out His wrath during the day of the Lord. First, the seven seals will be opened by Jesus. Then seven trumpets will sound. And finally seven bowls will be poured out. It's all God's wrath."

"Pastor, how can only the Lord be exalted during the fourth and fifth seals? Isn't this a time when the Man of Sin blasphemes our Lord? In fact, after the opening of the fourth seal, the false prophet will martyr a multitude of believers who refuse to worship the Beast. Please hear me. If the seals are God's wrath, then our Jesus would be responsible for empowering the Beast. Our Lord would be guilty of martyring His own. Saints, that's not possible."

Fear and Control couldn't wait any longer. The commotion felt like a bomb going off. With debates raging, Pastor Brown desperately tried to regain control.

"Now hold it right there. Mr. Corbin, the coming of the Son of Man can't be the rapture. Matthew 24:30-31 is Jesus coming with His saints at Armageddon. The Word of God is returning with His bride to destroy the Beast and his false prophet. Like in the days of Noah, unbelievers will be taken to judgment, those left will be saved."

"Pastor, may I compare the Word of God returning in Revelation 19 with the coming of the Son of Man in Matthew 24?"

"What for?"

"To see if they are the same event."

"I'd like that," he said with a wink.

"As I have already shared, Matthew 24 depicts the Son of Man coming for His elect who are being persecuted by the Beast. In verse 29, Jesus opens the sixth seal and the sun, moon, and stars lose their light. In this darkness, the Son comes in the glory of His Father. His angels gather the dead in Christ, then believers who are alive."

"You're so deceived," scoffed J.W.

"In Revelation 19 the Word of God returns and casts the two beasts into the lake of fire. Our Jesus will also kill all who followed them. This takes place after the seventh bowl judgment at the great day of God Almighty, Armageddon. Now, here's my question."

"We're waiting," mocked J.W.

"How can the Word of God returning at Armageddon be the same event as the Son of Man gathering His elect to heaven in Matthew 24? In Revelation 19, after the seventh bowl is poured out, no one is caught up to heaven. In Matthew 24:29-31 after Jesus opens the sixth seal, angels gather His elect to heaven. Let's be honest, these two events happen at different times each having different results."

"There is only one second coming," laughed Pastor Brown. "You've got Jesus coming back two more times."

A hush fell over the room. Before Stephen could continue, a teenager stood and asked to speak.

"If the sixth seal is opened before the rapture, and the wrath of God is poured out after the seventh seal is opened, then that means the elect must be gathered to heaven between the opening of the sixth and seventh seals." [20]

"That's unscriptural." blurted a pastor's wife. "There are no events left to be fulfilled. Jesus is coming like a thief in the night."

"Don't listen to this Yankee!" shouted an old timer.

"The elect in Matthew 24 isn't the body of Christ," howled another. "The elect are Jews living during the tribulation."

Through it all, some students were grasping the sequence of events for the first time. Chairman John Ryals wasted little time in taking control of the meeting.

"Please, please, may I have your attention? Before we close, I have a final announcement. We have several denominations represented here tonight. Unfortunately, none of our Committee members believe in the teaching you've just heard. I'm sure Mr.

Corbin is well received in Southern California with this new revelation. Those of us in Alabama certainly do not believe the Church will be martyred by the Antichrist. Trust me; this teaching is not of God. In spite of this unfortunate setback, I have asked Pastor Louis Cooper of Lakeview Assembly of God to be our featured speaker for the next two nights. So please invite your friends to come out and hear why Jesus can come at any moment. God bless you all."

As the crowd emptied out of the hall most were unaware of what really happened.

By the time Chairman Ryals asked him for the microphone, the Holy Spirit had already prompted Stephen to visit Bethany Assembly. At the same time, Billy B felt led to drive by his church before heading home.

LET NO ONE DECEIVE YOU

"Let no one deceive you by any means; for that Day will not come unless the falling away comes first, and the man of sin is revealed, the son of perdition."
II Thessalonians 2:3

Stepping out of his car, the Watchman spotted a heavy set man standing beneath the outside lights of the activity center.

"God bless you, Brother Corbin, they call me Billy B. I've been a deacon at Bethany Assembly for six years."

"Nice meeting you, Billy B, I'm Stephen."

"I must say your message packs quite a wallop. It was tough watching these kids arguing over the scriptures."

"It can get hectic when believers are challenged with the truth."

"Well, it took me a spell. But as you compared scriptures, I was able to see it."

"See what?"

"The coming of the Son of Man in Matthew 24 is the same event as the coming of the Lord in I Thessalonians 4."

"That's awesome," smiled the Watchman.

"What's with these preachers who kept interrupting you? Gee, I don't believe these kids even understood the questions you were debating, much less the answers."

"Michelle and I see this all the time. The lack of knowledge of the coming of the Lord is heartbreaking. Tragically, most pastors won't allow any meaningful debate."

"You got that right. You could just feel the spirit of Control oozing from the Seminar Committee."

"Even so, my brother, the Spirit of God is greater than any spirit, whether from man or from Satan."

"Amen to that. Hey, Stephen, do you think I could ask you some questions about what you taught tonight?"

"Sure, I'm always up for questions after I teach."

"When some of my kids from my church were asking me about Matthew 24, a youth pastor from Mobile kept interrupting and telling them it's no big deal."

"Actually, Billy B, Matthew 24:30-31, I Thessalonians 4:15-17, and II Thessalonians 2:1-4, each describe the same coming of the Lord for His saints. This is the most critical truth the spirit of Antichrist is trying to suppress."

"So we have entered the last days?"

"The final seven years 'til Armageddon began when the Beast brokered the false peace with Israel." 1

"Wow, Armageddon is really coming." 2

"Paul warned, 'Now, brethren, concerning the coming of our Lord Jesus Christ and our gathering to Him... let no one deceive you by any means; for that Day (of the Lord) will not come unless the falling away comes first, and the man of sin is revealed, the son of perdition.'" 3

"Isn't Paul saying the Man of Sin must reveal himself before the elect are gathered to heaven?"

"Yep, it's a warning for Christians living inside the Great Tribulation."

"So the saints getting the victory over the Beast will be the ones resurrected to heaven at the coming of the Son of Man?" 4

"This is what the early church believed, my friend."

"Hey, didn't you say the events inside the seven seals of the heavenly scroll represent the rebellion of man and Satan's wrath?"

"That's right."

"Well, in Revelation 6:12-16, the sun is turning black, the moon is turning red, and earthquakes are erupting. People are running for the caves in order to protect themselves. Then it says, 'The great day of His wrath has come and who is able to stand?' 5 Isn't this God's wrath erupting on earth after the sixth seal is opened?"

"The word 'come' in the Greek is *ethan*. It means it's coming. Those in darkness are hiding from His wrath that is coming at the seventh seal. Remember when Jesus was arrested in the garden by soldiers? Judas was leading them."

"Sure, Jesus was taken before Herod and Pilate."

"Jesus said, '...The hour has come; behold, the Son of Man is being betrayed into the hands of sinners.' 6 In other words, his trials before Herod and Pilate were coming. They had not yet happened. They were still future."

"I get it. When the sky goes black, the fear of God's wrath will grip the hearts of those who reject Him. For those not watching, Jesus will come like a thief in the night."

"Yep, the seals are the conditions which must be met before the scroll is opened. The scriptures never say the seals are God's wrath. The wrath of God doesn't come out of the heavenly scroll 'til all seven seals are opened."

Scratching his head, the trucker muttered back, "Now bear with me. So the sounding of the seven trumpets won't begin until all seven seals are opened, is that right?"

Stephen smiled.

"You see, if you don't make a distinction between Satan's wrath and God's wrath, you've got a serious contradiction on your hands."

"I can't believe I've never seen this before."

"The devil is going to deceive many Christians during the Great Tribulation. This is Satan's wrath against the children of God. Even so, this persecution is going to produce overcomers from every nation whose strength and obedience is in the Holy Spirit."

"That's a mighty strong word."

"Billy B, I want to encourage you to seek the Lord about becoming a Watchman."

"You mean like your calling and Pastor Mark's?"

"Yeah, you just pray and God will show you."

"Sure will. I wanna thank you for sharing with me."

"The spiritual warfare we felt tonight was intense. We need to form prayer teams to defeat the demons assigned to Bethany. How many intercessors attend your church?"

"Pastor has tried to teach on intercession. It's so discouraging. Only the youth have any desire to be used."

"That's okay. Let's remember the words of our Savior, 'The harvest truly is plentiful, but the laborers are few. Therefore pray the Lord of the harvest to send out laborers into His harvest.'" 7 Once we start praying, the Lord will raise up His prayer warriors. Can you set up a meeting with Pastor Mark?"

"Praise the Lord. This is so awesome."

"See you tomorrow and welcome to the fight."

For the past year, the trucker had fervently prayed to be used in a ministry which glorifies the Lord. His grateful smile was a reflection of his love for God.

"You were treated rather roughly tonight by the Seminar Committee. It's not always fun to be a Watchman, is it?"

"Billy B, if you hear and obey God, you will always make the right choice, no matter what the consequences. For the Lord, the highlight tonight was the fact some became Watchmen for the truth."

Waving goodbye, Stephen could sense his new friend's sincerity. The deacon from Bethany Assembly would now be responsible for what God had called him to do.

Pastor Mark Bishop was taking his time driving down Main Street. He loved seeing the rays of the sun slipping through the branches of the silver-leafed maple trees. The city was waking up to another brisk fall morning. Most were warmly greeting one another while shopping.

The events of the past few weeks had radically transformed Mark's life. He now looked at Bethany in a totally different light. Unsuspecting mankind, like in the days of Noah, was plunging toward an end time judgment called the day of the Lord. In a couple of years this bustling downtown would be no more.

Pulling into Sluman's Mark heard in his mind, "Asleep in the light."

"Hey, Pastor," hollered the attendant, "how ya doing?"

Ever since graduating two years ago from Lakeview High, Jimmy Curtis loved working at Sluman's Garage. Mark liked the lean rather bashful mechanic. He regularly invited him to visit Bethany Assembly. Jimmy always had an excuse, but that didn't stop the pastor from sharing the gospel.

"Heard about the prophecy seminar ya'll had last night," chuckled Jimmy. "A real barn burner, huh? Pastor, some are saying you're predicting the end of the world. Never seen so many folk wrangled up over the end times."

"What do you think, Jimmy, are things getting worse?"

"Aw, I ain't worried. How can anyone know anyway?"

"This Sunday morning I'll be teaching on the coming of the Lord. Would you like to come?"

"Sounds mighty interesting, Pastor, but I'm afraid I won't be able to make it. The Bethany Stock Car Series begins this weekend, maybe another time."

Waving goodbye, Mark wondered how many chances the young man would have before it was too late.

Wiping the grease from his hands with a rag, the mechanic curiously watched the pastor drive away. From behind Jimmy's restored 1966 Ford Mustang, the spirit of Control had only one thing on its mind. Shooting high into the air, the demon headed toward Bethany Assembly.

It had been a month since he received his vision of the ugly beast having seven heads and ten horns. The Friday evening prayer group had doubled in size since Mark dropped the bomb on that infamous Sunday morning. The youth had come early to seek the Lord in prayer. Near the back of the activity center, members from the men's prayer ministry were eating pizza and drinking coffee. Dwayne Pressley had their attention. Their loud laughter was not from God.

Rising from his knees, Pastor Bishop asked everyone to come together. Just then, Billy B and Stephen Corbin pushed through the double doors from the sanctuary.

"Good evening, Stephen," greeted a pleased Mark. "It's great you could join us tonight."

The laughter from the back of the center was suddenly replaced by nervous suspicion. One of the youth leaders had asked during their time of prayer for the Holy Spirit to send the Watchman with a message from God. While Mark motioned to Stephen to come forward, everyone quickly took their seats. The intercessors could sense an anointing as soon as the evangelist spoke.

"I've come here tonight with a divine exhortation. A month ago, your Pastor received a vision of the Antichrist brokering a false peace between Israel and the Muslims. The Holy Spirit gave me the same vision. Mark and I have been called to be Watchmen for the Lord. Our ministry is to prepare Christians to become overcomers during the Great Tribulation. 8 The Holy Spirit is right now enlisting Watchmen all over the world."

The moment seemed so surreal as the kids hung on every word. "Saints, when the Prime Minister of Israel signed for peace with

President Kayin last month, a seven year countdown to Armageddon began. The first seal has been opened and Satan has sent his conqueror to war against the saints. To overcome the Beast, we must prepare ourselves spiritually, physically, and emotionally. The Great Tribulation will begin forty-two months from the signing of the Jerusalem Peace Accord."

"Stephen, our youth have a lot of questions about what's ahead. How about a question and answer time?"

"Be glad to, Mark."

Immediately, an excited teenager asked, "Brother Corbin, could you explain the meaning of the name Antichrist?"

"The world leader who deceives mankind in these last days John calls the Antichrist. *Anti* means to take the place of. The Antichrist is given several other names in the Bible. In Revelation 13, John also calls him the Beast. In II Thessalonians 2 Paul calls him the Man of Sin, the Son of Perdition, and the Lawless One. In Matthew 24, Jesus calls him the Abomination of Desolation who invades Jerusalem. And in Daniel 7, Daniel calls him the Little Horn."

"How could our President be the Little Horn?"

"Under the guise of combating Islamic terrorism, Joshua Kayin physically subdued three Muslim nations, his first three horns. [9] This display of force pressured seven more Muslim nations to grant Israel the right to exist in peace." [10]

"How can we know for sure our President is the Beast?"

"Joshua Kayin has already gained the support of over one-hundred-twenty-five nations in his fight against terrorism. This is just the beginning. By the middle of the 70th week, Satan will give authority over every nation to the Beast. [11] During the Great Tribulation; Kayin is going to overcome many saints." [12]

"What about all these countries on the verge of war?" How does this fit into Bible prophecy?"

"After the second seal is opened, peace will be taken from this earth. Jesus exhorts us to watch for wars and rumors of wars. [13] Guys, we're moving toward a climax. We need to witness to every unsaved person we know." Shaking his head the Watchman solemnly warned, "In the past decade, the rising number of Christian leaders, pastors, and teachers denying the future rapture of believers is frightening. Deceiving spirits have already convinced many to turn away from their faith. [14] The lack of discernment by Christians who refuse to repent of habitual sin is far greater than we ever imagined. Even so, our Lord has given us a promise. For those who remain faithful, Jesus will physically deliver from the wrath of God." 15

As the kids praised the Lord, Stephen sensed a deep conviction of sin.

"The Holy Spirit just gave me this verse. 'But mark this, there will be terrible times in the last days. People will be lovers of themselves, lovers of money, boastful, proud, abusive, disobedient to their parents, ungrateful, unholy, without love, unforgiving, slanderous, without self-control, brutal, not lovers of the good, treacherous, rash, conceited, lovers of pleasure rather than lovers of God—having a form of godliness but denying its power. And from such people turn away.'" 16

The urgency from this passage was convicting hearts. Several were weeping. Suddenly Dwayne Pressley and Kevin Collins made a hasty beeline out the backdoor exit.

Refusing to be distracted, Stephen declared, "There is going to be a great separation within the next three and a half years."

"So how can we hear from God and not be deceived?" asked an uneasy ninth grader.

"Excellent question; the answer is holiness. In these last days, believers who refuse to repent of their habitual sin will be easily deceived. They will lack the spiritual discernment to identify the lies from the enemy. Paul's warning from the Book of Hebrews will become a personal nightmare. 'Beware, brethren, lest there be in any of you an evil heart of unbelief in departing from the living God... For we have become partakers of Christ if we hold the beginning of our confidence steadfast to the end.' 17 We as believers have a responsibility to repent of any sin which has taken root within our lives. We need to repent, so that we may be free to become overcomers in Jesus' name."

Bowing his head, the Watchman lovingly prayed for everyone to have the courage to be truthful. One by one, students were dropping to their knees. After Mark and Stephen raised their hands in worship, cries of repentance erupted.

"Lord, I've put it off too long," wept a teenage girl. "I've always hated my daddy for what he's done to my mama. Father, in Jesus' name, please forgive me of my bitterness and anger. As of today, I forgive my daddy for leaving us."

Near the back of the room, a group of boys were confessing their sins involving R rated movies. The boy leading in prayer quoted a scripture aloud.

"'But I say to you that whoever looks at a woman to lust for her has already committed adultery with her in his heart.'" [18]

"We were in bondage by just watching," shouted his friend. "Please forgive us, Lord. We want to be overcomers."

From her knees, a sobbing Hope Bishop cried, "This isn't a game. May we seek You with all of our hearts. Help us to love no matter how much others persecute us."

Turning toward Stephen, Mark excitedly shared, "I have never seen this group confess their sins like this before. His Word says, 'Confess your trespasses to one another, and pray for one another, that you may be healed. The effective fervent prayer of a righteous man avails much.'" [19]

Lance and Lee Ryan, current youth pastors at Bethany Assembly, had just recently graduated from Bible College. It was exciting studying for the ministry. Often times they would dream of seeing new converts living for Jesus. Most graduates would pastor churches scattered all across America. Some would become missionaries. Each were being sent forth to make an eternal difference for the kingdom of God.

Due to their love for people, ministry had always come easy for Lance and Lee. Both were from Georgia and both had deeply committed parents who loved the Lord. Throughout their childhood their parents faithfully shared with them the power of worldwide revivals. A revival was a powerful move of repentance by the Holy Spirit. The conviction of sin would spread from believers to the unsaved, prompting them to cry out for salvation. This was Lance's prayer to see Christians seeking after God no matter what it cost. He wasn't interested in becoming a famous evangelist or shepherding a church of three thousand. Lance Ryan wanted to experience a revival no man could take credit for. A move from God everyone could recognize. The Ryan's were aware of the critical role young people play in revival. They once visited a powerful revival in the mid 1990s. A small church suddenly exploded with the power of God. Millions of sinners were gloriously saved and filled with the Holy Spirit. It was easy to see how the youth, ages nine to eighteen, were so powerfully used to spread one of the greatest revivals America had ever seen.

The youth leaders of the Lakeview High Bible Club loved the Ryans. A former basketball star, the six-foot five Lance was a hit with the guys. After arriving in Bethany, he volunteered to work out with several sports teams at Lakeview High. Soon the good looking ex-jock, sporting a flattop haircut, became the unofficial chaplain for many students who didn't have a clue about heaven or hell.

Lee Ryan had long brown hair and deep brown eyes. Her beautiful smile could easily disarm a stranger. She quickly became a favorite with girls of all age groups. The Ryan's had a glow about them that could not be faked. The believers at Lakeview High knew they were for real. From day one, their top priority was a heaven sent revival. It would all begin in a charming farming town called Bethany, a town the Ryan's knew very little about.

Atop Bethany public library, the demons of Compromise, Lying, Control, Unbelief, and Fear, froze when they heard the rustling of his wings. It was a terrifying experience for them to see Satan face-to-face. The howling winds from this hideous angel grew louder as it hovered over the top of them. Without any warning, it swooped down upon his evil army of soldiers. His smell was so sickening some turned away; however, their reaction was much more from fear than revulsion.

"What have you done?" seethed the devil. "You're allowing this evangelist to form prayer groups. Because of your incompetence they are outlining our future attacks. I hate their pitiful pleas for discernment. I despise their eagerness to follow their convictions."

The spirit of Unbelief said, "Master, I believe..."

"Silence! I want their prayers stopped. Do you hear what they're calling this evangelist? I hate that name."

The spirit of Compromise bragged, "Master, the pastors in Bethany lack discernment and can be easily influenced."

Not wanting to be shown up by his peers the spirit of Lying bragged, "Master, I will personally sow lies about the evangelist to believers who gossip. It will take no time at all for the churches to turn against his end time message. Those who disagree with the Watchman can be..."

"What did you say?" shrieked Satan.

"What I meant, uh, this Corbin has enemies. There are two prophecy teachers, Tom Bray and Gerald Pierce, who speak lies against his ministry. Jealously has already gained a stronghold over each of them."

Perched nearby, the foul spirit grinned.

His greenish yellow tongue slipping out of his mouth like a giant banana slug, Satan sneered, "And what about you, Fear? What strongholds does this puny human have?"

The smallest of all demons wasn't prepared for such a confrontation.

Hastily it mumbled back, "I don't know, Master."

"Tell me, how many have you deceived in my world?"

"Yes, Master, you are the ruler of this world." 20

"To ensure victory you must sow false interpretations concerning the timing of His coming. We must continue to create a mindset of unbelief. They can't recognize the eternal consequences until it's too late."

"But the prayer warriors at Bethany Assembly..."

"Enough! Do I have to send more soldiers? I want you to stop Corbin from enlisting any more believers to pray. Take away his voice if you want. Fear, come to me."

The tiny demon weaved through the jealous horde. They tried to listen but it was no use, this wasn't normal procedure. If Satan had wanted this conversation to be private no one would have seen a thing. No, he wanted them to see Fear receiving its orders. Seething with envy, the demons fought among themselves as soon as the devil vanished.

Michelle had just brought breakfast up from the hotel lobby. Stephen had promised to take her out for a picnic. She was really looking forward for a drive in the country.

"C'mon, Honey, the blueberry muffins are hot."

Strolling back to their bedroom, she sensed something was wrong. Rushing into the bathroom, she could see Stephen clutching his throat. His lips were moving but no words were coming out. When he reached for her, she realized what had happened. Stephen couldn't talk. Holding him in her arms, Michelle began to intercede in Jesus' name.

The spirit of Fear wasted little time in maneuvering toward its next assignment—the Mark Bishop family.

SECOND SEAL : THE RED HORSE

"When He opened the second seal, I heard the second living creature saying, 'Come and see. Another horse, fiery red, went out. And it was granted to the one who sat on it to take peace from the earth, and that people should kill one another...'"
Revelation 6:4

American President Joshua Kayin rose to power out of relative obscurity. At first, most Muslims resented his high handed tactics in combating terrorism. Certainly his invasion of three nations was meant to be a wake-up call for those opposing Israel. 1 This military strategy was a tough beginning for his roadmap to peace. Most world leaders seriously doubted this man of war could ever stop the bloody struggle between the Palestinians and the Jews. That is, until he miraculously won the trust of several Muslim nations surrounding Israel. Almost overnight, the once hated American President had done the impossible. His charismatic speeches suddenly exuded strength and trustworthiness. Even skeptical leaders from the European Union were publicly praising Joshua Kayin as a visionary. For decades, the Middle East peace talks had moved from country to country. As a tense world watched, repeated attempts at a lasting cease fire between Israel and the Palestinians proved fruitless. Time and time again, expectations would seemingly rise only to be shot down by another suicide bombing. Any hope of a resolution was ebbing away. Negotiations were hopelessly deadlocked until the American President offered his roadmap to peace. Slowly the world began to believe.

It was a dream-come-true when the Prime Minister of Israel and the President of the Palestinian Authority seized a small window of opportunity. Political experts were astounded at the simplicity of Kayin's roadmap. For the vast majority, it was a beginning. Most remained cautious as new events unfolded daily. While the world reveled in its infatuation with its new hero, a heavenly event was coming, an event which would dramatically change the course of human history.

With the scroll in His right hand, the Lamb of God stood before His Father. Raising it above His head, He opened the second seal. Immediately, a fiery red horse was loosed. Its rider would rob the earth of peace by prompting people to kill one another. 2 The angelic host could only wonder how many would eventually die.

"Have the Russians gone crazy?" the popular News Anchor muttered to herself.

The Chicago newsroom was rocking with the announcement. She was desperately trying not to show any alarm.

"Good evening, this is News with Natalie Roberts. Our lead story tonight is from Siberia, Russia. Within the past hour, self-appointed President Alexi Rakmanoff has officially declared Siberia an Independent State. Since Siberian oil workers haven't been paid in six months, Rakmanoff has ordered a large portion of Moscow's oil supply to be cut off. The Siberian President has created a substantial army in order to defend against any Russian aggression. We have just learned that Siberia has officially applied for membership with the United Nations."

After cutting away for a quick commercial, Natalie was handed another news update of the Russian conflict.

"As you have just heard, Siberia's Alexi Rakmanoff has severed all political and economic ties with Moscow by announcing the formation of a new country. The President of Russia, Uri Esapenko, has renounced Rakmanoff's unlawful rebellion against his own people. Russian troops have already reached Kurgan and Chelybinsk in the Ural Mountains, cities touching the newly constructed borders of Siberia. We have just received news of a bitter division among the high ranking officers at the Russian naval base in Vladivostok. The United States Embassy in Moscow is advising all Americans to evacuate immediately. In response to this aggression, China has announced the doubling of its troops along the common border of Siberia. According to Pavel Skullus, an embedded reporter, Russian troops have just captured several garrisons of Siberian soldiers outside the city of Magnitogorsk."

With news agencies frantically gathering research, another shockwave exploded south of Russia.

"A skirmish along the border of North and South Korea has escalated into a small war," shared news reporter Seok Jang Jae. "South Korean casualties are said to be in excess of ten thousand. The civilian casualties are primarily the result of hostile bombing by North Korea. The evacuation along the bordering cities has become a hellish nightmare as thousands are fleeing for their lives. The South Koreans have reluctantly moved heavy artillery into the combat area. What direction these attacks will take is unknown at this time. Neighboring countries have issued pleas for a peaceful resolution. When asked about the possible use of nuclear weapons, the defense secretary from North Korea boldly declared his country would use whatever force is necessary in order to maintain security along their border. This is Seok Jang Jae reporting live from South Korea."

"Thank you, Seok, for that important update. At this point, the United States has no comment on either the Russian or Korean conflicts. Of course, the threat of nuclear war is certainly a possibility. Excuse me, we have another announcement. The General Secretary of the United Nations has asked the President of the United States to address its membership regarding America's intentions. He went on to say, "The world is looking to the United States for guidance in these trying times. Of course, our President's talk will be televised globally. This is Natalie Roberts from Channel 6 in Chicago. Please stay with us as we will continue to bring you fresh updates of the Russian and Korean conflicts."

Arriving at the United Nations building in New York, the President was escorted to the General Secretary's chambers. As he read over his notes, an urgent message was handed to him. After asking for his red phone, the Secret Service moved in for an official lock down.

Decisions influencing billions of lives were being made with split second precision. A fearful apprehension permeated the UN as the news was announced in several languages. The diplomats gasped as another newscast struck with even more alarm than the first two.

"From New Delhi, India, this is news anchor Omar Bhuta. Within the past hour, Pakistani rebels have captured four hundred hostages at a nuclear power base in Northern India. These rebels are threatening to destroy the cities of New Delhi and Jodhpur with short range nuclear missiles if their demands are not met. The Prime Minister of India has implemented peace talks with the President of Pakistan. All military units are on emergency standby."

In the background, a massive crowd herded behind reinforced barricades was anxiously awaiting any news.

"After hearing the intentions of the Pakistani rebels, millions of Indians are fleeing to the south. Our streets are overflowing with people praying for protection. At this time, the rebels are demanding the complete withdrawal of Indian forces from the country of Kashmir. The Pakistani Parliament is under intense pressure from these rebels to declare war on India if their conditions are not met. The Indian government has already made assurances that under no circumstances shall any Indian Special Forces attempt to regain control of the nuclear power base in Jaisalmer."

Across the street from the live newscast, the Indian Defense Council was reviewing the demands of the rebels.

"To avert any massacre," insisted the Defense Minister, "there must be a compromise. We must sign a peace treaty the United Nations will enforce."

The world had always suffered under the heartbreak of wars. For decades, the major powers not only survived, but triumphed over the fear of World War III. Only recently had defense experts advocated a financial system consisting of all nations. The earth was rapidly becoming an international community, a brilliantly assembled machine created to take orders from one leader.

Joshua Kayin smiled as he greeted the UN delegation. He knew the importance of this speech. Attempting to calm the fears of billions of people was no easy task. The American President looked confident.

"These are times when we can envision the horrific consequences of terrorism by a select minority. I can assure you I've been in contact with leaders of each side of the Russian, Korean, and Indian conflicts.

The only answer to this insane bloodshed is clear. In order to defeat such terrorism, we must become a united family. Today, I propose every nation on earth to join together..."

From behind the President, the spirit of Antichrist hissed, "The second seal has been opened. The rider of the red horse is loose."

Within a year, the deep-seated hate between ethnic groups erupted into thirty-three wars. The time was coming when the world would seek after a leader, a deliverer.

Jesus warned, "You will hear of wars and rumors of wars. See that you are not troubled; for all these things must come to pass, but the end [of the age] is not yet. For nation will rise against nation, kingdom against kingdom." 3

The cars just kept coming. While Julie Bishop and Lee Ryan served sweet tea, several teenagers were setting up folding chairs. Allie and Lindy Hart were passing out paper and pens for anyone interested in taking notes. No one could remember such excitement on a Tuesday night Bible study.

After an hour of praise and worship, Mark asked, "Lance, would you like to begin our study tonight?"

"Wow, I see some new faces with those special smiles."

"You can't hide the joy of the Lord, now can you?" gushed an excited Lee Ryan.

The laughter was coming from hearts who had just received Jesus as their Savior. For over a year, revival had spread to every service and Bible study connected with Bethany Assembly. While the city's religious crowd mocked the supposed move of God, the young people began to pray under a powerful anointing. Each study would begin with fervent prayer, followed by heartfelt praises to the Lord. The spontaneous worship was being led by kids who had no idea how the Holy Spirit would move. It was not uncommon for worship to last a couple hours. Pastor Mark called it 'the glory.' Of course, complaints opposing such fanaticism were common place.

A local pastor mocked, "These holy rollers think they're more spiritual because of their loud hallelujahs and emotional gymnastics. This glory they brag about is just a feel good experience which doesn't accomplish anything."

"The Bible teaches a church service should be conducted

decently and in order," challenged a popular worship leader. "My God is not the author of confusion. Besides, I would like to know how many souls are really getting saved."

The spirit of Jealousy had a field day when news of the revival spread to other towns. It wasn't long before carloads of youth were arriving early to seek after God.

"Pastor Lance, could you share the vision that the Lord gave you? There are some here who haven't heard it."

"Sure Lindy. It happened a year ago just after Pastor Mark received his end time vision. The Holy Spirit gave me a picture of revival spreading across America."

"What kind of picture, pastor Lance?"

"At first, I saw a dirty trough, the kind horses in the old West drank out of. Inside the trough was the anointing of the Holy Spirit. In front of the trough was a long line of ministers waiting their turn to drink. After drinking, they would return to their congregations with a supernatural anointing for revival."

Instantly whispers permeated the living room.

"In my vision some of the ministers became weary of the long wait. It was sad to see so many drop out of line, but it was easy to see why. There were three types of shepherds who refused to drink. The first were those promoting man made programs ahead of God's leading. The second refused to humble themselves in front of their peers. And the third group simply became impatient and left."

"Why would so many ministers do that?" asked a visitor.

"It's not a pretty picture, guys. The focus of many shepherds today is not real discipleship but the proud achievement of maintaining their own agenda. Even so, some ministers who stepped up to the trough actually dropped to their knees and received a double portion of the glory of God. This humility produced two different reactions from those waiting in line. For those who loved God, the excitement became even stronger. Many in this group had been praying for revival for many years. To see that it was within their grasp brought tears of joy. For those who refused to drink, such humility was a real turn off.

"Look how silly they're acting," laughed a preacher in my vision. "Their hyped-up show isn't honoring God. What a disgrace."

Within seconds the massive line was cut in half only to be replaced by hungry shepherds from overseas. The revival grew across America as millions received Jesus Christ as their Savior."

Suddenly his words were slower and softer.

"The fire of revival is spreading to those who seek after the Lord with all of their hearts. Eventually, the Christians who received from God will be persecuted by the Christians who refused to believe. A skeptical pastor in my vision said, 'Don't you see how deceptive it is? The reason I know it's not of God is the arrogance of those who experience this so called glory. My denomination doesn't approve of such manipulation," he bragged. "Besides, we have our own move of God which produces real fruit.'"

"You mean this is for real?" gasped a new convert.

Raising his hands to God Pastor Lance Ryan quietly wept. He couldn't go any further. The entire Bible study began to pray for pastors in America. The flame of revival had already touched such cities as Portland, Oregon; San Mateo, California; Tucson, Arizona; Naperville, Illinois; Philadelphia, Pennsylvania; and Deerfield Beach, Florida.

"But why would a heaven sent revival be opposed by the very ministers who prayed for it?" asked a confused student.

"Why God?" cried another. "Open our eyes, Lord, so we may see the truth."

With a deep sense of conviction, Julie Bishop shared, "The Holy Spirit has shown me the shepherds who refused to accept His anointing have no fear of God."

The weeping began like a small stream. Within minutes it became a mighty river of heart-felt confession.

"It's impossible," hissed the spirit of Pride. "The pastors in Bethany will never allow a real revival."

The intercessors discerning the evil intrusion rebuked the demonic visitor. An hour later, Pastor Mark concluded with a final prayer of thanksgiving. God was building a foundation of faith among young people to believe for the miraculous, overcomers who could expose the counterfeits of the enemy whether from the devil or from the traditions of men.

The Bishops and Ryans smiled after opening their eyes. Most still had their Bibles open and notepads ready.

"So you're still up for a Bible study?"

The chorus of amens was loud. Producing his notes, Mark was ready. His topic was on the disobedience of believers in the last days.

"Jesus warns believers living in these latter days to repent. Some will lose their first love. Others will worship idols, compromise with the world, become lukewarm, and eventually suffer spiritual death. 4 The habitual sinning of believers in Revelation 2 and 3 will be repeated by believers living in the days before the coming of the Son of Man. Their denial of the Lord is a warning to us. The Christians in Laodicea were promised to be spewed out of the body of Christ if they refused to repent. 5 Such rebellion has grieved the Holy Spirit right out of their lives. Jesus addresses those who perish under the deception of the Beast as well as those who escape at the coming of the Son of Man. 'Watch therefore, and pray always that you may be counted worthy to escape all these things that will come to pass, and to stand before the Son of Man.'" 6

"Escape what things?" asked someone near the front.

"To be exact, worshipping the Beast, his image, or receiving his mark during the Great Tribulation."

"Geez, this is intense."

Mark glanced at Julie. He could always count on her comforting smile.

"Revelation 14:9-11 spells it out. Many Christians are going to overcome the Beast by the blood of the Lamb and the word of their testimony. 7 Those that don't will be tormented with fire in the presence of the Lamb."

"But why would a Christian turn their back on God?"

"Their refusal to repent has opened them up to deceiving spirits and doctrines of demons. Tragically, many are going to have their consciences seared." 8

Standing to their feet, the students began to applaud.

"We praise You, Lord," cried Mark. "Only You can expose Satan's lies. May we become Watchmen for the glory of God." 9

CALLED BY GOD

*"And no man takes this honor to himself,
but he who is called by God."*
Hebrews 5:4

The sun glistened off the beautifully restored Temple. A twenty foot wall separating the Dome of the Rock from the Temple was a constant reminder of God's protection. Excitement filled the air as the people prepared themselves for the Sabbath. On this sunny fall morning, Rabbis greeted each other in the streets as families received gifts from one another. This would be a day to remember, a new day. The priests were preparing the incense offering with the utmost care. The red heifer to be sacrificed during the ritual purification was another miracle. Priests from the tribe of Levi had already secured the ramp leading to the top of the altar. Those attending today's history making ceremony represented countries from around the world.

As one priest positioned the microphone, another helped the ninety-two-year-old rabbi to the platform. Rabbi Ehud Reuben, a Holocaust survivor, was an Israeli historian with no equal. He was revered as a teacher who deeply loved his people and his heritage.

As he ascended the platform, a professor from Harvard University asked his guide, "Is Rabbi Reuben going to speak in this afternoon's ceremony?"

"This is so unexpected," his shocked guide whispered back. "Rabbi Reuben hasn't spoken publicly in years."

With the majestic Temple in the background, this revered Rabbi desperately wanted to participate in this historic moment.

"Dear friends of Israel. In the year 951 B.C., King Solomon was instructed by God to build our first house of worship. In 586 B.C., a Babylonian army swept through our beloved Jerusalem and set fire to our holy Temple. Some of our people were taken to Babylon, our Temple was abandoned."

The noonday sun highlighted the wrinkles on his face as he paused for a drink of water.

"In 70 A.D., a Roman army led by General Titus marched on Jerusalem and totally dismantled our Temple, which had been restored by 63 A.D." 1

Suddenly a teenager leaped onto the platform. Landing near the speaker, he boldly declared, "This is a new day between Jew and Muslim. It's a day when we can worship in our Temple while our neighbors can worship in their Mosque."

As the boy was escorted away, tears dripped down the cheeks of this Holocaust survivor. He had faithfully prayed for peace for over seventy years.

"It's true," confessed the old man. "We have entered a day when a Jew can say shalom to his Muslim neighbor."

The applause was deafening. The bloodshed had finally come to an end. Traumatized children could now play in the streets without any fear of being attacked. As the world was being rocked with wars, the Jewish people basked in their peace covenant with their surrounding Arab nations.

The glowing red light in the standby room was reflecting off his glass desk. The willowy silver haired preacher had two more minutes before the green light came on. He was proofing his notes for any mistakes. Arthur Lawrence's ministry had lasted for over thirty years. His popularity had grown primarily due to his teaching on the secret rapture of the saints. His books on prophecy never missed the bestseller lists. Some were even made into movies. In recent months, however, a vocal group of ministers had been warning Christians of the coming Antichrist. This wasn't new, Arthur personally knew several pastors who believed this. This was no big deal. What really irritated him were those who taught the Man of Sin must reveal himself before the church is raptured. After thousands of hours of comparing scriptures, the popular Bible teacher knew what he believed in. In his mind, it was scripturally impossible for the bride of Christ to partake in the Great Tribulation.

Glancing at his watch, he sincerely reflected, "Anyone who

believes a real Christian would take the mark of the beast is being deceived by the devil."

"Thirty seconds, Reverend," shouted the producer.

His make-up artist added a touch of hairspray to his shiny silver hair as he repositioned himself in his chair.

"3... 2... 1...," the producer silently mouthed. "Welcome to Countdown to Midnight. Tonight's show is on the imminent return of our Lord Jesus Christ. To help us grasp this comforting truth, here's Mr. Prophecy himself, Arthur Lawrence."

Focusing on camera # 2 the preacher smiled.

"Greetings everyone, in view of the recent events striking our world, I'm very excited to have this opportunity to come into your home this evening. The apostle Paul encouraged believers when he wrote, 'Behold, I tell you a mystery: we will not all sleep but we will all be changed—in a moment, in the twinkling of an eye, at the last trumpet. For the trumpet will sound, and the dead will be raised incorruptible and we shall be changed.' 2 My friends, this mystery is the rapture of the church to heaven. The apostle highlights the catching up of the saints when he wrote, 'For the Lord himself will descend from heaven with a loud shout, with the voice of an archangel, and with the trumpet of God. And the dead in Christ will rise first. Then we who are alive and remain shall be caught up together with them in the clouds to meet the Lord in the air. And thus we shall always be with the Lord. Therefore comfort one another with these words.' 3

"Saints, how can we comfort one another with the outbreak of over thirty-three wars around the world? That's right; our Jesus can come at any moment. He is our Blessed Hope and we will never be subjected to His wrath. I've been teaching for over thirty years on the day of the Lord, the final seven years of God's wrath. The day of the Lord will immediately follow the rapture, deliverance, and then wrath. As soon as our Savior catches up His elect the twenty-one judgments outlined in Revelation will begin. His wrath begins with the opening of the seven seals, followed by the sounding of the seven trumpets, and ending with the seven bowls. 4 The day of the Lord will begin when Jesus Christ opens the first seal which is the Antichrist coming to conquer on a white horse. According to Daniel, this deceiver will lead a ten nation confederacy from the European Union in signing a false peace with Israel. Soon after this treaty is signed, wars will break out all over the world."

Lowering his reading glasses, he paused and smirked.

"Now we all know the world has experienced two similar events in the past year. There are even some very sincere pastors advocating this is a sign we have entered the 70th week of Daniel and the beginning of sorrows. Saints, my heart is heavy when I hear such heresy coming from those claiming to know Christ. Some are even teaching Jesus will come for a purified bride because of persecution from the Antichrist."

For a moment the distinguished theologian wished these false teachers would just go away.

"Trust me, saints, first century Christians weren't looking for the Beast. No, the elect were looking for their Blessed Hope coming on the clouds of heaven. Be discerning, my friends. Jesus warned us of false prophets who will deceive many in these last days. Don't let the devil or anyone else make you doubt the Blessed Hope. All events leading up to the rapture have been fulfilled. For those who want to stay, God bless you, but I'm praying up, moving up, and finally, I'm going up."

The applause sign was flashing prompting the audience to cheer. The strain on his face was obvious. Within the past year more and more Christians were challenging, even attacking his secret rapture teaching. Fearful and confused, many were demanding answers from the Word. The applause died down after a signal from the producer.

"My time is almost up. In conclusion, only the blood of Jesus Christ can make His bride pure. You are not saved because of any lifestyle of works, but only by the grace of God. Jesus will never reject you once you are His child. Even if your life showed no fruit, you'd still be saved. Let's remember, saints, only Jesus can save a soul from the eternal lake of fire, and that is a gift not of yourselves. Those whom the Holy Spirit indwells are eternally saved and will be rescued from the day of the Lord."

His expression of deep concern was not the norm.

"Church, allow me to be very candid. How many of you can envision your children playing in the morning sunlight, and without any warning being thrust into the Great Tribulation? God forbid. Believe me; the elect will be delivered to heaven before the Man of Sin reveals himself to the world. There is nothing to fear, just keep looking up."

After a few moments, the lights on the set grew dim. The famous prophecy teacher greeted his audience by handing out autographed copies of his new best seller, 'At Any Moment'.

Pastor Mark Bishop reached over and turned the TV off. His prayer session with Stephen Corbin had lasted a lot longer than he had anticipated. Battle lines were being drawn within the leadership of the body of Christ. Arthur Lawrence's stinging rebuke would eventually force several Christian denominations to publicly announce their belief in the imminent return of Jesus Christ. For many who believed in a secret rapture, the very thought of the Beast overcoming the saints was not possible.

"The division among Christians is frightening," moaned Mark. "Kayin is doing the very things the Beast is supposed to do and the church isn't seeing it. What do you think, Stephen?"

"It's clear he is assembling a system to control the nations. The muscle behind his deception is the political support from millions of churchgoers. I can't believe the evangelicals who continue to judge Kayin by his supposed courage rather than by what he says or does."

"When President Kayin convinced a coalition of nations to invade several Muslim nations, most Christians backed him up. Christian leaders didn't even blink as he courted ambassadors from many nations under the guise of fighting terrorism. Even his push for Israel to give away its land for a new Palestinian State didn't seem to matter."

Stephen softly reflected, "I can't believe how many religions are uniting together under the banner of so called world peace."

"Pope Michael loves Kayin's roadmap for the Middle East. His vision for peace is really picking up steam. Both the Pope and President Kayin believe Christians and Muslims worship the same God. Talk about heresy."

"There won't be any peace until the Prince of Peace casts the Beast and his false prophet into the lake of fire." 5

Within the past year, the evangelist from California had witnessed a surge of divisive splits in churches. Even so, his speaking schedule for the next six months was almost full.

"So when are you returning to Santa Barbara?" asked a curious Mark.

"Not any time soon."

"But what about you're calling as a Watchman?"

"Since our first day here, Michelle and I felt this was a special assignment. For now, we have decided to make Bethany our home base until the Lord releases us."

"That's exciting news. I know our kids will be praising the Lord. Who knows, maybe you'll stay until the coming of the Son of Man."

Thomas Nelson Bray was called to be a minister at a very young age. Growing up in Kenya, Africa, his father and mother were committed missionaries. Both parents played a vital part in cultivating God's calling in their son's life. They knew the Lord was molding their young Tommy into a mighty man of faith.

Tragically, over the years, more and more parents were discouraging their children from entering the full-time ministry. It was true many missionaries were not well off when they retired. At times, friendships were strained by church edicts involving doctrine, discipline, and finances. Yet for the Brays and hopefully their son, the calling of serving the Lord would always be a joy.

During a heartfelt prayer time, Tom's father sadly confessed, "Lord, Your heart must be broken. Why would any parent steer his child away from the ministry. Just think of how many who have missed Your perfect will." 6

On his sixteenth birthday, Tom excitedly shared with his parents how God had called him to preach. From then on, there was never any doubt their only child would become a minister. At Bible College, while many of his classmates were crying out for souls during all night prayer meetings, Tom studied lesson plans, sermon outlines, and most of all, end time prophecy charts. This prize student knew what his peers revered. One's affirmation was often determined by what one taught, at least for Tom it was.

After graduating, he accepted a pastorate of a small church in Mobile, Alabama. While teaching part-time at a nearby Bible College, he met his wife to be, Ashley. A romance sprang up and two years later they were married.

His next ministerial position was a large church in Birmingham, Alabama. Tom was convinced this was God's will for his life. The highly educated membership exceeded one thousand members. Surely, he thought, this body would appreciate his exegetical interpretation of scripture.

To no one's surprise, his popularity within his denomination was growing. His next step up the ladder of success was a prominent congregation in Jacksonville, Florida. For leaders within his denomination, this was a jewel most aspiring pastors coveted. The beautiful redbrick sanctuary of Christ Cathedral, stood majestically erect among the well-groomed rose gardens, surrounded by hundred-year-old oak trees. The educational wing included classrooms with individual computers. Just recently, the church board voted to add a new indoor swimming pool adjacent to the well equipped gymnasium. More coveted than this was the prestige of the shepherd who preached from the mahogany pulpit rising high above the congregation. To be able to look down upon the sheep and proclaim the power of God's Word was a real adrenaline rush for the up and coming pastor. Through it all, his wife Ashley was watching. The more Tom achieved, the more character flaws she saw. She knew only God could expose her husband's selfish ambition: A sin that could be seen for anyone willing to look.

Every minister has a favorite area of teaching. For Pastor Tom Bray, it was the coming of the Lord. Of course, it was very rare for the respected orator not to be prepared when he spoke from the renowned pulpit of Christ Cathedral. But when given the opportunity to preach on the road or overseas, Tom would usually have to fight the urge to preach on the imminent return of Jesus Christ. This passion led the experienced pastor to write three books on the rapture of the saints. After shepherding Christ Cathedral Church for five years, the president of his denomination encouraged the popular pastor to pursue a full-time ministry as a revivalist, with a focus on end time prophecy. With his wife and two sons, Matthew and Samuel in tow, Tom established his new ministry headquarters in a delightful city in southeastern Alabama called Bethany.

The Reverend Thomas Nelson Bray quickly became an accomplished speaker at Prophecy Conferences all across the country. Backed by extensive research, he earned himself a reputation as a brilliant lecturer. As the years flew by, there was rarely a time when anyone would dare challenge his knowledge of the latter days.

Matthew and Samuel Bray were presently attending two very prestigious universities. Matt was pursuing a degree in New Testament

Theology with an eventual Doctorate in Biblical Languages. His dream was to become a Seminary professor. His younger brother was enrolled in a Bible/Administration double major. Sam wanted to become a college president, but their future ambitions would have to wait. Sitting on the sofa the brothers were discussing their research with their mother.

"Mom, Sam and I are very committed to what we believe...Yes, we have prayed over our conclusions."

Entering the family room, their father poured himself a cold glass of lemonade.

"Now, wasn't that a profound message my good friend Arthur Lawrence preached on Countdown to Midnight last night? If our pastors would just have enough backbone to teach the truth concerning the rapture we wouldn't have all this vacillating back and forth among the saints. The imminent coming of our Blessed Hope is so clear."

"Dad, Sam and I have been studying His coming."

Reaching over their proud father picked up his worn Scholfield King James Bible.

"Do you have any questions I might help you with?"

"Actually we'd like to share some of our conclusions."

Entering the family room, their mother took a neutral seat by the fireplace. Ashley had known for some time this moment would come. In her mind she prayed, "Father, I know my husband and my sons love You. I pray You will open our eyes to see the timing of Your Son's coming for His elect."

"It was a year ago when Sam and I began to research the subject of the coming of the Son of Man."

"Wonderful. The biblical foundation you've received must have put you head and shoulders above your classmates."

"Dad, Sam and I have come to the same conclusion while studying under professors from two different universities."

Relishing the idea of biblically sparring with his two sons, the prophecy expert asked, "What type of conclusion?"

Matt's eyes were fixed upon his father while Sam glanced over to watch his mother's reaction.

"Sam and I believe Matthew 24 is the most complete chapter on the timing of the coming of the Son of Man. While on the Mount of Olives His disciples asked, 'What will be the sign of Your coming and the end of the age.'" 7

Matt was expecting an interruption but received none.

"The most critical truth to understand is where the elect will be in the sequence of events which transpire before the coming of the Son of Man. Sam and I believe the events Jesus gave in Matthew 24:3-29 are the same events He gave John in Revelation 6:1-17."

"That's correct Matt. Our Lord is warning Jewish believers who are living during the Great Tribulation not to be deceived. Jesus prophesied, 'Then they will deliver you up to tribulation and kill you, and you will be hated by all nations for my name's sake.'" [8]

The teacher paused hoping his sons would not miss this important truth.

"Even though Israel is hated by the world, our Lord promises salvation to Jewish believers who endure until Armageddon."

"So Jesus' warnings to the elect are for Israel and not for the church?"

"That's right, Sam. In Matthew 24:32 our Lord uses an illustration of a fig tree to warn the Jews of His return. When the branches of the fig tree get tender, the summer is near. Jesus is warning the Jews who experience the events of Matthew 24 that the return of the Messiah is near. The Jewish people will watch for the signs like the tender leaves of a fig tree ushering in the summer."

"So you believe the fig tree represents Israel?"

"Absolutely, Israel is called the fig tree several times in the Old Testament. Furthermore, for the events of the tribulation period to transpire, the Jewish people have to be back in their homeland. In other words, the fig tree represents Israel's becoming a nation again after two thousand years."

"Dad, Sam and I believe Jesus is addressing the church in Matthew 24. In the New Testament, whether Jew or Gentile, the elect are always Christians. We don't see any biblical justification for having the fig tree in Matthew 24 representing the Jewish people."

"Check this out," offered an animated Sam. "How can Israel represent the fig tree when Jesus cursed the fig tree in Matthew 21:19 and commanded it to never bear fruit again? To us, the fig tree in Matthew 24:32 is referring to a time of approximation to warn Christians of His coming."

"Dad, Jesus is exhorting believers not to be deceived by watching for the events in Matthew 24:4-29. The elect that see these events will be delivered to heaven after the opening of the sixth seal."

Rolling his eyes, Tom scoffed, "Try proving that scripturally."

"Jesus has the elect living inside the Great Tribulation in Matthew 24:21-22. If the Great Tribulation begins in the middle of the 70th week, then how can the body of Christ be taken up to heaven before the 70th week begins?"

After an awkward silence, both sons braced themselves. Their father rose from his chair and began to pace. For Ashley, it was easy to see his irritation.

"Actually, I too had the same questions about the rapture when I was studying for the ministry. Ah, yes, the old post tribulation debate which wasted so much of our time. Time which could've been devoted to saving souls. To be perfectly honest, this type of interpretation comes from teachers who haven't been properly trained in eschatology. I respect your diligence in studying but your ignorance concerning Israel and the Church will eventually lead you down a path of deception."

"And what path is that?" asked Sam.

"A path into biblical error, simply put, the body of Christ and Israel cannot co-exist during the tribulation. This period isn't for the Church. Matthew 24 is about Jewish disciples during the seven year tribulation period and their deliverance by Jesus at the battle of Armageddon, Revelation 16:14-16 and 19:11-21."

"Dad, what about..."

"What's preventing you from understanding this? Matthew 24 and Revelation 6 have nothing to do with the rapture. Jesus can't be addressing the Church during the tribulation period because the saints are already in heaven. John represents the raptured Church being caught up to heaven in Revelation 4:1. The church is never mentioned again until Chapter 19. How can the Church participate in the seven year tribulation, which is from Revelation 6 through 19, when she's already in heaven?"

With no reply forth coming, the angry preacher stopped pacing and slipped into his favorite chair. After a few seconds, Matt broke the nervous silence.

"In Revelation 4:1 John is summoned before the Throne of Almighty God. There is no mention of a bodily resurrection in this verse. The gathering of the elect is a bodily resurrection. John was taken to heaven in the spirit not bodily."

A cautious Sam added, "When John reaches the Throne there are no other saints with him. The apostle receives spiritual revelation of what was to come. The gathering of the elect to heaven is for the redemption of the body. Scripture never says John represents the church in the last days."

A determined Matthew continued, "John is called up to heaven in 4:1. The apostle returns to earth by Revelation 10:1, just before the sounding of the seventh trumpet. Yet the bride doesn't return to earth 'til after the seventh bowl inside the New Jerusalem. 9 This means John can't represent the bride."

"If not in Revelation 4:1," laughed Tom, "then where do you see the church being caught up before God's throne?"

"The coming of the Son of Man for His elect will take place between the sixth and seventh seals in Revelation 7:9-14."

"Exactly where Jesus places His coming for us in Matthew 24:29-31," gushed Sam.

"Dad, we understand this is what you've believed all your life. Your seminars have become classics within our denomination's most respected churches. Sam and I admire your knowledge of Scripture. You know the twelve apostles were the founding fathers of Christianity. During the Lord's Supper, Jesus exhorted them to go and make Christian disciples teaching them to obey everything He commanded them. 10 Matthew 24 is important instruction for Christians living inside the Great Tribulation."

"Seems you two have received a dose of heresy from this new evangelist in town."

"The key is to compare all scriptures..."

"I already have. What are you two trying to prove? You know I'm personal friends with Gene Lloyd and Arthur Lawrence. These men have studied thousands of hours over every end time prophecy in the Bible. They know more about His return in their little pinkies than all your liberal professors. It's heresy to teach God will pour out His wrath on the church during the Great Tribulation. Don't you see what's happening? False teachers are taking away our Blessed Hope by placing the bride under the persecution of the Antichrist. I won't allow this false doctrine in my home."

Matt and Sam Bray knew what they believed; however, they didn't have any idea on how to communicate it without having an argument. After excusing themselves, the Holy Spirit assured them there would be other opportunities.

ANOTHER BEAST

"Then I saw another beast, coming up out of the earth, and he had
two horns like a lamb and spoke like a dragon."
Revelation 13:11

While holding his breath, the attendant asked, "How does it look,
your grace?"

His mind was a million miles away as he tried on his new
ceremonial robe.

"Be blessed for your excellent workmanship."

With his fitting complete, the Vicar of Christ paused and admired
the purple and scarlet robe in his full length mirror. Across the room,
a breathtaking view of the ancient city of Rome could be seen from
his picturesque window. Pope Michael had no doubt that this was
God's perfect will for his life. Even so, his heart was very heavy. He
had just finished reading several emails from South America.

"Some of these Protestant preachers reflect a peace and joy that
just radiates," wrote a priest from Brazil.

A Cardinal from Argentina pleaded, "When the anointing comes,
the crowds can exceed two-hundred-thousand."

It was obvious Protestant ministers were targeting millions within
the church with emotional messages of grace. From the Vatican's
perspective, this deceptively packaged gospel was an evil that had to
be exposed.

A woman sitting on a scarlet beast flashed in his mind. Dressed
in purple and scarlet, glittering with gold and pearls, her evil
fornication oozed from the golden cup she was holding. The
mesmerized kings of the earth were bowing before Mystery Babylon,
the Mother of Harlots. 1

This picture in his mind wasn't new. Pope Michael was having nightmares. The nightmare of a harlot drunk with the blood of the martyrs of Jesus kept coming over and over. This frail priest never missed a day praying to mother Mary for the interpretation.

Suddenly a beautiful white light saturated his office. In the far corner, standing within the brilliance, was a slender figure draped in silver. The captivated Pope dropped to his knees.

As a young priest he first heard of the white light experience while traveling on a mission in Southeast Asia. Even so, the brilliancy of the silver lady completely took away his breath. Her words were audible.

"God Almighty desires to use you. Through His love, He is going to bring His children from all faiths together. Be obedient to your calling as His Holy Seer. The world will have peace like never before. Remember, I am the Queen of Heaven."

Demons have been spreading their lies throughout the world since their fall from heaven. For some, their specific assignments had lasted hundreds of years.

"After all," howled the spirit of Compromise, "some religion is better than none."

"Yes," smirked Religion, "let's just add enough structure to their lives so they may believe a lie."

The evil spirits of Religion were more highly esteemed than other demons. They are responsible for thousands of religions which have drawn multitudes away from the Gospel of Jesus Christ. Their ultimate goal is for mankind to follow the traditions of men over the absolute truth of God's Word.

"Remember," jeered Religion, "everyone has their own interpretation of the Bible. Even the ministers don't agree on the words from the Son of Man. It's all a bunch of guesswork, no one really knows..."

The Lakeview High Bible Club had always been a small group of Christians. Under the new direction of Luke Appleby, the club was growing. No one had ever realized how important servant leadership was until Luke was voted in as president.

The after school meeting in room 104 was heating up. Luke

Appleby, Hope Bishop, Ned Henley, and Whitney Troy were all ears. Drew Henley, Ned's twin brother, was sharing.

"Ya'll, our President is too hot a topic to avoid. We just can't run and hide. A lot of kids are checking us out to see if we are for real."

"Especially the new converts," smiled Hope.

"Don't you think as leaders of the Bible Club we need to share about what's really going down?"

A puzzled Whitney muttered, "I'm losing you, Drew."

"We all saw this coming," added a solemn Luke. "Most in our school know by now what we believe. The problem is, declaring President Kayin as the Antichrist definitely carries a price tag. On the other hand, everyone's going to think we are wimping out if we don't take a stand."

"Bingo," grinned Ned, Drew's blonde twin.

"Do you guys think Kayin knows what he is doing? The Beast doesn't cut the deal with the devil until the fourth seal, right?"

A somber Luke replied, "Guys, we won't know for sure until the Abomination of Desolation invades Jerusalem."

"Hold up." Hope Bishop blurted out. "I gotta share this. At our prayer meeting last night the Holy Spirit warned me of an evil deception that's coming."

Opening his Bible, Drew nodded, "Let's hear it."

"The Lord gave me a vision of a beautiful woman riding a huge red beast. She was parading in front of the most powerful leaders in the world. Suddenly the beast grew seven heads and ten horns."

"That's the scarlet beast in Revelation 17."

"Yeah, Drew, but it was the beautiful woman riding the beast that blew me away. She was dressed in purple and red, had pearls and gold, you know, she was completely decked out. The world was captivated by her beauty, which most thought was holiness. So when the beast changed, so did the beautiful woman. She was transformed into an evil looking prostitute."

"Sounds like Mystery Babylon, the Mother of Harlots," affirmed Luke.

"Check this out. In my vision the woman turns her focus toward the religious leaders of the world. While mesmerizing them with her lies, tiny streams of blood began to drip from her lips. Several times she had to turn away. It got so bad she refocused everyone's attention back on the beast."

"What's it all mean, Hope?" asked a guarded Whitney.

"I believe the Lord is trying to warn us."

"Warn us of what?"

"Everyone was so into looking at the power of the Beast's system, they could care less about the harlot."

"What about it, Luke?" asked Drew. "This sounds like the religious harlot we studied last year. Doesn't the harlot help the Beast gain power?"

"It sure looks that way."

"So, who is this mystery harlot Luke?"

"Whit, the scriptures don't tell us her identity. But there are several clues when you compare scripture with scripture."

"What type of clues?"

"The first clue has the harlot representing a religious system possessing power throughout the world. This false religious system also has political power."

"Who could this be?"

"This harlot also has roots in the Babylonian religion."

"Luke, didn't the Babylonians worship a goddess mother?"

"Yeah, they called her Semiramis the queen of heaven. She taught her subjects to participate in mother/son idolatry."

"How did this cult come about?"

"Semiramis married Nimrod the founder of Babylon. This king convinced his people to build a tower used to worship the stars. God warned Nimrod of the consequences of this evil rebellion. When he refused to repent of it, God scattered the Babylonian people throughout the earth." 2

"God really did that?" gasped Whitney.

"When Nimrod died, the people worshipped Semiramis as the queen of heaven. 3 She became the mother of pagan idolatry.

"You mean they took this pagan religion with them?"

"Her teaching became the most dominant religion in the world. After Nimrod's death, the queen gave birth to an illegitimate son. Semiramis convinced the people Tammaz was their promised deliverer. 4 This was Satan's introduction of mother/son idolatry to the world. The heart of this mystery cult was an image of a mother with a baby in her arms. The people actually believed Semiramis miraculously conceived Tammaz. But even though she claimed her son as the savior of the world, it was she who was worshipped as the divine mother, the mother of god.

"This sounds like the Catholic church and their worship of

mother Mary," interrupted a stunned Whitney.

A reflective Luke continued.

"Babylonianism began as a mystery religion. The priests' hats were shaped like the head of a fish. They taught the doctrine of purgatory and encouraged the worship of idols. They even offered round cakes to Semiramis, the queen of heaven. 5 When Babylon was destroyed; the priests took their idols and fled across the sea. The evil seed of pagan idolatry eventually settled in a city resting upon seven mountains." 6

"What city sits on seven mountains?"

"It's Rome, Whit. The reason I believe this is because of the final clue. The harlot riding the beast is drunk with the blood of the saints. In other words, this religious system has persecuted and martyred Christians throughout history."

"So after all the clues what have we got?"

"In the last days this harlot is going to create a false unity by bringing all religious faiths together."

"That's Pope Michael's top priority. He gave a speech last week saying the only way to achieve true peace in the world is for all faiths to come together in unity."

"Whit, the goal of this harlot system is to resist the real gospel by eventually giving its power to the Beast."

"It makes sense, Luke," said Ned. "Yesterday in the Bethany Herald, the Religious Editor openly endorsed the World Religious Tolerance Act."

"Never heard of it, what's it say?"

"It's a religious law most European countries have adopted. It's now a crime to say someone else's religious beliefs are false. If you openly attempt to convert someone away from their faith into yours, you can be arrested."

"That could never happen in America."

"That's what the article was about, Whitney. Some Cardinals from the RCC are meeting with leaders representing several major religions in America. They're saying this law will help reduce religious hate crimes and further a spirit of tolerance among all faiths."

"So what's next, Luke?" asked Hope.

"What Ned just shared is pretty intense. You see the harlot will have her headquarters in Rome. For the first half of the final seven years, she will promote the Antichrist's system to power. When the world begins to worship the Beast, the scriptures say the harlot will be destroyed." [7]

As her friends shared, Hope slipped outside the room for a break. Down the hall, she could hear them arguing. This couple used to be close friends with Hope until the persecution over her father's vision erupted over a year ago. Across the hallway, several grungers were cutting up as three seniors walked by bragging about how far they had gone with their boyfriends over the weekend.

Pausing, Hope whispered, "Oh, Lord, this is all happening so fast. Is Pope Michael really behind the harlot in my vision? And how is this false religious system going to deceive the world?"

For a brief moment Hope doubted whether she could ever find the truth. But then she reminded herself of how faithful God had always been to her family.

"Jesus, I'm thankful I can trust You with my future. Please give me the eyes to see and the ears to hear what the Holy Spirit is saying."

Suddenly a passage came to mind.

'Then I saw another beast coming out of the earth, and he had two horns like a lamb and he spoke like a dragon. And he exercises all the authority of the first beast in his presence, and causes the earth and those who dwell in it to worship the first beast...' [8]

"Wake up, everybody!" she cried.

All Hope Bishop could do was to pound a metal locker out of frustration. Deep down she knew within a few years the sound of voices at Lakeview High School would be no more.

IF GOD BE FOR US

"What then shall we say to these things?
If God is for us, who can be against us?"
Romans 8:31

Lakeview High School had just let out. Students of all sizes and shapes were jamming the narrow hallways. The scenic grounds of the school meant nothing to these kids. Within twenty minutes the parking lot would be empty.

Slipping her backpack over her right shoulder, Hope sighed, "Wow, do I have a load of homework tonight."

"Me too," added a tired Lindsey.

As the two sisters turned the corner of Vaughn Road they could hear a group of teenager's coming their way.

"Hey!" yelled one of the boys, "look who we have here."

"Well, well, if it isn't the prophet's kids."

As the boys surrounded Hope and Lindsey, another teased, "maybe we should bow down and worship them."

"No, let's be nice," mocked Simon, "maybe they'll give us a word from the Lord."

"That's not funny." snapped Hope.

"Yeah, well your old man ain't so funny either when he teaches Christians are going to take the mark of the beast."

"Watch it, Simon; you could lose your salvation if you aren't careful."

"You don't understand, my father teaches..."

"Don't get super spiritual with me, Lindsey. My dad is pastoring a new church and I don't want some cult messing up what he is doing."

As one of the boys playfully tried to grab Lindsey's backpack, a

'66 silver Mustang turned the corner. After slamming on his brakes, the driver just stared.

"What do you think you're doing, hot shot?"

"These girls are making fun of my dad's church."

"Is that a fact? Well, I know Hope and Lindsey and that's kinda hard to believe. It's time ya'll be moving on."

The girls talked as Jimmy Curtis from Sluman's garage drove them home.

"Look what's happening, Hope."

"We've got to trust God, Lindsey."

"How do we do that? Everything is getting so weird."

"Dad will know what to do. When we get home, we'll tell him what's happening at Lakeview."

Jimmy was busy thinking. He could feel the tension in the town and he didn't especially like where things were heading. Pulling up in front of the Bishop's front lawn, the young man waved to the pastor who was raking leaves.

"Hey, Jimmy," greeted a smiling Mark, "looks like you've got a real handful."

Piling out of Jimmy's car, it only took a moment.

"Oh, Daddy," cried Lindsey, "there were some boys..."

"We're alright," added Hope. "We just need to talk."

"Why don't you go see your mother in the kitchen while I thank Jimmy for giving you a ride home?"

Both girls waved goodbye.

Turning toward the souped-up Mustang, the pastor noticed the mechanic's usual smile was strangely absent.

"Can you tell me what happened, Jimmy?"

"Your girls can fill you in better than I can. You gotta understand I arrived on the tail end of it. Seems like some boys were teasing your girls about what you've been preaching on lately. You know kids, Pastor; they can be pretty mean when they don't understand something."

"I want to thank you for protecting my girls."

"Forget it. I just hope you know what you're doing."

"What do you mean?"

"I was just thinking about how our town is reacting to your predictions. It's been going on for quite a spell now. I mean why get so many people riled up about end time events written in the Bible? No one knows for sure anyway, right?"

Crouching against his car, Mark waited until he got eye contact.

"Let me ask you a question, Jimmy. If you knew of a truth that is going to affect millions of lives for eternity, how much would you sacrifice in order to speak this truth?"

"Might have to think on that one for a spell."

Mark stood and smiled.

"Thanks again, my friend."

"Glad I was able to help." Pulling away from the curb he muttered, "I just hope our town can return to normal."

A few minutes later, seated around the kitchen table, Lindsey was the first to speak.

"These boys were mean, Daddy. They wouldn't even let us share what God has shown us."

"Hope, it appears the spiritual warfare at Lakeview is heating up. What exactly happened this afternoon?"

"It's about the word of knowledge I received from the Holy Spirit about the coming harlot. 1 Ned and Drew have been talking it up at school. This past month some kids started to bug us, it got even worse after Lindsey shared what the Lord had showed her."

"You remember, Momma, the vision I had of long lines of people taking the mark of the beast."

"Let's thank the Lord for sending Jimmy," shared a relieved Julie.

"Ditto," smiled Lindsey.

"I believe today's incident is a warning from the Holy Spirit. God is exhorting us to count the cost of what it will take to remain faithful. 2 Each of us has been called to be a Watchman to whoever is sent our way."

"Daddy, this one boy doesn't want to hear the truth."

"What's his name, Lindsey?"

"Everyone calls him Simon. He's the son of Pastor Allen Colson of Calvary Community Church."

"Okay, Lindsey, now what?" posed Julie. "What would Jesus do if He were in your place?"

"Our Jesus would love no matter how much it hurts."

"That's right, my little lambie," teased Julie as she reached over for a big hug.

"Girls, your decision to trust in Jesus is your choice. Your mother and I can't make it for you. The Great Tribulation is coming; a time when the body of Christ will be forced to take a stand for Jesus. The persecution of believers is going to increase all the way until the Son

of Man comes back with His angels." ₃

"Lindsey and I have decided to follow Jesus, no matter what the consequences."

"That's wonderful, honey," encouraged a hopeful Julie.

"Amen girls. Let's always remember, if we stand for the truth, God will always be on our side."

"Right on, Daddy," beamed Hope. "'If God be for us, who can be against us.'" ₄

Israeli Prime Minister Avi Rosen sat quietly as they debated the Jerusalem Peace Accord. Since the signing over two years ago, his cabinet had split into two factions. One side believed peace with surrounding Muslim countries was imperative. The other side, made up of older leaders, was convinced the peace accord was an evil deception.

"Our Muslim neighbors can't be trusted," demanded a conservative party leader. "They won't stop until they have captured our beloved Jerusalem."

"Utter nonsense," countered a liberal cabinet member. "Let us not forget how much we have given up to finally achieve peace! President Kayin's timely leadership in the invasion several Muslim nations was a reflection of his commitment to us. ₅ Look at how we benefited since signing of the Jerusalem Peace Accord." ₆

"It doesn't matter how many countries are forced to join," insisted a Holocaust survivor. "Our enemies won't be happy until they have killed every Jew in Israel."

The rise and fall of emotions throughout the six hour meeting was taxing the already weary Prime Minister.

"My brothers, what is happening to us?"

When the Jerusalem Peace Accord was signed, Avi Rosen had never seen such cooperation between the sons of Abraham. He knew without a comprehensive peace agreement every country in the Middle East was in grave danger. Then the conflict between Pakistan and India thrust the threat of nuclear war into the region. Several cabinet members wanted a hard-line policy implemented if a nuclear bomb ever exploded in northern India. For others, the top priority was to expose the evil intentions of American President Joshua Kayin and his Arab dominated Federation.

The hopeful Prime Minister asked well respected Rabbi Shimon Melchior to address the cabinet.

"My dear friends, I have come to warn you of an enemy whose face Israel cannot see. This adversary looks like a gentle lamb but can turn and attack us like a serpent. It appears we have become too complacent concerning our so called friends. I also believe we have put way too much trust in this American miracle worker."

A worried peace supporter interrupted, "Rabbi Melchior, look at how many ways we have profited since we agreed to peace. Even our enemies have blessed us with goods and services beyond our highest expectations. While the world has been plunged into wars for their disobedience, Israel has become the apple of God's eye. Eventually, Hashem will be praised by every Gentile nation."

Avi Rosen was desperately trying to satisfy both sides. The ultra Orthodox continually expressed their contempt for the ultimate compromise of allowing the Palestinians to call East Jerusalem their capital. On the other hand, the liberal wing of Judaism was ready to sidestep any religious law which would prevent a lasting peace.

The bags under his eyes reflected the constant pressure that never seemed to go away. It was a juggling act which had caused the Prime Minister many sleepless nights.

"Now, now, my brothers," reflected the concerned leader. "We must trust God with our future. I am aware of how uneasy our people are but I'm confident our military intelligence will alert us to any danger. Each morning I receive an up-to-date report of any suspected aggression from our neighbors. The Jerusalem Peace Accord has been honored by each member of the Middle East Federation. Because of this other countries are now seeing how powerful our alliance has become. Enough said. Rabbi Melchior, will you read us a blessing?"

The respected Rabbi stood and read from the Torah.

"'Dwell in this land, and I will be with you and bless you; for to you and your descendants I give all these lands, and I will perform the oath which I swore to Abraham your father. And I will make your descendants multiply as the stars of heaven; I will give to your descendants all these lands; and in your seed all the nations of the earth shall be blessed; because Abraham obeyed My voice and kept My charge, My commandments, My statutes, and My laws.'" 7

"I say we attack now," insisted the spirit of Lust.

"Let's be careful," warned Doubt. "They could…"

"What are they going to do? These believers don't care anymore."

Who would have ever dreamed how tolerant Christians would become toward blatant sin in these last days? Pornography was now a billion-dollar cash cow over the Internet. Demons were actively targeting the souls of teenagers through the perversion of porn. Bethany had the usual smut bookstores. For most, a little lustful entertainment couldn't hurt. But when the first homosexual church opened, the outrage from the churches was loud.

The spirit of Lust howled during the protest meetings.

"I love to hear Christians talk about what they're planning; since they have no intention of doing anything. Just look at how many millions have been possessed through porn. Even so, it sure didn't take much to convince the Ministers Association to be more tolerant in the areas of pornography and homosexuality, now did it?"

The foul spirit of Homosexuality just snickered.

"God wouldn't discriminate, now would He? Didn't Jesus die for the sins of all people?"

The office behind Sluman's Garage had been vacant for many years. Suddenly, there was a beehive of activity. One could hear workmen pounding nails and laying flooring. Curious onlookers tried to get a peek but all the windows were blacked out.

"Last time anybody used that office," scoffed a retired barber, "was for recruiting during the Vietnam War. Well, whatever they're selling, I ain't buying."

Many had questions but no one was getting any answers about the new office. The secrecy of the project was something these southern folk didn't cotton to at all.

"Wonder what they're hiding?" chuckled Jimmy as he locked up the gas pumps at Sluman's for the night.

THE MYSTERY OF THE WOMAN

'... I will tell you the mystery of the woman and of the beast that
carries her, which has the seven heads and the ten heads.'
Revelation 17:7

His mood darkened when he heard the knock at his office door. One
of his aides entered, waving some papers.

"Your Grace, I have the reports you requested. Please forgive me
for not..."

"May I have the numbers?"

"Your Grace, leaders from several major faiths are still dialoging.
They are very reluctant to make a public declaration for your inner
faith proposal."

"There has to be a way to show them how badly our world needs
peace. Men and women of faith must set the example."

"I agree your Excellency."

The holy father froze as the idea surfaced in his mind.

By the end of the month, leaders from over one hundred
religious faiths were summoned to Rome. Following their meeting,
the faithful crammed into Saint Peter's Square. The crowd was
singing, rocking back and forth, as they waited to hear. The noise was
deafening as the Vicar of Christ motioned for quiet. He shared how
God had spoken to these esteemed church leaders during a time of
fasting and prayer.

"Within the next twenty-four hours God has promised us a
miracle. May all families of faith to pray for God's perfect will."

World News agencies jumped on his prediction. Front page
headlines read, "God Promises a Miracle."

At Sluman's Garage, Jimmy Curtis was finishing an oil change for the religious editor of the Bethany Herald.

"Anyone with a lick of sense knows the miracles in the Bible ain't really true."

"Just a bunch of fairy tales," the editor muttered back.

"People expecting a miracle; the whole thing gives me the creeps," cursed the skinny mechanic.

"I pity them. I guess there will always be some who have to believe in some higher power in order to get by."

The world wouldn't have to wait long. The hysteria was unbelievable. Political officials, school teachers, housewives, teenagers— millions wept with joy. For a brief moment, the inhabitants of earth held their breath as they witnessed the miracle of miracles.

"It's Mary, the Queen of Heaven." announced an ecstatic Cardinal from Rome. 1 "Truly, God has sent us a miracle. Blind eyes have been opened, the deaf can hear, the cripple can walk, those vexed by demons have been set free."

"Just seeing my lady's face I could sense a supernatural peace," shared an overjoyed nun who confessed she was healed of cancer after praying to Mary. 2

"Praise our blessed Mother," wept a teenager. "May the spirit of Mary possess my soul for the rest of my life."

At first, the news reports focused on her beauty and holiness. But more than her physical appearance were her words. The world needed a message of hope amidst the harsh reality of war. Major newspapers printed her picture with her simple instructions: "God loves all people. The world is approaching difficult times. You must seek the wisdom which comes from above. When all faiths come together in true unity you shall have peace. I love you, Mary."

"This is our sign," praised a Catholic Archbishop.

Wasting no time, the Vatican officially announced the creation of The World Faith Movement. This ecumenical merger would include every major religion in the world. Leaders from Catholicism, Islam, Christianity, Judaism, Hinduism, even Buddhism, were asked to share how Mary's appearance has helped their lives. Demons of darkness were wooing religious leaders to sit at the feet of the false prophet.

The harlot would reach the pinnacle of her power with the help of an army of religious spirits. Soon, the World Faith Movement would ride the beast's system toward world domination. 3

Luke, Drew, Ned, Hope, and Whitney each arrived early to pray. The past few months had been a real roller coaster ride. Many kids at Lakeview High had accepted Christ. Even so, the battle lines between God and Satan were being drawn. For most Christians, persecution was something new. The devil wasn't happy about losing so many under his control. To combat this, those in leadership were being specifically targeted. Just calling yourself a Christian was easy. Learning how to defend against demonic attacks was something totally different.

"Hey, how are ya'll doing?" greeted a smiling Lance.

As the youth pastor and his wife, Lee, entered the activity center, they could sense the anticipation. Hope Bishop eagerly introduced some of her new friends.

"This is Donna, Alicia, and Richard. They each got saved at last week's meeting around the pole. You know, it's when we pray around the flagpole at our school."

"Congratulations, guys," grinned Lee.

While shaking their hands, Lance shared, "Everyone who wants to be a disciple must take the first step of being born again. After receiving the Holy Spirit, each of us must pick up our cross and follow God's will for our lives." 4

He paused to let it sink in. The Ryan's knew many youth were praying over His will for their lives.

"Lately we have been studying events which warn us of the coming of the Son of Man. Tonight we will... yes, Whitney, do you have a question?"

"Pastor Lance, I'm praying when you preach tonight you won't shift into hyper-speed when you get excited."

The room howled with laughter.

A smiling Lance meekly confessed, "Okay, okay, I'm guilty. Those who have heard me teach on the end times know how intense I can get. When I, or any of you, share on the events involving the second coming, we all need to remember to take our time. Now let's turn to Matthew 24:21-22. Jesus gave this teaching to some of His disciples on the Mount of Olives three days before he was crucified. Tonight, we're going to study a passage concerning the Great Tribulation. Jesus warned Christians, 'For then there will be great tribulation, such as has not been since the beginning of the world until this time, no, nor ever shall be. And unless those days were shortened, no flesh would be saved; but for the elect's sake those days will be shortened.' 5 Lately, some have expressed their confusion concerning what Jesus meant by 'but for the elect's sake those days will be shortened.'"

A freshman shared, "How about the smoke from all these wars blocking out the sun. Wouldn't that shorten the days?"

"She's joking," offered her embarrassed friend.

"Okay, everyone," proposed Lance, "Let's see what Jesus really means by this verse? What type of persecution is going to take place during the Great Tribulation?"

A confident Luke Appleby shared, "Jesus described a persecution which will cause many believers to betray and hate one another. Their love for Christ is going to grow cold. It appears many Christians are going to register for the mark of the beast during the Great Tribulation."

"So when does this begin?" asked a new convert.

"The Great Tribulation begins in the middle of the seven years; just after Jesus opens the fourth seal."

Seeing heads nod, the new convert asked, "So when does it end?"

"Did everyone hear that?" asked Lee. "The answer is super important."

"The seven seals, the seven trumpets, and the seven bowls, are set in stone," answered Hope Bishop. "They won't be shortened, right, Pastor Lance?"

"That's correct, Hope. The prophesied events you just mentioned won't change. Actually, the answer can be found by comparing Matthew 24:21-22 and 29-31, with Revelation 7:9-14. In these passages, Jesus has believers being delivered out of the Great Tribulation just before God's wrath begins. The Lord will cut short the Great Tribulation by removing the elect from the Beast's persecution."

"Hold up," blurted out a visitor. "I was always taught the church will be raptured before the Great Tribulation begins."

"Why speculate?" added Luke. "A good friend of mine warned me of Satan's wrath a couple of years ago. He said, "Bro, the Great Tribulation of believers will begin when the Abomination of

Desolation breaks his peace treaty with the Jews and invades Jerusalem. If we see this event, we know the mark of the beast is near." 6

As everyone scrambled to get it all down on paper; Luke couldn't help but smile.

"That's correct, guys," confirmed Lance. "A couple weeks after the Jews and the Middle East Federation signed for peace, wars broke out all over the world. Jesus warned us of the second seal when he said, 'And you will hear of wars and rumors of wars. See that you are not troubled; for all these things must come to pass, but the end (of the age) is not yet.'" 7

"I see it, Lance," grinned Drew. "Jesus taught the end of the age is the harvest. In the passage you just read, the red horse has robbed the world of peace and is having people kill one another. The elect are experiencing the second seal, when Jesus says the harvest (rapture) is not yet. In other words, believers couldn't be taken to heaven before the tribulation period because the church is here during the second seal."

"Wow, now this is heavy," blurted out another. "Lance, what about my parents who believe the events of Revelation won't be happening in our lifetime? Or my Sunday school teacher who believes these events took place in the first century."

"I'm afraid there are many in serious denial concerning the events Jesus warned us to watch for. 8 We must prepare for the coming persecution. We don't have much time before the rider on the black horse pays our world a visit."

A son of a popular Bible college professor to the left of Lance shared, "We've always had wars, no one knows for sure."

Their silence was a sign of maturity. Most already knew the answer. In less than a year, an unsuspecting Bethany will be plunged into the Great Tribulation.

"No one watching is going to be able to rationalize away the third seal, the black horse of famine."

A sympathetic Lee, Lances wife, shared, "Luke is saying the first half of the seven years concludes with a worldwide famine. The openings of the first three seals are the birth pangs."

"You mean like the pains a mother has before she gives birth to her baby?" asked someone from the back.

"Yep! The birth pangs will be followed by hard labor."

"So, Lee, what does the hard labor represent?"

"The Great Tribulation of the saints by the Beast."

"So when we see famines all over the world, the Great Tribulation is near?"

"That's right. Jesus also warns us to watch out for false prophets who will use false signs to deceive many." 9

"You mean like the mother Mary appearance?" interjected Hope. "Look at how many believers fell for that lie. Talk about a deceptive sign from the enemy."

"I have a question," asked a visiting youth pastor. "Doesn't Jesus say it's not possible for real Christians to be deceived?"

A calm Lance shared, "My brother, in Matthew 24:11, Jesus is warning us to be watching for false prophets who are going to deceive many believers. Matthew 24:24 is stressing how deceptive the signs and wonders of these false prophets are going to be. Only Christians spiritually ready will be able to discern the counterfeit." 10

"Whoa," added an excited Drew. "Believers who heed the warnings of our Savior won't be deceived but will endure faithfully until the end of the age (harvest)." 11

With hands going up all over the room, Lance smiled.

"Ok, let's end with this. Jesus answered His disciples' questions concerning His return by exhorting them to 'watch'. The sequence of events which precede His coming will help believers overcome during the Great Tribulation."

"So tell me, how is Jesus our Blessed Hope if we are all going to be martyred?"

Before anyone could answer, the angry pastor headed for the back door. His youth group reluctantly followed him out.

A determined Lance shared, "Let's remember, the persecution by the Beast will never rob the church of our Blessed Hope. It's just the opposite. The coming of the Son of Man will empower a multitude of believers to endure death so others may live eternally. 'Then I saw the souls of those who had been beheaded for their witness to Jesus and for the word of God, who had not worshiped the beast or his image, and had not received his mark on their foreheads or on their hands. And they lived and reigned with Christ for a thousand years.'" 12

An unwavering Luke reflected, "In my mind, if believers don't recognize the Beast during the Great Tribulation, what's going to prevent them from registering for his mark?"

A girl seated next to Lee whispered, "This is scary."

"Our Lord is faithful," encouraged Lance. "God has not given us a spirit of fear, but love, power and a sound mind. 13 Jesus exhorts us to watch so we may become overcomers through Him." 14

The Ryan's knew most of these kids weren't ready. The Bible study quickly divided up into prayer teams for the sole purpose of building up each other's faith. The black horse of famine was near.

Jason and Jackie Wylie were married just about the time the Bishops moved to Bethany. Both were graduates of the University of North Carolina. While Jackie worked as a nurse at the local hospital, Jason became the most respected defense attorney in town.

The Wylies first met the Corbins at a prayer meeting at Mark Bishop's church. Being members of Bethany Baptist, they would often slip over after their church service and join in with the prayer warriors at Bethany Assembly. What really intrigued this young couple was the supernatural healings which ignited the revival among the young people. It all began on a Friday night prayer meeting. No one really knew how the evangelist lost his voice. Some said he was burned out and needed a rest. A deacon started a rumor there was unconfessed sin in his life and God had withdrawn His protective favor. Jason remembered the serious look on Stephen's face when he motioned for the teenagers to pray for him. Forming a circle around the Watchman, they cried out to God to restore his voice. Within minutes a powerful heat touched him. Everyone was praising the Lord for His anointing. Then Luke Appleby received a word of knowledge.

"I believe the answer to Stephen's attack involves the discernment of spirits." 15

"I bear witness with the word Luke just received," confirmed someone from the back row. "When I pray, I sense the spirit of Fear coming against Brother Corbin."

The intercessors began to rebuke any spirits connected with fear.

Laying his hand upon Stephen's head, Luke prayed, "In the powerful name of Jesus Christ, we command you foul spirit of Fear to be gone. You have neither the right nor the power to continue to attack our brother in Christ."

Jason and Jackie Wylie led the cheering as Stephen began to sing, "God is my healer, God is my healer."

With everyone praising the Lord, one of the kids approached Luke.

"That was sure an awesome word your friend received."

"I don't know him; I thought you knew him."

Walking toward the exit the mysterious stranger had fulfilled his purpose.

"Hey, bro thanks for the word of knowledge."

Not bothering to reply, the stranger waved goodbye. 16

While Stephen shared with Lance and Jason about what God had shown him during the time he couldn't speak; Lee and Jackie led the kids in a Gideon march around the activity center. Never had such excitement ever come from the quiet church on the corner of Vaughn and Cherry.

The next morning, standing outside his new office behind Sluman's garage, the smiling priest greeted Pastor Dyer, Pastor Cooper, and Pastor Ryals.

"Welcome to our World Faith Movement office. It's so nice to put a face with a name."

Andrew Fleming had been a theology professor at La Salle University in Philadelphia for over thirty years. The recent appearance by mother Mary had profoundly touched his heart. After much prayer, the priest decided to resign and become a spokesman for the World Faith Movement. The WFM team assigned to visit Bethany included Catholic priest Andrew Fleming, Rabbi Daniel Stein, and Rebecca Grimm, a Unitarian.

The experienced priest could sense the pastors' uneasiness as they formed a semicircle in front of the new brick fireplace. For most folks, it was a shock to see outsiders transform their old Army recruiting office into a high powered voice for the World Faith Movement.

"Our slogan is one for all and all for one," joked Andrew while pouring coffee for each pastor. "Actually, I believe the WFM will inspire all faiths to worship God in their own way."

For over an hour the team shared a gospel tailor made to deceive. Carefully choosing their words, the trio shared the spiritual need for mankind to experience God's love.

"Yes, we appreciate your ideas fostering a tolerance of all religions," acknowledged a troubled Elmer Dyer. "But how can all faiths unite if we don't believe in the same God?"

Rabbi Stein pulled up a chair between the pastors.

"We know Christians, Muslims, and Jews, believe in one God. Of course, the majority of the world religions believe in many gods. Even with so much disagreement; we believe God is trying to save our world from total destruction. Mother Mary came to us with a message of hope and peace. The founders of the World Faith Movement consist of Pope Michael, a Catholic, Akim Maleek, a Muslim, and Joel Weiss, a Jew. Together, they have sought God and believe Mary was speaking the truth. We believe her love has the power to bring all children of God under the same umbrella."

A skeptical John Ryals asked, "Rabbi, if we don't agree the Bible is absolute truth, how can we have unity?"

"Pastor John, this in an historic time, God is asking His creation to become a reflection of His love. How can we love one another if we treat each other as evil? Peace for mankind can only be achieved through tolerance."

Ms. Grimm leaned forward and read, "'...You shall love the Lord your God with all your heart, with all your soul, with all your strength, and with all your mind, and your neighbor as yourself.' 17 I believe this passage applies to all people; as we seek to love God in our own way."

"Pastor Ryals, do you know Dr. William Burgess, senior pastor of Riverside Union Church in Memphis, Tennessee?"

"Why yes, father Andrew, I really admire him."

"Last month Dr. Burgess publicly endorsed the WFM. He thinks our world is plunging toward disaster. He believes the WFM, although not totally orthodox according to his view of God, has the potential to foster world peace."

Pastor Ryals had read about the WFM but never dreamed such a well respected colleague would ever endorse it. The spirit of Compromise continued to weave its deception as the team shared their vision for the world. It wasn't long before the pastors seemed reluctant to even ask the right questions.

THIRD SEAL : THE BLACK HORSE

"When He opened the third seal, I heard the third living creature
say, "Come and see." So I looked, and behold, a black horse, and he
who sat on it had a pair of scales in his hand."
Revelation 6:5

All of heaven heard the opening of the third seal. Standing before the
Lamb of God stood an emaciated black horse and its rider. The black
robed skeletal rider was holding a pair of scales.

One of the four living creatures declared with a mighty shout, "A
quart of wheat for a day's wages." 1

Soon, a rider on the black horse will reach earth with the power
to create famines; the likes of which no one has ever imagined.

It was during an early morning selling frenzy when the Dow
Jones mysteriously began its slide. At first, the stocks going down
were mostly high risk. But when the conservative stocks began to
plunge, all eyes focused on the big board at the New York Stock
Exchange. One by one, General Electric, General Motors, Microsoft,
AT&T, and a host of others joined the nose dive. Within hours, the
stock exchange experienced the worst panic since the 1929 crash.
Investors around the globe could only watch as their portfolios turned
to scrap paper. By the time the government could intervene, the
damage was irreversible. The Japanese, European, and Asian markets
followed with catastrophic losses. The constant drain of supplies in
multiple wars had depleted valuable resources. For many countries a
financial collapse was inevitable. 2

Then the President of the United States agreed to join forces with the World Faith Movement in the most powerful political religious merger ever seen. Meticulously, Kayin was assembling a foundation for a one world financial system. There would be a specific strategy for each country.

Reeling under the terror of wars, most nations were not unprepared for such utter devastation. Within months, a crippling famine would reach around the world. An army of demons was following the rider on the black horse. The goal of this evil horde was the ultimate control of mankind.

This meeting with the White House Staff was unique. A distinguished group of Christian pastors had come to share what God had shown them in prayer. The sound bite was highlighted with pictures. Thousands of languages, faiths, customs, and beliefs, were joining together as one. After their presentation one of the pastors asked to pray.

With other ministers huddled around Joshua Kayin, he prayed, "Father, we thank You for anointing Your servant for such a time as this. May You guide our President as he ushers in world peace through the defeat of worldwide terrorism."

Hovering above, the spirit of Pride bragged, "Who is like the Beast? 3 Satan will soon give him his power and authority over every nation. The Beast is coming to war and overcome many saints." 4

Positioned outside, a warrior angel prayed, "'Here is the patience of the saints: here are those who keep the commandments of God and the faith of Jesus.'" 5

"Who's going to pay for all this food?" gasped the accountant. "We can feed almost half the world."

Angrily slamming the phone down, he had no answer. Someone had to challenge such questionable purchasing of commodities. The accountant was horrified at the enormous amounts of food being shipped to cities throughout Europe, Asia, the Middle East, and Africa. The oil rich Middle East Federation had acquired more food, stocked and bar coded, than any other country in the world. Kayin's mission was right on schedule.

The beautiful halls were a remarkable sight. The paintings displayed its remarkable history. Even the furnishings held historical significance. The security of the world had been fought for on the floor of the United States Senate. For those visiting there were many wonderful memories to replay. But for the Senators today, only a fear of what could happen was gripping their hearts. No one ever believed the world could spiral so far out of control in just three short years. So many things had to go wrong at precisely the right time for the financial systems to fail so drastically. Answers to the curse of war, famine, and disease, were strangely absent. A closed door session would begin as soon as every Senator was accounted for.

As legislators were arriving, a Senator from New York openly warned, "This meeting could turn ugly."

Lobbyists could be seen scurrying down the halls trying to protect their interests. It was easy to see why. Soon, men and women of the United States Senate would be voting on legislation that could rescue billions from the greatest famine anyone had ever seen.

The Vice President of the United States opened the session by recognizing the respected Senator from North Carolina. All eyes focused on microphone # 2 as the Senator clutched the edges of the glass podium.

"Ladies and Gentlemen of the Senate, I come before you this morning to speak concerning the severity of the times in which we are living. Never before has our world experienced such fear, confusion, and hopelessness. If you take away a person's hope for the future, it's like letting them slowly die. Today we have one goal. This financial crisis which is spreading from country to country like an out-of-control fire must be stopped. The World ID Commerce Act, a worldwide system of buying and selling, is our only hope. 6 Without such a system in place; we could travel down a road ending in ruin."

"Mr. Chairman, Mr. Chairman, Mr. Chairman."

Fearing such a reactionary statement could breed more fear, a Senator from Massachusetts announced, "Our people need answers, not gloom and doom speeches!"

When the chair recognized the esteemed legislator from Florida, the loud buzz of confusion died down. Eugene McKnight has held office for twenty-eight years. His nickname among the lobbyists is Power Broker. He could make deals and propose compromises which could stop the McCoy's and Hatfield's from feuding.

"My fellow Senators, within the next month every nation on

earth will be scrutinizing the crisis we are now facing. We will need exceptional courage to make the difficult decisions to stop this misery. The only way for this to happen is to be empowered by a divine strength representing all faiths."

The applause was politically correct. Religious tolerance was a must for any Senator seeking re-election.

"I remember playing on my sixth grade basketball team with my three best friends: Timmy, Bobby, and Kenny. After twelve games, we were still undefeated. My three friends started every game while I sat the bench. Whenever we were leading by more than twenty points, the coach would reluctantly put Eugene, number six, in the game. It didn't matter to me because we were winning. The guys were so excited about the chance to capture our first city championship. We lived in a small town called Lake Bering. It seemed like everybody who was important turned out for the championship game."

"What is he up to?" whispered a Senator from Kansas.

"While the team was warming up, out of nowhere, the fear of failure hit me like a ton of bricks. Now listen, my friends. You and I know many of our greatest fears never come to pass. Think back when we faced the worst airline strike in history. American Airlines was near bankruptcy. Thousands could lose their jobs. The federally appointed mediators were unable to resolve the deadlock until two Senators offered to help. Everyone knew if they failed, the voters would not forget come election time. They risked their careers to bring a solution to this nightmare. They got the negotiations rolling, and within a month American Airlines was back in the air."

"He always has an angle," one Senator whispered to another.

"Now back to my story. My fear was that I would miss the last shot of the game and cause my team to lose the city championship. Most town folk would be okay about it; all they ever cared about was football. My brother's friends would call me a choker, so what, that didn't matter to me. What really scared me was facing Timmy, Bobby, and Kenny. The approval of our friends is hard to figure out sometimes. It can make us do things we would never do."

Edging forward in their seats, everyone was hanging on every word.

"We trailed throughout the game. With five minutes to go, each of our five starters had four fouls apiece. The coach's face looked about as intense as I had ever seen it."

"Standing up, he hollered, "Be ready, Eugene.""

"My hands started to sweat as I retied my sneakers for the fourth time. Then it happened. Timmy, Bobby, and Kenny, each fouled out within two minutes of each other. With a team of eight boys, the coach had no choice."

"Eugene, check in at the scorer's table."

"My family and neighbors cheered when they announced my name. I knew my best friends would be watching every move I made or didn't make. I could rebound, play defense, even dribble. My big weakness was shooting. With time running out, my team scored three straight baskets. We were down by one point with ten seconds left when the point guard from the other team was called for traveling. Our coach called time out. I wasn't part of his final instructions."

"Zack, take the inbounds pass and throw it inside. Galen, you take the last shot. Now remember, we have only ten seconds."

"With huge drops of sweat dropping from his forehead, it was easy to see our coach didn't have much hope of winning. When the huddle broke, the noise was deafening. Amidst the commotion, I looked back and saw their faces. I didn't want the glory. I didn't need any praise for winning the city championship. All Eugene McKnight cared about was the approval of his three best buddies.

"The inbounds pass went to Zack, our best dribbler. 10... 9... He maneuvered down the center of the court and was forced to veer to the left of the key where I was. He was trapped as they double teamed him. 8... 7... A quick shoulder fake pulled one defender out of position. Zack slipped between them and passed the ball to a panicked number six."

As the speaker scanned the audience, nervous laughs echoed through the hall.

"I had two choices. I could take a shot from ten feet or risk a pass to Galen on the baseline."

Looking into the eyes of men and women who could decide the destiny of six billion people, he paused again. For some Senators, the approval of man was everything. For others, it was the love of their family. Even so, Eugene McKnight was confident. When faced with the greatest fear the world could ever imagine he was convinced that his fellow Senators would vote for what is best for the people."

"6... 5... As Galen broke for the basket I faked the shot drawing the defenders to me. 4... 3... I made the pass. 2... As soon as Galen's hands touched the ball; he spun and shot. It hung on the rim as the entire crowd held its breath. The buzzer went off like an M-Eighty;

shattering the silence as the ball dropped in. The crowd went crazy as they raised Galen up on their shoulders. I remember my folks. I even saw some of my teachers cheering. But what meant the most were the words from one of my buddies.

"Way to go, Gene, you made the perfect pass."

"Ladies and Gentlemen of the Senate, I highly recommend the passage of the World ID Commerce Act. We must have the courage to do what is best for our country and the world. They deserve the perfect pass."

Everyone stood and applauded. Some wept with emotion; while others were summoning the courage to face what was coming. Not one Senator had any idea of the evil persecution that would soon cover America like a smoldering blanket.

While this emergency session dragged on, intercessory prayer groups were forming all over the country. The famine, which had lasted several months, had opened miraculous doors for the gospel. Bible studies were being held every night of the week. These meetings were not the usual, read two verses followed by an emotional story. No, the time had come for believers to demand the truth concerning the end of the age. 7

For most pastors in America, the warning to watch by a growing number of Watchmen was mainly ignored. For Mark Bishop, Stephen Corbin, Billy B, and Jason Wylie, it was gut-wrenching. Like sheep to the slaughter, most were already trusting in the sincerity of their pastors and well known teachers.

A very common excuse was, "I'm a Christian trying to raise my family. The preachers know a lot better than I do. If I can't trust my pastor, then who can I trust?"

One homemaker reasoned, "No man knows the day or the hour. If Jesus didn't know, why should believers worry about the timing of His coming?"

"It doesn't matter what the Bible says about the end times," admonished a Sunday school teacher. "No amount of debate will change anything. Let's just be ready."

For Watchmen around the world, it was terrifying to see so many believers accept such compromise as if it were from the Holy Spirit. The body of Christ could have been ready when the spirit of the

Antichrist split their families.

"Good morning, brethren," greeted a smiling John Ryals. "This morning's Bethany Ministers Association meeting has been requested by two of our members, Thomas Bray and Gerald Pierce. Both have had successful ministries in Bible prophecy for many years. Here is my good friend, Reverend Jerry Pierce."

"Thank you, John. Tom and I have come today to discuss a very disturbing situation. This past month, Mark Bishop and Stephen Corbin have made disparaging remarks about our Association's belief in the imminent return of our Lord Jesus Christ. They have attacked our motives as well as our character. As members of our Association they need to be held accountable for such false teaching."

The pressure of the moment seemed a bit much. The hypocrisy on his face would have become obvious if he had not motioned for Tom Bray to take over.

Stepping forward, the gray haired revivalist confidently affirmed, "I'm afraid Jerry is speaking the truth. For years, brethren have disagreed on the events taking place after the rapture. In fact, every minister within our Association believes in a future Antichrist. He will be given authority over every nation by Satan. We believe this evil leader will exalt himself above God during the Great Tribulation. Most of us even believe in the two Witnesses of Revelation 11:3. With all that said, it has always been a practice of our Association to treat our members with respect. But these so called ministers who deny our Blessed Hope, they're a different breed."

"Brother Tom," interrupted a puzzled Allen Colson, "how do Mark and Stephen deny the Blessed Hope?"

"C'mon guys, Mark Bishop never gave a hoot about the rapture until Corbin came with his new revelation. It's no secret he's convinced Mark former President Joshua Kayin is the Antichrist. It's like he's under Corbin's control. Even some of our teenagers are calling Corbin, 'The Watchman'. Sounds like a cult to me. Everyone doesn't have to agree with everything I teach, but the fact is, they're teaching a deception. No man knows the day or the hour; yet they teach a road map of events which supposedly warns the church of His coming. I don't know about you but I just can't sit by and not expose this dangerous heresy."

THE HOUSE OF GOD

"For the time has come for judgment to begin at the house of God;
and if it begins with us first, what will be the end of those who do
not obey the gospel of God?"
1 Peter 4:17

In the past decade, many pulpits in America adopted a seeker sensitive approach. The terrifying result was a Christian community that didn't understand accountability. Believers no longer confessed their sins to one another. Most knew very little about Bible doctrine. The average Christian prayed less than a minute a day. Sharing the gospel with the unsaved was mainly the clergy's responsibility. For the most part, the warnings of Jesus concerning the end of the age had fallen on deaf ears.

The Bishops remembered a Sunday morning just after arriving at Bethany Assembly. Among those praising the Lord was an usher hooked on porn, an openly racist couple, a teenager who had just had her third abortion, a recently divorced couple who refused to forgive one another and several who loved to gossip no matter who it hurt.

"Think of it," sighed Julie, "believers who hear His Word every week but have no intention of repenting." 1

Many pastors were guilty of teaching Christians they would go to heaven whether they confessed their sins or not. 2 The consequences of rejecting the conviction to repent had produced a lukewarm church. 3 Just the thought of Death and Hades attacking through the demonic power of the two beasts brought chills to Mark. His heart ached for ministers whose whole focus had become tolerance rather than repentance and holiness.

A popular evangelical leader recently taught Jesus never condemned anyone for their sin, but always reached out with His

Father's love. At a packed out Bible conference he shared, "Saints, once you are saved, your sin nature is destroyed. We aren't sinners; that's stinking thinking. 4 Irrespective of how we live our lives, God will never forsake His children." 5

"Lord," pleaded Mark, "only You can expose the teachers who are leading Your sheep astray. Allow the body to see with discerning eyes. Empower Your servants, O Lord, to stand for the doctrine of Christ." 6

He could barely hear the knocking on the door of his church study.

"Good afternoon, Pastor Mark."

"Welcome, Tom, please come in."

Offering the Reverend Bray a warm handshake, Mark realized how little he knew about his esteemed guest.

"The reason I've come today is because God has convicted me of saying some things I never should have said. Yesterday, Jerry Pierce and I met with the Bethany Ministers Association. Sadly, we pretty much maligned your ministry, your church, and your character. Even though I disagree with your post tribulation teaching, that doesn't give me the right to attack you or the reputation of your church."

Removing a handkerchief from his coat, he slowly wiped his forehead. He wasn't even trying to hide his shame.

"I was addressing the pastors. We were discussing how your teaching was confusing our youth. One thing led to another. Then a jealously came over me. It was more than that; it was like a presence that wouldn't go away until I said what it wanted. Then I just flat out called your church a cult."

This celebrated preacher was not discerning the spiritual warfare he was engaged in. Mark watched as tears welled up in Tom's eyes. The damage had been done. He knew it would take a lot more than a simple apology to the BMA to make things right.

"Tom, I forgive you for the lies you spoke against me. It took courage for you to admit you are wrong. I must tell you though; the spiritual warfare we are both experiencing is very powerful. Demons have been assigned to attack every spiritual leader in our town. The spirits of Jealousy and Lying which hit you so hard attacked my church last week. We must fight back in the name of Jesus."

The famous revivalist reluctantly agreed.

"Tom, I need to correct a misunderstanding the pastors within BMA have about me. First of all, my teaching isn't pre, mid, or post tribulation timing of the rapture. Each of these teachings has contradictions. In Matthew 24:21-22, Jesus has the elect being persecuted during the Great Tribulation. The Great Tribulation begins in the middle of the final seven years. This fact alone makes a pre-tribulation and a mid-tribulation rapture impossible. A post-tribulation rapture supposedly takes place at the end of the seven years. On His descent from heaven, Jesus catches up the saints as He returns for the battle of Armageddon. This means the saints never make it to heaven for either the judgment seat of Christ followed by the marriage of the Lamb to His bride. This is a blatant contradiction. My brother, the pre-tribulation and mid-tribulation rapture positions place the church in heaven before the coming of the Lord even occurs. In a post-tribulation rapture, the church never even makes it to heaven for the marriage of the Lamb!"

"Then when does Jesus resurrect His elect?

"In the middle of the 70th week, Jesus will open the fourth seal and the Great Tribulation will begin. The coming of the Son of Man with His angels for His elect will take place after Jesus opens the sixth seal. This means the resurrection must take place sometime in the second half of the seven years. 7 Of course; no man knows the exact day or hour."

"I'm glad you brought this up. Do you think we could take some time to discuss our Lord's coming?"

"Sure, what's on your heart?"

"Well, isn't your teaching a relatively new doctrine? Not many well known teachers ever taught Christians would be persecuted by the Antichrist during the Great Tribulation."

"You'd be surprised of the ones who did."

"Name one?"

"Charles Spurgeon, John Wesley, Matthew Henry, and John Wycliff, each taught the Man of Sin will reveal himself before the coming of the Lord Jesus Christ for His saints followed by the day of the Lord." 8

"What about the early church? Didn't the apostles teach Jesus could return at any moment?"

"Jesus taught a sequence of events which will warn believers of His coming. The resurrection of the elect will take place sometime between the opening of the sixth and seventh seals. Paul, Peter, and John, each taught this same sequence. In fact, not one church leader in the first three hundred years ever taught a secret rapture before the Great Tribulation."

"Whom are you referring to?"

"Justin Martyr, who lived from A.D. 100 to 168, taught the man of apostasy would persecute believers. So did, Irenaeus, who lived from A.D. 140 to 202, and Treutlen, who lived from A.D. 150 to 220. They each taught a future persecution of believers by the Beast."

With his arms crossed and his body erect, Tom asked, "So you're telling me the early Church didn't believe in the imminent return of Jesus Christ? Didn't Paul expect to be caught up in a twinkling of an eye when Christ returned?"

"He sure did. But before the elect are gathered to heaven, a falling away of believers must take place."

"Can you give me chapter and verse on that?"

"Jesus warned of a falling away during the Great Tribulation in Matthew 24:9-22 and so did Paul in II Thessalonians 2:3-4.

"So how does Israel becoming a nation fit into your sequence of events?"

"Before the coming of our Lord Jesus Christ can happen, the Jewish people have to be back in their homeland. Now you know God dispersed the Jewish people throughout the world because of their rebellion in 70 A.D. For almost two thousand years the Jews have not had a homeland. In 1948, Israel was miraculously granted Statehood. In 1967, the Jewish people regained control of Jerusalem during the Six Day War. These two events paved the way for specific prophesied events which must transpire before the coming of the Son of Man for His elect."

"I'd like to know the last event that takes place just before the rapture?"

"Like I said before, after the sixth seal opens, the sun, moon, and stars will lose their light. The Old Testament prophet Joel wrote, 'And I will show wonders in the heavens and in the earth: blood, and fire, and pillars of smoke. The sun shall be turned into darkness, and the moon into blood, before the great and the terrible day of the Lord comes.' 9 Joel saw this sign coming before the day of the Lord, God's wrath. In Matthew 24:29, Jesus describes this exact sign coming just before He gathers His elect to heaven. By comparing scriptures, it's clear this sign in the heavens must precede the coming of the Son of

Man, which is immediately followed by the day of the Lord. In other words, the body of Christ won't be delivered until the sun, moon, and stars lose their light."

"If this is true then a secret rapture isn't possible."

"Tom, there is a critical difference between a secret at any moment rapture and a visible rapture preceded by certain events."

"What about the promise of our Blessed Hope? How can the return of Christ be a blessing if the church must first suffer through the days of the Great Tribulation?"

"My brother, in Revelation 7:9-14, a great multitude of blood washed saints from every nation are going to get the victory over the Beast and his mark during the great tribulation. Our Blessed Hope will shorten these days by physically delivering those who do. Yes, we will face persecution from the enemy but the faithful will never experience God's wrath. Jesus will actually be more of a Blessed Hope in a time of great testing."

"He's coming as a thief in the night. No one knows the day or hour. Paul clearly taught imminence."

"Expectancy, Tom. In I Thessalonians 5:4, Paul says the day of the Lord should not overtake believers like a thief. The Lord is coming like a thief for those in darkness. It will be the sons of the day who will be watching for the events which warn of His coming. Jesus said, 'Now when these things begin to happen, look up and lift your heads, because your redemption draws near.' 10 Redemption in this verse means physical deliverance, the gathering of the elect to heaven."

"I've studied thousands of hours on the last days. To be honest, the Holy Spirit has given me a different interpretation for every one of your arguments."

"Yes, I'm very aware of your background. Your ministry experience is impressive. I also know there is not one scripture that teaches our Jesus will secretly catch up His elect before the Great Tribulation begins."

"So you believe in a road map of events warning the body of His coming?"

"That's correct. Right now, we are experiencing the third seal, the black horse of famine. In the middle of the 70th week, Michael will cast Satan out of heaven. 11 This arch angel will stop restraining the mystery of lawlessness. 12 Once Michael is taken out of the way, Jesus will open the fourth seal. 13 The two beasts will be given the power to kill one fourth of the world by Satan. The first Beast (Antichrist) and the second beast (false prophet) are going to war against the saints and overcome many." 14

"So you believe Joshua Kayin is the Beast and Pope Michael is his false prophet?"

"I do."

"How does your scenario change when Kayin isn't our President anymore?"

"It doesn't."

"This makes no sense. Why would a loving God allow the bride of Christ to be deceived by the Antichrist?"

Opening his Bible, Mark read, "'For the time has come for judgment to begin at the house of God; and if it begins with us first, what will be the end of those who do not obey the gospel of God? Now, if the righteous one is scarcely saved, where will the ungodly and the sinner appear? Therefore, let those who suffer according to the will of God commit their souls to Him in doing good, as to a faithful Creator.'" 15

"Judgment is for sinners; not for the elect. God's people cannot be judged for their sins; Jesus atoned for our sins on the cross. This means the body of Christ must be removed before the tribulation period begins."

"Tom, you create a serious contradiction when you don't see the critical distinction between Satan's wrath and God's wrath."

"What distinction?"

"The Great Tribulation isn't the day of the Lord. The Great Tribulation is Satan's wrath against Christians. 16 The day of the Lord is God's wrath against the wicked. 17 The Great Tribulation will begin after the fourth seal is opened. The day of the Lord begins after Jesus opens the seventh seal. This is when the heavenly scroll opens and God's wrath is poured out. Those who reject this truth are setting themselves up to be deceived."

"Real Christians will never be deceived!"

"Many already are. In America, we have Christians whose lifestyle consists of habitual adultery, homosexuality, racism, lying, drunkenness, hatred, and pornography. Paul warned those who live like this will not inherit the kingdom of heaven." 18

Mark knew only the Holy Spirit could make the truth come alive in Tom's heart. He patiently waited as the revivalist tried to reconcile what had just been shared.

"Well this has been a very interesting chat. I respect you for standing for such convictions. But I refuse to believe a child of God would deliberately deny the Lord. I don't see the mark of the beast coming in our lifetime."

"Tom, I believe Joshua Kayin is gathering..."

"Please allow me to finish. I believe your interpretations are way off. I wouldn't want to be in your shoes at the judgment seat of Christ. In fact, I'd bet my life the mark of the beast won't come in my lifetime."

At the urging of the Holy Spirit, Mark quietly prophesied, "Soon you will be given that very choice."

A preoccupied Tom never heard his reply.

"With God's help, I will ask for forgiveness for the remarks I have made against you and your church. Thank you for your time. Goodbye."

After closing the door, Mark bowed his head and prayed, "Lord, I know Tom loves You. Only You can change his convictions. Make him an overcomer for Your glory. I pray his family will never register for the mark of the beast."

The massive marble pulpit was glowing from hundreds of TV lights. The roar from the immense crowd was exhilarating. Never had so many religious faiths come together in such unity. Everyone could worship their God in their own way. Looking bigger than life in his purple and scarlet robes, Pope Michael raised his hands high. 19

"Brothers and sisters, I've come today with a message of hope from the very heart of God. The time has come to end all religious and political bigotry. Our world must conquer its fear of change. Next week former President of the United States Joshua Kayin and I will be meeting with the United Nations. This World Financial Summit has the potential to bring stability to our world. We earnestly covet your prayers. I believe God has allowed countries to fight one another so that we may all see the importance of becoming a one world community."

The media caught every word. A myriad of demons continued to fight over who would receive credit for the deception. The stage was being set for the two beasts to address over six billion people with a hollow promise of peace and prosperity.

THE MARK OF THE BEAST

'No one may buy or sell except one who has the mark or the name of the beast, or the number of his name.'
Revelation 13:17

"This is a Special Report. I'm Natalie Roberts reporting to you live from New York. A steady stream of financial leaders has been arriving this morning for the World Financial Summit. This international gathering will address the world's severe monetary crisis. The major item on the agenda will be the World ID Commerce Act. This projected financial system, which was recently approved by the United States, is expected to receive severe opposition from several major powers. Joshua Kayin, in a recent press conference, threw his support behind this new technology of checks and balances."

The former American President shared, "We, as a global village, must take bold measures to stop this famine which has destroyed so many lives."

Israel's Prime Minister, Avi Rosen, added, "This financial crisis is the greatest threat our world has ever faced. I can understand why President Kayin and Pope Michael, Leader of the World Faith Movement, have called for this Summit. Only a political/religious alliance has the power to stop this horrendous plaque. Our world needs a more secure system of merchandising and trading. I have the utmost confidence our leaders can agree on an acceptable solution."

The Anchorwoman gestured at the building behind her.

"In a related story, over one-hundred rightwing Christians were arrested earlier this morning for demonstrating against the World ID system. These protesters were condemning the proposed ID registration as the mark of the beast. 1 Some were even caught on camera predicting Joshua Kayin is going to deceive the world.

When asked about such threats, the head of UN security stated, "Our safety measures are airtight. No terrorist or Christian fundamentalist will be able to interfere."

The Media Center was packed with reporters covering the Summit. The Pope's aide pushed the pause button of the tape of this morning's demonstration.

"This isn't anything new," he scoffed. "These fanatics have been around for years. Don't you remember the right wingers who believed Ronald Wilson Reagan was the Antichrist because of the number of letters in his name?"

Laughter spread through the skeptical reporters.

"Each of you has a copy of today's press release. Pope Michael strongly recommends this Watchmen cult and its hysterical Antichrist allegations be ignored. This press release explains why prophesies of Daniel and Revelation have nothing to do with our present crisis. Several religious leaders from the World Faith Movement have publicly declared the prophecies concerning the Antichrist were fulfilled by A.D. 70."

The purpose of this meeting was not clear to most of the reporters, especially those still hung over from last night's party. It would take more than the three cups of coffee to be able to comprehend this morning's announcement.

"For example, during the year 168 B.C., a king from Syria named Antiochus Epiphanies, signed a peace treaty with Israel. He promised peace and prosperity for all Jews who would honor his treaty. With Israel living under his protection, he suddenly broke his promise and attacked them. This evil king then captured and desecrated the Holy Temple in Jerusalem. During this time, many Jews turned away from the Law of Moses and served Epiphanies. Daniel tells how this evil king accomplished his conquest." 2

Most were busy recording the aide's words to use as sound bites for their daily broadcasts. Others were furiously taking notes; highlighting their own interpretation of this bizarre press release.

"Now hear this sequence of events," exhorted the aide. "Epiphanies' armies desecrated the Temple, abolished the daily sacrifice, and set up an abomination of desolation." 3

"This sounds like the story line these Watchmen have been

feeding us," smirked a *New York Times* reporter.

"Precisely," said the aide. "Epiphanies signed a peace treaty with Israel and broke it by attacking the Jews. He then set up his image in their Temple and exalted himself above God. In other words, the prophecies in Daniel have already been fulfilled. All his Excellency is asking for is that our focus be on world peace. This can only happen by all of us remaining positive."

The world had never witnessed such an event. Virtually every nation was represented in one place, at one time, to resolve a world problem. To ensure success, former American President Joshua Kayin has already met with every voting member of the United Nations. Many were now convinced his economic proposal was the only viable option.

Even so, the World Financial Summit seemed to drag on and on. No real news was forth-coming from behind the closed doors. The reporters were extremely upset with the meager press releases they were receiving. Word finally came. Joshua Kayin would be making an official announcement. As soon as the doors were opened, the United Nations building was engulfed with reporters. Everyone was filming as the former American President stepped up to the microphone. Seated beside him was Pope Michael.

"Greetings of love to our World family. I humbly come before you in this urgent hour to propose a prosperity we have never experienced before. My vision includes peace and safety for every country. I believe in a world capable of laying aside its differences in politics, religion, and human rights. Proof of this is the success the World Faith Movement has had. This valuable grass roots organization has produced a membership consisting of Christians, Jews, Muslims, Catholics, Hindus, and Buddhists, to name just a few. In fact, it has grown so fast it's been difficult to keep up. What the World Faith Movement has done, we can too. Today I propose a World ID system which has the potential to completely defeat terrorism. By becoming one in mind and spirit, we will be able to eliminate the wars on our borders and put an end to these cursed famines. Trust me, the dying of innocent people must stop. Our only hope is to send a message of tolerance and love to the religions of our world. Ladies and gentlemen, I give you the New World Coalition."

The ecstatic reception was inevitable. Satan knew exactly what mankind wanted to hear. In a sign of unity leaders from the United States, China, Russia, Africa, India, North and South Korea, the European Union, Japan, the Middle East Federation, and Israel, joined hands. It would take several months for the plan to be implemented. A number of countries would resist at first, this was expected. The Prince of Darkness knew his New World Coalition would eventually grow into an enormous octopus, with tentacles powerful enough to control all its members. Every nation on earth would be forced to join. The religious harlot had completed her job. She had ridden the beast having seven heads and ten horns to a place of power among world leaders. Watchmen throughout the world were intensifying their message. Joshua Kayin was not a savior but an evil counterfeit. Time was running out for the Christian resistance movement. Soon, billions would be thrust into the valley of decision.

Mark Bishop loved sharing the gospel. There was no greater joy than leading a soul to the saving knowledge of Jesus Christ. After becoming a pastor, he realized it was one thing to have people accept Jesus as their Savior, and it was quite another to disciple them, love them, exhort them, and pray for them. The Bishops didn't need to be reminded of those who returned to the sins that held them in bondage before they were saved. 4

The past month had been a real drainer. To see the deception being proposed by the two beasts was tough to handle. Mark and Julie never doubted God would take care of them; it was just the harsh reality of seeing Jesus' warnings come to pass. Nearly two thousand years ago, the Son of God stood on the Mount of Olives and prophesied a future persecution of believers; a time when many coming in Jesus' name would deceive many. 5 The lack of discipleship in America would soon be exposed. Mark and his family spent all week fasting and praying in anticipation of the warfare this Sunday morning. Standing before his congregation, Pastor Mark Bishop knew his prayers had been answered. Their applause was such an encouragement. The saints were anxious to hear from the Lord.

Looking out over his parishioners he so deeply loved, he announced, "Our message this morning is entitled, *The Mark of the Beast*. Dear friends, I never dreamed of ever being in the position we are in today. We're at a point most Christians thought would never occur in our lifetime. A prophesied time when every man, woman, and child, must choose whom they will follow for eternity. I'm talking about a mark that can never be erased; an economic number Satan is going to use to deceive Christians. Tragically, in this dark hour, most believers are refusing to embrace the truth of Jesus' prophetic warnings..."

As her husband continued sharing, Julie couldn't help but reflect back on the past three years. Satan's attacks against believers were so obvious. So much precious time wasted. She could think of Christians who needed deliverance from demonic strongholds but didn't know how to get it. Of man-made programs that looked impressive but produced nothing eternal. Of youth groups whose focus was more on fun than pressing in after God. The Great Tribulation would erupt three and a half years from the day the Jerusalem Peace Accord was signed. 6 Even so, a large majority still had no idea what was happening.

Standing in front of the pulpit, Pastor Mark boldly shared, "We are warned of the mark of the beast in Revelation 13:16-17.' He causes all, both small and great, rich and poor, free and slave, to receive a mark on their right hand or on their foreheads, and that no one may buy or sell except one who has the mark or the name of the beast, or the number of his name.' 7 Jesus is warning Christians who will face persecution from the Beast and his false prophet. During the Great Tribulation, the false prophet will deceive a multitude of believers into taking the mark of the beast. John wrote, 'Here is wisdom. Let him who has understanding calculate the number of the beast, for it is the number of a man: His number is 666.'" 8

Those nodding their heads knew this verse by heart.

"Because of this persecution, many will fall away from their faith and will begin to betray and hate each other. Recently we witnessed Joshua Kayin introducing the mark of the beast as an economic ID. It won't be long before his false prophet insidiously implements this plan. Saints, are you hearing me?"

This type of preaching had already driven away those who were lukewarm. It was easy to see why.

"Let's examine the opening of the first three seals of Revelation 6:1-6. The arrival of Satan on a white horse, the red horse of war, and the black horse of famine are the beginning of sorrows. They have each transpired right before our eyes. The hour we are living in behooves us to live holy lives through the love of our Lord Jesus Christ. Look at how many have allowed their love to grow cold. Peter wrote, 'For if, after they have escaped the pollutions of the world through the knowledge of our Lord and Savior Jesus Christ, they are again entangled in them and overcome, the latter end is worse for them than the beginning. For it would have been better for them not to have known the way of righteousness, than having known it, to turn from the holy commandment delivered to them.' 9 Brethren, this passage is about those cleansed from the pollution and sin of this world. Now, how is one cleansed from this evil world?"

"Only by the blood of Jesus." shouted a teenager.

"By genuine repentance," offered another.

"That's correct. If blood washed believers go back into the world and are overcome by habitually sinning, then their end will be worse than if they had never known Christ as Lord. This passage is warning Christians not to deny their relationship with God by returning to a lifestyle of sin."

Nudging his friend seated next to him, a visitor whispered, "Are you hearing what I'm hearing?"

His friend whispered back, "He's got guts."

"In the Book of Hebrews, Paul gives us another example of how a believer can choose to follow or reject the Lordship of Jesus Christ. We must remember God never takes away our free will after we get saved. Paul wrote, 'For if we sin willfully after we have received the knowledge of the truth (salvation), there no longer remains a sacrifice for sins, but a certain fearful expectation of judgment.' 10 Now get this. The apostle is referring to himself and other Christians. He is warning believers not to willfully return to their lifestyle of sin. You and I have the free will to follow or deny our Lord. Paul highlights the severe judgment for those who 'trample the Son of God under foot and treat the blood of the covenant that once 'sanctified' him as an unholy thing.' 11 Now I ask you, what people are sanctified by the blood of Jesus?" 12

"Only Christians are sanctified."

"That's right, Whitney. The warnings throughout Hebrews are for sanctified believers. When believers choose to return to a lifestyle of sin they trample the Son of God underfoot and insult the Spirit of grace."

Looking out over the congregation, the young pastor could sense a heavy resistance coming from the older saints.

"Our Jesus promised, 'And this is the will of Him who sent Me, that everyone who sees the Son and believes in Him may have everlasting life; and I will raise him up at the last day.' 13 The word 'believe' means to continually believe in and seek after. Believers who faithfully follow Jesus will never be cast out. Jesus said, 'If you abide in My word, you are My disciples indeed.' 14 If implies a choice whether to abide or not. Brothers and sisters, the hour is late and many in the body of Christ are being deceived. I'm pleading with each of you not to register for the mark of the beast. Anyone who does will be tormented in eternal fire before the Lamb and His angels. Soon, a powerful delusion will come upon those who refuse to believe the truth and be saved. 15 As your pastor; I am accountable to God for teaching the truth, no matter what the consequences. I admonish each of us this morning to repent of any unconfessed sin and be obedient to the leading of the Holy Spirit." 16

"Preach it, Pastor." shouted an excited Luke Appleby, prompting the youth group to rise to their feet and cheer.

Clearly embarrassed the head usher yelled, "Down in front!"

Moving to the center aisle, Mark pleaded, "Now hear me out. I'm not preaching a perfection doctrine. No one can be saved by good works. We are saved by grace through faith. 17 The life of a believer should be a constant pursuit of Jesus; not one of bondage to sin but freedom in the Holy Spirit. Real faith produces real works. Let us pray."

Miraculously, the Spirit of God was setting people free from bondages that controlled them for years. As the worship team softly sang about the blood of Jesus, several disgruntled members rushed for the exit. The first person Mark met was a furious Harriet Jones.

"Pastor, show me one verse that says a real Christian can deny Jesus and go to hell? I don't think you can."

"In James 5:19-20, James says a brother who wanders from the truth through a multitude of sins can be brought back and his soul can be saved from death. Now we know a soul can't physically die. So this verse must be referring to a believer's soul being saved from eternal death."

"Is that so?" fumed the livid Sunday school teacher.

"Harriet, this passage teaches a Christian can bring back a fallen brother and save his soul from eternal death."

Spinning around, she rushed out vowing never to return again.

The soaring popularity of the WFM was sending shock waves through Christian homes. Recently, several Protestant denominations agreed to consolidate into one organization. Baptists, Methodists, Presbyterians, and Lutherans, were coming together as one.

"It's a good move for the Protestants," praised a representative from the Vatican. "No one religion has the total truth. Each faith has a measure of truth. As a member of the WFM, I promote tolerance toward those who disagree with my belief in God."

For some, membership with WFM was very controversial. The main advantage was financial. Many churches needed the stipend to keep their doors open. Self-preservation was now top priority; not the absolute truth of God's Word.

The world was being pressured to take a now or never attitude. The wave of optimism stemming from Kayin's speech was beginning to birth unbelievable changes. Decade long civil wars suddenly stopped. Old enemies were successfully negotiating new trade agreements with each other. Countries hardest hit by famine were being rescued from starvation by massive food shipments. Within the past three months, the entire supply of food Joshua Kayin stored up was dispensed throughout the world. In Brazil, a holiday was given in his honor. His lifesaving airlifts of food and medicine literally saved thousands of Brazilian families. In Ghana, massive crowds lined the streets to thank this beloved leader for his generous help. Almost overnight, the world was beginning to believe the charismatic American was a gift sent by God.

PARTAKERS OF CHRIST

"For we have become partakers of Christ if we hold the beginning
of our confidence steadfast to the end."
Hebrews 3:14

"Good morning, Jason, it's good to see you again."

The Watchman shook hands with the well-groomed attorney as they sat down for a sunrise breakfast at Bernie's Café.

Jason Wylie's heart was supernaturally touched the first night Stephen Corbin preached in Bethany. Even though they briefly met at Mark's church, the lawyer never really had the opportunity to share his experience with the busy evangelist. After finishing off some fried eggs and grits, the popular lawyer began their chat with a question.

"Stephen, in Revelation 3:5 Jesus exhorts believers to become overcomers. It says, 'He who overcomes shall be clothed in white garments, and I will not blot his name from the Book of Life; but I will confess his name before My Father and before His angels.' 1 So who or what are we to overcome?"

"I believe it will be the Beast and his evil agenda during the Great Tribulation."

"What's going to happen to those who resist?"

"Many will be martyred." 2

"Sounds like a real blood bath."

"It will be."

"What about Christians who don't overcome?"

"Any believer who worships the beast, his image, or receives his mark, their name will be blotted out of the Book of Life." 3

"Why aren't any well known pastors teaching this?"

"Jason, this teaching is new for most pastors in America. If you visit countries where saints are being persecuted, you'll find they believe what the early Church taught."

"Which is?"

"The Beast will war and overcome many saints during the fourth and fifth seals. 4 After the sixth seal is opened, Jesus will come back and His angels will gather up His elect."

"You mean the days of the Great Tribulation are going to be cut short by the coming of the Son of Man?"

"Absolutely, then I was preaching in Lithuania, I discovered something very interesting. Most churches started by American missionaries taught Jesus could come at any moment. When I visited churches without any missionary influence, they believed the elect would be delivered from the persecution of the Antichrist. Jason, believers who aren't prepared to face the Beast are in great danger."

"Stephen, this is intense. Thanks for taking the time to share with me. But before I go, could I share a testimony with you about my childhood?"

"I'd love to hear it," smiled the Watchman.

"Growing up I really loved my grandparents. I have fond memories of neighbor kids coming over for Grandma's blackjack pancakes and Grandpa's fiery sermons. He loved preaching on the rapture in their big barn. The end time charts he used were awesome. Hearing about the catching up of the saints at any moment was exciting stuff. A lot of my friends believed in a secret rapture but I never did."

"Me either," sighed Stephen.

"It's pretty amazing what's happened to our city since you preached your one night seminar," laughed the muscular lawyer. "You know, I was there that night."

"Really," grinned Stephen, "it seems like only yesterday."

"Since then, the Lord has dramatically changed our lives. Jackie and I now desire God's perfect will; nothing else matters." 5

Walking out of Bernie's Café they smiled and shook hands. Neither had any idea they were being groomed by God to become leaders of the greatest Christian resistance movement ever.

The prayer warriors were excited about tonight's Bible study. They had already spent two hours praying. They began by rebuking away any demonic spirits from interfering. Then they prayed for the

Spirit of revival. They finished by petitioning the Lord to save every unbeliever attending. The expectancy was infectious.

"Before I begin our study of God's Word tonight, does anyone have any questions or comments?"

A troubled Drew Henley asked, "Pastor Mark, some Christians at my school think your teaching is completely bogus. Since no man knows the day or the hour of His coming they say there can't be any signs before Jesus comes and gets us. If there were, then He couldn't come at any moment."

"Drew, in Matthew 24:4-29, our Lord highlights events and signs that must take place before the coming of the Son of Man in v30-31. When we see these events we will know His coming is near (v33). Jesus exhorts believers to be ready for the Son of Man is coming in an hour we do not expect (v44), an exact day or hour no man knows (v36). If this is true then how can Jesus come back at any moment?"

"Where do they get this secret rapture from anyway?"

"Drew, no one really knows who invented it. We do know a minister from the Church of England named John Nelson Darby popularized this teaching in the 1800's. For several decades, he used his eloquent preaching to promote this new revelation."

"But how could it become so popular so fast?"

"The year was 1859. It was a hot summer in Chicago. The long line of Americans waiting to get inside the rundown auditorium looked so out of place. The willowy teacher with bushy eyebrows and long sideburns spoke with a deep urgency. Most could see this man of God believed in what he was preaching. John Nelson Darby taught the coming of the Lord in I Thessalonians 4:15-17 was a secret rapture that could happen at any moment."

"So this secret rapture had never been taught before?"

"Not in America, Drew. Darby taught all the events leading up to coming of the Lord were fulfilled, which means Jesus could come at any moment."

"I don't get it. Where does it say that in the Word?"

"A lot of the listeners in Darby's day didn't get it either. The resurrection of the elect at the coming of the Son of Man isn't secret. Every eye will see Him. Yes, Ned?"

"So why do so many believe it now?"

"Ned, why can't Jesus gather His elect at this moment?"

"The gospel must be preached to every nation before He gathers His elect. 6 This will be fulfilled by the angel in Revelation 14:6 during the Great Tribulation."

"What about II Thessalonians 2:3?" added Drew. "The day of the Lord can't come until the Man of Sin reveals himself during the Great Tribulation. If the revealing of the Man of Sin is still future, then how can Jesus come today?"

"Some in Darby's audience asked these same questions. You see, in the 1800's, holiness and sound doctrine weren't a high priority. Most Christians were not concerned with the coming of the Lord. Because of this careless atmosphere, Satan sowed several major cults."

"What type of cults, Pastor?"

"You ever hear of the Church of the Latter Day Saints and the Jehovah Witnesses?"

"Mormons and JW's; talk about doctrines of demons."

"Yep, there was definitely a vacuum of unbelief for these types of cults to grow and deceive."

"Didn't Joseph Smith declare Christianity apostate?"

"He did, Drew. The Church Jesus Christ of Ladder Day Saints was created in the 1820's, the same time Darby taught a secret rapture of the church."

"What other doctrines did Darby teach?" asked Luke.

"The Plymouth Brethren, Darby's denomination, taught once a person was saved they can never be lost."

"What about free will?"

"John Darby didn't believe in free will. He taught God chose who would go to heaven or hell before they were even born."

"What about Christians who deny the Lord?"

"He taught anyone believing in Jesus and then lives in unconfessed habitual sin were never really saved."

An eerie silence captivated the room.

A perplexed Luke mumbled back, "And this was the preacher who convinced believers a secret rapture was true?"

"That night in Chicago, Darby gave an altar call. He challenged the jammed auditorium, "If Jesus returned tonight, how many of you would be left behind?"

"That sounds like last week's movie on the end times," gasped Whitney Troy. "What did the people do, Pastor?"

"The stampede to the altar was amazing. Soon many pastors were using this new teaching to motivate sinners to surrender their lives to God."

A smiling Drew shouted, "But no one can come to the Father

but by Him. Our Jesus is the Truth."

A girl seated next to Mark shared, "I don't get this. My daddy believes the doctrines of other religions are also important. Take the World Faith Movement for example. By bringing all the religions together, we can finally achieve world peace. Arguing over doctrine doesn't help; it just divides."

"She's right," affirmed her friend. "Look how Jesus loved everyone. He never argued over doctrine."

A solemn Mark respectfully asked, "I want everyone to listen up. 'Whoever transgresses and does not abide in the doctrine of Christ does not have God. He who abides in the doctrine of Christ has both the Father and the Son. If anyone comes to you and does not bring this doctrine, do not receive him into your house nor greet him; for he who greets him shares in his evil deeds.'" 7

"Whoa, that's not very loving."

"Paul warned believers will depart from the faith in the latter times because of doctrines of demons. This is a matter of heaven or hell. The Bible makes it clear there is only one doctrine that saves. Whereas all other religious doctrines are man-made, the doctrine of Jesus Christ is the only one which comes from above."

"What about Jewish people who love God? They don't believe in Jesus. Are you saying they won't go to heaven?"

"Jesus warned, 'He who has My commandments and keeps them, it is he who loves Me. And he who loves Me will be loved by My Father, and I will love him and manifest Myself to him...He who hates Me hates My Father also.'" 8

"Just because someone doesn't believe in Jesus doesn't mean they hate Him," scoffed the confused teenager.

"Paul wrote, 'Take heed to yourself and to the doctrine. Continue in them, for in doing this you will save both yourself and those who hear you.'" 9

With hands shooting up, a discerning Julie announced, "Tell you what, everyone write down your questions and Mark and Lance will try and answer them by this Sunday. Our Scripture promise tonight is, 'Nevertheless the solid foundation of God stands, having this seal: "The Lord knows those who are His. Let everyone who names the name of Christ depart from iniquity."' 10

"As we close tonight," concluded Mark, "I would like to ask each of you to pray about your future. Right now, God is calling Watchmen to warn the body of the eternal consequences of the Great

Tribulation. The decision to join the underground resistance won't be easy. Is there anyone who would like to pray about becoming a Watchman?"

Those raising their hands began to cry out in prayer. The Bishops immediately reflected back on Stephen's first admonition: "We just need to obey God. The Holy Spirit will raise up His prayer warriors."

ACCORDING TO THEIR OWN DESIRES

*"For the time will come when they will not endure sound doctrine,
but according to their own desires, because they have itching ears,
they heap for themselves teachers; and they will turn away their
ears from the truth..."*
II Timothy 4:3-4

Gene Lloyd Ministries had never paid for a thirty minute show during prime time. His prophecy organization had to downsize in order to raise the money for tonight's desperate appeal. Gene had always striven to be faithful to the Word; never attacking other ministers who disagreed with him. Nevertheless, his goal tonight was to expose false teachers who were preying upon the body of Christ. This emotional message wouldn't be easy. He would make one final plea to the unsaved while encouraging the saints to watch for their soon coming Blessed Hope.

"Tonight we interrupt our regularly scheduled broadcast to bring you, Countdown to the Rapture. Let's welcome well known author and prophecy expert Gene Lloyd."

The producer hit the applause button, triggering a canned response from a non-existent audience.

"Good evening, folks. Tonight, I've come into your homes with a message of eternal hope. Many of you don't know me from Adam. Actually what's really important tonight is the message, not the messenger. This message of hope I have for you is from the Bible. Jesus said, 'For God so loved the world that He gave his only begotten Son, that whoever believes in Him should not perish but have eternal life.' 1 My friends, if you pray to receive Jesus Christ as your Savior tonight, He will indwell you with the Spirit of God. God loves you. If you repent of your sins, He will write your name in the

Book of Life for eternity."

The cameraman moved in for a close up.

"There is another reason I'm here tonight. The Holy Spirit has given me a message of comfort to those who hold to the testimony of Jesus. Get ready, saints, our Blessed Hope could come at any moment. The night before He went to the cross, Jesus promised, 'In My Father's house are many mansions; if it were not so, I would have told you. I go to prepare a place for you. And if I go and prepare a place for you, I will come again and receive you to myself; that where I am, there you may be also.'" 2

"One more notch on the volume," whispered the producer.

"Listen church; don't believe these teachers who tell you Jesus can't come at any moment. It doesn't matter how sincere they appear. They are simply taking scriptures out of context to support their own false interpretations. For example, some confidently teach the coming of the Son of Man in Matthew 24:30 is actually the rapture. They believe Jesus is warning Christians about a series of events that must take place before He gathers His elect to heaven. Let's be clear; Matthew 24:30 is not about the rapture but those taken in judgment at the battle of Armageddon. The coming of the Son of Man is not the secret rapture of the saints; it's the glorious return of the Word of God with His saints to set up His Millennial Kingdom. John wrote, 'Behold, He is coming with clouds, and every eye will see him, even they who pierced Him. And all the tribes of the earth will mourn because of Him.'" 3

The annoyed preacher suddenly cast his notes aside.

"Let me ask you a critical question about the future of our world. Why should mankind be concerned about a future Armageddon? It's because the Word of God is coming back wearing a robe dipped in blood. 4 Jesus is going to split the Mount of Olives and then destroy the armies of the Beast. Don't be deceived, saints; we will not be here to be martyred by the Antichrist. It will be just the opposite. The bride will be with Jesus when He returns and casts the Beast and the false prophet into the lake of fire."

After pushing the applause button the soundman signaled.

"The Bible says, 'All who dwell on the earth will worship him, whose names have not been written in the Book of Life of the Lamb slain from the foundation of the world.' 5 Don't you see it? A real saint will never be overcome by the Beast. Praise the Lord, once your name is written in the Book of Life, it can never be erased."

The lights seemed hotter than normal to the experienced teacher. The commercial break came at just the right time.

"Listen up," announced the producer, "3... 2...1..."

"Church, I've taught for many years the body of Christ will be gone by the time the mark of the beast is forced upon the world. The events of the seven year tribulation period are highlighted in Revelation 6 through 19. I challenge anyone to find the Church mentioned anywhere in these chapters. The church is simply not there. And why is that? It's because she was caught up in Revelation 4:1. John saw, 'After these things I looked, and behold, a door standing open in heaven... Come up here, and I will show you things, which must take place after this.' 6 This has to be the rapture of the saints. Could it be any clearer?"

The producer signaled to Gene to lean back and relax.

"His coming is near; right at the door. For believers this is our day of redemption. For unbelievers, this could be your last chance to accept Jesus before being thrust into the day of the Lord." 7

A cameraman who once believed nervously shifted his feet.

"My friends, religion won't save you. Having family members who are believers won't save you either. You must be born again by the indwelling of the Holy Spirit. I beg of you; don't put it off another second. And for the saints, look up, your redemption is drawing near..."

"We interrupt this show," announced an excited Natalie Roberts, "for a Special Report from New York. After several weeks of debate, the United Nations has officially called for a vote on the World Commerce ID Act. This plan will have an impact on how we buy and sell commodities. What long term consequences it will have on our world's economy remains to be seen. Of course, many Muslim countries have already rejected the ID stipulation. Every person will be required to receive a microchip ID under their skin. Without an ID, a person won't be able to purchase or sell any bar coded goods. Some Wall Street insiders believe this provision has the power to kill this bill. When asked about removing this stipulation, former President Kayin was clear.

"ID registration will be the final weapon in the defeat of worldwide terrorism. I also predict this tiny microchip will lead the way in regulating our financial markets."

The sleepy pastor reached for the phone without looking. "Hello?"

"Hi, Pastor Lance, it's Drew. I know it's late but I had to call."

"No problem, bro. How ya doing?"

"Did you just catch Gene Lloyd's program?"

"I taped his show. He certainly had a lot to say, didn't he?"

"A lot to say," winced the scared teenager. "He's calling us false teachers. This is getting too weird."

"It's Paul's prediction of the last days. 'For the time will come when they will not endure sound doctrine, but according to their own desires, because they have itching ears, they will heap up for themselves teachers; and they will turn away their ears from the truth…'" 8

"Aren't Lloyd's books best sellers? Look at how many believers are mesmerized by his teaching."

"Do you think his presentation was biblical?"

"Not a chance, his interpretations are all messed up."

"Drew, do you remember the passage when Jesus referred to the days of Noah?"

"You mean Matthew 24:39? Noah and his family were the only ones who heeded God's warning and prepared themselves for the flood. They were delivered from God's wrath."

"Exactly, later Jesus said, 'Then two men will be in the field: one will be taken and the other left.' 9 The word 'taken' means to receive intimately unto one's self."

"The Son of Man is coming back with His angels. The angels will gather His elect to heaven. Those left will suffer His wrath like in the flood."

"You got it, bro. The dead in Christ will be gathered first, from one end of heaven to the other. Then angels will gather together the elect who are alive on earth. 10 The phrase 'gather together' means to gather upward. It's an upward gathering of the saints to meet the Lord in the air."

"Yep, deliverance then wrath, so what am I missing here?"

"Lloyd teaches everything in Matthew 24 is about the Lord appearing in heaven during the battle of Armageddon. He believes the coming of the Son of Man with His angels has nothing to do with the rapture."

"Is this for real?"

"He's deadly serious. Lloyd believes it's the absolute truth."

"But the coming of the Son of Man is the resurrection of the elect to heaven. There is no resurrection to heaven in Revelation 19:11-21. The Word of God doesn't come in the clouds, and there ain't no trumpet!"

"That's correct. No one will be eating or drinking and getting married when the Word of God returns in Revelation 19:11-21! 11 This can't be the coming of the Son of Man in Matthew 24:30-31. They're two different events; taking place at two different times."

"So why is this such a big deal to Lloyd?"

"Jesus warns believers to watch for the invasion of Jerusalem and the holy place (Temple) by the Abomination of Desolation. '...Whoever reads, let him understand.'" 12

"What does Jesus want us to understand?"

"The Antichrist must invade Jerusalem before the Son of Man comes for His elect. 13 Paul also warned the Man of Sin must proclaim himself to be God in the rebuilt Temple before our gathering to Jesus at His coming." 14

"But why do so many still refuse to believe this?"

"Drew, this exactly why Jesus warned, '...when the Son of Man comes, will He really find faith on the earth?'" 15

"The Great Tribulation is going to be a real dark time for believers, huh?"

"This isn't blind faith, bro. Yet you would have thought these worldwide famines would have changed a lot of hearts."

"Yeah, I've been trying to share at school but it ain't happening. Their heads aren't into it. Even my folks told me to cool it."

"All we can do is share as the Holy Spirit leads. He will give us the opportunities to reach those who desire to know the truth."

"This is deep. What do you think it will take for Lloyd to see it?"

"Hopefully after the Abomination of Desolation and his ten Muslim nations (horns) invade an unsuspecting Jerusalem. 16 Kayin has been trying to get this ID bill passed for months. Now's the time to be prayed up, that's for sure."

"I hear ya. Well, I just had to call. Thanks, Pastor."

"Let's be overcomers, Drew. Our Lord is faithful."

THE KINGDOM OF THE SON

'He has delivered us from the power of darkness and conveyed us
into the kingdom of the Son of His love.'
Colossians 1:13

Walking through the Lakeview High parking lot, Lance Ryan could
already discern the presence of demonic activity. A couple of times
within the past year students were expelled for practicing witchcraft
on school grounds. The big outrage came last January when the
school janitor found a cat drained of its blood behind the Industrial
Arts building. After several complaints, the school principal was
forced to tighten security.

The youth pastor could hear the baseball team warming up while
the tennis team ran wind sprints, most left as soon as the final bell
rang. It was not the type of school to hang out with friends.

Strolling down the paper scattered hallway, Lance mumbled to
himself, "Everything looks normal enough."

Turning left at the principal's office he could hear excited voices
coming from room 104. With so many rumors about the former
American President being spread about, members from the Bible
Club decided to invite kids to come hear about the last days.

"Give me wisdom, Lord," Lance quietly prayed while slipping
between students standing outside room 104.

Bible Club President Luke Appleby raised his hands and
welcomed everyone to the meeting. Standing directly behind him,
Lance knew this was a divine appointment. Of the sixty students
present, most were not Christian. Lining the far wall of the classroom
were the grungers. On the opposite wall was a skinhead gang called
the Neighbors. While Luke was answering questions, Lance spotted
four girls seated in the back row. With their heads bowed; they

appeared to be praying. They obviously preferred not to be noticed. The demons of Death, Lying, and Fear had just been summoned by the four girls dressed in black.

"So what do we have here?" smirked Fear.

This foul spirit wasted no time sowing its evil lies. 1

"I'm sick of these Bible meetings," cursed the spirit of Lying. "Let's just attack them and be done with it."

"Not without permission from above," countered Death.

Lance greeted the students with a big smile.

"I'm here today to share with you about the end of the age; specifically the events warning us the coming of the Lord is near. Before we begin, I'd like to pray."

Most watched with blank stares but curious hearts as Lance bowed his head and closed his eyes.

"Father, I thank You for allowing me to share the timing of Your Son's return with these students today. May You open their eyes to see the truth of Your gospel. By the power of Jesus Christ, I bind every foul spirit of the enemy. I take authority over the spirits of Witchcraft, Unbelief, Death, Lying, and Fear. In Jesus' name, I rebuke..."

Death and Lying departed as soon as they sensed the presence of the Holy Spirit. The supernatural grip squeezing Fear was something they wanted no part of. As Lance ended his prayer, warrior angels swept through room 104. Fear was long gone, along with the three Satanists performing curses from the back of the room. The fourth girl, Amy Phillips, was well known around Lakeview. She always wore black and had several tattoos. Her favorite tattoo was a tiny dragon located under her blonde bangs. She affectionately called the dragon lord Nimrod. After her friends slipped out, she took a seat in the third row. Simon Colson, who was seated in the second row, looked away when their eyes met.

"A popular teaching being taught in your school is that all religions worship the same God. Recently we have witnessed the growth of a new religious group called the World Faith Movement. Its goal is to create tolerance among all faiths. So what has the world gained by such a merger?"

Sporting a spiked haircut trimmed in orange, a grunger playfully joked, "It looks pretty phony to me."

A member of the Neighbors shouted, "All these religions playing nice don't prove nothing. It's just the same old religious crap."

"You guys are right. The reason you are here today is not to learn more about manmade religions but to experience the truth about God. Before I believed in Jesus Christ, I was also wearing a mask. You know what I mean: the drugs, the sex, the music, and the clothes. I'm talking about the mind games you play on each other. Some of you still think the way to live is a better party, a better drug, and a better partner. Yeah, it was fun at the beginning; that's the way sin is. After awhile the newness wears off. The loneliness becomes oh too real, now doesn't it? Then it hits you; there's got to be more to life than this."

"Here we go again," blurted another grunger. "Just dress right; cut your hair, walk the straight line with loving big brother, and Jesus will love you."

"Not so, bro. It's the spirit of Religion which says, be a good person, go to church, don't get caught in any big sin, and you'll make it to heaven."

"Give us one difference between what Jesus taught and all these other religions?" challenged Tanner Harrison, the gang leader of the Neighbors.

"Jesus Christ is the Son of God who died for our sins. Whoever follows Him will receive eternal life. 2 Believing in man-made religions will only lead to eternal death."

A concerned Hope Bishop asked, "Lance, can you kinda explain about the persecution that's coming?"

"Sure, Hope, but before we do I'd like to share what Jesus Christ has already done. First, we must realize Jesus has already come to pay the price of sin. He overcame sin's power and redeemed those who will eventually choose to follow Him. He did this by defeating Satan."

"Are you sure, Rev?" laughed Tanner. "Look what the devil has been doing to kids in America."

"Please save me." mocked another. "We're getting higher, watching grosser films, the sex is great, and everybody says it's cool. Most say we'll grow out of it."

Lance patiently waited for their laughter to die down.

"What about it? Are you into the path you're on? Are you happy? Are you ready to live life with a real purpose?"

"Right on, preacher," mocked a grunger. "I've got a purpose. I'm going to party until I drop dead."

"Is this what you want? I'm not here to impress or get something from you. If you choose not to be real, I'm outta here."

"No, Lance, you're right," muttered Amy Phillips as she subconsciously blew her blonde bangs over Nimrod. "Life isn't fun or fulfilling. It's like being in bondage to something and not knowing how to get free."

"Okay, listen up. Just before Jesus willingly went to the cross, He promised He would someday return. So His disciples wanted to know when He would come back. They asked Jesus what would be the sign of His coming and the end of the age. Jesus answered them straight up. He gave two signs which would appear in the sky just before He returns."

"What signs?" asked a curious Tanner.

"The sign of the end of the age is when the sun, moon, and stars lose their light. 3 Then Jesus Christ will explode across a black sky coming in the glory of His Father. 4 His angels will be with Him." 5

A frightened Amy asked, "Pastor, how close are we?"

"The coming of the Lord is a period of time when specific events take place. It begins when the Son of Man delivers Christians from the wrath to come." 6

"What other events warn us of Jesus' return?"

"A world leader will be given authority over every nation." 7

"You mean Kayin's war on terrorism?" grinned Tanner. "Look at how many nations are supporting his bogus plan."

"You got it. You see, when the Bible predicts specific events, the only way you know they are true is if they come to pass. Jesus predicts the future attack of Jerusalem by an evil leader called the Abomination of Desolation. 8 This leader, who is also called the Beast, will soon force all people to take a mark on their hand or forehead. Without this mark, no one will be able to buy or sell anything."

Simon Colson nervously asked, "Could the ID chip the United Nations is pushing be the mark of the beast?"

"It's possible, let's be watching. The hour of testing of Christians is near." 9

Immediately, Lance discerned a spirit of Rebellion manifesting in several students.

"So why is God so upset?" asked a tormented Amy. "Isn't He responsible for allowing evil to reign?"

"God allowed Satan to become ruler of this world because of man's rebellion. The reason for testing is because of the lukewarmness of Christians. Once the Great Tribulation begins, it will be easy to see who loves the Lord and is willing to die for Him."

"Will this mark of the beast be like mine?"

After showing Nimrod under her blonde bangs she winked. The laughter among the grungers was normal. They loved to see the slender witch cut up.

"Listen up," Lance shouted. "Once a person takes the mark of the beast their fate is sealed for eternity."

"Isn't this microchip like our national ID cards?" asked a suspicious junior. "It's just a way to identify people so we can buy and sell. My daddy thinks it's a great way to stop identity theft."

"Don't be deceived, anyone who registers for it will become part of the Beast's system." Sensing an urgency Lance pleaded, "The only way you're going to make it through the coming persecution is to believe in Jesus Christ as your Lord and Savior. You must ask Jesus to forgive you and follow the leading of the Holy Spirit. It begins with a step of faith. For real, how many want to follow Jesus with everything they've got?"

Hope Bishop and Luke Appleby could hardly believe their eyes. Almost all the kids were raising their hands for salvation. Amy Phillips unashamedly wept after praying for the first time since she was a little girl. It looked so out of place to see members from the Neighbors giving up the knives they were carrying. Two grungers looked relieved as they took turns destroying their satanic jewelry. Amidst all the excitement, a confused Simon Colson left unnoticed.

The demons were waiting. Their prescribed pecking order was always a big deal. Religion, Pride, Compromise, Lying, Fear, Death, Lust, Suicide, Unbelief, Control, most everyone was present. Of course, Denial was always late.

These demons knew what was at stake. This was a moment the underworld had always dreaded. The consequences of this war would determine the destiny of billions of people. If Jesus ever returned to Jerusalem they would lose control of a world which was handed to them when Eve sinned. At times, angels from above couldn't resist reminding them of the days just before the sounding of the seventh trumpet. 10 These foul spirits hated this prophecy and would do anything to stop it.

Their ears burned with the sound of his entrance. The pressure of the moment was unmistakable. Pacing back and forth, the devil was in deep contemplation. No one dared speak when their Master was in such a worked up state.

"The time has come for your final assignments before the Great Tribulation. Upon my signal, we will attack Michael. Don't be fooled by what the angels are saying. Doesn't His Word say I will lead the whole world astray?" 11

"Yes, Master," affirmed the spirit of Religion. "That's what the Book says."

The spirit of Pride asked, "Isn't this war in heaven conditional? Personally, I'm looking forward to destroying them. I detest their lack of rebellion."

"Each of you will accompany me. Be alert. We don't know what the One from Above will attempt. We do know He cares very deeply for these puny humans; so the more believers we deceive the better."

Their hideous shrieks were common place. Once Satan's piercing red eyes met theirs they jumped to attention.

"For those of you who are here when the Man of Sin reveals himself, be relentless. Use every ounce of deception you possess, every lie you have perfected, every destructive strategy that has ever worked. We must explore every opportunity allowed from the One Above."

"Think of it," bragged Control, "when we win this war we'll control all of heaven."

"Yeah," whispered Doubt, "that's if we win."

Testimonies from last week's Bible Club meeting were the talk of the school. A growing number of kids appeared uneasy. Seeing Amy Phillips in a white dress with a pink ribbon in her blonde hair was a bit much. Her beautiful smile radiated her newfound freedom. Only her Christian friends knew her spirit guide, Nimrod, had been cast out of her. They understood her transformation. For everyone else it was just a big joke.

"Look at her," ridiculed a jealous cheerleader. "She's getting more attention playing the goody little Christian rather than when she acted out her evil witch charade."

While most kids couldn't help but laugh, a lonely figure near the stairs wasn't joining in. He had watched Amy take a stand for Jesus in front of her friends, her teachers, even those who cursed her. He knew this change was nothing to be laughed at.

As Commander of the Neo Nazi gang called the Neighbors, Tanner Harrison was facing a crisis. His gang of thirty soldiers had grown under his leadership. He still remembered the hot summer night when it happened. His bedroom windows were wide open. There was a full moon out. He was lying on his bed in baggy shorts. The humidity was so high he couldn't sleep for more than an hour at a time. It was close to two in the morning when the evil presence appeared in the dark corner of his bedroom. Its smell made him sick to his stomach. All he could do was call out to God for help. Finally, the demon spoke with an audible voice.

"Do not be afraid. I have a message from my Master. He has been watching you. Your leadership skills can be used to train a group of soldiers who will stand for the truth. My Master will send messengers to explain the purpose of your group and what will be expected of you. Remember, you will be rewarded by being obedient to the Prince of Darkness."

The next day an executive from a bank in town encouraged Tanner to accept his calling. An hour later, a man in his early twenties shared with the boy during study hall. He carefully outlined the objectives of a white supremacy group called, The Neighbors.

The mysterious stranger whispered, "This is an opportunity of a lifetime."

Tanner watched as the messenger disappeared behind a crowd of students. At first, the lonely teenager didn't trust his offer. But the more he entertained the demonic realm, the more intoxicating his assignment became. The power of evil began to draw him closer; his will to resist gradually weakening. Once Tanner Harrison made the commitment to lead, the demons of Fear and Hate took control of his life and all who swore to follow him.

While watching Amy share her love for God he suddenly got it, the demon controlling her was gone. Such freedom was something he always dreamed about.

The spirit of Hate knew something wasn't right. Instantly the demon flooded Tanner's mind with lies.

"Her happiness is only for a season. By the next full moon she'll return to her coven."

Confusion, Despair, and Fear, were alerted to the gravity of the situation. Amy Phillips was now a coveted assignment. To see a new believer return to the power of darkness is something every fallen angel craves to see.

To most students at Lakeview High, the Neighbors were just social misfits trying to gain attention. Their hate propaganda was like a fantasy being acted out. Since they really never hurt anybody, the small group was mainly ignored. Tanner Harrison knew better. Satan was planning to use his gang as an evil weapon. Each was led to believe they were in control of their own destiny. It wasn't long before Tanner and his soldiers were brought under control by the same demons indwelling the girls at the witches' coven. While Amy's spirit guide was a dragon, Tanner accepted one called Wolf. This demon taught the naïve recruit how to astral project outside his body. Wolf would always be waiting.

Running up the stairs, Tanner knew Amy would be attending her history class. Despair was gradually gaining a stronghold over the gang leader, believing the lie from Wolf he would never be free.

He immediately spotted the happy blonde witnessing to a group of students in front of her locker.

"Hey, Amy."

"What's up, Tanner?"

When he tried to answer, Wolf appeared in his mind.

"She's pretending; she's still a witch. She won't understand anything you tell her. I'm your only true friend. She doesn't like you any better than the others."

"I need to talk to you. It's really important."

"Stop this," screamed the demon in his mind. "I forbid you to interfere with assignments, our Master..."

"How about lunch? We can walk over..."

"She can't help you," growled Wolf. "Why would God ever accept you?"

"No, you don't understand. You're going to be..."

Suddenly, he felt dizzy.

"It's okay, Tanner, the Holy Spirit is greater than these spirits trying to intimidate you. Their threats are a big bluff. God has the power to deliver you from the power of darkness into the kingdom of His Son. 12 Are you hearing me, Tanner? You can be free anytime you want. No demon in hell can ever win against the power of the Holy Spirit."

As the bell rang, Amy slipped her friend a note.

Taking off, Tanner headed for his favorite hangout; the lunch tables behind the Industrial Arts Building.

BEWARE OF FALSE PROPHETS

"Beware of false prophets, who come to you in sheep's clothing, but inwardly they are ravenous wolves."
Matthew 7:15

Five years ago, the Bethany Ministers Association was formed as a gesture of unity. Its purpose was to bring pastors together in a serious effort to understand their doctrinal differences. In recent years, the debate over the Lord's coming was like a festering sore within the religious community. As a result, the rapture had become a heated topic at BMA meetings. One pastor told his congregation a person wasn't even saved unless he believed in the imminent return of Jesus Christ. For most believers, even the hint of Christians experiencing persecution by the two beasts was unacceptable. The BMA membership became even more divisive after Pastor Mark Bishop publicly announced the Great Tribulation was near. The members were greeting one another as John Ryals leisurely approached the pulpit.

"Welcome, brethren. The purpose of our monthly open forum is to discuss a biblical doctrine within our ministerial guidelines. Today, I have selected a doctrine with quite a wallop; the rapture of the church. The past few years we have all seen the tragic consequences when one toys with a biblical doctrine. Due to the confusion over the timing of the rapture, I have asked Reverend Bishop of Bethany Assembly to teach on this subject this morning. Pastor Mark, please come."

As the young pastor walked to the front he couldn't help studying their faces. Some of these ministers were once close friends. To see their contempt was not easy.

"Thank you, Pastor John. I would like to begin by defining the popular pre-tribulation rapture position. Those who teach this view believe the resurrection of Christians has been imminent since the days of the apostles. This view teaches Jesus will catch up His elect before the final seven years leading up to the battle of Armageddon. Many teachers have nicknamed this time, the tribulation period. They teach this seven year period in Daniel 9:27, includes the seven seals, seven trumpets, and seven bowl judgments from the Revelation of Jesus Christ. The critical question we face today is when will the church be caught up during these judgments? Of course, those who teach the pre-trib view believe the entire seven years is God's wrath. Since the elect are promised not to suffer His wrath, this means the rapture must take place before the tribulation period begins."

Oddly enough, there was no talking; one could hear a pin drop.

"As you all know, for almost three and a half years, I've taught the Beast will war against the saints during the Great Tribulation before the resurrection from God's wrath. I would like to give a short overview for those who have never heard this taught. I teach the biblical position church leaders taught in the first century. They believed the Great Tribulation, the persecution of the elect by the Abomination of Desolation, would be cut short by the coming of the Son of Man. After Jesus opens the sixth seal, He will come back with His angels. These angels will first gather the dead in Christ. After this, the elect who are alive will receive their glorified bodies and be taken before the throne of God in heaven, Revelation 7:9-14. Since the Great Tribulation is initiated by the opening of the fourth seal in the middle of the seven years, this means the coming of the Son of Man for His saints must occur sometime in the second half. Of course, no man knows the exact day or hour. The Great Tribulation is the wrath of Satan against the children of God. This persecution will be carried out by the Antichrist and his false prophet. The day of the Lord is God's wrath against the children of Satan. The day of the Lord will begin after Jesus opens the seventh seal and the heavenly scroll opens." [1]

To Mark's surprise several ministers were taking notes. Across the room, an angry J. W. Brown could not believe what he was hearing. To give such heresy any acknowledgment was unthinkable. Indeed, the spiritual warfare had begun.

"As you can see, it's critical to understand whether the seven seals are the wrath of God or the wrath of Satan. Revelation 6:1-17 describes the first six seals and Revelation 8:1 describes the opening of the seventh seal."

Paul Bortolazzo

To Mark's far right, several P.K.'s (pastor's kids) were seated at a small table. A blonde, green-eyed, five-year-old named Julia was drawing in her coloring book.

"In Matthew 24:4-8 Jesus exhorts believers living during the beginning of sorrows to watch for the events of the first three seals on the outside of the scroll in Revelation 5:1. The first seal is Satan coming to conquer through false teachers. The second seal represents wars and rumor of wars. When the third seal is opened famines will spread around the world. In the past three and a half years, this is what we have experienced, the beginning of sorrows."

"Here it comes," chuckled a minister under his breath.

"The content of the fourth seal is critical to see. This seal contains a pale horse whose rider is called Death. Following close behind is Hades. They are given the power to kill one fourth of the world by the beasts of the earth. 2 Now, who are these beasts?"

"As if we care," laughed a pastor out loud.

"In the Revelation of Jesus Christ, 'beast' either refers to the first Beast, the Antichrist, or the second beast, his false prophet. Now how will these two beasts persecute one fourth of the world?"

A visiting minister candidly shared, "The Bible says the second beast will make the world worship the first Beast by receiving his mark."

"That's correct. And what type of people will refuse to take the mark of the beast?"

"Christians," shouted Pastor Allen Colson.

"Amen. This is why the opening of the fourth seal takes place in the middle of the seven years. At this time, Michael will cast Satan and his angels out of heaven for good. 3 The devil will empower the Abomination of Desolation to break the peace with Israel by invading Jerusalem with his armies from his ten horns. 4 This is the beginning of the Great Tribulation. Once the Beast gains authority over the nations, he will convince the world to receive his mark. 5 After the fifth seal is opened, martyrs slain for their testimony of Jesus will cry out to God asking Him to avenge their blood."

An interested youth pastor asked, "How can you prove scripturally the mark is given after the fourth seal?"

Mark nodded; there was no hesitation in his voice.

"There are martyrs after the fifth seal because the mark of the beast was accepted by the nations after Jesus opened the fourth seal. The persecution during the Great Tribulation will be a threat to only those who resist the Beast and his system. Of course, any person saved or unsaved, who takes his mark will be tormented with fire in the presence..."

In the back of the room stood Dwayne Pressley and Kevin Collins, former deacons from Bethany Assembly. Kevin just shook his head in disgust.

"I don't get how he can just spew out such fear. How can anyone respect him for what he is doing?"

"He can stay and be martyred by the Antichrist if he wants to," laughed Dwayne. "But we're outta here."

"The next event is the opening of the sixth seal; when the sun, moon, and stars, lose their light. In Matthew 24:29-31 this sign appears before the coming of the Son of Man."

The spirits of Fear, Compromise, and Control, were poised, patiently waiting for the perfect time to attack.

"Now is there anywhere else in scripture where we see the sun, moon, and stars, losing their light?"

"That would be Joel 2:30-31."

"That's correct, Pastor Dyer. The Old Testament prophet predicted this sign would come just before the day of the Lord. 'The sun will be turned to darkness and the moon to blood before the coming of the great and awesome day of the Lord.' 6 Now what is the day of the Lord?"

"The catching up of the saints."

"You're close," smiled Mark.

"God's wrath," answered several pastors simultaneously.

"Yes, Isaiah also prophesied the sun, moon, and stars, would lose their light just before God punishes the world for its evil during the day of the Lord. 7 In Matthew 24 29-31, our Lord Jesus taught the sun, moon, and stars, would lose their light just before His coming. Now we know from Jesus' own words His coming and His wrath are back to back events; just like the days of Noah and Lot. 8 Deliverance for believers; followed by wrath for unbelievers. The coming of the Son of Man and the day of the Lord are back to back events. Each will come like a thief to an unsuspecting world. By comparing scripture with scripture, the events involving the resurrection of the elect to heaven fit together perfectly."

"Who does this young whippersnapper think he is?" whispered a retired minister.

The pastors were already losing interest. Several were reading their Bibles; not bothering to listen. Little Julia had just finished drawing a yellow scroll with seven purple seals.

"In Revelation 7 between the opening of the sixth and seventh seals, two events will take place. First, a vast multitude of believers from every nation are caught up to God's throne. After this event, 144,000 Jews are sealed for protection from God's wrath, which will be poured out after the seventh seal is broken."

Trying to regain their attention, the Watchman paused.

"There is a question we must ask ourselves about these Jews from the twelve tribes of Israel. If all seven seals are God's wrath, then why are 144,000 being sealed for protection from God's wrath just before the seventh seal?"

After scanning the audience, Mark knew he would have to answer his own question.

"In other words, why aren't the 144,000 being sealed for protection from God's wrath before the first seal?"

"Who cares?" snapped a pastor. "It's not what you know about the end times, it's who you know."

"No amount of speculation can change anything," affirmed his associate. "God has won the victory. I'm more concerned believers remain under the blessings of God."

"What about saving souls? What good will it do to argue over the timing of the rapture? You're just wasting our time."

A determined Mark knew what he was facing

"The reason why the 144,000 are sealed right before the seventh seal is obvious. The seals are not the wrath of God. When the final seal is opened by Jesus, the heavenly scroll will open, and His wrath will judge a Christ rejecting world. Actually, the fourth and fifth seals of the Great Tribulation are Satan's wrath against the saints. 9 The Beast will persecute anyone refusing to follow his evil plan."

The interaction between pastors seemed to be picking up. To an outsider, it looked like a meaningful discussion. But in reality, the majority had already labeled Mark Bishop as a full blown heretic.

"What about the multitude gathered out of the Great Tribulation in Revelation 7:9-14?" the Watchman boldly asked. "They are standing before His Throne and praising God for their salvation. They are holding palm branches in their hands. This can only mean they have received their glorified bodies. My brothers, this is a picture of Jesus cutting short the Great Tribulation by the resurrection of His blood washed saints to heaven."

There wasn't one pastor who looked happy; Mark knew it was time to close.

"Jesus promises to shorten the days of the Great Tribulation for the elect's sake. When the seventh seal is broken, there will be thirty minutes of silence in heaven. I ask you, what's the purpose of such silence?"

He could hear their discussions but no response was forth coming.

"This silence signifies a very solemn moment. The scroll containing God's final wrath is about to be opened. The angels holding the seven trumpets are ready to sound off. But before the opening of the seventh seal; reapers are sent forth by our Blessed Hope to gather up His elect."

Their upraised hands seized the moment.

"Yes, Pastor Cooper from Lakeview Assembly of God."

"Mark, how can the vast multitude in Revelation 7 be the catching up of the saints? That's not possible. The Church was already raptured in Revelation 4:1. The believers martyred during the Great Tribulation are the ones who missed the rapture."

"Pastor Cooper, if the Church was caught up to heaven in Revelation 4:1, then the Church should be ready to welcome the martyrs when they arrive before God's throne in Revelation 7:9. Is that right?"

"Absolutely."

"In Revelation 7:9-14, there are only three groups present when this multitude from every nation arrives in heaven. There are angels around the throne, the twenty-four elders, and the four living creatures. Let me ask you, where is the resurrected body of Christ?"

"Well, I..."

"Pastor Bishop," interrupted an irate Elmer Dyer. "Regrettably your backwards logic overlooks a very significant truth. The most important motivator to inspire believers to holiness is the imminent return of Jesus Christ. Anything other than a pre-tribulation rapture simply promotes a license to sin. Many will just wait until they see the sign of the end of the age and then repent. Your teaching takes away the hope of the imminent return of Christ. This interpretation is literally destroying the faith of millions of believers. Is this what you hope to accomplish?"

"Pastor Dyer, the return of Christ is not the most important motivator for me to live a holy life. The main reason I live a holy life is because I love the Lord. Christ said if we say we love Him, then we will keep His commandments (teachings). Actually the believers at my church who are watching for the invasion of Jerusalem by the Antichrist are on fire for God. They are winning more souls, praying with greater fervency, and building up one another's faith."

"Let me ask you a hard question, Pastor. Isn't it true, that you've lost over one half of your congregation since teaching this new interpretation of the rapture? Let's be honest; even your so-called revival has run out of gas."

"The spiritual warfare is against those…"

"Then why have so many left your church and are joining ours?"

"Pastor Dyer, allow me to ask you a question. Can anyone know the exact day of the rapture?"

"Nope and you're a liar if you think you can. In Matthew 24:36 Jesus said, 'But of that day and hour no one knows, not even the angels of heaven, but My Father only.'" 10

"So the coming of the Son of Man represents the rapture of the saints to heaven?"

"No, no, no. Matthew 24 has nothing to do with the rapture. Jesus is describing the Word of God and His angels coming at the supper of the great God, Armageddon."

"Then how can you use Matthew 24:36 to refer to no one knows the day or hour of the rapture?"

"Mark, you're twisting of scripture can only…"

"You don't want the coming of the Son of Man to be the rapture because the Antichrist attacks Jerusalem before the saints are gathered to heaven. 11 This means the elect can't be taken to heaven until the Man of Sin (Antichrist) reveals himself during the Great Tribulation." 12

Their resistance to the conviction of the Holy Spirit was ebbing away. An incensed J. W. Brown couldn't wait any longer.

"Excuse me, Mr. Bishop; your whole line of reasoning on the timing of the rapture is meaningless. Matthew 24 was not written to Christians because it says false prophets will deceive many. We know from scripture, Christians can never have their salvation taken from their Father's hand. Jesus said, 'My sheep listen to my voice; I know them and they follow me. And I give them eternal life, and they shall never perish; neither shall anyone snatch them out of My hand. My Father, who has given them to Me, is greater than all; and no one is able to snatch them out of My Father's hand.' 13 The elect in Matthew 24 are unsaved Jews during the tribulation period."

After the well respected pastor took a seat; all eyes quickly refocused on the young pastor's reply.

"Pastor Brown, Jesus is stressing relationship in this passage. Those who continually hear His voice, who continually follow Him, are His sheep."

Glancing at their faces, Mark could discern a thin veil covering their eyes; a spiritual deception preventing them from seeing the truth.

"Please allow me to be candid. Our discussion today involves much more than the gathering of the elect to heaven. The real issue we are debating is the salvation of a believer. For those of you who have never studied it; the secret at any moment rapture was popularized in America in the 1860's during the time of the Civil War. Many pastors embraced this Trojan horse myth in order to strengthen their view a believer could never deny the Lord. Jesus clearly taught the opposite in Matthew 24. He warned us of believers falling away and betraying one another..." 14

"Pastor Mark, may I speak?" interrupted another pastor. "I too believe Christians have free will. But the falling away of believers can only happen after the body of Christ has been raptured."

After silently praying for the leading of the Holy Spirit, Mark shared, "Don't you see, many Christians don't even believe in a future world leader empowered by Satan. You all need to listen to this. I believe more believers are going to register for the mark of the beast than those who refuse. For those who overcome Jesus promises to make a pillar in the temple of God (New Jerusalem). 15 Christians who deny their Lord by receiving the mark of the beast will be blotted out of the Book of Life for eternity." 16

The demonic oppression coming against Mark was stifling.

"This day I stand before you as a Watchman with a warning from God. Ezekiel prophesied, 'When a righteous man turns from his righteousness and does evil and I put a stumbling block before him, he will die. Since you did not warn him, he will die for his sin. The righteous things he did will not be remembered and I will hold you accountable for his blood.'" 17

"It makes sense now," shouted an angry pastor. "He denies the assurance of salvation for a believer."

"In the past forty-two months, many have been deceived through the counterfeit signs and wonders of the false prophet. I warn you all, the ministers of the World Faith Movement are wolves in sheep's clothing. 18 The WFM has even set up an office across from Sluman's

Garage. They have come to deceive your parishioners."

His time was up. Mark knew the next sixty seconds could have eternal consequences.

"The World Faith Movement is the disguised harlot of Revelation 17:3. The ten horns of the scarlet beast is the Antichrist's Middle East Federation. The harlot is riding the beast's system to power. God is pleading with you to open your spiritual eyes. The Beast is Joshua Kayin. The World ID he has proposed is the mark of the beast. I'm begging you not to register for an ID number. Those who receive the mark of his name will be lost for eternity. 19 If you do not take a stand against..."

Quickly striding toward the podium Pastor Ryals shouted, "Hold up, son." Grabbing the microphone, he whispered to Mark, "That's enough."

The distain on the Chairman's face was easy to see.

"Gentlemen, it's obvious Mr. Bishop is sincere in what he believes. But when you start with a false premise, you always end up with a false conclusion. The Bible clearly says a believer's name can never be blotted out of the Book of Life. That means any verses that appear to say a believer can deny Christ must mean something else."

"Finally," cringed an angry pastor who was praying for John Ryals to take over.

Perched beside him, the spirit of Control just smiled.

"Mark, are we to believe you and this evangelist Corbin have suddenly found this truth and we have all missed it? Somehow you two are His chosen spokesmen, while God allows the rest of us to be blinded to this truth? This must mean you're the anointed Watchmen for God and we are the unenlightened shepherds. Do you deny this?"

John never looked in Mark's direction for a reply.

"My brothers in Christ; you don't have the truth if you have a contradiction. First of all, the rapture must take place before the tribulation period can begin. This means the day of the Lord begins at the opening of the first seal, not after the sixth seal. Secondly, Matthew 24 is telling Jewish people to flee their homes not believers in Jesus. And finally as Christians, we are exhorted to watch for our Blessed Hope, never the Abomination of Desolation. It saddens me there are believers in our town being seduced by this doctrine of demons. After this morning's tirade, obviously Mark has no intention of repenting. I can only recommend he resign from our Association."

Without any delay, a voice count was taken. The only member

abstaining was Pastor Allen Colson. The pastor from Calvary Community sat motionless while pondering Mark's interpretation of the coming of the Son of Man.

Turning away, Chairman Ryals snorted, "Well, that's it. You have our decision on what you taught."

While gathering his notes, Mark felt led by the Holy Spirit to give one last warning.

"My brothers, our former President didn't invade several Muslim nations to remove evil dictators. He was actually gathering his ten horns. 20 By displaying such military strength the Little Horn persuaded these Muslim nations into accepting his roadmap to peace with Israel. 21 Soon, after the opening of the fourth seal, Joshua Kayin will reveal his true identity by proclaiming to be God. For the sake of your families and congregations, don't register..."

Exiting the conference room, a confident Pastor Elmer Dyer shook his head and muttered, "He just doesn't get it."

While walking out, Mark noticed Pastor Allen Colson intently going over his notes. Near the podium raced a laughing little Julia, clutching her drawing of a yellow scroll with seven purple seals.

It was a foggy, cold night as they aligned themselves along the edge atop the World Faith Movement Building.

"Where is he?" cursed the spirit of Control. "I hate these stinking interruptions."

"I know we messed up this time," whimpered Doubt.

"We are all here except you know who?" laughed Confusion.

"What's so great about Fear?" challenged Jealously. "You think such a ugly little imp is something special?"

"You know how our Master has been treating Fear."

Positioning to strike, the demon's fangs slowly appeared under its bluish red lips.

"Why don't you tell us?"

Edging toward the other side of the roof, Confusion choked, "You're right; Fear ain't so special."

"Why do we always have to wait?" screamed Lust.

"You know why," hissed Pride. "Our Master loves to make grand appearances."

Hearing the deafening shriek from the east, the demons turned away as a howling wind preceded his arrival.

"He's awfully high," reflected Lying, who was fully prepared to defend itself from any false accusations from his peers. "He may be coming from the heavenlies." 22

His shadow covered the top of the building. Extending his wings the devil purposely knocked several demons off the roof. The sense of urgency their Master usually exuded was surprisingly absent.

"Greetings soldiers of darkness. Your assignments are coming along very nicely."

While Satan was flattering his pawns of destruction, Fear purposely arrived late so everyone could see him.

"I'm going to love this rebuke," whispered Pride.

His red eyes focused on the smallest of all demons.

"Tell us, Fear, how is your special assignment coming?"

"Just as you planned, Master."

"Are you believing this?" cursed Jealousy.

"Yesterday was such a masterpiece! I had to come and see the results for myself," bragged the devil.

"Do you mean how I split the charismatic fellowship on Cherry Avenue?" interrupted Jealousy.

"How about the Neo Nazi group I created?" bragged Hate.

Their constant verbal volleyball was a great annoyance to their Master.

"No, you idiots, I'm talking about the Ministers Association meeting. These pastors missed the truth even when it was right under their long religious noses. Let's remember, believers can be extremely faithful if they're able to discern the truth of our attacks. For those of you who encounter the gift of discernment; don't get careless. The time will come when your work will bear the fruit of evil. Soon, without even understanding the consequences of their decisions, a multitude of believers will depart from their faith."

Anticipating the days Great Tribulation by the Beast against the saints, the evil spirits roared with delight.

HAVE I BECOME YOUR ENEMY

"Have I therefore become your enemy because I tell you the truth?"
Galatians 4:16

Bertha's Coffee Shop was usually full on weekday mornings. Not today due to the heavy rain. The smell of fresh sweet potato pie was in the air. Smiling waitresses were casually circling tables looking for coffee refills.

As Julie sipped her green tea; a lethargic Mark stirred his coffee. Last week's grilling was still on his mind.

"My heart aches for them and their congregations."

"Was there anyone who was receptive?" asked Julie.

"Allen Colson of Calvary Community seemed to be listening. I rechecked my notes. There is nothing more I could've said that would've changed their beliefs."

"It's all in God's hands now, honey."

While gently squeezing Mark's hand Julie spotted the Colsons walking toward their table.

"Good morning," greeted the nervous pastor. "Do you think Marsha and I could join you for some fellowship?"

"Certainly, Allen."

Grabbing two chairs from another table a hopeful Mark smiled.

"Last week, I bought a tape of your presentation. Marsha and I have been studying your interpretation of the coming of the Son of Man. After comparing the scriptures you listed, we have some questions if you don't mind."

"That would be great."

"Jesus promised, 'Then they will see the Son of Man coming in the clouds with great power and glory. And then He will send His angels, and gather together His elect from the four winds, from the farthest part of earth to the farthest part of heaven.' ₁ This is our Lord's coming for His saints, right?"

"That's correct. Old and New Testament believers who have died will receive their resurrection bodies first. After this, believers who are alive on earth will be gathered by angels to receive their resurrection bodies."

A stunned Allen stared for a moment.

"So His coming in I Thessalonians 4:15-17 is the same event as the coming of the Son of Man in Matthew 24:30-31?"

"It's amazing so many believers missed this. Say, have you ever studied the words alive and remain in I Thessalonians 4:17? Those alive and remain until the coming of the Lord will not precede those who have died in the Lord."

"Sounds kinda funny, Mark," reflected Marsha. "If a believer is alive then obviously he remains."

"Remain in this verse means survive."

The dazed couple was slowly putting it together.

"So believers who survive the Great Tribulation will be caught up to heaven by angels?"

"Exactly, Allen. Jesus gave a general description of six events which precede His coming in Matthew 24:4-29. John filled in the details of these six events in Revelation 6."

"We see this now. Jesus has the elect gathered to heaven in Matthew 24:29-31 between the sixth and seventh seals. In Revelation 7:9-14, John saw believers from every nation arrive in heaven between the sixth and seventh seals."

"The days of the Great Tribulation will be shortened by the deliverance of the church," added an excited Julie. "This is exactly when Jesus said His angels gather His elect to heaven."

"Are these the martyrs saved after the rapture?"

"Marsha, there is no mention this multitude will ever be ever martyred," said Mark. "These believers are caught up to heaven with resurrection bodies. Check it out; they are thanking the Lord for their deliverance."

"It's strange I never looked at it this way before," muttered a dazed Marsha.

"What about now?" asked a curious Julie.

"For me, the real eye opener was studying early church leaders like Irenaeus, Justin Martyr, Tertullian, and Hippolytus, who all taught believers would face the Beast."

The Bishops could sense the anointing of the Holy Spirit. They knew that this was more than just a visit.

"Allen, you wouldn't believe the warfare my family has received since last week's forum. The demons coming against us and anyone connected with us is escalating."

"Why such attacks from the enemy?"

"It must be my comment in the Bethany Herald last week that ignited the explosion."

"We missed it, Mark. What did you say?"

"It's much worse than we ever imagined. Satan is desperately trying to suppress Jesus' warnings. I wrote to *The Herald* exposing Kayin's agenda to control the nations. As of today, almost every world leader is supporting his goal to spread democracy. 2 A famous Christian leader representing thirty million evangelicals just prophesied God is using Joshua Kayin to bring peace to our world. No wonder so many still refuse to believe he is the Antichrist."

"Those are mighty strong words," posed Allen.

"Paul wrote, 'Have I therefore become your enemy because I tell you the truth?'" 3

"I guess the truth doesn't need defending," sighed Marsha.

"Most pastors are required to study the Book of Revelation in Bible College or Seminary," continued Mark. "Tragically, a majority are just regurgitating what they were fed."

"I'm afraid I'm on that list," confessed Allen.

"The body of Christ desperately needs Watchmen. The opportunity for revival is running out. Once the mark of the beast is launched worldwide; the delusion of God will come. Tragically, the faithful will be much smaller than we ever thought."

The couple from Calvary Community was speechless.

"Mark, how does the World Faith Movement fit into end time prophecy?"

"Scripture warns us of a harlot riding the beast during the first half of the last seven years. This deceptive harlot is drawing major faiths of the world into an evil religious system of tolerance."

"You must mean the WFM out of Rome?"

"The harlot will oppose Christianity by substituting a counterfeit in its place. After the Beast makes the world worship him; the harlot will be destroyed." 4

"So the appearance of Mary was not from God?"

"Amazingly Pope Michael used her demonic apparition to form

the WFM."

"But the Pope's reputation is skyrocketing?"

"During an intense time of prayer, the Holy Spirit warned Julie and me. Did you know this Pope visited several Muslim countries just before the WFM was established?"

"For what reason?"

"To encourage Muslims worldwide to join the WFM."

"How did I miss this?" winced Alan.

"Pope Michael is the false prophet of Revelation 13:11. It's no coincidence he pushed the mother Mary deception. Such an endorsement can only point to Satan."

"So you actually believe our former President is the Beast?"

"The Beast had to convince ten Muslim nations (horns) surrounding Israel to agree to peace. He began by physically subduing three horns. Kayin was backed by the harlot as he convinced seven more horns to join him in his vision for the world. Anyone can see it; it's just connecting the dots."

"But Joshua Kayin claims to be a Christian," pleaded Marsha.

"So did Hitler. The Furor claimed Jesus as his Savior; that the blood of Jesus cleanses him from all his sins."

"This is a nightmare," Allen honestly confessed.

"Do you see what we are up against? The traditions of men have permeated the pulpits of America. To combat this compromise, God is going to send an angel to declare the gospel to every nation, tribe, tongue, and people. 7 This heavenly assignment will fulfill Jesus' words: 'The gospel of His kingdom will be preached in the whole world as a testimony to all nations and then the end will come.'" 8

Sitting silently; they could hear the rain bouncing off the windows of the cafe.

"Marsha and I so much appreciate your ministry as Watchmen. You have certainly paid a price for it. Thank you so much for sharing with us. We plan to fast and pray concerning the things you've taught us. It's clear we must speak the truth of Jesus' warnings no matter what the consequences."

"Julie and I will be praying for you both. The Corbin's are also available to help in any way they can."

Both pastors stood with a new respect for each other. While exchanging phone numbers, Marsha and Julie excitedly praised the Lord for arranging such a divine appointment.

"A divine appointment indeed," smiled Mordecai.

Neither the Bishops nor the Colsons were aware of the warrior angel supernaturally protecting their conversation from any interference. The demonic spirits patrolling this side of the city knew better than to try and interfere.

By sixth period, Lakeview High was buzzing.

"Hey, Luke, have you heard the news from the twins?"

"Not a clue, Jake."

"The twins are saying Joshua Kayin is the Antichrist. They believe he is demon possessed. They're actually predicting he's going to attack Israel and take over the world."

Two girls standing behind Luke couldn't help but laugh.

"No joke, Drew's telling everyone the Middle East Federation is going to break the peace treaty they signed with the Jews. Hey, I like the twins. Last month, they stood up for me when a teacher accused me of stealing food out of the cafeteria. But if they continue to share this end times stuff; they're going to be labeled as fruit loops."

"What if it's the truth?"

Rolling his eyes, Jake shared, "Whatever. Look, if the twins want to share future Bible prophecy, they just need to be more careful. Some of the teachers are pretty hot about it. Kayin is like a hero to my math teacher. Check it out; she believes the two beasts of Revelation are animals."

Both boys smiled as they waited for the noise in the crowded hall to die down.

"What about you, bro? You've heard the gospel from Hope and me. Do you believe Jesus is everything He says He is?"

"You mean Jesus is the only way to heaven?"

"That's right. Jesus said, 'I am the way, the truth, and the life. No one comes to the Father except through Me.' 9 Only Jesus has the power to save a soul for eternity."

Luke was silently praying for Jacob Thomas Jamison, affectionately called Jake by everyone at Lakeview. Just over a year ago, the Jamison family moved to Bethany from Fort Jackson, South Carolina. Jake's father was a sergeant in the Army. Their latest move was their fifth in nine years. Even though Jake was new, he immediately was accepted by several clicks. Nevertheless, behind all his jokes and funny stories was a seventeen-year-old desperately searching for some sort of meaning in life.

"Honestly, Luke, I have a problem with this whole Jesus thing. How do you know He died on the cross two thousand years ago? Christians are just living by blind faith. You can't see Jesus; you can't touch him, you can't talk to Him. So how do you know He's real?"

"Before I accepted the Lord I had the same questions. The only way I ever got any answers was through a personal relationship with Jesus Christ. When you are born again by the Spirit of God, He will guide you into the truth."

"What are you talking about?"

"I don't have to see Jesus physically to believe in Him. When I got saved, Jesus started to take away my fears."

"What fears? You're Senior Class President, Captain of the basketball team, and President of the Bible Club. You've been offered a full scholarship to Auburn University. What could you possibly be afraid of?" pleaded the outsider.

"You know things can look good on the outside but on the inside a person can be in bondage. Before I got saved, I was scared of dating, taking tests, even competing in sports. I was afraid no one would like me if they ever got close enough to know me. Jesus changed all that. He gave me a confidence I never had before. I made a 180 degree turn from being someone who had no purpose; to being someone who loves life but more important, loves God."

"So your first move was a step of faith through repentance. Then after you ask Jesus to be your Savior and receive the Holy Spirit, everything changes?"

"A new creation my friend, old things pass away; everything becomes new." 10

The school bell rang signaling their next class.

"This sounds kinda strange, Luke. I'm from a military family. Everything is by the book. You've got to prove every belief, every action. I don't know what to think. But thanks for sharing with me."

"Would you like to hear some more about the end times? I'm meeting Jessie Hyatt and Damien Haley behind the gym at three o'clock to discuss some of their questions.

"Wow, Jessie is interested? Ok, I'll see you there."

It was a little after three when Luke arrived. Hope Bishop was already in a heated debate.

"Jessie, if you want to discuss what the Bible says about end time events, fine. Just leave my daddy out of it."

"It's not that simple. Your father is teaching the mark of the beast is right around the corner. He says anyone who registers for an ID is going straight to hell."

"It's true. Satan is going to give authority over all the nations to one man. A religious leader is already assisting him by promoting a tolerance among all the religions."

"Sounds good to me," challenged Jessie. "Just look at how many have been helped by the World Faith Movement."

"The goal of the WFM is to deceive the entire world."

"Oh, get a life," snapped an annoyed Damien Haley. "The WFM isn't evil. Who made you judge and jury?"

Glancing over at Luke, Hope thought about leaving.

"I heard the twins preaching this nonsense during lunch," taunted Damien, as two of his friends looked away and laughed. "Everyone's calling them the space cadets."

After taking a seat next to Hope, Luke shared, "Ned and Drew were speaking the truth of what's going down. They knew they'd be persecuted for preaching straight up. It's one thing to share about God's love; warning people of Satan's wrath is a different story."

"Drew believes Satan's wrath comes before God's wrath."

"I do too, Jessie. The ultimate test will be offered to everyone. There's a good possibility your friends, your relatives, even your folks may end up receiving the mark of the beast."

Taking off with his friends, an aggravated Damien yelled out, "Hey, Luke, what have you been smoking lately?"

"This is just too much," muttered Jessie. "See ya."

"C'mon, can't you stay and let us share the whole story?"

"My daddy says without a major change our world is going down the tubes. He is hoping this ID Bill passes."

Sensing her inner struggle, Hope softly asked, "So what are you going to do, Jess?"

Looking away she whispered back, "Who knows?"

As Hope and Luke prayed for Jessie; Jake was making his way across the parking lot. All afternoon he kept wondering what it would be like to be a Christian. Reaching the gym, he suddenly veered toward the bus departure area.

After Jake caught the last bus, the spirit of Control smiled. This demon knew God was calling the boy.

"As long as he is open," bragged the foul spirit, "the more opportunities I'll have to deceive, now won't I?"

THE WHOLE ARMOR OF GOD

"Put on the whole armor of God that you may be able to stand against the wiles of the devil."
Ephesians 6:11

There was a much bigger crowd for the Tuesday night Bible study. Mark had invited the evangelist from California to preach. With teenagers practically sitting on his feet, Stephen started the meeting by having everyone read Acts 26:16-18.

"Tonight let's see what it means to be a witness for the Lord. In the book of Acts, God called the apostle Paul to be a witness. In Acts 1:8, witness actually means martyr."

Raising her hand, a Lakeview cheerleader named Cindy Johnson requested, "Brother Corbin, can I ask you a question?"

"Love to hear it."

"Some of my friends and I are pretty confused over Christ's second coming. We were always taught Jesus delivers His saints before the seven year tribulation period begins. My pastor believes, I Thessalonians 4:15-17, is the rapture because Jesus never touches the earth. Seven years later, in Revelation 19:11-21, Jesus comes back physically with His saints at the Battle of Armageddon. This is His second coming; not the rapture."

"Cindy, your answer can be found by examining what Jesus accomplishes during His second coming. The main reason the church has never understood the second coming for two thousand years is because they have not allowed Jesus to define His coming in His own words. This also includes the teachings of Paul, Peter, and John. By comparing scriptures, you can see Christ's coming is much more than a singular visitation. 1 It's actually a time period in which specific events take place. Ever since Jesus ascended, teachers have tried to fit the events of Christ's second coming into a singular visit."

"How come, Stephen?"

"It's because the Bible never speaks of two second comings. It speaks of the coming, His coming, or Your coming. The scriptures only refer to one second coming. The stumbling block is due to the misunderstanding of the word 'coming'.

"But how can the rapture be part of His second coming if Jesus doesn't touch the earth?" posed the confused cheerleader.

"Cindy, let me explain it through a story. Let's say you and Hope decide to eat at Max's this Friday night. Hope arrives at your house in her car. She honks the horn and you come out and get in. She then drives to Max's. Now, did Hope come and get you?"

"Of course," grinned Cindy.

"Did she go into the house?"

"Nope."

"So she took you away without coming into your house?"

"So Jesus doesn't have to touch the earth when He catches up his saints?"

"It makes no difference whether Jesus touches the earth during the resurrection of His elect to heaven. Paul is clearly addressing the second coming of our Lord in I Thessalonians 4:15."

"There's only one second coming," interrupted one of Cindy's friends. "With your interpretation, it sounds like there is a second and third coming. What's up with that?"

"In I Thessalonians 4:15, Paul is teaching on the coming of the Lord. In the Greek, Parousia means coming. Coming in this verse is a noun not a verb. Parousia means an arrival with an ensuing presence. It's more than one appearance; His coming is a process. Paul is referring to the first phase of Christ's coming. The Parousia of the Lord has a beginning and an ending. His second coming is kinda like His first coming."

"What do you mean?"

"Okay, let's check out His first coming. Jesus was born in a manger, spoke the truth at twelve, and was baptized at thirty. He then performed miracles, preached the gospel, was put on trial, was crucified, rose from the dead, and ascended into heaven. His first coming wasn't just a trip from heaven to earth but a time period in which Jesus fulfilled His Father's will."

After seeing their puzzled faces, Stephen knew he needed a better explanation.

"Here's another example. Let's say Michelle and I have a speaking engagement in Nashville this Sunday. I preach twice on Sunday and we return to Bethany on Tuesday. Our coming included everything we did while we were on the trip. We preached twice, we counseled two couples, and we taped a radio show on Monday. Do you see what involves our coming to Nashville?"

While taking notes, an excited Lindy Hart shared, "I get it. The rapture is the first visit of the coming of the Lord. 2 The final visit of His coming is when the Lamb of God returns with His bride inside the New Jerusalem to rule over the millennium. 3 During His second coming, the Son of God will complete His Father's will."

"So why don't other church leaders teach this?" Cindy skeptically asked.

"Maybe it's because they're convinced they have the truth," reflected Stephen. "I've met a lot of pastors who choose to ignore Jesus' warnings on the last days for fear of losing their job or causing a division within their congregation."

Off in a corner sat a bewildered Simon Colson. The struggle over his soul was raging. As the group thanked the Lord, the young teenager headed for the backdoor.

Mark and Julie were thrilled. To their right, several students were answering Stephen's questions in rapid fire succession. To their left, others were fervently praying for unsaved families and friends. The Bishops could see their passion growing; a passion strengthened by the truth of God's Word through the power of the Holy Spirit.

It was a little after eleven when everyone shared their final goodbyes. While the guys were rearranging the furniture, there came a quiet knock at the front door.

"I'll get it," yelled Julie.

As the door swung open the frightened teenager just stared.

"Hey, Whit, what's up?"

"Is it too late to talk?" It's alright with my folks."

"Sure, come on in."

Entering the living room, she took a seat across from Julie and Michelle on the Bishop's oversized sofa.

Whitney Troy had been a believer for six years. But it wasn't until the Bishops arrived that she really responded to God's call on her life. The super thin teenager had long blonde hair and dark blue eyes. A friendly girl, Whitney was becoming an effective witness for Christ. Her friends would always tease her about her habit of raising her eyebrows really high when she got excited.

"Is everything okay?" asked a concerned Michelle.

With her hands folded in her lap, Whitney confessed, "Tonight's teaching really hit me. I mean all anyone ever talks about are all these famines. I must admit, seeing so many starving people has been super scary. Yet since the white, red, and black horses have come, God has answered so many of our prayers. Although some kids have backslid and returned to partying and drugs, we have seen tons get saved this past year. What really freaks me out is the coming invasion of Jerusalem by the Abomination of Desolation. This persecution is for keeps, isn't it? What I mean, uh, how can I know God will be with me when the mark of the beast becomes law?"

Michelle comforted the worried teenager by sitting beside her on the sofa.

"Whit," shared Julie, "Jesus gives us a promise of protection in Revelation 3:10. 'Because you have kept My command to persevere, I will also keep you from the hour of trial which shall come upon the whole world, to test those who dwell on the earth. Behold, I am coming quickly. Hold fast what you have, that no one may take your crown.'" [4]

"I know this verse is about the coming of the Lord. What I don't get is this hour of trial testing those living on the earth."

"The hour of trial represents the Great Tribulation, Matthew 24:21-22."

"So how are we kept from it? Most Christians at my school believe this is a promise to deliver the body of Christ from the hour of trial. They believe the church is going to be raptured before the Great Tribulation even begins."

"Whit, the key to unlocking the meaning of this promise is the phrase, 'keep you from.' In the Greek, it means to deliver from the midst of danger. The only other time Jesus uses this phrase is in John 17:15. Jesus is praying to His Father for the protection of believers from Satan. "'I do not pray that You should take them out of the world, but that you should keep them from the evil one.'" [5]

"I see it. We won't be delivered before the hour of trial. Jesus is promising to deliver us out of the midst of the Great Tribulation."

"Whit, this is the message of the hour for those who face the Antichrist and his false prophet."

"So how have we persevered?" she innocently asked.

"We have persevered through the beginning of sorrows."

"So what have we kept?"

"We have kept his Word and not denied His Name," shared Michelle. "Like the faithful church of Philadelphia in the first century, we have persevered for the sake of Christ's name. Jesus said, 'But he who endures to the end (of the age) shall be saved.' 6 Remember Whit, saved in this verse means physical deliverance, not salvation."

With her eyebrows raised high, the slender teen squealed, "Which means those who stand firm in Jesus against Satan's persecution will be rescued."

"That's right. 'For God did not appoint us to wrath, but to obtain salvation through our Lord Jesus Christ.' 7 The word 'salvation' means to be physically delivered. At the coming of the Son of Man, angels will gather His elect out of the Great Tribulation to heaven."

"Wow, what an awesome promise."

"So how will the elect be tested during the Great Tribulation?" asked Julie.

"After the fourth seal is opened, the mark will be forced on the world and everyone will see who the overcomers are." After a long pause, Whitney asked, "What about when the seventh seal is opened and God's wrath is poured out on the world? Is this a test or a divine judgment?" Before Julie or Michelle could answer, the excited teenager answered back, "Wait a second. God's wrath is never a test; it's a divine judgment."

"Excellent," encouraged Julie. "So is the Great Tribulation a test from Satan against believers or is it the wrath of God?"

"It's a test drawing a line between believers who follow the Christ and from those who follow the Antichrist."

"Amen, God has promised to guard us during this hour of trial. At the trump of God the Son is going to come back and bring us safely out from the midst of this danger."

"So the Great Tribulation can't be the day of the Lord."

"Go, Whit."

"So don't let anyone take your crown is a warning not to deny Christ?" 8

"I'm afraid so. This promise is for those who overcome and remain faithful. Anyone who denies the Lord by worshipping the Beast will lose their crown and their name will be blotted out of the Book of Life for eternity. 9 So let's trust in His promise, even though we don't know how He's going to do it."

A solemn Michelle couldn't help but reflect on the utter

magnitude of this truth.

"What awesome sharing. May I ask you one more question?"

"Sure, Whit," smiled Julie.

"What about those that are martyred?"

"Whit, as we speak there are believers exposing the Beast. Many will be martyred for their testimony of Jesus. Think of it, a remnant of overcomers will pay a great price to remain faithful. But their sacrifice is small compared to what our Heavenly Father did by sending his only Son so that we might be saved."

"Let's end with a wonderful promise," encouraged Julie. "'Therefore do not cast away your confidence, which has great reward. For you have need of endurance, so that after you have done the will of God, you may receive the promise.'" 10

Amy looked excited as she shared with the Ryan's what God had just given her.

"That's right, Lance. I'm planning to visit the witches' coven and share my salvation with Serena."

"Amy, how did you first get involved with witchcraft?"

"When I was a kid the craze was children books filled with witches and curses. Casting spells and controlling one's spirit was so much fun. It was super addictive."

"So you found out witchcraft was the manipulation of someone else's spirit?"

"Yep, I was good at cursing those who tried to hurt me. I learned a ton about witchcraft from the children's books I bought. When I was introduced to Wicca during my freshman year at Lakeview, I was ready for some real action."

"And now?" asked a troubled Lee Ryan.

"Since receiving the Holy Spirit, I now know Serena used demonic manipulation to control me. It all started when we were studying the power of spirit guides. Each girl at the coven has one. After a while, most of us believed we would die if we didn't obey."

"So who was your spirit guide?"

"Nimrod. Serena chose him for me. Spirit guides are demons who indwell their victims through doorways of opportunity. After seeking God, it was easy to see how Satan deceived us. All the girls at the coven were sexually abused at a young age."

"This is heavy stuff, Amy," Lee softly shared. "Do you feel intimidated when you are with Serena?"

"Yeah, especially when I refuse to obey her."

"How about when you tried to achieve things on your own? Did you feel inadequate, maybe insecure?"

Amy loved her new freedom to tell the truth. Such transparency was so liberating.

"It usually started with her put downs. Then I'd feel confusion coming from Nimrod. You begin to feel like you don't know how to do anything."

"Serena wants you to trust her," cautioned Lance. "She uses the spirit of witchcraft through manipulation. She'll use guilt and fear in an attempt to control you."

"It's like you're replaying a tape recorder of my life at the coven," yelped a giddy Amy. "Now I can see Serena's tricks for what they really are, lies from the devil."

The Ryans knew how serious this situation was but did not want to frighten the young convert.

"Amy, we'd like to go with you."

"Would you, Lee? I appreciate it. To be honest, I'd rather not get any of my Christian friends involved."

"Serena will try to intimidate you. Since this will be a spiritual confrontation, she will attack Christianity by highlighting the so called superiority of Wicca."

The Ryans were already feeling the burden to intercede.

"The key to victory over controlling spirits," Lance slowly shared, "is not to submit to them in any way. To break the chain of control from Serena and her satanic coven, you must use the power in the name of Jesus. If any demonic spirits attempt to regain control of your life, resist them by pleading the blood of Jesus. Remember, Amy, Serena will attempt to force her will upon you by manipulating your emotions."

"Thank you both so much. This morning I studied Ephesians 6 and prayed over my spiritual armor. I prayed for the helmet of salvation to protect my thought life. I asked for the breast plate of righteousness in order to stand in God's righteousness and not my own. I petitioned for the belt of truth so I may speak freely and truthfully. I asked for my feet to be shod with His peace. And finally, I asked for the shield of faith and the sword of the Spirit, which is His Word, so that nothing Serena throws at me will prosper. [11] Guys, I know God will free me from the coven's demonic influence."

"Amen, girl." shouted Lee. "'The Lord is faithful, who will establish you and guard you from the evil one.'" [12]

ONLY HE WHO NOW RESTRAINS

'For the mystery of lawlessness is already at work; only he who
now restrains will do so until he is taken out of the way.'
II Thessalonians 2:7

The Bishops loved to worship God. Sunday was a day for loving the Lord by believers not ashamed to be called radical. To experience the presence of the Holy Spirit was a gift from heaven that should always be treated with appreciation. The joy of watching people coming forward to be saved by the Holy Spirit was indescribable. Altar workers would pray for believers to be baptized in the Holy Spirit and speak in tongues. Those sick would come to be to be healed. Intercessors trained in deliverance would pray over those being attacked by the enemy. To Mark and Julie, it was a demonstration of God's power promised to those who believe.

While taking a seat in her favorite pew, Emily Teeter whispered, "If you ask me, Pastor Mark went too far when he said believers will have the choice to take the mark or not. The Bible never says believers will worship the Beast and lose their salvation."

"Emily, what about Revelation 13:16-18 and 14:9-12?" asked a concerned Allie Hart. "Why are believers warned not to take the mark if there was no chance they could?"

"Tell that to everyone who has left our church."

As the worship team began to sing a soft melody of songs about Jesus, Allie tried to reply but the seventy-year-old Sunday school teacher cut her off.

"If Pastor had just stayed on the rapture, everything would've been okay. Once he announced Joshua Kayin is going to invade Jerusalem with the nations from the Middle East Federation, he might as well have written Ickabod across the front door of our church." 1

Mark looked rested as he stepped up to the pulpit.

"Good morning, saints. May our Lord be praised for what He is going to accomplish in our lives this morning. The message the Holy Spirit has given me for today is entitled, *Who is the Restrainer?*'"

For some in the audience, this would be a day of reckoning. The tension was evident, to say the least.

"In A.D. 49, the apostle Paul wrote his first letter to the Thessalonians highlighting the future coming of our Lord. He made it clear when God blows His final trump; those who have died in Christ will receive their new resurrection bodies. Then believers who are alive on earth will be caught up to heaven with them. This was the mystery Paul was referring to. You see, Old Testament saints believed in the resurrection from the dead. It's the catching up of those who are alive at His coming that was a mystery. It wasn't long before some teachers confused the Thessalonians by teaching they had missed the coming of the Lord and had entered the day of the Lord, God's wrath. In response, Paul sent a second letter assuring them the day of the Lord will not come until the Man of Sin is revealed. [2] This happens when the Man of Sin sits in the Temple in Jerusalem and exalts himself above all that is called God." [3]

Immediately Mark could sense resistance.

"But before this world leader defiles the Temple the restrainer must be taken out of the way. 'For the mystery of lawlessness is already at work; only He who now restrains will do so until He is taken out of the way.'" [4]

The left side of the sanctuary was lined with teenage intercessors. They were poised and ready.

"Today's message provides a critical link in the chain of events warning us of the coming of the Lord. From scripture, we know the Beast cannot break the peace covenant with Israel until the restrainer is taken out of the way."

Emily leaned over and whispered to Allie, "The restrainer is the Holy Spirit. Only He has the power to restrain the mystery of lawlessness."

"So who is this restrainer preventing the Beast from attacking Jerusalem and taking control of the world? Many pastors teach only the Holy Spirit through the church has the power to hold back the mystery of lawlessness."

"That's what the Word teaches." shouted a choir member.

"Since the Bible doesn't tell us who the restrainer is, let's compare scriptures to determine his identity. Let's begin with a timeline of events which will precede the restrainer and the Beast. We know the 70th week of Daniel began when Joshua Kayin brokered a seven year peace treaty with Israel and his Muslim horns. Half way through it, he is going to break this treaty by invading Jerusalem with armies from these ten nations. 5 This is when Satan will convince the nations to support the Beast in his takeover of the world. It will be the second beast, the false prophet, who will initiate the mark of the beast worldwide. The horrific result will be a falling away of many saints not ready to overcome. But before all this can happen, the restrainer holding this evil back must stop. Now, who in scripture is presently upholding Israel against the spirit of the antichrist?"

Several youth knew but didn't want to interrupt.

"The answer is Michael the archangel. In Daniel 10:21 he is called the one who upholds or restrains the enemies of Israel. In Daniel 12:1 Michael is called the great prince who protects the children of Israel."

A disgusted Emily whispered to Allie, "I've never heard this interpretation before. Have you?"

"Let me be perfectly clear," cautioned Mark. "The Bible doesn't say the restrainer will be taken out of the world. It says he will be taken out of the way. Michael, the special guardian of Israel, is the restrainer who will be taken out of the way. Daniel 12:1 says Michael shall stand up or stand still at a time of trouble believers have never experienced before. Before the Great Tribulation can begin, he must stop protecting Israel. In II Thessalonians 2:7 Paul wrote of a restrainer taken out of the way just before the Man of Sin reveals himself at the beginning of the Great Tribulation. Do you see the connection? Both Daniel and Paul are warning believers living inside the 70th week of the one who will restrain the enemy right up until the Great Tribulation begins!"

"Preach it, Pastor!" shouted an excited Drew.

"In Revelation 12:7 exactly in the middle of the 70th week, Michael the restrainer and his angels will throw Satan and his angels out of heaven for the final time. The devil will no longer be able to accuse the saints before God. Satan will come down to earth to vent his wrath against Israel and the church. The woman in this chapter represents the 144,000; the first fruits from the remnant of Israel. 6 They will be hidden in the wilderness for the second half of the seven years. Not able to attack Israel, Satan will then make war against her offspring, those having the testimony of Jesus Christ." 7

"That's us!" shouted Ned, Drew's brother.

"For those of us who are born again, we are ready to be with the Lord if we die. But being saved doesn't necessarily mean we are ready to overcome the persecution from the Man of Sin. This is why Jesus exhorts us to watch and not be deceived."

The ovation from the youth group was loud and spontaneous. Most were on their feet praising the Lord.

"In closing, the Great Tribulation is near. Many Christians in America still deny this reality. While attending a prayer conference in Tuscaloosa last year, I had the opportunity to discuss this subject with another pastor. When I brought up the mark of the beast, he insisted the church would be long gone before the mark is given. I then asked about those who would face the Beast and his false prophet during the Great Tribulation. What if they get saved but then deny their Lord because of the persecution? The pastor confidently shared, "If one becomes a child of God, they can never lose their salvation, even if they are tricked into taking the mark of the beast." He then shared the testimony of a missionary who had just visited his church. The speaker shared a heartbreaking story of two missionaries ministering in Africa. A few months earlier, they were arrested for openly sharing the gospel. Both were sentenced to die unless they publicly denied Jesus as their Savior. One missionary refused and was killed. The other denied the Lord in order to save his life."

"I said, 'That's not God's will.'"

"The pastor angrily responded, "Don't you realize he had a family? He had no choice; his very existence was at stake. We are all sinners. We all fall short of Jesus' example. God understands when each of us strays from doing the right thing. Who are you to judge? Do you sin?"

Mark paused before continuing.

"Listen to me, saints. Telling a believer they can deny Christ and repent later is never God's will. The World ID System our former President is promoting is the mark of the beast. Nowhere in scripture does the Holy Spirit war with Satan. Soon, Michael the arch angel is going to throw Satan out of heaven. The question is whom will you worship, the Antichrist or Jesus Christ? For those who choose to live under the authority of the beast's system you will not suffer any persecution. Of course, when Jesus returns, you will know whom you have denied. John wrote, 'And now dear children continue in Him so that when He appears we may be confident and unashamed before

Him at His coming.' 8 Jesus warned, 'Therefore whoever confesses Me before men, him I will also confess before My Father in heaven. But whoever denies Me before men, him I will also deny before my Father who is in Heaven.'" 9

"So what's the purpose of the Great Tribulation, Pastor?"

"The compromise of believers in these last days is without debate. 10 Satan is going to deceive many Christians during the fourth and fifth seals. Our Lord exhorts us to overcome by watching and living holy lives. 11 After our Blessed Hope cuts short the persecution by the Beast, mankind will suffer God's wrath. As believers, we must follow Jesus even if it means martyrdom!" 12

As the morning service closed, Julie Bishop was desperately interceding for several families who were exiting for the final time.

Her hands clinched, her heart broken, she cried out, "Lord, why can't they hear what the Holy Spirit is saying?"

"Reverend Bray, Matthew is waiting to see you."

"Thank you, please send him in."

The Reverend Thomas Bray's spacious office was adjacent to his new high tech TV studio. An entire wall was decorated with plagues and mementoes from twenty-six years of full time ministry. It was very impressive for visitors. But to his oldest son, the accolades were beginning to sound hollow. He had always had a close relationship with his dad. The famous prophecy teacher was praying Matthew would follow in his footsteps.

"C'mon in Matt."

"Hi Dad, just caught the tail end of your new prophecy video. Your secretary is reviewing it on her computer."

"We just wrapped it up. Truthfully," he chuckled, "radio was a breeze compared to TV. You know I'm not getting any younger."

"The Lord has lots left for you to do, Dad. What's the title of your new video?"

"The Coming of the Son of Man, it's a commentary on the events Jesus gave His disciples on the Mount of Olives. This will be a blessing to those struggling with the false prophecies and visions being spread around town."

"What do you mean?"

"Have you ever heard of Pastor Mark Bishop?"

"Sure, he pastors a Pentecostal church on the Eastside."

"Three and a half years ago, he had a vision of our former President brokering a covenant of death with Israel. He teaches Joshua Kayin is the Antichrist."

"Yeah, I heard about it."

"So has the entire religious community. I've already met with the BMA, even talked with Pastor Mark. Nothing but a miracle will change his mind. His false teaching is no secret. He teaches the elect will be caught up after Jesus opens the sixth seal. He believes we are living inside the final seven years before Armageddon. As of today, we are experiencing the famine from the third seal."

"It's only going to get worse. The world has never seen so many starve to death."

"These famines can't be God's wrath during the tribulation. It's the out of control spending by super powers and these pointless wars that have drained our world's economy."

"Have you tried sharing..."

"I gave him the scriptures. He refuses to see the truth. Most of the pastors are ignoring him. I can't do that. This is why I created this video."

"Sam and I believe..."

"Actually, you and your brother helped me to see how important this video will be to the body of Christ."

"So you're teaching the Son of Man in Matthew 24 represents the Word of God coming with His bride in Revelation 19?"

"It's biblical, Matt."

"In Matthew 24:30-31 the Son of Man is coming back and His angels are going to gather His elect to heaven."

"Son, you need to compare all verses..."

"What about one taken, one left, in Matthew 24:40?"

"Matt, when the Word of God cuts short Armageddon, the unsaved are taken away to eternal punishment. The believers who survive the day of the Lord will enter the millennium. Jesus said it would be like the days of Noah, the wicked were taken, and Noah and his family were left."

"Dad, no one is taken to eternal punishment at Armageddon. The unsaved aren't resurrected out of Hades to stand before the white throne judgment until after the millennium. In Matthew 24:40 Jesus is describing the resurrection of the elect to heaven."

"You're twisting the scriptures, Matt. The secret catching up of believers is in I Thessalonians 4. The events in Matthew 24 are referring to Armageddon, not the rapture."

"What about the gathering of the elect by angels in Matthew 24? The word gather in verse 31 is *episunago*. Epi is a preposition meaning upon. Sunago means gather. When used together it means an upward direction. This is the gathering of His saints to heaven at the coming of the Son of Man between the sixth and seventh seals."

"Can't be, son!" objected Tom. "The elect in Matthew 24 are Jews saved during the Great Tribulation."

"According to Daniel 9:24-27 and Romans 11:25-27, the Messiah doesn't redeem His Jewish remnant until the fullness of the Gentiles is over at the end of the 70th week. The elect in the New Testament are Christians."

Looking away, his famous father appeared pale.

"Does this mean you and Sam reject the imminent return of our Blessed Hope?"

"Dad, if the church is in Matthew 24 and the events Jesus highlights take place inside the 70th week, then how can the church be taken in a secret rapture before the 70th week begins?"

Not even noticing the full moon, memories flooded Amy's mind as she walked the dirt road lined with sycamore trees. It had been two years since her first visit to the witches' coven. The initial party was very friendly. Everybody seemed to be having fun. At school, all the girls involved in the coven wore black and had a passion for the history of Wicca. Their favorite meeting place for lunch was behind the Industrial Arts Building. Of course not everyone could become a member. For girls who had a desire to learn, Serena would share her passion for supernatural power.

Amy's goal was twofold. First, she would renounce any involvement with the coven to her mentor, Serena. Second, she planned to share her conversion to Christ with the girls. Even though Pastor Lance objected she go alone; deep down Amy knew Jesus would protect her. 13

By the time she arrived at the old cottage, the other twelve girls were already preparing themselves for tonight's ritual. Amy wondered what had ever attracted her to such an extreme group. Immediately, the Holy Spirit brought back the painful memory of her abuse by a neighbor at the age of seven. Her parents never understood why their bundle of sunshine suddenly lost her smile. Virtually overnight, the little girl's personality changed from outgoing and playful, to that of a secluded loner.

"Hi, Amy, how you doing?" greeted a smiling Serena.

The old witch could sense something was wrong with her favorite pupil. Closing the front door behind her, she silently summoned Amy's spirit guide to manifest. Serena's goal was to enslave the teenager to the spirit world. Amy had been an excellent student from day one. Her mentor was optimistic for her future.

"Can we talk, Serena? I would like to share with you a tremendous blessing in my life."

While silently preparing herself the witch knew what do.

"Let's use a meditation room where we can be alone."

As they walked down the dark hall, the peace of God seemed to rest upon Amy like a mantle across her shoulders.

"This blessing happened when four of us from the coven attended a Lakeview High Bible Club meeting. Pastor Lance taught on future Bible prophecy. He highlighted the two signs warning us of Jesus' return for His saints."

Her excitement was upsetting to her skilled mentor.

"Amy, you don't actually believe Jesus is coming back again? Everyone knows, once a person dies, he or she may never cross back over into this life."

To keep her pupil off balance, the experienced witch needed to re-establish her authority. Her control over Amy was never a problem with Nimrod's assistance.

While searching for her little brown leather New Testament the distracted teenager mumbled back, "Lance spoke of Jesus' resurrection from the dead. He also highlighted the events which warn us of His coming."

"My dear, everyone knows Wicca was a religion centuries before Christianity. In fact, many of the events of the Bible aren't meant to be taken literally. For example, I don't know of anyone who actually believes in an ark filled with thousands of animals." Before Amy could reply, she sarcastically asked, "You can't possibly believe God flooded this earth because mankind was so evil?"

"Lance talked of an Antichrist who will attempt to stop Jesus from regaining control of earth."

"That's nothing new. I've heard about the coming of the

Antichrist for years now. Christian ministers who believe our world is evil pompously predict God is going to bring judgment by fire. Actually, the very opposite is happening. Mankind is reaching a higher plain of spirituality bringing in worldwide peace. Joshua Kayin is a respected leader who has the vision, the courage, and the love, to bring about such harmony."

"That's just it. Joshua Kayin is the Antichrist."

Jumping to her feet, Serena shrieked, "And what proof do you have for such an ugly accusation? Before you answer me, how do you know Jesus will come back? Ever since the beginning of creation the things of this world have gone on just like they always have." 14

"Well, uh," muttered the naïve convert, "I don't know the verses at this time. I have a lot of studying to do."

"Why would anyone think Joshua Kayin is evil?"

"Satan is going to give the Beast authority over the nations..."

"You must be joking, Amy. You don't actually believe in such a fairy tale?"

Lifting her blonde bangs off her forehead, she calmly said, "Enough to do this."

The witch gasped.

"What have you done with Nimrod?"

"I had him removed. Last week I accepted Jesus Christ as my Lord and Savior. I've repented of my sins. I'm free; I'm a new creation in Christ."

"Stop this right now. Your oath to Nimrod can never be broken. Amy, you may think you've had a real experience with God, but I assure you, you'll only be disappointed."

"Through Jesus' name, I rebuke you spirit of Control out of my life. It's over, Serena. I am totally free from Satan's control, your control, and any influence from this house of witches. I'm not intimidated by you anymore or the spirits indwelling you. The blood of Jesus protects me; what protects you?"

"Enough of your nonsense! I never want to see you again."

Scurrying out the back door the bitter witch never looked back.

Nimrod hovered near the back of the room. The foul spirit could feel it. The power of darkness over the girl was no more.

As Amy slowly walked down the hall toward the main foyer, not one girl was in sight. Pausing at the front door, she turned around and boldly shouted, "Is there anyone who would like to hear how Jesus has forgiven me and saved my soul for eternity?"

The only reply was an eerie silence.

"Father, I pray in Jesus' name for You to supernaturally open the eyes of these girls. Let them see how Satan has deceived them. The devil has used the abuse each girl has suffered as a channel to control them. It wasn't their fault. Father set them free by Your love. Grant them a real peace; a peace which can only come through repenting of their sins and believing in Your Son. I commit each girl into Your loving arms."

Closing the front door behind her, the former Witch could faintly hear the sound of weeping coming from the top of the stairs.

HE WHO OVERCOMES

The secret meeting at Billy B's home had taken two months to arrange. Each Watchman was handpicked by either Mark Bishop or Stephen Corbin. Trained to detect any surveillance, most parked their cars a mile away. Some had been Watchmen for years. Others had just received their calling, like the Changs, Shiners, and Machovecs.

Without uttering a greeting, Stephen dropped to his knees. Fervent prayer was a common denominator among Watchmen. Many were crying out for the salvation of those who still could be saved. Others were praying for the discernment of believers against deceiving spirits which had captivated so many. After a powerful breakthrough in intercession, Stephen shared the details of the camp.

"As you all know, everyone here tonight has been called to be a Watchman for the Lord. Until now, the persecution has been minimal. Once the mark is introduced our inside sources tell us everyone will be given six months to voluntarily register. After this grace period, the mark will become mandatory. The New World Coalition will issue specific sign up dates in alphabetical order. Approximately sixty days after the mandatory sign up begins, those who refuse to register will be arrested. Heavy fines and jail time will be used as deterrents. Eventually, any one subverting this ID system will be put to death."

Most questions were coming from those who never believed a world leader could ever control all the nations.

"Saints, we need to realize the critical role the Holy Spirit will play in the safety of our families. We cannot allow our emotions to dictate how severe a situation appears to be. Obedience is always better than sacrifice."

The evangelist was aware of those who had just learned the truth. The betrayal on their faces was proof enough.

"For example, some of your pastors are saying Joshua Kayin is a man of God who has simply lost his way. This is a blatant lie from the spirit of antichrist. Scripture says Satan will give his power, his throne, and his authority, to one man. 1 Paul calls him the Man of Sin. 2 John calls him the Beast. Jesus calls him the Abomination of Desolation. Satan's beast kingdom is portrayed as having seven heads and ten horns. 3 The seven heads represent seven leaders, along with their kingdoms who failed to destroy the nation of Israel throughout history. John sees another head. The eighth head consists of ten nations who will give their power to the Antichrist." 4

"Stephen, how about a quick rundown of these seven heads?"

"Sure Billy B. The first head was the Pharaoh of Egypt who attempted to destroy Moses and his people. God divinely intervened by opening the Red Sea and drowning the Pharaoh and his army. The second head was Assyria. Led by the wicked King Tiglathpileser, the Assyrian army captured ten of the twelve tribes of Israel in A.D. 722. The third head was Babylon. King Nebuchadnezzar and his Babylonian army destroyed Solomon's Temple in 586 B.C. and took the Jewish people captive back to his homeland."

"So the first three heads failed to destroy Israel were Egypt, Assyria, and Babylon," the trucker slowly repeated. "Who are the other four heads, Stephen?"

"The fourth head was Persia. This kingdom, under the control of the evil Haman, tried to destroy Queen Esther's people in 539 B.C. The fifth head was Greece, led by the infamous Alexander the Great. After the invasion of Israel in 330 B.C., the people of Israel were required to speak Greek instead of Hebrew. They were forced to worship idols in an attempt to turn them away from the one true God. The sixth head was Rome. Rome's evil emperor, Domitian, persecuted the Jews more severely than the previous five head kingdoms. John the apostle spoke of five heads that had fallen. They were Egypt, Assyria, Babylon, Persia, and Greece. In A.D. 96, when John supernaturally received The Revelation of Jesus Christ, Rome the sixth head, was still in control of Israel. The apostle then saw a seventh head kingdom that had not yet come. But when it did come, it was for a short time." 5

"So who was the seventh head?"

"What country since the first century persecuted the Jews worse than Rome?"

"You mean Nazi Germany?" asked a Watchman near the back.

"I do," said Stephen.

"So these seven heads represent seven rulers who tried to destroy Israel?"

"That's right. The Scriptures predict the Beast is the eighth head and is of the seven. This world leader will soon lead the armies coming from his ten horns against Israel. All nations from the Middle East Federation were once part of the Roman Empire. 6 Scripture says, 'So they worshiped the dragon who gave authority to the beast, saying, who is like the beast? Who is able to make war with him?'" 7

The humid evening seemed so surreal. Everyone in Billy B's jammed living room knew the time for debate was over.

"Listen up," insisted a hopeful Stephen. "We need to warn believers to be watching for the false prophet. Pope Michael is going to be given the power to kill those who refuse to worship the Beast. This deceiver will have every country create images of Kayin. When these images are in place, demonic spirits will possess them. 8 Let's not underestimate the satanic power controlling these two leaders. Their goal is to stop the fulfillment of Bible prophecy. When the Word of God returns at Armageddon both will be cast alive into the lake of fire." 9

"Amen to that," grinned Billy B.

"After Michael casts Satan out of heaven, Kayin is going to cut a deal with the devil. 10 He will be given authority over every nation. He will have the power to war against the saints. We know God has given us the strength to be faithful 'til the sun, moon, and stars, lose their light. The Holy Spirit will lead us until the Son of Man comes back in the glory of His Father."

Praises went up as Stephen asked Mark to speak.

"Thank you, my brother. Once the mark is accepted by this Christ rejecting world, we won't have much time. For over a year, volunteers have secretly been preparing our camp. At this moment, our Watchman Camp is totally operational. By this Friday, we will begin receiving our first campers. Your camp contact in Bethany will be called the Mole. For security reasons, once you leave for the camp no one can follow you. The Watchman leadership has created a barter system which will supply everything necessary to sustain our campers. Of course, if any of us are arrested, heaven is waiting."

For the next two hours, Mark Bishop shared the layout of the secret campsite. It was hidden deep within caverns outside the city of Birmingham, Alabama. Most attending this meeting would safely be inside within forty eight hours of the introduction of the mark. For some, the choice to leave wasn't hard at all. For those who had family members who refused to come, it was a total heartbreak. The words of Jesus had a new sense of urgency: "Anyone who loves his father or mother more than me is not worthy of me; anyone who loves his son or daughter more than me is not worthy of me; and anyone who does not take up his cross and follow me is not worthy of me. Whoever finds his life will lose it, and whoever loses his life for My sake will find it." 11

The farm looked deserted as cars pulled up without the aid of their headlights. Preparations already were underway. The old barn was being transformed into a Neo Nazi shrine. While some interns strung lights across the crossbeams, others set up chairs. Propaganda consisting of books, pictures, and leaflets, were displayed on tables near the podium. Tonight was no ordinary gathering. The Neighbors' Commander, Tanner Harrison, had called an emergency meeting.

The sentries had their orders. No outsiders would be allowed in under any circumstances. For some, it was the ultimate fantasy to be acted out. For others, it was a cause as important as life itself.

Tanner appeared uneasy as his soldiers lined up in two lines facing him and saluted. The uniforms, the long black boots, the swastika emblems, the short haircuts, everything was in place. Tonight's agenda was an exhortation from their Commander.

Throughout the barn the demons were waiting. Most were perched on crossbars high above the seats. Wolf had warned them of Tanner's rebellion. These evil spirits also knew of his contact with Amy, a recent defector from the coven.

"No problem," bragged Fear as he circled the inside of the barn. "He is in our territory tonight. Besides, Wolf is fully capable of regaining its subject."

Everyone stared as Tanner approached the portable stage. He knew the consequences of such betrayal but refused to look over his shoulder for the rest of his life. Picking up the microphone, he scanned the soldiers who deeply respected him.

"I have called this meeting to share with you the future direction of our family."

"Let's hear it, Tanner!" yelled a lieutenant seated beside the interns.

"We all joined the Neighbors with a desire to make a difference. We saw injustices, yet nothing was being done."

"Paint the picture, Commander!" hollered a new recruit.

"We each received visitations from our spirit guides convincing us the power we have is supernatural. At first, it was pretty exciting, a real adrenaline rush. But after a while, this power started to drain me. I felt empty; especially when I was alone."

"No way," challenged a defiant second in command.

No soldier was ever allowed publicly to reveal a weakness, especially from anyone in leadership.

"Recently, several of us were led by our spirit guides to disrupt a Bible club meeting at Lakeview High School. When Pastor Lance prayed, I felt something inside of me. Wolf urged me not to go but I wanted to hear the preacher."

"That club is full of stinking Jews. Did you purposely break the rules of our family?"

While everyone gawked in disbelief, Tanner boldly replied, "Me and six others."

Motioning to join him; the dedicated soldiers walked up and stood in front of the stage.

"Life is not about obeying manmade rules. It's about finding the truth from above and living it out."

Speaking out of turn an intern dangerously confessed, "Commander, we already have the truth. You taught us that."

"There is only one truth, Reg. 'For God so loved the world that he gave His only begotten Son, that whoever believes in Him should not perish...'" 12

"What's he talking about, Reggie?" whispered another intern. "Aren't we all Christians?"

"While Lance spoke of his relationship with the Holy Spirit, I realized my involvement with the Neighbors wasn't producing a life of peace. Actually, we've been taught to spread fear in order to manipulate those who are weak. In the hands of someone who is not free, intimidation is an effective tool."

Suddenly, several soldiers jumped up and began to call out curses. This manifestation of hate was no joke.

"Hear this!" demanded Tanner. "After the pastor laid down the coming events, the seven of us felt the presence of God. I have never felt anything like it."

All six soldiers started to clap.

"Those of us standing before you tonight have become believers in Jesus Christ. He is our Savior and Lord. Salvation is open to anyone who will follow the Son of God."

"Why should we?" mocked a soldier. "Jesus was a Jew."

"It begins with a step of faith. We did it; so can you."

The noise level rose as small groups talked privately. The six formed a circle to pray for their friends then Tanner raised his hands and spoke for the final time.

"I know an altar call isn't exactly what you were expecting tonight. In fact, some of you have no intention of giving up the hate the devil uses to control you. The truth is every one of us has a choice concerning our eternal destiny, either heaven or the lake of fire." After a deep breath, Tanner bravely announced, "I hereby resign as Commander of the Neighbors. As a new creation in Jesus, I publicly renounce Satan, Wolf, and all other spirits of darkness. My brothers in Christ and I don't fear any attacks or threats from the devil or his demons. For any who desire to be free from these foul spirits, the seven of us will be outside. Jesus is just a prayer away."

And with that, seven ex-Nazi's walked out of the barn. Those inside were speechless. The power of God had swept the barn clean of any demonic influence. It wasn't long before several soldiers removed their swastika armbands and stepped outside to pray with their friends.

Taking charge, the second in command led the remaining soldiers in a hasty retreat out of the old barn. That night on a deserted farm in rural southeastern Alabama, ten more Nazi's surrendered their lives to God. After praying, the young boys began to rejoice. Really, they were no different than any other teenagers. Each boy was searching for the truth; a truth they could believe in.

"Tanner," asked Reggie, "whatever led you to face the family straight up and challenge us to believe in Jesus?"

Pulling her note from his wallet Tanner asked for a light. After Reggie fired up his Zippo, the ex-Commander read: *Dear Tanner, words cannot express the love and freedom I've found since believing in Jesus as my Savior. And to think, the enemy of our souls sent us to the Bible Club to disrupt what God was planning. I remember how troubled you looked when you left. At first, I didn't understand the burden tugging at me. Later I realized I was supposed to pray for you. That night I met with some of my new Christian friends, we prayed for the spirits of Fear and Hate to leave you. Afterwards I received a word of knowledge. The Holy Spirit spoke into my mind, 'The things which are impossible with men are possible with God.'* 13 *God is calling you, my friend. Don't let Satan deceive you any longer. Our Jesus loves us. Tanner, be a leader for what is right. If we stand for the truth, God will always be on our side. Love ya, Amy."*

Tanner's search for the truth was over. God would now direct him. As the boys jumped into the back of his red pickup truck, they could hear a loud howl in the distance.

"Hear that? Sounds like a wolf. Tanner, we don't have wolves living in this area, do we?"

The ex-Nazi smiled.

"Not anymore, Reggie, not anymore."

AS YOU SEE THE DAY APPROACHING

'...not forsaking the assembling of ourselves together, as is the manner of some, but exhorting one another, and so much the more as you see the Day approaching.'
Hebrews 10:25

She paused for a moment after peeking inside his dimly lit study. Mark sensed something was wrong as he rose from his knees.

"Are you praying, Mark?"

"My prayer time is over, honey, what's up?"

"The girls just left for school. When I heard a knock at the front door I thought Lindsey forgot something. When I answered it a government official introduced himself and showed me his badge. He's from Homeland Security. He wants to speak with you."

"Did you invite him in?"

"He's in the living room. Has an easy going smile; couldn't be more than twenty-five. I'm so sorry, Mark, I didn't mean to..."

"It's alright. While I was praying the Holy Spirit assured me He was with us. Let's go see what he wants."

"He only wants to speak with you."

"Ok, can you intercede for me in our bedroom? If he attempts to arrest me use the window to the backyard. Wait until lunch time before picking up the girls. Act as natural as you can. You know the way to the camp."

"But we are so close to leaving."

His gentle embrace was his way of saying everything was all right. He waited until she disappeared into their bedroom.

The relaxed officer stood and extended his hand.

"I'm Mark Bishop, nice to meet you."

"I'm afraid I'm not allowed to give you my name. I'm with

Homeland Security. My badge number is..."

"That won't be necessary. How can I help you?"

"Reverend, my jurisdiction covers religious subversive groups. Any group or individual who openly advocates the breaking of any federal laws is subject to arrest."

"I'm not aware of any laws that I..."

"Reverend, your apocalyptic teaching is no secret to my department. My superior has no problem if you teach our former President is some sort of Antichrist taking over the world. Calling the Pope a false prophet is no crime either. But when you deliberately encourage citizens of the United States to resist mandated security measures, then Homeland Security has a problem."

"Are you referring to the future microchip?"

"We call it the World ID Commerce Act. Reverend Bishop, my visit today doesn't have to be hard. I've personally read your sermons on the mark of the beast. Preach up a storm this Sunday if you want to. But from now on, if you encourage or threaten any man, woman, or child, to subvert our ID security law, then I'll have to arrest you. Our department won't warn you again. This also goes for your wife and your two daughters."

"Everyone please be seated," sighed the sixty five-year-old teacher. "C'mon, c'mon, we don't have all day."

Room 206 was buzzing with the news of this morning's guest speaker, the commander of a Nazi gang called the Neighbors.

"Your homework assignment was to select an active hate group in the state of Alabama. Your grade will reflect how well you highlight the group's objectives and the specific types of people that tend to become members."

Cleaning his glasses with his wrinkled tie, Mr. Olson was ready for the usual stream of meaningless questions.

"Class, this morning we'll be examining the history of white supremacy groups in America."

There was a rush of anticipation in the air. The prospect of opposing sides clashing was a real possibility. Yet, the already tired professor didn't have a clue of what would soon break forth in his usual boring third period history class.

"Yes, Heather, what is it now?"

"I'm afraid I don't understand the assignment."

Rolling his eyes he asked, "And why is that?"

"Well, some of my friends say the Neighbors believe Jews and Blacks are evil."

"Go on."

"What I mean to say is, uh, Reggie Lincoln was once a member of the Neighbors and he's a really great guy."

The scattered laughter was the norm.

"All right, settle down everybody. Actually, Heather's observation of today's topic is very appropriate. Of course, this is a voluntary discussion. Anyone who feels today's subject matter is not acceptable to their belief system can go to the library."

After taking a seat behind his cluttered desk, the slightly bent over teacher lowered his reading glasses. No one had moved.

"Well, well, well, it seems like we have some genuine interest in hearing Mr. Harrison this morning. I've asked him to explain the general makeup of his former hate group called the Neighbors. After his presentation, Tanner will take any questions you might have. Now guys let's show a little self control."

The ex-Nazi walked toward the front with an uneasy stride. Down in study hall, Amy Phillips and Reggie Lincoln were interceding for their new brother in Christ.

"Ignorance can be a scary thing," Tanner candidly shared while laying his Bible on the podium. "Three years ago I transferred to Lakeview. At first, I didn't fit in. I wasn't a jock or into theater. My grades were average. I didn't have any hobbies. I felt pretty alone. No one talked to me much, so I didn't talk either. This went on for a couple of months. I knew if I didn't find something to be part of I'd be labeled a loser."

Some students were becoming restless. They were thinking; get on with it, racist.

"Then one day I started to study the history of the white race in America. That's when I decided to form the Neighbors. At first, it was a rush. Being in charge of soldiers who respect you is addictive, especially for someone who had never had such power."

"What type of power, Tanner?" asked Heather.

"The Neighbors was a hate group promoted by demons."

Hands shot up as several began talking at once.

"Class!" barked the gray haired teacher. "Absolutely no more interruptions. Go ahead, Tanner."

"I know a lot of this is going to sound extreme. A few weeks before I started the Neighbors a spirit visited me."

"Yeah, right," coughed a grunger.

"It was a hot night and I remember waking up after having a bad nightmare. About two in the morning I felt a presence..."

Tanner looked confused; not quite sure on how to explain what he had experienced.

"Anyway, I could hardly breathe. Then I got on my knees and cried out to God. That's when I heard it."

"Heard what?" called out someone from the third row. "Don't stop now, dude, this is better than the Tea Party freaks."

The nervous laughter eased the tension. Tanner could sense their impatience. Most were trying to figure out if he was telling the truth.

"This is no joke. The voice was supernatural. I could feel its presence. Somehow I was drawn to it. I didn't understand at the time. But now I do, I was after power."

"Aren't we all," taunted someone from the first row.

"It told me I could do great things. I believed because I wanted to. Later I found out the name of this spirit guide was Wolf."

"Cool," laughed someone aloud.

"It's not cool. That's when the bondage took hold of me. After forming the Neighbors, I surrendered to Wolf. We believed in the protection of the white Angelo Saxon race. We felt superior as we looked for ways to promote our hate. But the more I got into it; the emptier I felt. I knew there had to be something more to life than just pumping yourself up and putting others down. The day Lance Ryan came to speak at the Bible Club, I felt dead inside. Hope Bishop invited our gang to come and hear the pastor share on the coming of the Lord. When I showed up with a few of my soldiers we were hoping to blow their minds. You see, Satan taught us the key to controlling people is fear. People will respect you if they fear you."

"Do you really believe that, Tanner?"

"Not anymore. Lance shared how Jesus gave His life so all who follow Him may receive eternal life. During his message Wolf kept harassing me. He threatened me if I didn't leave. But something stopped me, another voice; a peaceful voice greater than Wolf's."

"So you found religion?" yawned a cheerleader.

"I'm not talking about manmade religion. The Bible says, 'For the grace of God that brings salvation has appeared to all men, teaching us that, denying ungodliness and worldly lusts, we should live soberly, righteously, and godly in the present age, looking for the blessed hope and glorious appearing of our great God and Savior Jesus Christ.' 1 Religion can't save anyone. Only Jesus Christ, God's Son, can grant salvation."

"Stop this!" interrupted an irate Muslim. "Allah doesn't have a son. You have no right to dogmatically..."

"I have renounced my belief in white supremacy and Satanism. I've asked Jesus to forgive me of my sins."

Another itching for a fight asked, "Do you expect us to believe you are now a loving disciple of Jesus after you and your racist buddies have spread your stinking hate propaganda all over our school?"

"What about it," Tanner?" pressed Heather.

"Don't you see it? He was starving for acceptance from his racist clones before he realized how hopeless it was. He saw the end coming, so he bailed and joined up with the holy rollers."

"I now know a person can't be a Christian and a racist at the same time. How can you say you love God, who you can't see, if you can't love your brother, who you can see?" 2

"May I speak?" interrupted a black football player. "Get a grip, Harrison, everyone knows about the racism in Bethany. Just look at the all white churches. Many of them claim to love God but deep down they hate my people. You'd have to be blind not to see the prejudice in their hearts."

"What about the black churches?" challenged a skinhead. "You don't think they're prejudice?"

"Hold up!" hollered Tanner. "All kinds of people go to church. They get baptized in water, accept the doctrines of their church, even help the poor. But people playing church doesn't prove they're really saved. Real believers don't promote hate. Right now I publicly repent of my actions with the Neighbors. As Christians we are to exhort one another in love as we see the day approaching." 3

"What day?" asked a curious Heather.

"The only way to be ready for the day of the Lord is to watch for the events that warn of His coming. Soon, Jerusalem is going to be invaded..."

After the bell sounded, several students surrounded Tanner with questions. The gray haired teacher was gathering homework assignments when their eyes met.

"Thank you, Mr. Olson for allowing me..."

"Young man, when I asked you to share about your former white supremacy gang, I was hoping to hear some gory details. Some need to hear how destructive hate can be. I haven't decided if your presentation was about hate or the second coming of Christ."

"Hope I didn't get you into any trouble," Tanner awkwardly confessed.

"What are they going to do to me?" the bent over teacher chuckled under his breath. "Besides, your talk kept their attention better than any I've heard in years."

"So what do you believe, Mr. Olson?"

"You mean about Jesus?"

Tanner nodded, refusing to be distracted by the students coming in for the next class.

"I was brought up Lutheran. When I joined the Army at nineteen, I left the church, haven't been back since. But you're not talking about churchgoing, are you?"

"No sir, I guess what I want to know is..."

"It's a relationship you have with Jesus, isn't it?"

"Yeah, not just a duty to gain the approval of others."

The old man's smile seemed so out of character.

"If you believe Jesus is the Son of God, are you going to ask Him for forgiveness of your sins and spend eternity with Him in heaven?"

"Tanner, I asked Jesus to be my Savior halfway through your testimony. After school I'm going to buy me a Bible. I've got some serious reading to do."

"You really mean it?"

Amidst the cheers from Room 206, the ex-Neo Nazi offered the newly converted history teacher an extra special high five.

FOURTH SEAL : THE PALE HORSE

'So I looked, and behold, a pale horse. And the name of him who sat on it was Death, and Hades followed with him. And power was given to them over a fourth of the earth, to kill with sword, with hunger, with death, and by the beasts of the earth.'
Revelation 6.8

The tribes of Judah, Reuben, Gad, Asher, Naphtali, Manasseh, Simeon, Levi, Issachar, Zebulun, Joseph, and Benjamin, were all accounted for. 1 For the past month, members of this remnant had been secretly slipping away to hide in the Jordanian wilderness. Somehow they knew their beloved Jerusalem was in grave danger. It was as if God was drawing them away for their own protection. Tucked away in their safe haven they took turns petitioning Hashem for His will for their lives.

This night, sitting around huge fires in dug out sand pits, a Rabbi from the tribe of Levi motioned for quiet before reading from the Book of Revelation.

"'Now a great sign appeared in heaven: a woman clothed with the sun, with the moon under her feet, and on her head a garland of twelve stars.'" 2

Looking over these from the twelve tribes of Israel he paused.

"Then being with child, she cried out in labor and in pain to give birth. And another sign appeared in heaven: behold, a great, fiery red dragon having seven heads and ten horns, and seven diadems on his heads. His tail drew a third of the stars of heaven and threw them to the earth. And the dragon stood before the woman who was ready to give birth, to devour her Child as soon as it was born. She bore a male Child who was to rule all nations with a rod of iron. And her Child was caught up to God and His throne.'" 3

Without any warning all 144,000 men stood to their feet and started to praise the God of Abraham, Isaac, and Jacob.

With a loud voice the Rabbi boldly proclaimed, "'Then the woman fled into the wilderness, where she has a place prepared by God, that they should feed her there one- thousand-two-hundred and sixty days.'" 4

A member from the tribe of Judah asked to speak.

"Ezekiel prophesied, 'I will bring you from the peoples and gather you out of the countries where you are scattered, with a mighty hand, with an outreached arm, and with fury poured out. And I will bring you into the wilderness of the peoples, and there I will plead My case with you face to face...I will make you pass under the rod, and I will bring you into the bond of the covenant.'" 5

A multitude of angels were lining up behind Michael. There was no talking, no strategy sessions, no instructions on how to defend. Each angel knew the importance of this war. For millenniums they had heard the evil threats from Satan. He had made many boasts but in reality Lucifer was still just an angel. His ultimate goal is to defeat Jesus by the sounding of the seventh trumpet. 6

Suddenly the dragon hovered above his evil army. The demons were slandering one another as usual.

"Enough! The time has come to thwart what has been decreed. I summon you to join me. Come let us defeat Michael and his armies."

Those who once worshiped before the Throne of God shot effortlessly into the heavenlies. Michael and his fellow angels could hear the advancing horde. Such aggression meant nothing. Humans could be intimidated but not the angelic host from heaven. From his left, Michael spun to face what had once been God's favorite. Satan cursed him. Lunging forward the Archangel struck the Devil casting this foul spirit down to earth. 7

A loud voice in heaven declared, "... Woe to the inhabitants of the earth and the sea. For the devil has come down to you, having great wrath, because he knows that he has a short time." 8

Every angel looked forward to this moment of victory. Their radiance was glorious as they bowed before the Father. For over six thousand years, the angelic host had fought those cast out of heaven. To see one third of their fellow angels following Lucifer was piercing.

9 The demonic onslaught mankind would have to suffer was heartbreaking. Nevertheless, it would soon be over. The Father would choose three angels to carry out His will. Dressed in pure bright linen with golden bands fastened around their chests, the angelic host patiently waited. 10 From His Throne the Father announced His decision.

"Glory will preach My eternal gospel to every nation, tribe, tongue, and people. 11 Amad will announce the destruction of the Babylonian harlot who deceived the nations with her fornication. 12 Ian will warn mankind not to worship the Beast. 13 Those who do will drink the wine of My wrath. They shall be tormented with fire in the presence of holy angels and the Lamb."

Deep within the caverns outside Birmingham believers were lining up. The identity of each overcomer was checked and recorded. This was just a beginning. The leadership knew there be would more. While everyone inside cavern #1 gathered round, Mark Bishop turned on his microphone.

"Michael will soon cast Satan and his angels out of heaven. 14 The Archangel will then stop restraining the mystery of lawlessness. 15 The Lamb of God will open the fourth seal and Satan will give his power, his throne, and his authority to the Beast. 16 This is the green light Joshua Kayin and his ten horns (nations) have been waiting for. Once they capture Jerusalem, the Great Tribulation of saints will commence. 17 The Abomination of Desolation is going to announce his true intentions from the rebuilt Temple just north of the Dome of the Rock. Later, the second beast will implement the ID system introduced by the United Nations. 18 Pope Michael is going to perform great signs in the presence of the first Beast to promote this lie. 19 Because mankind has rejected the truth, God will send a strong delusion to those who trust in the Lawless One. 20 Anyone who worships Joshua Kayin, his image, or receives his mark, will be tormented in fire for eternity." 21

"Oh, Lord, it's happening right before our eyes," wept a wife who chose to leave her unsaved husband. 22

"Tonight, we are going to study the two Witnesses of Revelation 11. Simply put, God has promised to send two prophets. For forty-two months they will prophesy."

A teenager couldn't help but ask, "Wow, this is such a mind game. Who could they be?"

"The Bible doesn't say. These two men of God will have the power to harm their enemies with fire, have the power to stop it from raining, have the power to turn water into blood, and have the power to strike the earth with plagues." 23 The world will be convicted by their testimony for forty-two months."

"So when do these dudes show up?"

"They will begin their testimony the same day Kayin's armies break the peace treaty by invading Jerusalem."

"So what happens when their testimony is over?"

"The Beast will kill them. 24 Mankind is going to schedule parties to celebrate their death. But three and a half days later, Jesus will bring these prophets back to life. They will then ascend into heaven while their enemies look on in astonishment."

"Our Lord is faithful!" shouted a twelve-year-old boy.

"Amen," affirmed Mark. "Let us intercede for all who need to hear the truth from the two Witnesses."

The excitement of the heavenly host was growing. Standing before the Throne was the Lamb of God. When He opened the fourth seal, the immense power of the pale horse spewed forth. Its rider Death was closely followed by Hades. 25

"Beware," warned a warrior angel. "'Seek the Lord while He may be found, call upon Him while He is near. Let the wicked forsake his way, and the unrighteous man his thoughts; let him return to the Lord, and He will have mercy on him; and to our God, for He will abundantly pardon.'" 26

The Holy Father stood.

"'For My thoughts are not your thoughts, nor are your ways My ways. For as the heavens are higher than the earth, so are My ways higher than your ways, and My thoughts than your thoughts... So shall My word be that goes forth from My mouth; it shall not return to Me void, but it shall accomplish what I please, and it shall prosper in the thing for which I sent it.'" 27

In the past three and a half years, nations relentlessly attacked each other. Amidst the heartache of these wars, Israel slept under the protection of a peace treaty signed by her Arab neighbors. Initially, most Jews resisted Kayin's roadmap to peace. A piece of paper couldn't change the hate between Jews and Muslims. The mistrust of Israel's neighbors would never really go away. Even so, Jewish children could now play in the streets without any fear. Amazingly, the former American President Joshua Kayin was now being revered as a man of peace.

It was a typical Sabbath morning as the sun rose above the Temple Mount. Suddenly, hundreds of tanks were moving across their unsuspecting borders. 28 Air strikes from Syria and Iran struck with uncanny precision. The high tech jets Israel purchased from the United States were hit before they could even get off the ground. The casualty count of Jewish soldiers was soaring. The world watched in horror as Israeli blood flowed freely in the streets. As Kayin's armies surrounded Jerusalem; families could be seen fleeing with just the clothes on their backs. 29 Sons and daughters watched as their parents were shot. As homes were ransacked, businesses looted, and synagogues destroyed, those who survived the Holocaust remembered. They could see the same Hitler-like hate in the eyes of these Arab soldiers. The possessed Abomination of Desolation was invading Jerusalem, the apple of God's eye. Tragically, Isaiah prophesied of Israel's covenant of death with her enemy in the last days. 30 Another holocaust was coming. 31

WHO EXALTS HIMSELF ABOVE ALL

'Who opposes and exalts himself above all that is called God or
that is worshipped, so that he sits as God in the temple of God,
showing himself that he is God.'
II Thessalonians 2.4

"This is News with Natalie reporting to you from Tel Avi. Earlier this morning ten nations from the Middle East Federation invaded an unsuspecting Jerusalem. 1 Missiles from Syria and Iran have crippled Israel's defense systems. Israeli military bases have been rendered useless."

Adjusting her earpiece, she paused. Straining to hear she looked dazed.

"It's official. This unwarranted attack by Muslim nations is being led by Joshua Kayin. At this moment, he is accompanying a delegation of leaders into Jerusalem. According to our sources, he will announce his terms for surrender from the Knesset. Prime Minister Rosen is awaiting their arrival. Let's go live to this historic moment."

"I'm Joel Friedman reporting live from the Knesset in Jerusalem. This vicious assault by the Middle East Federation is a clear violation of the Jerusalem Peace Accord. Incredibly, the United Nations has refused to publicly condemn this slaughter of..."

The gunfire forced the reporter to hide behind his news truck. His cameraman looked petrified as Joel signaled for a close up shot. Without any warning, news reporters rushed out of the Knesset.

A fellow reporter hollered, "C'mon, Joel, Kayin is going to speak from the steps of the restored Temple on Mount Moriah." 2

Glory's arrival on earth attracted several religious spirits. Their assignment was to prevent this angel from preaching the gospel to every nation, tribe, people, and tongue. 3 For every good plan God institutes, Satan counters with his own evil deception.

Glory's first visit began near Mount Herman in Caesarea Philippi. His mission was clear. Jesus prophesied concerning the last days, 'And this gospel of the kingdom will be preached in all the world as a witness to all nations, and then the end will come.' 4

While preaching the gospel, Glory was shocked to see the immense popularity religious traditions had over the absolute truth of God's Word.

The Temple was locked at every entrance. Each vessel of honor was hidden. White sheets covered the altar, the laver, and the porch, leading to the Holy of Holies. In order to stop any unauthorized entry, a priest was stationed at every entrance. The High Priest looked very majestic as he slowly ascended the steps leading to the Beautiful Gate, the main entrance to the Temple. He was wearing a robe with a golden breast plate featuring twelve precious stones representing the twelve tribes of Israel. With a nod of his head, seventy priests gathered behind him. He could vividly remember the day when worship was reinstated in the rebuilt Temple. With Gentile armies surrounding them, it seemed like a distant memory. An aggressor was once again attacking a people whose hearts have grown cold to the God who loves them.

As his entourage surged up the Temple Mount, the Man of Sin appeared. Strolling toward the Beautiful Gate, it seemed as if the world was holding its breath. The priests were calling out prayers for protection as the Abomination of Desolation approached. With the sound of enemy fire in the background, their eyes met. After a long pause, the High Priest spoke first.

"You are not welcome here. You have broken the Jerusalem Peace Accord. This is our Holy Temple and your armies will not..."

Kayin's lips formed an evil smile as his soldiers moved in. Within seconds, the priests were forcibly removed. Those reporting looked disoriented. Without any delay, the former American President strode into the Court of the Women. In front of him was the Nicanor Gate, with the chamber of lepers to his right and the chamber of oils to his left. Passing through, he entered the Court of the Israelites. With television cameras recording his every move, he stepped into the Court of Priests. The Jewish people could not believe what was happening. Their Holy of Holies, a symbol of holiness and purity, was being violated by an abomination that would soon cause a desolation. And they were powerless to stop it.

"Hear me people of the world," Kayin boldly announced. "I've come today with a new vision for peace. For years, we have seen the spread of war, famine, and disease. It is time someone acknowledges the truth concerning the future of the human race. I've asked several world leaders to stand with me today. We have come to acknowledge the desperate need for harmony among the nations."

With just a wave of his hand, a mighty rushing wind of evil flooded the Holy of Holies. Several soldiers stepped forward and placed an image of Kayin beside their new ruler. The world leaders within the Temple knelt beside his image and held hands as a sign of unity. Kayin bowed his head. The power of Satan was exploding over the airways; supernaturally touching all watching or listening.

"As of today, I plan to lead a New World Coalition of nations which will put a stop to war. As a world family we can work together to end all prejudice, hunger, and disease. For all who support my vision, I am promising you a new world of peace and safety." 5

Back at the Watchman Camp, Luke read aloud, "Then he opened his mouth in blasphemy against God, to blaspheme His name, His tabernacle, and those who dwell in heaven. It was granted to him to make war with the saints and to overcome them. And authority was given to him over every tribe, tongue, and nation." 6

Prayer warriors responded by hitting the dirt floor in tearful intersession for those who still could be saved. The delusion from God was coming to those rejecting the love of truth for the pleasure of unrighteousness. 7

On the same day the Beast was worshipped by the world, the two Witnesses dressed in brown sackcloth appeared atop the Mount of Olives. As they walked down the Kidron Valley, people stopped and stared.

"Papa, who are they and what do they want?"

"Quickly, go and find our Rabbi. He will know the right

questions to ask."

His son took off running for the nearby synagogue.

The two prophets paused in front of a crowd of onlookers blocking their path. The taller one spoke first.

"'Blessed are those who are persecuted because of righteousness sake, for theirs is the kingdom of heaven. Blessed are you when they revile and persecute you, and say all kinds of evil against you falsely for my sake. Rejoice and be exceedingly glad, for great is your reward in heaven, for so they persecuted the prophets who were before you.'"
8

Over the jeering crowd, an old man shouted, "Who do you think you are?"

"We are witnesses for God Almighty."

"Why have you come to us?"

"Our message will bring freedom to your soul. Behold, the Messiah has come but your forefathers rejected him. He is coming again. Not as a Lamb to be slaughtered but as a Righteous Judge. Jacob's trouble (Great Tribulation) has begun. 9 For those who repent, they shall worship the Lord."

"If you're from God," scoffed a college student, "why do you wear such filthy clothes?"

"We are the fulfillment of the Word of God. Two Witnesses shall prophesy for forty-two months. The Word will never return void but will accomplish its purpose for which it was sent." 10

"What are your names so we may tell our leaders?"

"Be still. Jesus is the only begotten Son of God. He is our Redeemer, our Messiah, and our King. Open your eyes so that you may see the truth. Today is your day of Salvation."

"They speak heresy! They must be stoned!"

Those who picked up rocks were knocked to the ground by a flash of fire. 11

"Joshua Kayin isn't the Christ; he is Antichrist. Whoever worships him, his image, or takes his mark will..." 12

The taunts from the crowd were so loud no one could hear the prophet's warning. The spiritual warfare was mounting as they headed for the Wailing Wall.

Within a month, ambassadors from every nation were invited to Kayin's headquarters in Jerusalem. His lobbyists were working round the clock as the foundation of his New World Coalition was being methodically laid. The Beast's propaganda campaign was actually being jumpstarted by Pope Michael's counterfeit miracles. For decades, the spirit of the antichrist had brainwashed mankind. Salvation only by believing in Jesus would ultimately be rejected. The demons of Religion and Compromise continued to tighten their grip of bondage upon those who had already surrendered. The Beast smiled as he waved to the audience.

"I, Joshua Kayin, welcome you all to our first New World Coalition Summit. Each of you has received an outline of our newly proposed global laws. The implementation of these laws will rescue our world from its path of destruction. What we need is a new high tech financial system. This fiscal measure will ultimately be responsible for saving mankind."

"President Kayin," interrupted a delegate from France.

Immediately the prophet cut in.

"May I remind our delegates to address our leader as Lord Kayin."

The French delegate said, "Yes, of course. How can we possibly..."

"Excuse me. Please hold your questions until the end of our presentation."

"I'm afraid I must object to..."

"Remove him."

Kayin continued as the delegate was taken away by guards.

"There will be plenty of leeway to negotiate a reasonable policy for all nations. Today I have established a World Committee chaired by Pope Michael. This Committee is subject to my authority. It will oversee the implementation of all legislation approved of during this summit."

The possessed leader cautiously examined the leadership for any hint of rebellion.

"The first action of the NWC Committee will be to officially dissolve the World Faith Movement. 13 The responsibilities of the WFM will now be under my authority. Now is the time for action. In order to ensure success we must move decisively."

The demonic cloud engulfing Jerusalem was overwhelming. By the end of the day, the dissolution of the World Faith Movement was completed. Thousands of religions would now look to Joshua Kayin for direction. Religious leaders were encouraged to accept a stance of tolerance for the safety of their people. Within months, the Beast would command the world's worship. 14

After a final delegate vote; the World ID Commerce Act became law. Speculation varied on who would sign up first. This was virgin territory. Still, it would only take a signature from a representative of any country to receive financial support.

"It's a law," announced Channel 6 Anchorwoman Natalie Roberts. "The NWC Committee, chaired by Pope Michael, has recognized the European Union as its first member, followed by, the United States, Israel, Japan, the Middle East Federation..."

Arriving in Rome, Amad immediately perceived the Babylonian harlot drunk with the blood of the saints. 15 The queen of heaven had intoxicated mankind with her blasphemy and the filth of her adulteries.

"The Beast's ten horns will hate the harlot and make her desolate," decreed Amad. 16 "She is no more because she made the nations drink the wrath of her fornication."

Jewish families were gathering for prayer in a secret camp just across the Jordanian border. A great-grandfather asked to speak before evening prayer.

"My heart is very troubled tonight. This assault on our families and friends has brought back bitter memories of my internment. The ovens at Auschwitz killed ten thousand prisoners a day. I remember the Nazi guards laughing at our sufferings. I once questioned an order, so they decided to punish me. They tied my hands above my head to a tall post. I was hung this way for hours. I couldn't move my arms for a week. A year later, a guard stripped me naked and threw me in a room filled with cold water up to my ankles. After two days, I struggled to keep my sanity. There were times they crammed forty prisoners into one prison cell. It wasn't long before their cries of mercy rang out. I asked then and I ask you now, what type of evil could possess a man to do such a thing? Some guards even delighted in the suffering of children who lost their parents. When I walked out of Auschwitz, I made this pledge. If I ever see this evil again, I would do everything within my power to expose it."

Reaching over, he put his arm around his grandson.

"Our people are in danger as long as Kayin leads the NWC. Anyone submitting to his agenda becomes his pawns."

"Grandfather, I think most of my friends are going to register."

"Everyone will have to make their own choice."

"Have you heard what the two Witnesses announced at the Wailing Wall? It was the same day Kayin desecrated our Holy Temple. They're saying Yeshua is the Messiah."

The ninety-two-year-old Holocaust survivor winced in pain.

"Let us all ask Hashem to show us the truth. We must ask for protection from the evil visiting our people."

"Grandfather, do you think the Messiah will come soon?"

"Let's pray so," he tenderly replied.

THE SMOKE OF THEIR TORMENT

'And the smoke of their torment ascends forever and ever, and they have no rest day or night, who worship the beast and his image, and whoever receives the mark of his name.'
Revelation 14.11

In America, having your own ID number was just the next step in fighting terrorism. For many, registration was just another excuse for having a party. In Times Square, over a million Americans wore party hats and blew whistles while waiting to receive their IDs.

After getting an ID on his forehead, a senior from Georgetown University declared, "It's a brave new world."

A reporter from Miami witnessed the most novel idea. The marriage ceremony lasted two minutes while those in line cheered. The young couple from Boca Raton exchanged wedding rings after receiving IDs on their right hands.

The Los Angeles Times, The Chicago Tribune, The Washington Post, and The New York Times each published editorials praising this new financial policy. The spin by the media was creating an atmosphere of trust the NWC desperately needed. Even so, trouble was brewing among religious sects refusing to register.

"It's only his image." shouted a steelworker from Bethlehem, Pennsylvania. So what if he says he speaks for God. He ain't hurting anybody, look what he's doing. I'll not only bow; I'll kiss his feet."

Just after the lunch bell rang, Jessie Hyatt and Jake Jamison decided to take a walk to Max's Barbecue.

"This is so weird, Jess. Look what's happened since the New

World Coalition took over!"

"Hope Bishop, Luke Appleby, Whitney Troy, Ned and Drew Henley, they're all gone. And they didn't even tell anybody. Even our principal had no clue."

"I wonder if they joined the Christian resistance."

"I wouldn't doubt it. It's obvious they believed in the last day scenario they were preaching."

"Do you really think there's anything to it?"

"When I talked to my folks they laughed me out of our family room. Later, when I showed them some verses, they totally flipped out. My daddy called those who left school a bunch of cultists."

"Forget that. Luke wasn't deceiving anybody. He was just taking a stand for what he believed in. Think about it, Kayin broke the peace treaty he brokered with Israel. All the nations are caving into his demands. The two Witnesses are testifying, and now no one can buy or sell anything unless they have an ID."

"Are you saying Luke was right?"

"I don't know. I just wish he were here so I could ask him some more questions."

"What type of questions?"

Slowly Jake mumbled back, "You're right Jess, guess there's nothing more to ask."

After implementing the first phase of his global strategy, NWC Leader Joshua Kayin's approval rating reached an all time high. Suddenly countries were making dramatic recoveries in trade, commerce, and productivity. The war machines of America, the Middle East, North Korea, China, Russia, and the European Community were now funneling their money into helping one another. Never before had the world seen such an amazing recovery of the International Stock Market. The new ID system would make identity theft go away. The spectacular results promised by Joshua Kayin were coming true. The fruit from his innovative ideas had convinced most of his truthfulness.

Ian was several times stronger than Glory and Amad. His mission would involve the most powerful demon of all, the spirit of the antichrist. Ian knew he would not be allowed to give his message without a fight.

With deep conviction, the angel declared, "'If anyone worships the beast and his image and receives his mark on his forehead or on his hand, he himself shall also drink of the wine of the wrath of God...'" 1

"Don't listen to such fear tactics," hissed the spirit of the antichrist. "Your top priority is the protection of your family!"

World leaders were carefully monitoring the progress of the new ID system. As the most powerful super power, it was critical the United States set a positive example. The American youth had always been a trend setter in clothes, music, movies, even drugs. The devil knew how important it was to keep them deceived.

"If His power from above ever fell on America," challenged the spirit of Deception, "it could then spread to the Russians, the Chinese, even the Europeans. Don't you understand how vital it is to deceive the American youth? Having an ID must look cool so young people can express their individuality."

The Pressleys had just finished dinner when Dwayne invited everyone to meet in the family room.

"As you all know, ID stations have been set up in several locations around Bethany. For the first six months, anyone can register. After that, everyone nineteen and over will receive a notification slip of their sign up date. A second notification will be sent a week before. Now, I've studied a great deal on the subject of microchip technology. There is nothing to fear."

He wasn't getting any eye contact from his wife Gloria or his two daughters Rachel and Anna.

"The NWC is encouraging families to register together. For our convenience, I'd like to get our ID's at the first available opportunity. Are there any questions, girls?"

"I'm scared, Daddy," cried Rachel. "Some kids I know are really freaking out. They believe this ID system is evil. Luke Appleby, Whitney Troy, Ned and Drew Henley, have even left school. Daddy, they believe Joshua Kayin is the Antichrist. Luke believes anyone who registers for an ID number is denying Jesus. What if he is right? I don't want to lose my salvation."

"Calm down, honey."

"What if it's true? We believe our salvation is forever, right? Didn't we leave Bethany Assembly because Pastor Bishop taught Christians receiving the mark of the beast will spend eternity in the lake of fire?"

"Yes, that's why we left. The Bible says once you become a Christian, it's for eternity. Now before you take it to an extreme like your friends are doing, let's just remember last Sunday's sermon."

"Wasn't it on eternal salvation?"

"That's right. Pastor Ryals proved a real Christian can never commit the blasphemy of the Holy Spirit."

Even though Rachel and Anna sensed something was wrong, deep down they had always trusted in their father's wisdom.

"What about Christian who backslid?" asked Gloria. 2

"Do you remember Pastor Alton Graham from Grace Harvest Church in Orlando? This man of God teaches believers are sealed until the day of redemption. Why would God promise us eternal salvation and then take it away? Only Jesus was sinless. Once you become a child of God, no sin can take away your salvation." 3

"But Luke sounds so convincing," cried Anna.

"Girls, if it were possible to deny our faith, wouldn't God warn us in his Word? There isn't one verse that says a believer can ever be erased from the Book of Life." 4

Nodding, Rachel whispered back, "Okay, Daddy."

"Besides, what can a microchip the size of a piece of rice do to our faith? Now how about a movie?"

Softly the Holy Spirit spoke to her spirit, "My child, you ran well. Who is hindering you from obeying the truth? This persuasion does not come from Him who calls you." 5

While his girls got ready to go, the phone rang. It was Kevin Collins, a former deacon from Bethany Assembly.

"Hey, Kevin, what's going?"

"I'm good. So what's your take on these ID stations?

"Pretty exciting stuff, Kayin is one sharp cookie. The financial package the NWC has proposed looks tight. He's going to be a great leader... Kevin, are you there?"

"Yeah, on the surface he's impressive. But I have some questions about the ID number."

"Like what?"

"While shopping at Winn Dixie today, my wife was approached by some members from Bethany Assembly. Their handout really upset her."

"Imagine that," yawned Dwayne.

"It says anyone registering for an ID is denying Christ."

"How is that possible?"

"Well, isn't the ID system Kayin's plan?"

"Sure is."

"For some, the comments made by Pope Michael about dissolving the WFM just don't add up."

"Incredible," scoffed Dwayne. "Our former President has intervened to bring our world back from disaster with the help of some international financial geniuses. His plan is designed to bring down walls since Babylon. The only reason for such respect is to bring about a harmony the World Faith Movement couldn't achieve. Some don't agree with his unusual theology but most religious leaders have decided to be tolerant and give our ID System a chance."

"Dwayne, doesn't the Book of Revelation say..."

"I know, I know, Revelation 13 and 14 warns believers not to take the mark of the beast. Tell me, how many people do you know who have 666 as their ID number?"

"I don't know of any."

"The handout your wife received probably labels Joshua Kayin as the evil Antichrist, is that right?"

"That's what they're feeding us."

"Has Kayin ever said he is God?"

"Well, if you put it that way..."

"Let's be logical. If Joshua Kayin is the Antichrist, then why are so many pastors registering? Even prophecy experts like Gene Lloyd, Arthur Lawrence, and Tom Bray, are encouraging believers not to submit to the spirit of Fear."

Not totally convinced, the officer asked, "When do you plan to sign up?"

"Maybe this weekend. Would you like me to talk with your wife?"

"That's ok; it's just another scare tactic from Satan."

"We're going out for a movie. Wanna join us?"

"Won't be able to but I do want to thank you for the encouragement."

"No problem, buddy, what are friends for?"

IF THEY PERSECUTED ME

"Remember the word I said to you, a servant is not greater than his Master. If they persecuted Me, they will also persecute you."
John 15:20

The two Witnesses stood before an angry crowd near the outskirts of Bethlehem. The conviction from their testimony was for those who had ears to ear.

"Hear the Word of the Lord. 'And it shall come to pass afterward that I will pour out My Spirit on all flesh; Your sons and your daughters shall prophesy, Your old men shall dream dreams, Your young men shall see visions. And also on My menservants and on My maidservants I will pour out My Spirit in those days.' 1 Tonight, we have come to testify. The day of the Lord is near. We see multitudes in the valley of decision. 2 The sun, moon, and stars are going to lose their light.'" 3

"Heed this warning," shouted the other Witness. "'When He opened the fifth seal, I saw under the altar the souls of those who had been slain for the word of God and for the testimony which they held. And they cried with a loud voice, saying, "How long, O Lord, holy and true, until You judge and avenge our blood on those who dwell on the earth?" Then a white robe was given to each of them; and it was said to them that they should rest a little while longer, until both the number of their fellow servants and their brethren, who would be killed as they were, was completed.'" 4

"Tell us." shouted someone from the crowd. "Who are these slain?"

"John saw believers martyred for the Word. Beware of the Beast has been given authority over every nation. Many who refuse to take his mark will be slain for their testimony of Jesus Christ!"

While crossing over Vaughn Road heading for his house, Simon Colson never dreamed his life could become so complicated. Growing up, he couldn't remember a time when he had a real father and son talk. He knew all about his father's busy schedule. Besides, he thought, some of the members of the church really needed help. Being a pastor's kid, Simon was brought up to believe whatever his father taught. If he ever asked a question, his father would always have an answer. He would instruct his son on how to say it, when to say it, and why he should say it. Throughout his childhood, he learned never to question his father's counsel. When faced with friends who disagreed, the boy would often lash out, not really knowing how to handle the situation. But it was clear now. Simon had never really understood what he believed. Like a sponge, he had soaked up thousands of sermons. But he never knew whether the messages were true or not.

He had met many pastors' kids. Most of them were not very happy as far as he could tell. Then he met Joshua Hirsh at a summer camp. Joshua, the son of Pastor Benjamin Hirsh, was unique in Simon's eyes. It didn't take long for the kid from the Westside to break through the walls of protection Simon had built up over the years. It didn't seem to matter how many mind games Simon played, by the end of the camp, the two had become close friends. Joshua taught Simon consistent obedience to the leading of the Holy Spirit was the only way to keep one's relationship with God on track. Joshua knew what he believed and his goal in life was to obey God.

Entering the backdoor, the young teenager stumbled over several cardboard boxes scattered across the kitchen floor.

"Hey, what's all this?"

Looking anxious, both parents stepped into the kitchen.

"Where have you been?" Marsha blurted out.

Before he could answer his father added, "Have a seat, Simon, we need to talk."

Wondering what he might have done wrong, the teenager took a seat at the kitchen table. His mother sat across from him as his father paced with his arms tightly folded.

"As you know, son, we've had a lot of changes in the past four years. We moved and you had to switch schools and make new friends. Our new church was completed this past year and you know how busy that kept us. Of course, your mother had to rest to recover from the virus she caught last Christmas."

"What are you trying to say, Dad?"

"Well, there's no easy way to say this. Your mother and I have been fasting and praying over this ID System. I'm afraid this is going to sound pretty extreme."

"After what I've heard these past few months, I'm pretty much up for anything."

"Do you remember the evangelist from California named Stephen Corbin? He was invited to teach on the rapture by the Bethany Ministers Association."

"Yeah, I was sitting near the Seminar Committee. Boy, were they hot with that preacher."

"What do you think of his interpretation on the timing of our Lord's return?"

Simon thought for a moment.

"The part about Jesus not coming back until certain events happen was interesting. Some of the kids at our Bible Club really got into it. That is until their parents found out. Then it died out; at least for most it did."

"Your mother and I have been studying the passages he taught on. We believe his view has real merit."

"That so?"

"We also feel Pastor Bishop's messages on the Great Tribulation are scriptural. Jesus' warning to believers not to be deceived has eternal consequences."

Getting up, Simon leaned against the refrigerator and casually asked, "So who's going to deceive believers?"

"The Man of Sin."

"That ain't right, Dad. You've always taught the body of Christ will be gone before the Man of Sin reveals himself. We're looking for our Blessed Hope, not the Antichrist!"

"I'm very sorry, Simon, my teaching was wrong."

"Wrong? After all these years you just say, oops, I was wrong?"

"Once your mother and I yielded to His leading, the Holy Spirit revealed the timing of our Lord's coming. In Matthew 24:21-31, the Great Tribulation of the saints by the Antichrist is cut short when angels gather the elect from heaven then earth. In Revelation 7 believers are delivered from the Great Tribulation and taken before God's Throne. They have resurrection bodies, son. John is describing the coming of the Son of Man for His elect exactly where Jesus placed it in Matt 24:29-31. These are Jesus' words not mine."

"So you think the ID registration is the mark of the beast?"

"This isn't easy for us either, Simon. At first we denied it too. We now believe Joshua Kayin is the Man of Sin and when he stepped into the Jerusalem Temple he fulfilled the prophecy in II Thessalonians 2:4."

"Mom, what if..."

"None of us can ever register, Simon, never."

"What about the Thompson's, Garcia's, and Warner's?"

"Everyone must decide for themselves. I've left a note explaining our decision to leave the church. My secretary will read it to our congregation this Sunday."

"Where will we be?"

"We will be gone, honey," shared a determined Marsha. "Our packing is almost done. No one knows we are leaving or where we are going. In a few months the mark will become mandatory. They will begin by targeting those who don't have an ID. Anyone who refuses to register will be arrested. Eventually, they will be martyred."

"I figured that was coming," smirked Simon.

"I'm glad you understand," sighed his father. "Now let's finish packing. We need to be on our way before dark."

The confused teenager followed his parents upstairs. He waited until his father entered their walk-in closet. While his mother was gathering articles from the bathroom, Simon raced to his bedroom. It would only take a minute as he jammed some extra clothes into his backpack. Sitting down at his desk, he pulled out the middle drawer and flipped it over. Grabbing an envelope of money which was taped to the drawer, he stuffed it in his pocket. Ripping a piece of paper from his notebook he started to write.

"Dear Mom and Dad, I don't want you to worry about me. I need to find the truth about the coming of the Lord. So I've asked the Holy Spirit to lead me. I know your decision to leave the church took courage. I want you to know that no matter what happens I will always love you. Til He comes for us, Simon."

Cracking open his bedroom door, he listened. Sneaking down the stairs he paused at the kitchen table before propping his note up against a vase of wilted flowers.

Silently slipping out the backdoor, he whispered, "I'm sorry, Mom, this is something I've just got to do."

The established ministries of Gene Lloyd and Arthur Lawrence were completely overwhelmed by the sheer volume of calls. Believers were begging for some sort of direction on what to do. Most had over six months to decide whether to register or not. Names beginning with A through C would be the first to face mandatory registration. Tragically, most Christians were clinging to a spirit of rationalization; following whatever direction the majority was taking. The Beast had made his move to deceive. Who would even dare come against the propaganda machine of Joshua Kayin now? 5

The announcement was a shock to the Christian community. Gene Lloyd Ministries was pre-empting normal TV coverage to present a statement concerning the NWC ID System.

"Good evening. I come to you tonight with news every believer in America needs to hear. After reviewing events of the past few months, I must say I'm a little perplexed. I have studied eschatology for many years. I feel God has given me a sound grasp of events concerning these last days. With the way things currently are, uh, there is a chance my teaching on the rapture of the church needs to be revised. I'm confident the Holy Spirit will speak to us concerning this new ID System. I don't want to cause any alarm but there could be serious consequences for those who refuse to register."

Pausing he wiped his forehead with a handkerchief before taking a deep breath.

"I want to make one thing perfectly clear; neither NWC Leader Joshua Kayin nor Pope Michael have ever publicly declared they are God. These two world leaders are merely acting as advocates for religious faiths around world."

Staring into the camera with troubled eyes he concluded, "Let's all seek God for direction as new events unfold daily. God bless you."

The long line was moving forward at a steady pace. Simon could see those ahead of him receiving their embedded chips. It's no big deal, he thought. It takes less than a minute, no pain, no bump, not even a scar. Most of his friends at school were already bragging about having their own IDs. Some had even memorized their individual numbers. Stepping forward, Simon wondered if Joshua Hirsh would be registering this week. Then he recalled something his buddy told him at summer camp.

"Remember, Simon, if we're here when the Beast seizes control of the nations, don't be deceived into taking the mark of his name. 6 It doesn't matter what he achieves. It's a one way ticket to hell!"

It seemed like everything Joshua had taught him was the very opposite of what his father believed.

"No one really knows," Simon muttered under his breath.

"Next please," yawned the bored agent.

"My name is Simon Colson."

"Our files show you are sixteen, Simon. Is your family with you today?"

"I've come alone."

"May I please see your parent's permission slip?"

"I don't have one."

"Simon, to register you must be accompanied by a parent or have their written permission. Is there a reason your parents aren't with you today?"

Avoiding eye contact, he mumbled back, "Registering is against their religious beliefs."

"Young man, this is a mandatory law. For the safety of your family, you all need to report here tomorrow morning so I can register each of you. How does that sound?"

"Real good, ma'am."

"Simon, are your parent's first names, Allen and Marsha?"

After nodding he watched as the agent scribbled their names in a red file on her desk.

Heading downtown, Simon tried to shake off a feeling of despair. While waiting at a light, the Holy Spirit brought Joshua to mind. He could see his friend so clearly.

"What am I going to do now?"

His walk down Main Street seemed to last forever. The loneliness of the moment gave Simon a yearning to know God better. Then it hit him. He had to find Joshua. His good friend would have the answers he so desperately needed. Picking up his pace toward the Hirsh's house he headed for the Westside of town.

LET NOT YOUR HEART BE TROUBLED

'Let not your heart be troubled;
you believe in God, believe also in Me.'
John 14:1

Simon was exhausted he after reaching their home. As the sun dropped behind the Alabama hills, he stepped up to their front porch. Cupping his hands above his eyes he peered through their front window.

"They're gone too!" he gasped.

Tired and hungry, he slouched on a wooden swing resting on the Hirsh's porch.

"Oh, Lord, they could be anywhere?"

The answer came to Simon as he drifted off to sleep. The Hirsh's had left to become Watchmen.

Driving down Main Street, Matt and Sam Bray knew the friendly atmosphere of their cozy town was missing. The peaceful summer days had been replaced by the annoying supervision of ID agents.

"Seems like everything is right on schedule, huh, Sam?"

Looking out his window, Matt's younger brother sadly muttered back, "Jesus warned, 'See I have told you beforehand.'" [1]

Over the past year, the sons' belief Christians would experience the Great Tribulation was totally rejected by their father. Even so, their heated debates had really inspired their mother to search the scriptures for herself.

Pulling into the driveway, they fervently prayed for the Lord to supernaturally reveal the truth to their father.

"Hey, folks, we're home."

Each son received a warm hug from both parents.

"Matt and I are up for some real R and R," grinned Sam. "Sorry, Mom, afraid you've got some serious laundry work."

They gladly joined their parents for a home cooked meal of meatloaf, black eyed peas, corn-on-the-cob, and mashed potatoes. It was a real treat compared to dorm food.

Their father spoke first.

"Ya'll won't believe this I've got some great news. Yesterday we as a family received an early sign up date from our local ID office."

"How come, Dad?" asked a tense Sam.

"It's a privilege given to members of the Bethany Ministers Association. By signing up early, we'll miss the heavy lines the NWC is expecting. We can register as a family this Saturday morning."

Matt slowly lowered his fork; his eyes focusing on his brother, then on his mother.

"Sam and I have decided..."

"Of course you can register yourselves, you're certainly of age."

"It's no secret where we stand. Sam and I believe Joshua Kayin is the Beast. Anyone who registers for an ID will be receiving the mark of his name. They will be denying Jesus as their Lord."

He tried to interrupt but his oldest son cut him off.

"Dad, this time you need to listen. Sam and I will never worship Kayin, his image, or register for his mark. We have both withdrawn from school. After we get you and mom settled in an underground camp, we plan to join the resistance movement and become Watchmen."

Sliding his chair back, Tom stood and shouted, "Have you lost your minds! If you want to give up everything we have worked for, God's calling on your lives, the respect of family and friends, your reputation within our denomination to follow this Watchmen cult, go ahead, but leave your mother and me out of it."

"They're right," cried Ashley. "The ID System is a form of worship our Lord wants none of us to be a part of it."

Turning toward her in anger, he was blocked by the presence of his two sons.

"I won't be registering either, Tom."

"Do you realize what you're doing? Refusing to register opens you up to arrest. If you break this law, ID agents will track you down like dogs. How can you defy God by choosing to follow this cult?"

The stress of the moment was almost too much for his high blood pressure. Stepping around her boys, Ashley embraced her husband.

"God will take care of us, Tom, just like He always has."

The popular preacher was so upset he was unable to discern the power of God radiating from her face.

"Well, I need some time to pray about this."

As their devastated father retreated upstairs, the boys quietly cleared the dirty dishes from the dinner table.

At first, he sat motionless in his dimly lit study. Kneeling to pray, it seemed as if his ministry was on trial. Then it all made sense.

"This is a test. That's it, a test from God."

After serving her boys homemade peanut butter cookies and vanilla milkshakes, Ashley made her way up the stairs to his study.

"Tom, would you like to have some cookies with us..."

After downing his milkshake, Sam muttered, "What's taking Mom so long?"

Suddenly Matt felt a prompting from the Holy Spirit. Bounding up the stairs, he called out, "Hey, Mom."

Stepping into his father's study, a shocked Matt saw his mother slumped prostrate across the floor. Leaning down to comfort her, he saw a note slip from her fingers.

"What's wrong, Mom?"

"Hurry, Matt, your father's gone to register."

Her words felt like a slap in the face.

Racing down the stairs, he shouted, "Let's go, Sam."

The new Watchmen had just received their first assignment from the Lord: their own father.

The religious leaders were feeling the heat from the NWC. A sizeable number of Jews had not yet registered. The time had come to explain such rebellion.

Shimon Melchior, a respected leader of Israel's Orthodox Party and his two closest advisors looked anxious. This meeting was top secret. Clearly, each party considered their own agenda top priority.

As Kayin entered his office, Pope Michael followed close behind signing documents. Trying to hide their obvious distain, the Jewish leaders bowed. The Rabbi's opening statement was intriguing.

"So you believe the two Witnesses are heretics?"

"They're prophesying against the NWC..."

"We're aware of their false predictions," snapped the false prophet.

"They are calling Lord Kayin the Son of Perdition."

"When did this happen?"

"Yesterday just outside of Nazareth."

The Jewish leader knew the exact day the two Witnesses arrived at the Wailing Wall. It was a day Israel would never erase from their memory. The repeated gunfire, the pleas for mercy from an unsuspecting people, the smell of decaying flesh permeating their streets. 2 Missiles launched from Syria and Iran rarely missed their targets. A land promised by God as an inheritance in these last days was now being held hostage by Gentile invaders.

His weary eyes met Kayin's. He was being forced into a corner he didn't like. Melchior had no doubt this deceiver had the power to stop the two Witnesses.

His hands clasped behind his back, Pope Michael shared, "I believe these well dressed prophets arrived the day the Middle East Federation took control of Jerusalem."

The false prophet could see their agitation. He knew what they were after. He wanted these fanatics dead too.

"Let's be up front with one another, shall we? Ever since the implementation of our ID system in your country, the NWC has faced widespread resistance. Now we are not accusing you of any conspiracy. The fact of the matter is we also want the killing of innocent people to stop. I believe you can help us reach the ears of your people."

"The holocaust of my people must end."

"Shimon, we are reasonable men, are we not? You must know the Jerusalem conflict between Muslims and Jews was the result of many years of hostility. Let's focus on the peaceful result of this ugly disaster."

One of the advisors dryly asked, "Such as?"

"Look at the world leaders supporting our vision. Most people desperately want a message of hope for their future."

"What future do you see for Israel?"

"The invasion of Jerusalem was the final piece of the puzzle which brought the NWC into existence. Leaders from America, Russia, China, India, Japan, and the European Union, have all said as much. As long as bloodshed ruled the Middle East, the entire world was in danger."

"The pre-meditated assault of our people has..."

His patience was wearing thin. The false prophet had no time for such dialogue. Leaning forward, he uttered, "Many of your people are starting to believe in these Witnesses. You're losing control, my friend. Trust me; you won't receive any of your financial requests from the NWC unless a large majority of Israeli citizens register. You've got until the end of this year."

Heading toward the last ID station, Sam could barely maintain. Most were enjoying the popular Summer Rodeo. It was family night featuring the tasty chili cook-off. The cotton candy machine was spinning while kids lined up to try and hit Cowboy Clyde with a banana cream pie. A newlywed couple was celebrating after winning a weekend trip to Hilton Head, South Carolina.

"I don't see him, Matt."

Approaching the Eastside ID Station, Matt replied, "For as the days before the flood, they were eating and drinking, marrying and giving in marriage, until the day that Noah entered the ark, and did not know until the flood came and took them all away, so also will the coming of the Son of Man be." 3

Suddenly Sam spotted a man slumped over an old park bench.

"It looks like, Dad."

After Matt hit the brakes, Sam jumped out. Reaching the lonely figure an overwhelming fear filled his heart.

"Did you register, Dad?"

Matt arrived just in time to hear his father's confession.

"No, boys, I just couldn't do it."

Wiping his tears away, Sam pleaded, "Dad, we've got to take a stand. The fig tree is budding. The saints alive at the opening of the sixth seal will be delivered. The fifth seal, the martyrdom of the saints, is next. We have to endure until the coming of the Son of Man."

"We love you, Lord," praised the relieved preacher.

"Dad, this happened when you were pastoring at Christ Cathedral. I was just a young boy. One day I came home after an argument with one of my classmates. It was about something in the Bible that scared me. So I asked you if everything you taught was true.

Deep down, I knew you would tell me the truth."

Both sons couldn't help but laugh.

"You surprised me with your answer. You said, "No, son, the only one that is one hundred percent right is God.""

"I remember like it was yesterday," smiled Tom.

"That's what the Holy Spirit is saying to you now. Just because you taught a secret rapture before the Great Tribulation doesn't mean everything you taught was wrong. Some of the greatest ministers who ever preached were wrong on specific points of theology. I mean, what about Charles Spurgeon? Isn't he one of your favorites? Look at how many lives his ministry touched, yet he taught a Christian could never deny the Lord."

"The Christians registering still believe that," cringed Matt.

"You guys are right. During these past few hours I've been more transparent with God than in my entire life. I truly believe the Holy Spirit was waiting for me to humble myself and repent so He could show me the truth."

After each son sat down beside their father, Matt asked, "What do you mean, Dad?"

"Some call it the Messiah complex. You see, when the Lord opens a door of ministry for you, you can sense His anointing to accomplish that specific goal. It's very exciting at first. Gradually, without realizing it, instead of relying on God I began to live off the experiences of my past. The need for His anointing became secondary. Believers were growing but God wasn't being glorified because the control was in my hands. The Lord called me to be His spokesman so I thought I had to have all the answers. It seemed so easy. In time, I was blinded by the compliments coming from those I ministered to."

"The approval of man can really be a trap, can't it?"

His voice beginning to crack with emotion, Tom confessed, "Sam, after arriving here I sat in the car for a long time. I was so deceived. I was actually thinking about registering rather than having to admit I was wrong. Just imagine how many believers don't even believe in the mark of the beast due to what I've taught. I owe you so much for your willingness to stand up to my threats. You stood for Jesus no matter what I threw at you. Your mother was even willing to risk our marriage. She is far more courageous than I ever was."

"C'mon, Dad," grinned Matt, "let's go home and tell Mom."

As they rushed to their cars, the line was already stretching around the block.

A man waiting in the line asked, "Say isn't that Tom Bray, the famous prophecy teacher?"

His friend answered, "It sure is. He must've just registered with his two sons. You know, his teaching was such a blessing to our church. Remember when all the churches were arguing over the timing of the rapture?"

"Sure do. I so much appreciate my pastor for having Reverend Bray come and teach his three day prophecy seminar. God's plan for the last days became so clear. Even my twelve-year-old niece understood it. We are so blessed to have Bible teachers like Tom Bray that are speaking the truth no matter what the consequences."

"Next, may I please have your name and..."

Lying prostrate in her husband's study, Ashley prayed, "Lord, there are many things I want to confess. Tom and I have just been going through the motions. It seemed effortless as we moved from one promotion to another. Even though we took it for granted You always provided for us, protected us, led us. Lord, please forgive us of our pride."

The famous preacher's wife could barely confess her sins. The approval of man had always been a top priority. The depth of her sobbing was anchored in the reality she would never be able to go back and make it right. She could see flash backs; situations in which she could have made a difference for the Kingdom of God but chose to let it pass.

"Father, I ask forgiveness for my disobedience that has grieved You. I've played these games way too long, and now the eternal destiny of my husband is in jeopardy. Jesus, I beg You, please don't let Tom take the deceiver's mark."

The forgiveness she was feeling was followed by an overwhelming peace.

Then these words came in her mind, "'Let not your heart be troubled; you believe in God, believe also in Me.'" 4

From the driveway she could hear, "We're home, Mom."

Jumping up, a strengthened Ashley ran down the backstairs. After she reached the kitchen door he grabbed her waist from behind and lifted her off the ground. Immediately she knew God had answered her prayers.

"Thomas Nelson Bray, you're such a mess."

Clutching his beautiful wife in his arms, he gratefully whispered, "Oh, Lord, I praise You so much for opening my eyes to Your truth."

ANOTHER HELPER

*'And I will pray to the Father, and He will give you another Helper,
that He may abide with you forever.'*
John 14:16

"How many times do I have to tell you, Jessie?"

"Daddy, my friends believe…"

"Hold it right there, young lady. Your mother and I have heard enough of this religious propaganda from your so-called friends. What do you want from us anyway? You know we don't believe in these rightwing interpretations about the end of the world. Don't you see, little one, no one really knows the future?"

"It's a crazy world, Jess. Your father and I thought the 1960's were a rough time. Families were fighting over the Vietnam War, drugs, sex, and rock music. But things today are even more confusing than they were back then."

"Don't forget the college riots," added a smiling Jon Hyatt, Jessie's father.

"Are you kidding? I could never forget that, darling. After all, that's where you and I first met."

"Is that true, Mama?"

"Jess, you're father and I lived pretty sheltered lives until we stepped onto the campus of the University of Alabama. It was like an exciting new world. We had the freedom to embrace new ideas. Our eyes were opened to the injustices being promoted by leaders who cared more about their agendas than helping people. This gave us a cause; a purpose worth fighting for."

"After all this time, Jess, I can still see your mother standing in the middle of a riot in front of the ROTC building. Shelby had absolutely no fear on her face."

"I was scared to death," she chuckled.

"Well, I couldn't tell. Anyway, I was really attracted to your mother. Shelby wasn't afraid to stand up for what she believed in. Even when the police shot tear gas at us, a lot of people ran away but your mother stood her ground."

"So you were willing to sacrifice for what you believed in," Jessie quietly reflected.

"That was many years ago. Times have changed."

"How is that, Mama?"

"We were just a small minority trying to convince a huge majority to open their eyes to the truth. We thought we could influence our country. Our pleas just fell on deaf ears. I imagine we looked pretty fanatical. In hindsight, who knows if we made any difference at all?"

"That's just the point I'm trying to make. It doesn't matter what the majority believes. What matters is whether or not your beliefs are the truth."

"Yeah and your truth may not be my truth," Jon answered without any emotion. 1

"But what about our former President and the NWC..."

"For God's sake, Jess, give it a rest. We've heard enough about Joshua Kayin deceiving the world. What you need to learn is to stop pushing your beliefs on others. Honestly, some things are just not worth fighting for."

"He's right, Jess, by this time next year the NWC financial system will include every nation. There will be no more wars or famines, just a world where everyone can be his or her own person. Who could ask for anything better?"

"A time of peace and safety," Jon cheerfully predicted. 2

More confused than ever, Jessie whispered back, "I sure hope you're right."

"Jake, can you hear me?"

"Out here in the garage, Mom. I'm lifting weights."

"Your father is coming home. We need to be ready to go by six o'clock."

"But Jess and I were going to our first Bible study tonight."

"Your father advised us over two weeks ago we would be registering tonight. Now you know how he is. If we try to change plans on him, you know what'll happen."

As Jake ran up the stairs to change clothes; a demon arrived through the window over his bed. Opening his bedroom door, he could feel another presence. The Spirit of God had come in response to someone's prayer. As the teenager paced back and forth, both voices spoke in his mind.

"You don't want to disappoint your parents, now do you? Besides, you're young; your whole life is ahead of you. Tonight is your first step to being on your own."

The manipulation could be felt but not seen.

"What should I do?" he muttered.

"Fear not, Jake. The Lord will guide you as you follow Him. He will take away your fears. Today is your day for salvation. 'Therefore, if anyone is in Christ, he is a new creation; old things have passed away; behold, all things have become new.'" 3

"Be careful, you don't want your friends to think you're some fanatic. Think of the good times you're going to miss. Look at those you know who have registered. They're doing just fine."

"Jake, 'if you love Me, keep My commandments. And I will pray the Father, and He will give you another Helper, that He may abide with you forever.'" 4

"Look who's coming up the stairs," whispered the demon. "You'd better hurry."

"Jake, are you ready?"

"Come on in, Dad, I'd like to talk for a second."

Taking a seat on the floor with his back leaning up against Jake's bed, he cautiously asked, "What's up, son?"

"Dad, all my life you've taught me that if I lived by a proper set of rules; I can achieve anything I wanted."

"That's correct."

"Well, this past year I've made some new friends at Lakeview. Now, I know I gave you a hard time when we first arrived here. I'm really sorry about the way I acted."

"Believe me, Jake, I understand. Don't forget, I was once an army brat too. Your mother and I are very proud of you for reaching out and making new friends."

"That's just the point; most of my friends are gone."

"Hey, that's life. People move for many reasons. Look at us, in the last nine years we've moved five times."

"I'm not talking about a regular move. I'm trying to tell you they've all vanished. Luke, Hope, Whitney, Ned, Drew—they all left after the NWC took over. You know, when everyone started to register for their ID's."

"You mean those weirdo's are hiding in the hills of Alabama?"

"Dad, they're taking a stand for what they believe, just like you taught me to do."

"There's no need to talk about this anymore. I doubt any of them will ever be heard of again."

Sergeant Jamison stood. His eyes looked stern. Jake groaned. He could tell from his father's stance he was about to receive another lecture on personal responsibility.

"Jake, as a soldier I've sworn to uphold the Constitution and to obey the orders of my superiors. Congress has voted for our country to become a member of the NWC. NWC Leader Kayin believes sometimes you have to implement desperate measures in order to achieve your goals. I support his vision of peace through the NWC just like his war against terrorism. And what I support, I expect my family to support. Understood?"

"But Dad..."

"You should have never involved yourself with this religious click. Your mother and I know how convincing they can sound. But it's all conjecture. Even the pastors from the Bethany Ministers Association believe a person's individual ID number has nothing to do with Bible prophecy. It was in yesterday's Bethany Herald."

"So, you know what I'm talking about?"

"Why, of course. My Company Commander is worried sick. His son refused to register and went AWOL last week. This scenario is pretty sad and it all could have been avoided if his family had just gone by the rules."

"What rules?"

"My Commander should have briefed his son on the responsibility of every American. If you break the rules, you suffer the consequences. It's that simple. Are you ready to go, son?"

"I guess so."

"Okay, then. I'll meet you and your mother out back. We'll register and then hit Max's for some barbecue ribs."

The sergeant was pleased their talk had gone so well. Moments later, while his father was backing out of their driveway, Jake could hear his phone ringing through his open bedroom window.

"C'mon, pick up the phone."

"What's wrong, Jess, isn't Jake home?"

"Guess not. We were supposed to go to Bible study tonight. That's strange; it's not like Jake to forget something he was looking forward to. Mamma, would you be mad if I passed on dinner? I promised Jake a ride tonight."

"Can't it wait, Jess? Dinner will be ready in ten minutes. I thought you said he wasn't there."

"Maybe he just couldn't get to the phone. His father won't allow him to have a cell phone."

"Okay, take my car, if Jake's there, bring him back for dinner."

"That sounds great, Mama, I'll just be a few minutes."

"Oh, yeah," smiled Shelby, "I've heard that before."

The ID station the Jamison's picked was jammed with college student's home for break.

As they parked in the last available parking space, Jake asked, "Dad, I need to tell Jess I won't be making the Bible study tonight, think I could use the phone across the street? I won't be long."

"Okay, we'll save you a place in line."

After ringing their doorbell a third time, she muttered, "How strange; I know Jake asked me for a ride."

The Jamison home was dark; their car was gone. As she drove away, she sensed her best friend was in danger.

Shelby was cutting the roast when the phone rang.

"How ya, Jake, did Jess catch you? Are you coming over for dinner tonight?"

"Afraid not Mrs. Hyatt, is Jessie there?"

"She left for your house a couple of minutes ago. You must have just missed her."

"Thanks for the invite, Mrs. Hyatt, but my family has decided to register tonight."

"Well good for you, Jake."

"Can you tell Jessie I'll call her when I get home?"

The line seemed to be growing as he crossed the street.

"Did you get her, Jake?"

"No, Mom, we're playing phone tag."

"Son, we all agreed we would register tonight."

"I know, Dad, everything's cool."

"I'm home."

"Dinner's ready, Jess. Why don't you wash up? Oh, Jake called and said he couldn't make it tonight."

"Did he happen to say why?"

"What do you think, Jess, should I use the neat candles you bought for me at last week's garage sale?"

"Mama, please. Did Jake say why he wasn't coming?"

"He said his family was registering tonight. You know, your father also thinks signing up early is a good idea. Now, our official sign-up date doesn't come until..."

The tall brunette spun and bolted for the door.

"Jess, what's wrong?"

Reaching the car, she knew it would take at least five minutes.

"Oh, Lord, let it be the right ID station."

Turning onto Vaughn Road, she begged, "Please warn, Jake."

Reaching the Eastside station, she frantically scanned the crowd.

"Where is he?" she shouted.

They were next in line.

From the passenger's side window she desperately yelled, "Hey Jake! We need to talk!"

He had never seen her like this.

"Dad, I'll be right back."

"Sorry, Jessie will have to wait. We are next up."

"It'll only take a second, okay?"

"Jake..."

"Look, Dad, I'm having some doubts about..."

"What's the big deal; it will take less than a minute. How about you go first?"

Jake wanted to do what was right, not for his country, his family, not even for Jessie. He somehow wanted to do it for God.

"Jake, your father is asking you a question."

"May I please have your name and your National ID Card?"

Frantically honking the horn, Jessie never let up. Jake took off running. Before his father could react, he felt the grasp of her hand.

"Let him go, honey, Jake needs to find his own path."

After a deep breath, the Army sergeant agreed.

"My wife and I would like to register. Our son has decided to register with his friends."

As Jessie's car disappeared out of sight, the spirit of Compromise cursed, "Oh, so close."

Parked in the Jamison driveway, she just stared.

"What now?"

"I have no idea, Jess."

"If your parents registered, agents will be paying you a visit."

"I know, I know, it's all happening so fast. Before we make any more moves, we need some answers."

"How is that possible? Everyone who believes the ID system is evil has disappeared."

"Not everyone. I heard a rumor at school about Lance and Lee Ryan. Some believe they are part of the underground resistance."

"Ok, it's gonna take me a little time to get my stuff together. Avoiding my folks won't be easy. Tell you what; I'll meet you behind Max's in three hours."

THE PATIENCE OF THE SAINTS

'Here is the patience of the saints; here are those who keep the
commandments of God and the faith of Jesus.'
Revelation 14:12

His secretary locked the office front door and closed the blinds. From
his phone he punched in a number. Slowly the wall behind his desk
opened; revealing several THX computers. While his secretary
carefully typed in new names, the passionate lawyer silently prayed.
Jason Wylie, code name Mole, had become the contact for believers
leaving Bethany for a resister camp outside of Birmingham.

The Mole was quickly becoming a legend. There were so many
stories; it was hard to determine fact from fiction. Once while hiding
twenty-two believers, Jason calmly directed two ID agents outside his
office to another part of town. Another time the persuasive attorney
somehow convinced a judge to give four underage resisters another
chance to register. After they were released all four escaped to a
Watchmen Camp near Pensacola. But the story that really earned the
respect of the saints was when Jason risked being caught by stopping
the beating of a female resister by a drunken agent. The Mole was
becoming a key player in the budding Christian resistance. 1

After receiving their sign up date, Kevin Collins and his wife
decided to take the day off and register. Arriving at the ID Station, the
couple saw some friends.

"Hello, Pastor Brown, Mrs. Brown. Nudging his wife, Kevin
softly whispered, "You see, dear."

Noticing several members from their church, she felt a little better. Pastor Elmer Dyer was also in line but he didn't look too happy about it.

At the first desk, everyone was required to identify themselves by showing their National ID card. Then each person would take an oath of allegiance to the NWC. At the next desk, an anesthetic is applied and a microchip is embedded under the skin of the right hand or forehead, depending upon one's preference.

A false peace came over Kevin as he watched the pastors receive their ID's. Afterwards, he could hear Pastor Dyer nervously laughing over a story shared by Pastor Brown.

"Look at them, honey, these preachers love God. They are faithful to their families and they've helped so many over the years."

Stepping up, he wondered why he had ever had doubts over such a simple procedure. As Kevin extended his right hand, a man in an old yellow Chevy drove up.

The driver leaned out his window and yelled, "Don't register; it's the mark of the beast!"

Before any agents could react, the Chevy sped away.

"Thank you for your cooperation," smiled the agent.

It happened so quickly, the former deacon hardly noticed.

"I think they're tracking our every move."

"Did you hear anything when you answered the phone?"

"Not a peep," said a nervous Lee.

No one needed to tell Lance the risk. It wasn't easy for the Ryans to watch as several friends successfully escaped to different Watchmen Camps in their state. Yet when they prayed, all they could see were faces of children searching for the truth. It took a prayerful fast for the young couple to appreciate their calling from God. The Holy Spirit would lead them. Snatching young ones from the jaws of damnation was now their passion. They didn't have any kids but in the coming months they would become the spiritual parents of hundreds of children.

A middle aged couple had just joined some overcomers interceding for children on the run. They were crying out for conviction to fall on those planning to register.

Warren Johnson knew the Holy Spirit had led him to this camp near Jackson, Mississippi. The camp outside Birmingham was receiving way too much traffic. The risk could be disastrous. Even so, his heart was still broken over the mix up which left their daughter behind in Bethany.

"How could we ever lose her?" cried Joyce, her mother.

Suddenly, Warren sensed a cloud of oppression coming against his daughter.

"In the name of Jesus, I rebuke the spirits of Compromise and Lying away from my precious one. Wherever our Cindy is, Lord, You are faithful to protect her from the evil one's lies."

At that very moment, Dwayne Pressley, his wife Gloria, and their two daughters, arrived at the Eastside Station in their new silver Land Rover. The NWC was setting up stations in every city in America. For everyone's convenience, stations were now open twenty-four seven. The Chairman of the ID system had just announced a two-hundred dollar bonus for families registering this month.

"Honey," grinned Dwayne, "with this bonus we can refinish the antique sofa your mother gave us last week."

Reaching the back of the line, Dwayne's daughters spotted a friend from Lakeview High School.

"There's Cindy Johnson. Now that's creepy."

"What is, Rachel?"

"She's alone, Daddy. I guess her parents gave her permission; Hey Cindy."

The petite cheerleader didn't move a muscle. Tears running down her red cheeks, she pretended to look forward, her shoulders beginning to shake ever so slightly.

An older lady standing behind the Pressley's leaned over and spoke to Rachel.

"Young lady, haven't you heard the news? Last night, Congress dropped the age requirement to register."

"Really, when does it start?"

"Immediately."

For some, the new ID stations were scary; like a scene out of a science fiction novel. Cindy's tears were beginning to subside as she got closer to the front.

"Good morning," greeted the cheerful agent. "May I please have your name and your National ID card?"

"Hi, I'm Cindy Johnson."

"Miss Johnson, our records show you are seventeen."

"That's right, ma'am."

"Are your parents with you?" she suspiciously asked.

"No ma'am."

"Our ID files have no record of your father or mother. Why haven't they registered?"

"Well, uh, I don't believe they will."

Lowering her glasses, she asked, "And the reason?"

"I'd rather not say."

"Cindy, this law is strictly enforced by our agents."

"Yes ma'am."

"Do your parents still reside at 449 Fulton Road?"

She fought to maintain her composure as a demon flooded her mind with lies.

"Not anymore."

"For you to register I must have your parent's address and phone number."

"Can we move a little faster?" yelled someone in line. "My niece is late for her soccer game."

"Miss Johnson, are you okay?"

Before Cindy could reply, a warrior angel arrived. Immediately the spirits of Compromise and Lying departed.

"I'm all right, thank you. I have their new address in my car."

"Make it quick." snapped the annoyed agent.

Stepping out of line, she jogged across Vaughn Road and unlocked the front door of her parent's car.

"Hey, Cindy, it's Rachel. What are you doing after..."

The young teenager had other plans. After starting the engine, she tore out of the parking lot.

A motorcycle agent took off after the underage resister. Since mandatory registration was approved, sirens were installed to help alert ID agents to any lawbreakers. The high pitched shrill was the perfect scare tactic.

"Daddy, what's going on?" screamed Rachel.

"It's okay, girls; we're almost there."

"Daddy, why is that agent chasing Cindy?"

Dwayne motioned to his wife and daughters.

"I don't know the Johnson's very well. I know they're Christians; that's about it. Who knows why Cindy freaked out? Trust me; this ID system has nothing to do with the Bible. We cannot afford to panic. I'm not prepared to lose my job, my reputation, everything we've worked for because of the theatrics of some religious fanatics."

It took a few more minutes before they reached the desk.

"May I please have your name and your National ID card?"

"I'm Dwayne Pressley. This is my wife and two daughters. We would like to sign up for the two-hundred dollar family bonus."

"Of course, Mr. Pressley."

Minutes later, as Dwayne guided their Land Rover out of the parking lot, Rachel blurted out, "I want to go home!"

"Sure, honey, I just need to cash this check first. There's nothing worse than being stiffed by the government."

"Momma, I feel so empty."

Reaching over to comfort her daughter, Gloria knew something was very wrong.

"What do you mean, Rachel?"

"It's like how I felt before I became a Christian." 2

As Dwayne waited for the corner light to change, one could hear a loudspeaker blaring in the background.

"Next, may I please have your name and your National ID card?"

FIFTH SEAL : SLAIN FOR THE WORD OF GOD

'When He opened the fifth seal, I saw under the altar the souls of those who had been slain for the word of God and for the testimony they held.'
Revelation 6:9

Standing to the right of the Throne, the Lamb of God opened the fifth seal. The altar was filled with souls slain for the Word of God and the testimony of Jesus Christ. 1 The angelic host knew what was coming.

The shock was almost too much to bear. Family members wept as ID agents dragged the young rebel away. Within minutes news reached the ears of the world.

"This is World News live from New York. Earlier this afternoon, a junior from Syracuse University named Eric Bachman was arrested for not having an ID. He was taken to a security station, where he refused to register. A NWC spokesman repeatedly warned Bachman of the consequences of such rebellion. The head of ID Security was forced to order the young man's execution at 4:02 p.m."

Turning to an aide he asked, "Was Bachman a Christian?"

"Yes, Lord Kayin, he was studying to be a minister."

Making his way to speak with reporters the Son of Perdition bragged, "Bachman will make a perfect example of those resisting my plan." Erupting in mock laughter, "yes, Christians all over the world will soon be running to my ID stations like scared rabbits."

Every nation was given the opportunity to watch the replay of the execution. It wasn't long before Congress was buried under a deluge of phone calls, emails, and faxes. Massive demonstrations followed. United States Senators and Congressmen had totally misjudged the reaction of the American people.

During a street protest in Albany, New York, an angry eighty-year-old grandmother hollered, "Is our new World Leader going to let our boys die like this?"

Protest on college campuses swelled in support of their fellow student. Advisors for the NWC knew how volatile this situation was. Joshua Kayin needed to be compassionate yet firm in his address from Jerusalem. Within the hour the Lawless One would attempt to convince the world, especially America, that ID registration was necessary for the financial stability of every nation.

The eyes of the world were glued to their TVs as their World Leader read a prepared statement.

"Earlier today a college student from the United States, named Eric Bachman, was executed for refusing to register. We grieve at this loss of life as our prayers go out to his family. Unfortunately, the New York Security Force has informed us this young man was labeling our ID registration as a weapon of evil. Tragically, several agents had to physically restrain Eric from hurting himself. It appears he was mentally disturbed."

Pausing, Kayin could sense the importance of this newscast.

"This is why the New World Coalition has produced a new video. This valuable presentation explains the reasons why every citizen needs to have an ID. The best way to combat fanatical terrorism is for our nations to come together in unity. In no way do I condone the execution of innocent lives, but we cannot jeopardize our future by allowing terrorists to choose what laws they wish to obey. My fellow citizens, this ID plan is crucial for your safety. In order to maintain security, the NWC has enacted a new law. Unfortunately, there is no other alternative. Any refusal to register is now a treasonable offense. Anyone who refuses regardless of age, race, or religious preference, will be executed. Students planning to resist; I implore you to rethink your position. The destiny of our world depends on a unified front. I ask you for your trust in these trying times. Good night and God bless."

The spirit of Compromise seemed pleased while perched upon the right shoulder of a smiling Joshua Kayin.

It had been weeks since Jake's parents registered for the mark of the beast. After three attempts of trying to reach the Ryans, the two teenagers were on the verge of panic. Hiding behind a neighbor's garden shed, they moved to where they could see the Ryan's house. A half block away, two agents were sipping coffee in their squad car. They had not moved in two hours.

"We've got to warn the Ryans."

"It's too dangerous, Jess," whispered Jake.

"How about phoning them from Max's?"

"No way, the NWC has bugged the phones. We've got to reach them without being observed. Look, they're leaving."

The NWC squad car was pulling away from the curb. They waited until the car was completely out of sight.

"Ok, let's go."

Grabbing Jessie's arm, Jake abruptly pulled her back. Glancing right, he pointed to a parked unmarked truck.

"What about it?"

"Why would agents leave unless they had some back up? That truck arrived five minutes ago. No one has left it. I think it's time we get out of here."

The NWC Committee had just convened in Geneva, Switzerland. These leaders had come to evaluate how the world was adapting to mandatory registration. A committee member from Kenya had the floor.

"My country simply can't afford this expense."

"I agree," added a representative from North Korea.

"Need I remind you of the alternative to this plan?" interrupted Pope Michael. "Do you remember the days when your young men died in worthless wars and your children went to bed hungry? To ensure success, we must enforce the mandatory acceptance of this financial system. If we fail, life as we know it will cease to exist. Do I make myself clear? As of today, individual countries will be responsible for setting up images throughout their cities, airports, schools, movie theaters, sports arenas, even their homes. 2 In addition, I have established a new Internet law. All commercial, organizational, and educational sites have been modified so only those registered can use them. This means a person must have a valid NWC ID in order to access any site. Within thirty days, no one in the world will be able to use the Internet without first acknowledging the authority of Joshua Kayin."

The committee sat in stony silence as the false prophet explained the penalty for those who resist. For some, the silence of the committee would have been suspicious, but to this frail priest it was meaningless.

While Lee was preparing dinner in the kitchen, Lance heard a faint knock followed by muffled voices. He lifted a blind before opening the backdoor.

"Jake. Jessie. C'mon in."

Before they could answer, the former youth pastor motioned for silence. Leading them into the living room, he turned up his stereo.

"It's so good to see you two."

"You're being watched!" blurted out a shaken Jessie.

"It goes with the territory," smiled Lee.

"Have you seen the stakeouts coming and going?"

"Most of the time."

"Why haven't they arrested you?" asked a wary Jake.

"That's a good question," answered a solemn Lance.

"I'm scared, Lee. Jake's parents have registered, and I've heard through the grapevine mine have too."

"Well, Jessie, we were all warned this wasn't going to be fun and games. You know, it's for eternity."

"That's why we're here; we've got some questions."

While feeding their hungry guests the Ryan's explained how Satan introduced the NWC through the Antichrist. Years earlier, under the guise of fighting fanatical terrorism, the American President first got the world's attention by invading three Muslim nations. 3 The Beast then used the influence of the World Faith Movement to gather more power. 4 Eventually, the United Nations approved his roadmap of peace between Arab States and Israel. 5

"Once Joshua Kayin convinced the nations to register for the number of his name, the Great Tribulation of Christians erupted. At the same time, God raised up a worldwide Christian resistance movement in order to help believers overcome." 6

With tears in her eyes, Jessie shared, "If this is true, then a majority of the world is going straight to hell."

Taking the frightened brunette's hand, Lee gently shared, "The bottom line is this: either you choose to believe in the evil propaganda the Beast is dishing out or you trust in the words of a loving God."

"Lee is saying there is no gray area for an overcomer in Jesus."

"We get it, Lance. It's easy to say but it's hard to believe when your family and friends aren't buying it."

Peeking around the curtain to see if any surveillance units were watching, the tall pastor appeared calm.

"Jesus said, "Enter by the narrow gate; for wide is the gate and broad is the way that leads to destruction, and there are many who go in by it. Because narrow is the gate and difficult is the way which leads to life, and there are few who find it."' 7

"Let's go, Jess, I need some time to think."

"Before you go we need to ask you something. Would you go to heaven if you die tonight?"

"If you're asking us if we've become Christians, the answer is not yet. It's a big step."

"We can pray right now," encouraged Lee. "In fact, we can hide you in a camp just a few hours from here."

"I just don't want to be a hypocrite. It seemed like the Christians were the first in line to register."

"Jessie, even if every Christian at your school received the mark of the beast that still wouldn't make Jesus any less real."

As the two teenagers got up to leave, Jessie whispered back, "You know, Lee, that's something Luke Appleby used to say."

IN THAT HOUR

"…But whatever is given you in that hour, speak that; for it is not you who speak, but the Holy Spirit."
Mark 13:11

Stephen Corbin arrived at Lakeview High during lunch time. The Watchman had come in response to the Spirit's leading. A subtle nudge prompted him to change his plans for the afternoon. From the backdoor of the gym he could hear voices from the bleachers. The uneasiness of the students was not a good sign. From here on out; the Watchman needed to be extra careful. The Spirit of God must guide his every move. Stephen would often meditate on Jesus' exhortation: "But when they arrest you and deliver you up, do not worry beforehand, or premeditate what you will speak. But whatever is given you in that hour, speak that; for it is not you who speak, but the Holy Spirit." 1

He discretely sat down on the far left side of the old wooden bleachers. Another Watchman was sharing the gospel with about thirty students. Stephen had heard about this young man but had never met him.

David Cowley had been a youth evangelist for seven years. After graduating from Bible College, the preacher was anxious to serve God. His first position was in a Pentecostal fellowship in Yuma, Arizona. For some, the hot summers would have been too much, but not for David. This was an opportunity to disciple warriors for Christ. It wasn't long before the senior pastor exhorted him to tone down the intensity of the meetings.

"David, this is the Southwest. We don't want our kids called fanatics."

The rebukes from leadership never let up. After God closed the door, David moved to Chicago to become an evangelist. The teenagers loved his style of preaching. His no nonsense messages would often appear harsh, but to David, they were like life preservers being thrown to those crying out for help. This evangelist wanted to see the power of God transform lives. The young people needed to experience the presence of God, not emotional orchestrated songs or well thought-out programs which looked good but produced nothing. There was a fire in David's belly and he was committed to sharing it with any who would listen.

"Listen up. I've answered your questions the best I can. Without Jesus as your Savior and the Holy Spirit guiding you, you're never going to make it. Satan has given the false prophet the power to kill those who refuse to worship Kayin, his image, or take his mark. If you do any of these things, you'll spend eternity in the lake of fire." 2

Some kids left as soon as they heard the lake of fire.

"NWC agents have taken off the gloves. If you refuse the mark and take a stand for Jesus, you might physically die, but you will receive eternal life."

"Might die!" yelled a football player. "What about the dude who refused to register? They sure wasted him, I ain't going like that."

"Go register then," laughed his friend, "most have anyway."

From the back of the bleachers someone asked, "Has anyone seen Jessie Hyatt or Jake Jamison lately? I heard an ID agent was asking questions about them last week?"

"And what ever happened to Cindy Johnson?" interrupted a fellow cheerleader. "The Bethany Herald reported she refused to register. A motorcycle agent tried to catch her but she got away. Some are saying her parents are resisters."

"That's so bogus. I grew up with Cindy. She would never do anything like that. Not something that stupid."

Several others shook their heads in agreement.

"It's pretty lame all right," added another. "Without an ID, your life is pretty much gone. No family, no parties, no graduation, no future. Why would anyone want to throw all that away?"

Rachel Pressley couldn't take it any longer.

"Wait a second. I was there when Cindy refused to register. She took off..."

Slumping over she could only bury her face in her hands.

"Listen to me," pleaded David. "I've given you the verses on His return. Jesus said, 'When you see these things happening, know that it is near—at the doors.' 3 Now what events is Jesus talking about?"

A convinced Simon Colson answered, "Jesus is referring to the first five seals of Matthew 24:4-12 and Revelation 6:1-11. The first seal was Satan coming to conquer the nations. The second seal was wars. The third seal was famines. In Matthew 24:8, Jesus calls these three events the beginning of sorrows. After Jesus opened the fourth seal, the worldwide persecution of Christians erupted. The fifth seal will show the martyrs in heaven that refused to take the mark of the beast. In Matthew 24:21-22 Jesus calls this time of persecution, the Great Tribulation. For four and a half years we have watched these five events unfold right before our eyes. The next event is the sixth seal, when the sun, moon, and stars, go black. In Matthew 24:29 Jesus calls this blackout the sign of the end of the age. In Matthew 24:30 the sign of His Coming will appear..."

They had come in response to a tip. Someone reported a Watchman named David Cowley was on school grounds. Their dragnet of the main building produced nothing. As they passed by the gym, a cheer could be heard coming from the bleachers. When the doors flew open; sunlight flooded the gym floor.

"Freeze!" yelled an agent.

Everyone scattered. Most headed for the hallway exits, while others escaped through some first floor windows. A few kids sprinted to the top of the bleachers and escaped through the windows leading to the roof over the auto shop.

The armed agents cautiously approached the speaker.

"David Cowley, we have a warrant for your arrest for teaching propaganda to underage children."

With no hesitation, the agents cuffed him, taped his mouth, and led him away. Stephen Corbin never moved during the arrest.

He had waited long enough. The teenager squeezed through an opening between the first and second rows. He would use the window in the bathroom for his exit.

"It can't be," Simon whispered to himself. "But why didn't God protect David? Lord, if it be Your will, please allow this man of God to help me find Josh."

The Watchman was quietly interceding.

"Brother Corbin, is that you?"

"Yes, I'm Stephen Corbin. Are you okay?"

"Am I glad to see you. What's up with all these agents? Where do you think they're going to take David?"

"Probably to the downtown ID Security Station."

"I'm Simon Colson."

"Nice to meet you, Simon."

"My father used to pastor at Calvary Community. Last year I tried to register but I was turned away for being underage."

"Praise the Lord."

"This happened after I found my folks packing. My Dad told me a secret rapture before the Great Tribulation was a myth, Joshua Kayin is the Beast, Pope Michael is his false prophet, and the NWC ID is the mark of the beast."

"Must have been a hard pill to swallow all at once?"

"No kidding."

"So what do you believe now, Simon? Taking a stand for Jesus isn't easy. Have you ever met Ricky Jackson; the star running back from your football team?"

"Sure, everybody knows Ricky."

"He is now a committed Watchman. Several weeks ago, after being threatened, Ricky's father told ID agents where his son was hiding."

"No way."

"Jesus prophesied believers will be betrayed by parents, relatives, and friends. Some will even be put to death." [4]

"Yeah, I just never thought it would happen in my lifetime."

"Simon, do you know Jesus as your Lord and Savior?"

"Yes sir, I love the Lord with all my heart. He's become so real to me in this past year. I've lost so much that used to be important to me: my home, my school, my friends, even my church. I can still remember dozing off on the Hirsh's front porch."

"How do you know the Hirshs?"

"Joshua and I met at Bible camp. Do you know them?"

"Sure do," smiled a giddy Stephen. "The Hirsh's are part of a Watchman camp up north. The same camp your folks have been living in for almost a year."

"You really mean it?"

Arthur Lawrence had sold millions of books on the end times. His TV programs were being produced in over twenty languages. He had always enjoyed walking on the edge of controversy. But this was different. The incessant calls were taking a heavy toll on his staff. The nonstop pressure was almost too much to take.

"That's right; hold all my calls until I can relax enough to think. What do these people want from me anyway? Can't they find His will for their own lives?"

"Reverend Lawrence, you have a call from..."

"What did I just say?"

"I understand but this is your good friend Thomas Bray."

Pushing the button on his speaker phone he playfully teased, "It's about time I heard that strong baritone voice. How's my favorite prophecy teacher?"

"I appreciate you taking my call, Art. I know your schedule is tight. I've really been praying for you and your family."

"I always have time for you and Ashley. So how are Matt and Sam doing with their Biblical studies?"

"The Holy Spirit is leading them in a new direction."

"It's politics, isn't it? I've always suspected this."

"Matt and Sam have withdrawn from school, forfeited their scholarships, and have become Watchmen in the resistance. For now they're focus is rescue."

After a long pause, Arthur angrily snapped, "I have no time for such nonsense. Do you realize how much pressure my family and I have been under? It's been a nightmare."

"That's why I've called."

"Just spell it out for me, Tom."

"They are good boys, Art. We could learn a lot from their studies on the coming of the Son of Man."

"Get to the point, I'm a busy man."

"The point is the mark of the beast, my friend."

"So Matt and Sam have convinced their old man we're in the Great Tribulation. Kayin is the Antichrist and Pope Michael is his false prophet. How am I doing?"

The dead silence between old friends was awkward.

"Deep down you know my boys are right."

"Okay Tom, let me be honest with you. Yes, I've had some doubts. So what? Lots of ministers are searching for the truth concerning the timing of the rapture. What God really wants is for all of us to be on the same page."

"It's the message of the hour to the saints, Art. Ashley and I have had an encounter with the Holy Spirit. It was like my ministry, my motives, and my false teachings, were lit up like fireworks. Almost overnight, Ashley and I could see clearly with spiritual eyes."

"Tom, what's gotten into you? False teaching, spiritual eyes, you're not sounding very rational."

"Christian leaders have totally underestimated the power of the traditions of men. Those ignoring the conviction of the Holy Spirit have been deceived. Understanding the events warning of His coming can only come from supernatural revelation."

"I'm not willing to go that far. I'm writing a new book. We need to be consistent in interpreting events..."

"There's no time for another book. Look out your window. They are receiving the mark as we speak."

"What are you suggesting, Tom?"

"You need to invite Gene Lloyd to join us at my TV studio. The three of us need to warn believers that if they submit to Kayin they'll be denying Jesus as their Lord."

"That's treason. Not a chance. Gene would never agree to such a hasty judgment. Don't you think comparing notes is more in order?"

"Can't you see what is happening? We were wrong in teaching the rapture comes before the Great Tribulation. The apostasy of Christians Jesus and Paul warned of is right now. Have you registered?"

"Not yet."

"Why not? It's just a silly number Satan wants to put on you for eternity."

"I'll say it one time. I'm not going to risk my reputation just because you feel we have entered the Great Tribulation. Do you understand me, Mr. big shot orator?"

"Oh, I understand the approval of man alright. The problem is the end doesn't justify the means, now does it?"

"You're making it a lot worse than it really is."

"It's been awhile since I've discerned the truth. By the way, here's a scripture the Holy Spirit just impressed on me. 'Let no one deceive himself. If anyone among you seems to be wise in this age, let him become a fool that he may become wise.'" 5

"What's that supposed to mean?"

"Jesus warned of those coming in His name and deceiving many. 6 I never dreamed our Lord was referring to the betrayal of the body of Christ by apostles, prophets, evangelists, pastors, and teachers. Ashley, Matt, Sam, and I, have decided to stand for Jesus against the

NWC. You should do the same, Art. Goodbye."

After hanging up the phone, the famous teacher fell to the floor and wept over his rebellion. Deep down, he had no intention of repenting. Over and over, he kept repeating, "We all just need to be ready, everybody knows Jesus can come at any moment." 7

FOR EVERYONE WHO BELIEVES

'I am not ashamed of the gospel of Christ, for it is the power of God
to salvation for everyone who believes.'
Romans 1:16

Throughout the world, more and more were being martyred for their testimony. Everyone knew the risks for openly sharing Jesus Christ. That didn't matter to Carl Russell. He would share the gospel at football games, malls, family picnics, rock concerts, anywhere people would gather. This Sunday afternoon the local symphony orchestra was warming up for an outdoor concert at George Wallace Park. Boldly stepping in front of the six-foot stage, Carl turned his megaphone way up.

"Jesus said, 'Therefore whoever confesses Me before men, him I will also confess before My Father who is in heaven. But whoever denies Me before men, him I will also deny before my Father who is in heaven. Do not think that I came to bring peace on earth. I did not come to bring peace but a sword. For I have come to set a man against his father, a daughter against her mother, and a daughter-in-law against her mother-in-law; and a man's enemies will be those of his own household.'" 1

This experienced Watchman knew he was reported as soon as he mentioned the name of Jesus. ID agents would be arriving at any moment. But there had to be someone in the crowd who had not yet taken the mark or worshipped Kayin's image.

"My friends, these words apply to our lives. We have all witnessed the evil deception of Joshua Kayin. As a believer in Jesus, I challenge anyone who has not yet registered, to reject this deceiver. He was never a man of peace. Deep down in your soul, you know the words of Jesus are the truth."

"You're too narrow-minded." shouted a retired minister. "Your type of Christianity might be right for you, but not for others. Besides, all faiths worship the same God."

Most of the crowd applauded and cheered.

"Is there anyone here who hasn't registered for an ID?"

"How dare you call Joshua Kayin a deceiver!" shouted a veteran of the Iraqi war. "You could care less for the soldiers who gave their lives for world peace?"

"He's really a messenger from God," taunted a teenager. "Tell us, Mr. Prophet, when will the world end?"

The mean spirited crowd roared with laughter. Tragically, most had already made their choice of whom they would follow for eternity.

Carl could see flashing blue lights heading toward the front of the gazebo. Before witnessing, this Watchman would always have an escape route mapped out in his mind. With one quick move, he ducked under the platform. Making his way through some trees, he disappeared over a wall separating the park from an old shopping mall. There would be another day for Carl Russell to share the gospel. For a Watchman living in Washington, DC, she would not be as fortunate.

Munching on cheap hot dogs and cold fries, they shared while pretending to watch a pee wee soccer game.

"Jake, do you think the Ryans are for real?"

"Don't know, Jess. Most at school liked them. They certainly believe what they teach. As far as their end time scenario, who knows?"

"That's our problem. Who can we trust?"

"I trusted Luke Appleby."

"Yeah, and no one seems to know where he is."

"I heard a rumor he made it to a Watchmen Camp."

"So what's stopping the Ryans?"

"They're still rescuing kids who haven't registered."

"Each day more and more arrests are being made. Sooner or later, we're gonna get caught."

"Maybe if we ask around we could catch a ride to one of these Watchmen Camps."

"Talk about long shots," sighed Jessie.

"Who knows," grinned Jake, "maybe someone is praying for us."

"Ok, Frank, everyone's accounted for. You can go ahead and shut down the outside power."

The Birmingham Camp, hidden deep within abandoned caverns, had become a haven for those seeking protection. Many were called as full-time Watchmen; while others tended to the details of caring for a growing number of campers. The caverns, which had been blocked off from public access for years, were almost full. Those without critical skills were taught how to dig and shore up emergency exit tunnels. Each night was set aside for praying, teaching, and fellowship. Tonight's meeting would begin with an exhortation from Pastor Mark Bishop.

"Ok, our study tonight is Matthew 24:45-51. This story is about the coming of the Son of Man and the choices believers will make before He returns. Who wants to read?"

Ned Henley stood.

"'Who then is a faithful and wise servant, whom his Master made ruler over his household, to give them food in due season? Blessed is that servant whom his Master, when he comes, will find so doing.'" 2

"So who does this faithful servant represent?"

"A believer washed in the blood of the Lamb."

"Yes, Ned. A faithful servant is a believer who is obedient to his Master's will. Keep reading bro."

"'Assuredly, I say to you that he will make him ruler over all his goods. But if that evil servant says in his heart, my Master is delaying his coming, and begins to beat his fellow servants, and to eat and drink with drunkards, the Master of that servant will come on a day when he is not looking for him and at an hour that he is not aware of, and will cut him in two and appoint him his portion with the hypocrites. There shall be weeping and gnashing of teeth.'" 3

Luke Appleby raised his hand to speak.

"This servant thinks his Master won't be back any time soon; so he begins to take advantage of those in his care. While he is committing unconfessed habitual sin, his Master returns. Since the once faithful servant refused to follow His Lord, he was assigned a place in Hades where there is weeping and gnashing of teeth."

"Very good, Luke, any comments?"

A teenager named Alice shared, "I know this might sound a bit strange to you, but all my life I've been taught this story represents two servants. The faithful servant is a believer and the evil servant is a person who had an opportunity to get saved but rejected it."

"Okay, Alice, after hearing Luke's interpretation now what do you believe?"

"Well, it's pretty clear there is only one servant in this story. He was faithful for a while but began to rebel and hurt those in his care. When the Son of Man returns with His angels, this servant is denying the Lord. At the coming of the Son of Man this unbeliever will be assigned a place where there is weeping and gnashing of teeth."

"This is scary stuff, saints," reflected a solemn Mark. "For many believers even the suggestion a Christian can deny their faith in God is unthinkable. 4 So, Alice, what made you change your mind?"

The brave teenager slowly stood and faced her peers.

"When Joshua Kayin and his armies invaded Jerusalem, my whole family got together. Each of us shared what we believed about the NWC and its ID registration. Then God sent a Watchman into my life who explained the timing of our Lord's coming, but even more importantly, the truth concerning my salvation."

Intercessors were already praying as tears fell from her deep brown eyes. Many within the camp knew what Alice was going to say. They had suffered the same fate.

"Even though I disagreed with my folks that night I...I... never dreamed they would register for the mark."

Several friends circled the perky redhead as she wept.

Another teenager stood.

"Mark, can I share my testimony?"

"Okay, everybody listen up."

"I would like to thank the Lord for opening my eyes. I was in my own little world, living a sinful lifestyle the apostle Paul warned believers not to live. The Holy Spirit was convicting me to repent and turn away from it. I refused, even though the Word of God clearly warns, that those sleeping around will not inherit the kingdom of God. 5 I stand before you today as a saint who has repented of my habitual sin against God. By His grace through faith; I am now free.

The applause was electrifying. Only those closest to her knew how much it took for her to publicly testify.

"Awesome testimony," affirmed Mark. "Saints, our time is short.

We must pray for the salvation of those who can still be saved. Very soon, the sky is going to go pitch black. This is when our Blessed Hope will return in the glory of His Father. His angels will be sent forth to rescue His elect before the wrath of God is poured out."

Sara Cassie Whitaker grew up in a popular suburb just outside of Alexandria, Virginia. Just recently, the single thirty-one-year old was appointed to a high security position at the Pentagon. It had always been her dream to serve her country within the confines of the nation's capital. God had led her every step of the way.

The rush hour traffic inched along as a light mist of rain fell on her windshield. Her Pentagon ID had always gotten her through the local checkpoints before. As she approached their flashing blue lights, she felt the conviction of the Holy Spirit. Her escape route was in jeopardy. Her contact had warned her not to wait too long. The resister camp in rural Maryland was almost full. The underground tried to warn Sara of tonight's roadblocks. She never got the message. NWC security was becoming tighter in order to reduce the growing number of resisters. Now she was trapped on a major highway with a checkpoint coming up. The young Watchman prayed as she tried to compose herself.

"Good evening, ma'am." Clicking on his handheld scanner, he asked, "May I see your ID number?"

"I'm afraid I haven't signed up yet. My schedule at the Pentagon has been crazy. This is my Pentagon ID..."

The agent abruptly cut her off.

"Please step out and put your hands on the hood. According to NWC policy, you're under arrest for failing to register for your personal identification number."

Sara got out waving her Pentagon badge. The agent brushed it aside; handcuffing her wrists behind her back.

"You will be taken to a detention center where you will be formally charged. If you want these charges dropped, you can register there after paying a $5,000 fine."

Later that night, the ID agents at the Washington DC Regional Detention Center were losing their patience.

"My name is Sara Cassie Whitaker. I work at the Pentagon. My national clearance number is..."

"Quit this charade, Whitaker," pressed the agent. "Your position at the Pentagon means nothing to us. The only way you are getting out of here alive is having an NWC ID."

As Sara silently prayed, she felt the peace of God.

"Tell me, what's your reason for not registering?"

"I'm afraid I'm going to have to report you to my..."

"You shut your mouth. We know you're working with the underground resistance. I don't like it but we will be willing to make a deal with you. If you lead us to the Watchmen Camp you were going to, you can go free. No strings attached."

"Such a deal," she whispered back.

"That's it." shouted the interrogator. "We just got a green light from the Captain. Make an example of her."

Two agents hustled the resister outside in full view of those being detained. She made no effort to resist as they pushed her up against a reinforced brick wall. There they secured her wrists to two iron rings.

"Is your name Sara Cassie Whitaker?" asked the agent.

"Yes, it is."

"Are you a resident of Alexandria, Virginia?

"Yes, I am."

"Under Article 21B, each citizen of the United States must be registered with the NWC. Do you have an ID?"

"No, I do not."

"Are you willing to register at this time?"

"No, I am not."

Sara had spiritually prepared herself. Her countenance looked peaceful, even angelic.

"Under what grounds do you refuse to register?"

"I am a believer in Jesus Christ, the Son of God. He alone is my Lord and Savior. I will not worship any other. Everyone listen to me. Do not register. It is the mark of the..."

Those watching recoiled in horror as blood splattered all over her white blouse. Screams from the crowd subsided into heavy weeping. As they shielded their eyes from the atrocity, the agent holding the gun shouted, "This is what happens to those who refuse to obey the law."

It wasn't long before most of the detainees registered and were released.

A Washington, DC reporter solemnly announced, "Sara Cassie Whitaker has joined an ever increasing number of resistors who are challenging the national security of our country. She was executed for the capital offense of treason for refusing to comply..."

"There's another one. The black sedan, two cars back."

"Are they agents?"

"Can't tell Stephen," sighed Michelle, "been with us through our last two turns."

"Ok, just to be safe let's pull over."

Stephen made two random turns before pulling into a twenty-four hour Gas Mart. Simon got out; pretending to fill the tank.

"They're coming," whispered Simon.

The father and son were arguing as they got out and went inside the store.

The relieved teen let out a big moan.

"Yes, Lord," praised Stephen.

"Another false alarm," Michelle apologized.

"Don't be sorry, baby, you've spotted two for sure and I'd rather dodge ten false ones than miss the real one."

"Thanks honey."

"This one scared me so bad I've got to go."

"Ok, Simon," laughed the Watchman. "I'm up for a pit stop too. But let's hurry, we're almost there."

It had been a nerve racking journey, consisting of unmarked turns and constant back tracking. Camp lookouts strategically placed along the route, continued to report their progress to the camp.

From the driver's seat, Stephen shared, "Simon, from here on out I'd like us to be even more cautious. If you see anything suspicious, let me know at once."

All three watched with anxious eyes as they headed down the highway.

Jason Wylie stepped outside his Bethany Law Office for a quick breather. Every day more and more families were contacting the Mole. His job was to coordinate a scheduled departure date for several Watchmen camps. It was critical each family leave precisely on time. This procedure would prevent a massive overload like the ones which exposed two Mississippi camps. Equally as important, Jason had to be positive that each prospective camper didn't have the mark. The mini ID scanners he had obtained off the black market were extremely expensive; as well as very dangerous. Anyone caught with one would be arrested no questions asked. Security within the Alabama camps was particularly tight. Jason was aware of at least three surveillance teams combing the countryside for resister camps.

The main objective of a Watchman camp was to provide protection for young children and senior saints. The second objective was to enlist intercessors around the clock to pray for unbelievers to repent and obey the warning of the Gospel angel, Glory. 6

"You catch their license plate, Joe?" asked Frank Donnelly as he checked his schedule sheet.

"How's GOJ 316 sound?"

"It's the Watchman's car, all right. Praise the Lord; the Colson boy is with them."

As the Corbins cruised through the final checkpoint, a loud cheer erupted throughout the camp. Leading the cheers were Allen and Marsha Colson. They had always believed they would see their son again. As soon as the car came to a complete stop, Simon jumped out and ran into her arms.

"Oh, Simon, you made it."

"I'm a Watchman, Mom. Jesus took care of me."

"We're so proud of you, Son."

Reaching over Allen gave his son the biggest hug he had ever received.

"Gee, you mean you're not mad at me for what I did?"

"You turned to the Lord and the Holy Spirit led you here. That's all that matters."

"It's crazy out there, Dad. Do you remember Pastor Brown and Pastor Dyer?"

Shooting a fearful glance at Marsha, he asked, "What have you heard?"

"They both took the mark. Their congregations did too. Most Christians are registering. The deception of the Lawless One is greater than anybody ever dreamed." 7

Looking away his father sadly confessed, "The lack of discernment among believers is horrific."

"Just like the days of Noah, huh, Dad."

After sharing with his family, Simon was engulfed with

overcomers eager to hear any news from the outside. A line quickly formed. The Hirsh's waited while other parents described their missing children. When Simon saw Ben and Ida, he burst into tears.

"Pastor Hirsh, Mrs. Hirsh, you made it. You won't believe this, but God used Joshua to save my life. It's a long story; where is he?"

Ida quickly turned away.

"Is Josh, ok?"

Ben was searching for the right words.

"Joshua is not here anymore. When we first arrived at the camp, we sat down with your parents and they told us what had happened to you. The day you left, they went searching for you. They already had a scheduled departure time, so they tried to contact the Mole and have it changed. Unfortunately, the NWC somehow learned your parents were not going to register because of their religious beliefs. A warrant was issued for their arrest. When your parents found the Mole, he insisted they leave for this camp. No one knows how the agents got tipped off."

Hanging his head, the teenager turned away and confessed, "Dad, you don't understand. I told them you weren't going to register. I was confused and angry. It happened so fast."

"It's okay, Simon, at least we now know it wasn't an informant."

"So Pastor Hirsh where is Josh now?"

"When he found out you were searching for the truth, he hid in a delivery truck that was leaving our camp."

"But why would he do that?"

"He went looking for you," wept Ida. "His note said he was willing to risk his life for you. That's how much you mean to him."

"No, this can't be right. God would never allow this to happen. Would He, Dad?"

It took a while before he spoke.

"I've been doing a lot of soul searching, Simon. I haven't been the father you deserved. Instead of allowing you the space to learn how to be guided by the Holy Spirit, I pushed my own beliefs on you. Your mother and I can see how God has stretched you; teaching you lessons we never would have allowed you to learn. You already know the answer to your question. Yes, God will allow painful consequences as a result of our own decisions. Joshua knew the risks he was taking when he left to find you. We are praying a Watchman will pick him up before any ID agents do."

"Listen to me, Dad. The agents are not as concerned with

underage resisters as they are with adults. I know God will lead me to Joshua if you let me go find him."

"Sorry, son, once a resister enters they are never allowed to leave, camp rules."

Walking toward them, Stephen Corbin shared, "There are exceptions. As Watchman Commander, I can leave for emergencies involving the security of our camp."

"You mean Joshua is a security risk?" blurted Simon.

"You could say that. If agents capture Joshua he could lead them to this camp."

"But, Stephen, why do you need my son?"

"Being the same age, Simon would have better contacts for our search. He also knows the places where Joshua might hide."

"How about it, Dad, I know God will lead us to Joshua?"

Allen Colson was already pacing. This was new territory for him. Looking up, he could see the Hirshes praying. How hard this must be for them, he thought. Yes, just as hard when my son was lost.

In his mind he heard, "Remember the ninety-nine sheep Jesus left in order to recover one? You can do no less." [8]

He could feel his heart beating. The struggle within his spirit was raging. How could he give up his only son?

"Father, we have no idea where Joshua is, but You know. Help me to hear the heart's cry of my son. I pray You will guide Stephen and Simon to Joshua's side. Give Marsha and me the faith to let go and trust You. In Jesus' name amen."

"Our Lord will protect our boys." shouted Ben Hirsh.

"Don't worry, Mom, if we stand for the truth, God will always be on our side."

Cheers spread through the camp. The news traveled fast as intercessors lifted up the name of Joshua Hirsh.

A pumped up Simon was ready.

"When can we leave, Stephen?"

"When the Mole gives us clearance, I suggest you get in some warfare praying before we leave."

The Corbins could only wonder if the young Watchman was up for the task laid before him. Only time would tell.

A GOOD SOLDIER OF JESUS CHRIST

'You therefore must endure hardship as a good soldier of Jesus Christ. No one engaged in warfare entangles himself with the affairs of this life, that he may please him who enlisted him as a soldier.'
II Timothy 2:3-4

Slipping into the passenger seat of Stephen's van, a baffled Simon couldn't hide his growing frustration.

"He's not here. We've been to his high school, old man Jenkins' deserted farm, the river crossing, on top of the Go Cart Center, even our hideout at George Wallace Park. There's no sign of him. This is weird. No one has seen him in months. He's just disappeared."

A concerned Stephen knew Simon was struggling with the lies of the enemy. Scanning the street he prayed, "C'mon, Josh, hang on buddy. We're going to find you."

Cruising by the Eastside ID Station both Watchmen instinctively stiffened. Looking straight ahead they avoided any eye contact.

"Could I ask you a question, Stephen?"

"Sure, what's on your mind?"

"Is it all worth it? You know, following God's calling for your life? Is it really possible to fail?"

Looking away, Simon wished he'd used a better choice of words.

"When God grants a believer a specific calling, He will always empower him or her to fulfill His purpose. Simon, although you have seen many believers second guess your father's decisions as a pastor, it is only God who will be the real judge of what was really successful. For example, God commended Enoch, Noah, and Abraham, for their faith, yet none of them received what had been promised. 1 In other words, my friend, obedience to the leading of the Holy Spirit doesn't always bring immediate results."

"So it's not always a picnic?"

"There's a cost in obeying Jesus. Is it worth it? Absolutely. Tragically, many never fulfilled His will because of their refusal to deny their own sin nature." 2

While checking out the solemn faces on Main Street, the weary teenager mumbled back, "Yeah, I can relate. But how do you know what God's calling you to do?"

"Speaking for myself, I can't imagine doing anything other than teaching His Word. The desire to serve the Lord is a gift, Simon, a gift from God."

With his arms crossed and head down, he confessed, "But look what I've done, God has rebuked me so many times."

The Watchman couldn't help but glance over at the young boy who was becoming a man of God.

"Let's learn from the apostles. Paul wrote, 'My son, do not despise the chastening of the Lord, nor be discouraged when you are rebuked by Him; for whom the Lord loves He chastens, and scourges every son whom He receives.' 3 God desires a holy relationship with us but not so perfect that we never sin. John wrote, 'If we say that we have not sinned, we make Him a liar, and His word is not in us.' 4 In other words, we all sin and fall short of God's perfection. John also wrote, 'Whoever has been born of God does not sin, for His seed remains in him; and he cannot sin, because he has been born of God.'" 5

"Gee, Stephen, these verses seem to contradict one another. What is God really saying?"

"For those who abide in Him; they have a relationship. We all sin and fall short. But as Christians we do not habitually sin against our Lord. Those who continually sin with no repentance cannot abide in His grace." 6

"So God will empower us to live holy lives as we continue to follow Him?"

"You got it, bro. The Lord exhorts us never to give up but become overcomers through Him."

Turning left off Main Street, the driver of a yellow Chevy signaled to Stephen. The Watchman maneuvered between two cars and parked on the left side of Sluman's garage.

"Good to see you again, Stephen."

"You too Carl, here's a current list of resistors."

While scanning the list, the younger Watchman informed Stephen of a resistance meeting being held at the closed down Bethany Assembly Church.

"It's really the Lord we got to meet like this."

While watching two agents patrolling the other side of the street, Stephen asked, "We're looking for a seventeen-year-old named Joshua Hirsh. He's five ten, weighs about a hundred and fifty, and has blue eyes and brown curly hair."

"Yeah, I know Ben Hirsh's boy. I remember getting a tip last year about a teenager fitting Joshua's description. One of our downtown contacts thought she spotted him. My guess is he's been arrested. It's getting really ugly, Stephen. Christian families are terrified. They are turning each other in to avoid any confrontation with the authorities. Pretty much dog-eat-dog if you ask me."

"What is the Lord leading you to do, Carl?"

"Proverbs 11:30 is my calling, Simon. My favorite scripture is, 'The fruit of the righteous is a tree of life, and he who wins souls is wise.'" 7

"Have you ever thought about coming to the camp?"

"I'd like that. Heard you have twenty-four seven intercession that's incredibly anointed. Thanks, but my place is winning souls until the Son of Man returns with His angels."

"The Lord is with you, Carl," encouraged Stephen.

Steering his van away from the garage, they headed toward Bethany Assembly. At the stoplight, Simon looked in his rearview mirror. Two ID agents were approaching Carl from his blind side.

"Stephen, what are Carl's chances of getting caught?"

"Pretty high."

"I thought God promised to protect the saints during the Great Tribulation?" 8

"Simon, have you ever heard of Chernobyl; a Ukrainian city located near the border of Russia?"

"Wasn't that where a nuclear reactor blew up and millions of people got exposed with radiation?"

"That's right. Ten years ago, Michelle and I had the opportunity to visit the Ukraine. We were invited to preach in a nearby city called Chernigov. After visiting with the minister of health, Igor Kiroff, we found out most of the kids in the city had either cancer or anemia. Many under the age of ten would die within three years."

"What happened?"

"A year later I visited some churches to recruit teams to come to Chernigov and share the gospel. During a presentation in Arizona, an officer from the United States Army interrupted me. He told the congregation a visit to Chernigov for more than a month would be like receiving one thousand x-rays from a dentist. When I told him that was correct, he asked me why I would want to send anybody into such a mess."

"Why would you?" asked the shocked teenager.

"Her name was Axanna. She was nine, had red hair and freckles. She lived in an orphanage in Chernigov with two-hundred other children. On my first visit, she asked Jesus to be her Savior. I can still remember her excitement after she received the Holy Spirit. The little redhead had all sorts of questions about heaven. She asked if her friends Galina, Sasha, and Tanya, could also go to heaven."

"That's pretty cool, Stephen. Did you get a chance to pray with her friends?"

"No, I didn't, they all died six months earlier. I promised to come back and give Axanna a doll. As we were leaving, she took my hand in hers and asked me, "Can Jesus take away the pain that's in my stomach?" You see, Axanna had cancer. She wasn't able to sleep due to the pain."

"What happened to her?"

"Four months later, I arrived at the orphanage with a beautiful doll wrapped in a big red bow. Ivan, the administrator, asked me if we could go for a walk on the grounds. As we watched the children playing, he expressed how much Axanna loved me. Ivan's eyes filled with tears as he shared how the little red head with freckles died in her sleep just three days earlier."

Stopping at a light, Stephen paused.

"Only God can reveal the cost of a soul for eternity."

Simon could not believe how fast his life had changed. Turning back was not an option anymore. He was now willing to give his life for his best friend.

After parking several blocks away; both Watchmen approached on foot. Reaching Bethany Assembly, they paused and stared. Every window in the deserted church was broken. There were no cars in the parking lot. The brown grass was choked with weeds. *Beware of false prophets* was scrawled across the church's beautiful redwood sign.

The Watchman knocked on the entrance to the pastor's study. He couldn't hear anything. Then the door swung open.

"Stephen," whispered the shocked Mole.

As soon as the door was secured, they greeted each other.

"We've got to talk, bro. The NWC has been getting a lot of flack over so many underage resisters. The Bethany ID Force has doubled. They're searching for you, Stephen. Seriously, they plan to make an example of you in order to divide the resistance movement."

His warning seemingly had no affect on the evangelist.

"Thank you, my brother. The reason Simon and I are here today is to find a teenager named Joshua Hirsh. Do you have any evidence he's been arrested?"

"We have no record of him."

"He's been to the Birmingham Watchmen Camp. We need to find him as soon as possible. Please alert all remaining Watchmen. It's top priority, Jason."

"You got it, Stephen."

Intercessors were quietly seeking the Lord as they entered the church's activity center. Only Jason knew how scared they were.

"They have their departure times. I was just going to give them directions to the camp. You know it's no accident you're here today. Could you give them a message of encouragement? Would you?"

He took his time shaking hands with all sixteen believers.

"Good afternoon, I'm Stephen Corbin. I greet you in the precious name of our Lord and Savior Jesus Christ."

A lady in her mid forties asked, "Are you the Watchman from California?"

"I'm one of many Watchmen speaking the truth of our Lord's return. Let me ask, how many of you were expecting to be caught up before the Abomination of Desolation invaded Jerusalem?"

Everyone raised their hand.

"The Holy Spirit has supernaturally opened your eyes to the events warning us of the coming of the Son of Man. Even though the enemy tried to deceive you..."

Stephen could see a shadow pass by a broken window.

"Jason, hide in the basement."

"But I..."

"Move it, bro, you know what's at stake."

Within seconds the Mole disappeared.

"Quickly, let's go to..."

Before anyone could respond, agents stormed through the side entrance with their weapons drawn. As a demonic presence filled the room, the Watchman motioned for everyone to stay calm. Simon hid under a table near the water cooler.

"My name is Doyle Mercer. I'm the Commander of the Bethany ID Security Force. Now listen carefully. Your sentry across the street is dead. Whether or not you live is entirely up to you. Now who wants to give me the location of the Watchmen Camp you were planning on visiting?"

The flashing blue lights from the agents' cars were reflecting off the broken glass windows as the overcomers sat motionless. The younger children began to cry as they pressed closer to their mothers.

"Look at them, Chief, they don't know anything."

As Mercer conferred with his agents, the spirit of Death positioned itself behind Simon. At that moment, the young boy caught a glimpse of Stephen's face. He expected to see fear. When their eyes met, the Watchman smiled.

Immediately the Spirit of God spoke, "'Simon, Simon, indeed, Satan has asked for you, that he may sift you as wheat. But I have prayed for you, that your faith should not fail; and when you have returned to Me, strengthen your brethren.'" 9

After receiving thumbs up sign from Stephen, Simon relaxed.

Drawing his 9 mm from his holster, Doyle stepped forward and grabbed a teenager seated in the first row. Pulling her to her feet, he placed the barrel of the gun to her temple.

"Okay little lady, just tell me the Watchman in charge of this get together and I'll let you live."

In utter horror, she pointed at him.

Turning toward the evangelist, Mercer couldn't help but smile.

"Well, well, well, if it isn't the infamous Stephen Corbin."

"Let these people go, Doyle, they know nothing about the resistance."

"No problem, tell me where I can find the Mole and they can go free."

"No way."

"I didn't think so. Well, boys, we finally got the Watchman. Under the jurisdiction of the New World Coalition ID System, I am required to ask you why you haven't registered."

"I'm a Christian. Jesus Christ is my Lord and Savior. I hereby refuse to worship anyone other than the only true God: the Father, the Son, and the Holy Spirit."

The overcomers began to cheer.

"Silence!" shrieked Doyle.

The agent closest to Stephen cocked the trigger to his gun and placed it to his head.

"Corbin, I must ask you to reconsider your decision under the penalty of death."

The agents heard him praising God for the honor of being a Watchman. Simon suddenly remembered the first martyr of the early church. Stephen courageously gave his life for speaking the truth about the Son of God. 10

"Not much has changed," Simon whispered to himself.

The Holy Spirit strengthened Stephen Corbin's soul as he worshipped. It would be his last act on earth and his first in heaven.

Lifting his cuffed hands in praise, he prayed, "Father, reveal Your love to those who can still be saved. Strengthen the overcomers. And I know You will take care of my lovely Michelle."

It only took one shot. The overcomers recoiled in shock. The Watchman lay dead in a pool of his own blood.

"Everyone shut up!" fumed Doyle. "This is the end of the road for all who continue to resist. We know who you are. You've got until tomorrow to register. For those who don't, it's your own fault."

Within the hour, a local news agency announced the execution of a resister from Santa Barbara, California, named Stephen Alan Corbin.

"Hello, this is the Ryans. May we help you?"

"Hey, Lee, this is Damien Haley. How are ya'll doing?"

"Super, Damien, what's up?"

"Well, uh, I need to talk with Lance. Is he in?"

The teenager's voice seemed nervous, almost halting.

"Lance should be home soon. How can I help you?"

"I just need to talk. I know something is wrong with me. I'm working late tonight. Do you think Lance could meet me behind the Industrial Arts Building around ten?"

"Sure. How about inviting Jessie and Jake?"

"Don't know about that; haven't seen them in a while. Besides, I'd feel more comfortable if it was just me and Lance. Of course, it would be great if you could come too."

The sobbing by the children was too much. Simon had to get away. Exiting through the sanctuary, he headed for Main Street.

"Why now, God?" he pleaded. "So many depended on Stephen and what about his wife?"

Amidst his tears, the voice of God seemed silent.

"Even if I find, Joshua, how will we make it back to camp?"

Bethany never looked so lonely.

Reaching Main Street Simon prayed, "I need Your help."

As the distraught teenager let a car go by, the Holy Spirit spoke, "'You therefore must endure hardship as a good soldier of Jesus Christ. No one engaged in warfare entangles himself with the affairs of this life, that he may please him who enlisted him as a soldier. And also if anyone competes in athletics, he is not crowned unless he competes according to the rules... Consider what I say, and may the Lord give you understanding in all things.'" 11

"Yes, Lord, I'll never give up. Nothing can stop me. Even though I can't see it yet; somehow You'll make a way."

Back at the Watchmen Camp, Simon's parents were desperately interceding for their son.

"Wow, honey, the Holy Spirit just gave me a verse for Simon."

"Let's hear it?"

"'For He shall give His angels charge over you, to keep you in all your ways. In their hands they shall bear you up, lest you dash your foot against a stone.'" 12

A worried Marsha confessed, "Allen, I'm losing it. It's so hard for me to believe that God will send an angel to protect our Simon."

Crossing the intersection next to Max's BBQ, Simon continued his search, completely unaware of the warrior angel, Mordecai, walking right beside him.

THESE SIGNS WILL FOLLOW

'And these signs will follow those who believe.'
Mark 16:17

Cindy Johnson had lost track of time since her getaway from the Eastside ID Station. Life before the NWC takeover was now a distant memory. After several narrow escapes from ID agents, the exhausted cheerleader from Lakeview High hid in a boxcar at the old train station. That's where she met Ray, Jay, and Faye.

Ray Largent and Jay Wilson were freshmen at Lakeview High when they both refused to register. They briefly met during fall orientation but never traveled in the same circle of friends. Faye Braun was a junior at Cornwall Jackson High School, Lakeview's cross town rival. She first met the boys while hiding in a closed down church. Ray and Jay managed to talk her into leaving just moments before ID agents arrived. They never talked much about their families but tonight was cold and foggy, huddled together in dirty blankets, they began to reminisce.

"So, Cindy, what's your story?" asked a curious Ray.

"You mean how I got here?"

"Yeah, like, where's your family?"

"I don't know where they are. We were supposed to meet at Max's and then make our way to a Watchmen Camp. When I arrived, two agents were just waiting for something to happen. I couldn't risk it, so I left. When I came back my folks never showed up."

"Then what?"

"I wasn't ready for the persecution. Satan's lies almost got to me. My mom and dad were gone. My close friends who registered were doing okay. The voice tormenting me told me it would go away if I would just register."

"Old slew face is such a filthy liar."

"Yeah, Ray, this demonic voice was so subtle. I was just about ready to take the oath to Kayin when the Holy Spirit opened my eyes. I've been on the run ever since."

It wasn't hard to spot an underage resister, the circles under their eyes, the sweaty wrinkles on their forehead, the shaking hands from the constant fear of being caught. The pain of losing one's family had caused many to give up.

"What about you, Ray?" asked a curious Cindy.

"Well, my old man really flipped out when I told him I was joining the Christian resistance movement."

"He was pretty mad, huh?"

"In spades. It's hard to believe. My family never missed Sunday morning church. The problem is my father really trusts Pastor J. W. Brown of Bethany Presbyterian."

Cindy lit up.

"My parents know the Browns. Are they okay? I've been praying they would make it to a Watchmen Camp."

"C'mon, Ray," whispered Faye, "you have to tell her."

"What's wrong? Are the Brown's in trouble with the NWC?"

Faye Braun knew the young teenager from the Eastside was in way over his head. The tall blonde was the only believer in her family too. After becoming a Christian, Faye got involved in a Messianic congregation on the Westside. The pastors, Ben and Ida Hirsh, lovingly became her spiritual parents. Joshua Hirsh also played a major role in her discipleship. In fact, it was Joshua who pleaded with Faye to hide with them in a Watchmen Camp. After praying and fasting, Faye felt led to wait for another time. Even though no one could see it, God was preparing her to help rescue underage resisters.

"Cindy, this isn't a pretty picture. Pastor Brown and most of his congregation registered during the six month voluntary period."

"That can't be. What were they thinking?"

"Seems like a big blur now, doesn't it? I'll never forget the day my family got their sign up date."

The naïve cheerleader was beginning to feel her friend's pain.

"What was it like, Faye?"

"My mom accused my pastor of brainwashing me. Of course, my dad was convinced I was in a cult."

Sitting on a tomato crate across from Cindy, Jay sadly shook his head. Jay Wilson became a Christian at the age of seven. At twelve, he was rated the number one back-stroker in his age group in America. Later that year he developed severe asthma and had to give up his goal of someday swimming in the Olympics. Most of his friends knew how much swimming meant to him. Jay's relationship with the Lord was, at best, lukewarm. With his idol of swimming cast away, the boy started to seek after God. During a prayer meeting, Jay prayed for the baptism of the Holy Spirit. After speaking out in tongues, the former swimmer was instantly healed of asthma. The power to witness was like a fire within him. It didn't matter where he was, or who he was talking to, Jay Wilson was a walking testimony.

"Yeah, Faye's father spilled his guts to ID agents investigating her disappearance. It didn't take him long to report her, now did it?"

"How is this possible?" cried Cindy. "How can so many Christians be so deceived?"

"It's really pretty simple," Jay calmly shared.

"Simple. What's simple about it? Wonderful Christian people are being deceived, millions of them, with no chance of repentance if they receive the number of his name."

"Cindy, I'm talking about Satan's strategy to deceive believers during the Great Tribulation. A few years back I started studying the coming of the Lord for His saints. The more I studied, the more I shared."

"That's why we call him Rapture Man," teased Ray.

"I memorized so many rapture verses hardly anybody could debate me."

"Oh, Rapture Man, let's not forget Joshua."

"You got it, Faye. I remember the first time I met Joshua Hirsh. It wasn't long before we were debating the coming of the Lord."

The drained cheerleader wasn't crying anymore.

"Could you share it with me?"

"We first met at a Bible Quiz competition. I really respected Joshua because of his strong witness for Jesus. What bothered me was his belief the church would face the persecution of the Beast. So I asked him, 'Why does your church believe the rapture occurs in Revelation 7:14; while my church believes it takes place in 4:1?'"

"What did he say, Jay?"

"Josh said the Holy Spirit will reveal the truth to anyone who is open to hear it." 1

"I've heard that one before," winced Faye.

"My pastor, Elmer Dyer, said that about believers who didn't believe in a secret rapture."

"What verses did Joshua give to prove his point?"

"He surprised me, Cindy. Instead of comparing the passages on the coming of the Son of Man, he brought up the signs Jesus said would accompany those who believe."

"Didn't Jesus say believers will cast out devils, speak with new tongues, and lay hands on the sick?" 2

"That's right."

"So is your church open to deliverance, speaking in tongues, and healing?"

"Not a chance. When I received the gift of tongues, our deacons just laughed it off and said it was not for today."

"What about when God healed you of asthma?"

"Pastor Dyer said there was no way to know it was from God."

"So his problem was unbelief?"

"As far as I can tell it was just a form of godliness but denying the power. Josh was saying if someone is open to the signs following a believer, then the events warning us of the coming of the Lord should be easy to see." 3

"But so many..."

"You're right, Cindy. The deception is big time. The devil knows exactly what he's doing."

"What do you mean by that?"

"If you were the devil, and your time to deceive the saints was almost up, what deceptions would you use?"

"I'd trick Christian leaders into teaching the body of Christ will be resurrected before the Antichrist appears."

"There it is!" blurted Ray. "And how about deceiving Christians, who believe they are eternally saved, into taking a mark that denies their Lord?"

"A smooth move to deceive," muttered Jay. "Combine these two teachings and you pretty much have the falling away of believers during the Great Tribulation." 4

"You once believed Jesus could come at any moment. What changed your mind?"

"Cindy, it came down to either believing my pastor or the Word of God." 5

"Yeah, those having ears to hear the Spirit will overcome."

Pausing, the young Watchman painfully concluded, "Tragically, when it's all over, every person who denies Jesus by taking the mark will be without excuse." 6

After getting permission, the young man took a walk into the hills overlooking the well hidden caverns. Thoughts of regret were plaguing his spirit. A continual flashback of what could have been was a tactic from the devil every overcomer had to defeat. For some, it would require many hours of warfare praying. For Luke Appleby, it would become one of the greatest challenges of his life.

"Oh, Lord, I wasted so many opportunities."

The prayer covering over the Watchmen Camp certainly limited the attacks from the enemy. Even so, a demon had come with strict orders to stop Luke from praying.

"It's alright, my son," whispered the spirit of Lying, "you did everything you could. Trust me, you need to rest."

Suddenly a burden of intercession gripped Luke's heart. "But who do you want me to pray for?"

The two teens asking questions about God surfaced in his mind.

He gasped, "Satan is attacking Jake and Jessie."

Kneeling in the dirt, he prayed with all his heart.

"You're too late," hissed Lying. "They both received the mark of the beast. And where were you when they really needed your help? You abandoned them; just hiding out protecting yourself. They'll be burning in fire while you're enjoying heaven."

"In the name of Jesus, I rebuke you foul spirit. Be gone. Lord, I lift up Jake and Jessie and commit them into Your loving arms of grace. May You save their souls for eternity. I pray a divine appointment for them; an appointment no demon in hell can stop."

"Honey, I'm home."

"I'm in the kitchen."

Lee was putting the finishing touches on Lance's favorite dinner: roast beef with applesauce, mash potatoes and sweet peas.

Gently slipping his arms around her waist he knew something was wrong.

"What's up, Lee? Are you okay?"

"Damien Haley called. He said his life is really messed up. He wants to meet with you at the Industrial Arts building tonight at ten."

"Praise the Lord. What an awesome answer to prayer."

"Lance, there is something wrong with this whole thing. I can feel it. I don't think you should go."

"Talk to me."

"Damien's voice sounded funny, as if he was nervous about something. Who knows, maybe he was loaded. I don't know why; it just feels wrong."

"You know the rules. We don't witness to anyone who is high. Can you call him back? I'll meet him tomorrow at noon behind the abandoned factory on Cherry."

"Sure, I've got his work number right here."

Stepping into their living room, Lance turned on his favorite praise music. Moments later, a puzzled Lee sat down beside him on their oversized couch.

"So did Damien agree to meet me?"

"I'm afraid not. He wasn't there."

"I thought you said he gets off work at ten?"

"I talked with the manager. He fired Damien two weeks ago. He caught him stealing from his store. I'm telling you, honey; something's not right."

"Sounds like Damian's in trouble. If he is, we can't ignore him. We have to help him if we can. You know that."

"But, Lance..."

"I'll tell you what. After we spend some time in prayer, I'll go over and check out the high school ahead of time, just to make sure everything is cool. Okay?"

"What if it's a set up? Who knows what type of kids Damien's been hanging out with lately? Please, can you take another Watchman with you?"

Reaching for a hug, he shared, "Sweetheart, I won't go alone. If it will make you feel better, I'll take Lamar with me. Everything will be fine. God is with us."

FOR THE HOUR IS COMING

'Do not marvel at this; for the hour is coming in which all who are in
the graves will hear His voice and come forth—those who have
done good, to the resurrection of life, and those who have done
evil, to the resurrection of condemnation.'
John 5:28-29

The walls of the cave were lined with kids who loved the Lord. Mark
Bishop was fielding questions about heaven.

"That's right, guys, let me read it. 'For the Son of Man will come
in the glory of His Father with His angels, and then He will reward
each according to his works.' 1

A young believer curiously asked, "What type of rewards?"

"Paul calls this the judgment seat of Christ. 'For we must all
appear before the judgment seat of Christ that each one may receive
the things done in the body, according to what he has done, whether
good or bad.' 2

"What does he mean good or bad?"

"From the very moment the Holy Spirit indwelt your human
spirit, every action, every word, every motive, will be judged. Each of
us will give an account of our actions to God." 3

"Mark, I have a question. I got saved a month ago so all this is
new to me. If believers are judged at the judgment seat of Christ in
heaven, then when are unbelievers judged?"

"My brother, the apostle John saw the dead resurrected out of
Hades. They are standing before the great white throne. The works of
every unsaved person will be judged by Jesus.'

With hands going up throughout the cave, Luke stood.

"Mark, most here have never heard of the judgment seat of
Christ, much less the great white throne. Do you think you could

show us when each judgment takes place?"

It only took a couple of seconds before the pastor was surrounded by eager voices.

"Ok, let's begin by reviewing the purpose of each judgment. During the judgment seat of Christ, which follows the resurrection at the coming of the Son of Man, all who were ever saved will be judged by Jesus. After the millennium is over, the unsaved in Hades will be resurrected before the great white throne. Then Jesus will judge their works before casting them into the eternal lake of fire."

"So Hades is not the lake of fire?" asked a new convert.

"That's right; the lake of fire is called the second death."

"So these two judgments aren't the same event?"

"Correct; they take place at different times."

"So when does the judgment seat of Christ begin?"

A confident Luke answered, "After the sixth seal is opened, the Son of Man will come with His angels and reward each according to his works. This is the resurrection of believers to heaven followed by the judgment seat of Christ."

"Doesn't the apostle Paul say a believer's works can be burned up? He will suffer loss in heaven but he will still be saved." [4]

"Try 1 Corinthians 3:10-15. Paul is talking about believers who laid a foundation in Jesus Christ. All works built on this foundation will be rewarded. All works of the flesh will be burned up. This is one aspect of the judgment seat. To understand the overall purpose you must compare all verses on this judgment."

"What do you mean, Mark?"

"How many like taking tests?"

From the mouth of the cave, someone playfully joked, "It all depends what it's going to cost me."

"Tragically, most Christians never got the opportunity to take this test. The passages I'm going to read either refer to the judgment seat of Christ or the white throne judgment. You make the call."

Their excitement echoed off the ceiling of the cave.

"Jesus said, 'Do not marvel at this; for the hour is coming in which all who are in the graves will hear His voice and come forth those who have done good, to the resurrection of life, and those who have done evil, to the resurrection of condemnation.'" [5]

A puzzled girl asked, "Jesus is talking about the resurrection of the dead in Christ. But is this all people or all believers who are resurrected?"

"It's either the white throne judgment or the judgment seat of Christ."

"You said Jesus judges all unbelievers at the white throne judgment. And only believers will experience the judgment seat of Christ. This is confusing."

"It doesn't have to be," said a solemn Mark.

"I think it's the judgment seat of Christ."

"Why can't it be the white throne judgment?"

"It's simple. No believers are taken to heaven during the white throne judgment."

"A direct hit young lady. Ok, let's now try an Old Testament passage. Daniel prophesied, 'And there shall be a time of trouble such as never was since there was a nation, even to that time. And at that time your people shall be delivered, everyone found written in the book, And many of those who sleep in the dust of the earth shall awake, some to everlasting life, some to shame and everlasting contempt.'" 6

An intercessor sitting to Mark's right stood. "This is the resurrection of the dead in Christ at the coming of the Son of Man. This has to be the judgment seat of Christ. If it is, then who are these who are going to suffer everlasting contempt?"

"Wait a second." challenged an angry Sunday school teacher. "The judgment seat isn't about a person's salvation; it's only about rewards. Jesus said, '...he who hears My word and believes in Him who sent Me has everlasting life, and shall not come into judgment, but has passed from death into life?'" 7

"Everyone, I'd like to share a story with you Jesus taught Peter, James, John, and Andrew, on the Mount of Olives. This happened three days before He was crucified. The passage is Matthew 25:14-30. It goes like this. Three servants were given talents according to their ability. After a long time their Lord returned to settle their accounts. Two servants were found faithful. The third servant was judged wicked. This wicked servant was cast into outer darkness where there is weeping and gnashing of teeth. In this story Jesus is either referring to the judgment seat of Christ or the white throne judgment?"

An intercessor answered, "There are no believers at the white throne, so this must be the judgment seat. But how can that be?"

"Guys, at the judgment seat of Christ every believer who built upon a foundation of Jesus Christ will be rewarded. Those who denied the Lord will be cast into Hades." 8

The irate Sunday school teacher hollered, "Where did Jesus ever teach the unrighteous would be separated from the righteous at the judgment seat of Christ?"

"Try Matthew 25:30-46. After the Son of Man comes with His angels He will sit on His throne in heaven. Those gathered up from the nations will stand before Him. Jesus will then separate the goats from His sheep. The saved will receive everlasting life after the unsaved will go away to everlasting punishment."

"That's so wrong. This is Jesus sitting on His throne during the millennium. The people who survive Armageddon will be gathered before Him. The Son of Man will separate the sheep from the goats. The saved will inherit the kingdom prepared from the foundation of the world. The unsaved will go away to everlasting punishment. Everyone listen up. The sheep and goat judgment takes place on earth not in heaven."

"My brother, can I ask you some questions about the coming of the Son of Man?"

"Sure, Mark, you can ask all the questions you want."

"What happens right before the coming of the Son of Man?"

"The sun, moon, and stars lose their light. Matthew 24:29-31."

"Is this event found anywhere else in scripture?"

"It's the sixth seal in Revelation 6:12-14. Joel and Isaiah also have the sun, moon, and stars, going dark right before the day of the Lord, God's wrath against the wicked." 9

"And when is a multitude from every nation delivered from God's wrath and taken up to His throne?"

"That would be Revelation 7:9-14. The saints will be caught up out of the Great Tribulation between the opening of the sixth and seventh seals."

"Are you sure?"

"Positive," chuckled the confident Sunday school teacher.

"You're right. The Son of Man coming in the glory of His Father and His angels is the deliverance of believers from His wrath to come. After the resurrection, Jesus is going to sit on His throne and judge every person that was caught up."

"But, Mark, how can you..."

"Please allow me to finish. At the coming of the Son of Man, Jesus doesn't sit on His throne on earth. The Lamb of God doesn't rule with His bride from Jerusalem until the first day of the Millennium. 10 Jesus doesn't judge the unsaved on this day. The great white throne of the unsaved doesn't take place until after the millennium." 11

"So what kingdom do believers inherit at the judgment seat?"

"The Holy City, the New Jerusalem." 12

"So where do these goats go?" laughed the teacher.

"Those who denied the Lord will go to outer darkness; where there is weeping and gnashing of teeth. After the Millennium, the unsaved will be resurrected out of Hades. They'll be judged by Jesus at the white throne judgment and cast into the lake of fire."

"You can't prove this from just one passage," scoffed the teacher.

"My friend, in Matthew 24 and 25, the context is the coming of the Son of Man followed by the judgment seat of Christ. To highlight the judgment seat, Jesus uses three parables, the faithful servant who becomes unfaithful (Mat 24:45-51), the ten virgins (Mat 25:1-13), and the three servants given talents (Mat 25:14-30). In Matthew 25:31-32 the Son of Man comes with His angels and then sits on His throne in heaven. There is only one coming of the Son of Man. This is the resurrection followed by Jesus sitting on the Bema Seat during the judgment seat of Christ."

"It's easy to see it in Matthew 24:45-51," offered Luke. "The story is about a faithful servant who beat his fellow servants while his master was away. Jesus warned, 'The master of that servant will come on a day when he is not looking for him and at an hour that he is not aware of and will cut him in two and appoint his portion with the hypocrites (unbelievers). There shall be weeping and gnashing of teeth.' 13 This has to be the coming of the Lord followed by the judgment seat of Christ."

Mark was scanning the crowd to see if they were getting it.

"Can you name me one Christian leader who taught this interpretation of the judgment seat?" asked the stunned teacher.

Pausing, the former pastor replied, "Tragically, most apostles, prophets, evangelists, pastors and teachers never warned the saints of the eternal consequences of the coming of the Lord followed by the judgment seat of Christ."

"You can't be serious," he scoffed.

"Saints, the judgment seat is much more than rewards for works. Only those who do the Father's will enter the New Jerusalem for eternity." 14

"It's clear the judgment seat of Christ takes place in heaven. So tell me how can an unsaved person be caught up to heaven?"

"Sure, let's study another story Jesus used to describe the kingdom of heaven. In Matthew 22 our Lord describes His wedding. Many are called but few are chosen. When the king visits the wedding he sees a man without a wedding garment. The king sends this man into outer darkness where there is weeping and gnashing of teeth." 15

"Pastor Mark, doesn't the wedding of the Lamb to His bride in heaven follow the judgment seat of Christ?" 16

"That's correct, Luke. Paul warned believers concerning the judgment seat, 'Knowing therefore the terror of the Lord, we persuade men...'" 17

"Why would he use terror when referring to the judgment seat?" pleaded the teacher.

"The apostle Paul is warning believers of the eternal consequences of the judgment seat of Christ. 'Beware, brethren, lest there be in any of you an evil heart of unbelief in departing from the living God...For we have become partakers of Christ if we hold the beginning of our confidence steadfast to the end.'" 18

Another camper asked, "Didn't Jesus talk about a harvest?"

"Jesus warned the end of the age is the harvest. 19 This harvest represents the resurrection followed by the judgment seat of Christ. At the harvest, the Son of Man will send forth His angels and gather out of His kingdom all who were ever saved. The righteous will shine forth in the kingdom of their Father. 20 Everyone who practiced lawlessness will be cast into a furnace of fire where there be wailing and gnashing of teeth." 21

The Sunday school teacher was spinning.

"So who are these people practicing lawlessness?"

A college student stood and shared, "To be gathered out of His kingdom means they were saved at one time. At the judgment seat their denial will be exposed by Jesus."

Raising his hand the teacher could hardly control himself.

"What about Matthew 7:21-23? Jesus said, 'Not everyone who says to Me, Lord, Lord, shall enter the kingdom of heaven, but he who does the will of My Father in heaven. Many will say to Me in that day, "Lord, Lord, have we not prophesied in Your name, cast out demons in Your name, and done many wonders in Your name?' And then I will declare to them, "I never knew you; depart from Me, you who practice lawlessness."'" 22

"What do you think everyone? Is this passage referring to the judgment seat or the white throne judgment?"

"It can only be the judgment seat of Christ."

"How come, Luke?"

"Only believers can prophecy, cast out demons, and do real wonders in Jesus' name. The ones crying Lord, Lord, were once saved. It's Jesus who says they denied Him by practicing lawlessness."

Mark tenderly asked, "This is a lot to take in, isn't it?"

"Keep going," yelled several campers.

"Mark," pressed the teacher, "Jesus says He never knew them. This means they were never saved. This has to be the white throne judgment."

After Luke reread the passage, Mark Bishop patiently waited for the sharing among some of the intercessors to die down.

"What did Jesus mean when He said, I never knew you? The Greek word translated 'knew' is *ginosko*. It's like the intimacy between a husband and wife. Paul wrote, 'But if anyone loves God, this one is known (ginosko) by Him.' 23 In Matthew 7:23 Jesus doesn't intimately know those crying Lord, Lord."

"Right on," affirmed Luke. "Only those who do the will of the Father will enter the kingdom of heaven. 24 The only day believers enter the kingdom of heaven is at the coming of the Son of Man with His angels. No believers enter heaven at the white throne judgment."

The silence lasted for awhile. This profound truth the Spirit of God had just brought forth had always been there.

Standing up, a young man in his twenties asked, "I've gone to church all my life. So why wasn't I ever taught this?"

The hill above the football field provided a perfect lookout of the Industrial Arts building.

"What do you think, Lamar?"

"I don't see anyone but it's still early."

Lamar Minnich and Lance Ryan grew up together as best friends in a small town in southern Georgia. Both accepted the Lord at a summer church camp when they were in junior high. After entering high school, Lance responded to God's calling on his life. Tragically, Lamar took a one eighty and backslid. After several years of rebellion Lamar didn't want to live anymore. He was at a party high on speed, when the fear of God gripped him for the final time. When he woke up the next morning, he felt led to call his old buddy, Lance Ryan.

Before the day was over, Lamar was crying out for forgiveness on the living room floor of the Ryan's home in Bethany, Alabama.

"What do you think Lance?" whispered Lamar.

The muscular teenager was sitting on a lunch table behind the Industrial Arts building.

"See anyone else?"

"He's alone."

It was crunch time and Lamar didn't like it. It was too risky. What made him nervous was his friend. Lance didn't seem to care.

"C'mon, let me go with you?"

"He's expecting me, bro; can you stand watch? If anything goes wrong, give me a signal with your flashlight. I'll meet you in the alley next to the tennis courts."

"I don't like it, Lance. Why can't you meet him in the daytime? And what about this heavy fog?"

"Tomorrow might be too late. Damien is reaching out for help. God will lead us."

Just after the mark was introduced, Lamar became a Watchman for the Lord. It was Lance who invited his best friend to move to Bethany and team up in rescuing underage resisters. The bond between these two young men was like David and Jonathan. Either one would risk his life for the other.

There was a circle of fog surrounding the moon. The smell of barbecue was in the air. Staring into the darkness Damien sat perfectly still. It was ten after ten. His hands were shaking as he lit another cigarette. The young man was already thinking Lance was a no show. Then he heard footsteps coming from the football field.

Flicking his cigarette away, he whispered, "You can do this."

"Hey, Damien."

"What's up, Pastor Lance."

Taking a seat on the lunch table facing Damien the Watchman prayed for discernment.

"Got your message. Sounds like you need some help?"

"Lately, it's been pretty rough."

"Let's talk. You know the Lord can make things right."

"Is Lee with you?"

"She's at home. You know my wife has really been praying for you. To be honest, we just don't get it. You've seen Jesus transform some of your closest friend's lives. What has kept you from believing in Jesus as your Savior?"

Damien began to shake. The bitterness bottled up inside him began to pour out in heavy sobs. Knowing how bad the bondage was, Lance got up and sat next to him.

"What's up with that?" gasped Lamar while wiping the sweat from his forehead.

He could see dark figures jogging toward the Industrial Arts building from the school parking lot. Lamar began flicking his flashlight.

"Lance, what are you doing? Turn around! Turn around!"

He couldn't wait any longer. It would take a full minute at top speed to make it to the benches. As Lamar started to run, he prayed for a miracle.

Interrupting a rambling Damien, a determined Lance asked, "Hold up. Do you know what a word of knowledge is?"

The puzzled boy shook his head no.

"It's when the Holy Spirit tells you something you would have no way of knowing. You're not being completely honest with me, are you? What are you hiding, Damien?"

"Huh, what do you mean?"

"You can fool a lot of people, my friend, bt you can't fool Jesus. He sees right through your lies and says, "Come unto Me, and I will give you everlasting life." 25

As the strangers turned the corner, Lance heard a muffled cry from the football field.

"It's a trap, Lance, it's a trap!" screamed Lamar.

Jumping off the bench, the teenager moved away.

"Freeze, Ryan. You're under arrest."

Lance turned and stared. His eyes seemed to burn a hole in Damian's heart. Two agents quickly handcuffed the pastor and taped his mouth. It only took a few more seconds before Lamar reached the tables.

"Hold it," yelled an agent. "He's packing."

As Lamar skidded to a stop, shots rang out.

"That's no gun," screamed Damien. "The dude had a flashlight. It's only a flashlight, you idiots."

The agents ignored the snitch as they frisked the dead body. They hated hired informants. As necessary as they were; they had no use for traitors on either side.

"Well, did he have an ID?"

"He was a resister alright. I'll get the truck so that we can bring them both in."

The head agent turned toward Damien.

"Okay, Haley, you can pick up your reward money tomorrow at the usual drop-off spot. And by the way, hotshot, the reward was for a couple. If you want top dollar, you'll need to deliver Ryan's wife."

As they hustled Lance away, one of the agents could see the betrayal in his eyes.

"What's the matter, Pastor," he mocked, "don't you know the name Damien means devil?"

With the agents gone, the young man slumped down against the concrete wall.

"You're such a Judas," whispered the spirit of Suicide. "Just think, for thirty pieces of silver you sold Lance out." 26

The demon was already weaving its web of deception. Within the hour, it would attempt to indwell its victim.

Getting up to leave, he couldn't get Lee Ryan out of his mind.

"Oh, God," he shrieked, "You've got to help her."

A group of United States Senators, led by Eugene McKnight of Florida, took their assigned seats as Joshua Kayin and Pope Michael made their entrance. Their meeting was a mere formality. The outcome was already agreed upon.

"Welcome to Jerusalem. The NWC expresses its appreciation for each of you for meeting with us at this crucial time. Of course, operating as a one world financial system has helped us to recognize the inherent needs of specific countries. Whenever special requests are received, we do our best to answer them with the utmost expediency. Today you will be helping billions of people who desperately need someone to care."

Handing the microphone to his prophet, the Beast took a seat looking out over his guests.

"We have a detailed agenda we will be discussing with you today. Let me remind you not to introduce any new topics. Only those on the list will be addressed."

As aides passed out the agenda, Senator Eugene McKnight asked to address the delegation.

"As leader of this fact finding mission from the United States, we have come to congratulate the leadership of the NWC. A coalition that now encompasses every nation. This unity is a direct result of the global vision of Lord Joshua Kayin."

Each Senator stood and applauded.

"The peaceful coexistence of former hostile countries is truly a miracle. While it took some leaders a little more time to come around, it was well worth the wait. Nations are cutting back on their military arsenals in order to strengthen our worldwide economy. As members of the NWC, we can now declare peace and safety for our world." 27

Raising his glass the Senator offered a toast.

"Even so, I am very troubled by a report I've just received from Israel."

Kayin's smile dissolved into a thin line of anger.

"Israeli intelligence has detected a build-up of weaponry on its borders. I have come to ask..."

"Enough!" screamed the false prophet. "You're out of order. You have deliberately broken..."

"But we have come..."

Security quickly escorted the frightened Senator from the room. With all eyes focused on the Man of Sin, he rose to his feet and smiled.

"My friends the initial vision of the NWC was established to benefit all people. The rebellion you just witnessed is unacceptable. Do I make myself clear? The deployment of troops in specific Middle East countries is to help maintain security over resisters who continue to defy our ID system. If there was ever a time when we needed to trust one another, it is now."

After his arrest, David Cowley was fingerprinted and assigned a bed at the county jail. Cell block C was filled with Christians arrested for purchasing bar coded goods without an ID. One exception was David's cellmate. No one was sure about him, he hardly ever talked. The Watchman did notice the stranger on the top bunk perk up when someone would pray.

Resting on his bunk, David was daydreaming about his days at Bible College. Everyone was so excited the morning of graduation. The scenes from that day were crystal clear.

"David, we know God has great things for your life," praised one of his teachers.

"She's right," admired his mother. "Just imagine, someday you'll be a respected leader in your denomination."

"Remember, son," bragged his father, "you make the right decisions and someday you'll fill some big shoes."

The filthy smell from his cell brought him back to reality. Being incarcerated was no big deal to David. He had preached in prisons all over Illinois. For most, it was a terrifying experience. The harshness from the guards toward anyone professing Christ was growing. Eric Bachman, the first martyr under the NWC, was purposefully singled out because he was a Watchman. Within months of his death, many overcomers willingly gave their lives for their Savior.

Bowing his head to pray, David whispered, "Lord, only You can strengthen those on the verge of caving in to the threats of the devil. Grant them the discernment not to entertain his lies."

The young Watchman was amazed at the number of people arrested who were not trained in spiritual warfare. Who would have ever dreamed such anemic believers would be called upon to spiritually fight near the end of the age? Righteous anger gripped him as he thought of pastors who boldly taught the church would never face the Antichrist.

"They looked good in their Sunday morning clothes," reflected David, "but their disregard of Jesus' warnings to the elect will send a multitude to the eternal lake of fire."

"No one believes that," whispered the spirit of Lying.

"Most won't get it until they actually see the flames," hissed the spirit of Fear.

"Lights out!" yelled a guard on the night shift.

The demons loved the darkness.

"The key to tormenting believers," boasted the spirit of Confusion "is to find a weakness and then wait to attack at the most vulnerable moment."

"Look how they struggle with our threats," sneered Lying. "I love fighting for the control of a human spirit. The most thrilling part is when they surrender. It's amazing to see how ignorant humans really are. They actually think they can free themselves from our attacks through their own strength. They don't even try to use scripture against our attacks. Most have no clue."

At night, David could hear their nightmares. At any moment, believers could be making a decision affecting their eternal destiny.

"Remember, son, you make the right decisions and someday

you'll fill some big shoes," taunted Lying. "Look at all those who believed in you, David. You could have really made a difference in so many lives that desperately needed your help. And now look at you," cursed the demon. "Just another burned out preacher no one listens to. You're not going anywhere; you might as well just give up."

Most welcomed the early morning breakfast call. As the prisoners marched in, those on kitchen duty started dishing out the food. After breakfast, prisoners from cell block C would get to exercise in the main yard for sixty minutes. It was the only time they could talk in private. As each inmate passed through the metal detector; the normally hostile guards seemed almost friendly. David immediately sensed an evil presence.

"Oh, Brother Cowley," laughed one of the guards. "Have you heard the latest news about the resistance movement?"

David knew this avowed atheist very well. He was bad news to anyone who openly professed Christ.

"I guess you're going to tell me anyway."

"You betcha; they got him."

"Got who?"

"Corbin. That's right, Davey, the Watchman is dead. They wasted him in a church; right in front of some resisters. Man, I miss all the fun."

Most of the prisoners heard every word. Demons were already sowing their lies. David headed for the privacy of the courtyard.

An elderly prisoner shouted, "I told you they're going to destroy the resistance. It's just a matter of time."

David motioned for everyone to huddle up.

"We must trust God; do you understand? It's late in the game, guys. Don't entertain these demonic voices. God will never leave us nor forsake us. 28 The sign of the end of the age is almost here."

"What about my daughter? My little girl is all alone."

"In the first century, a remnant of Christians refused to bow to an evil leader claiming to be God. Caesar fed these men, women, and children, to the lions. Jesus said, 'Therefore whoever confesses Me before men, him I will also confess before My Father who is in heaven. But whoever denies Me before men, him I will also deny before My Father who is in heaven.' 29 If we aren't willing to count the cost, should it even mean the lives of our children, Jesus will stand before His Father and deny knowing us."

Looking at their terrified faces, David's heart ached.

"When you signed up for this ride, you knew the cost. You knew the devil would threaten to kill your children in an attempt to make you deny Christ."

One of the younger guards, who overheard David speaking, approached the Watchman from behind.

"Now ain't that a touching speech. Cowley, when they put a gun to your head, you'll worship Kayin just like everybody else. Wait and see; you're no different."

Suddenly, David's cellmate tackled the guard from behind. Pressing his face into the dirt, he whispered, "I have a message for your stinking Kayin. Tell him I spit on him and his evil plans."

Another guard moved in and struck the prisoner from behind.

"Give him a week in the hole." yelled the officer in charge. "That'll teach him to ever touch a guard."

As they dragged his unconscious cellmate away, David felt led by the Holy Spirit to pray for him for the entire seven days.

The Bethany Herald featured the front page story. At 2:37 a.m. this morning, Lance Christopher Ryan was executed. By refusing to register, the rebellious pastor broke the NWC Law of Unification. Reportedly, a member of the Christian underground resistance, Ryan showed no remorse before his execution.

"Hello, this is Jason Wylie, may I help you?"

"How have you been, Jason? This is Lee."

"Lee, are you ok?"

"The Lord is faithful. Is there somewhere we can meet?"

"Remember the spot where Lance and I used to talk?"

"Perfect."

"Give me one hour."

"Thank you, my friend."

Lee Ryan returned to her corner table at Bertha's Coffee Shop. She knew it was just a matter of time before an ID agent arrived. Just after being served lunch, she discretely got up to use the restroom. Her food was never touched.

MY TWO WITNESSES

'And I will give power to my two witnesses, and they will prophesy
one thousand and two hundred and sixty days,
clothed in sackcloth.'
Revelation 11:3

NWC Leader Joshua Kayin had just finished meeting with a
delegation from the European Union. Under the careful supervision
of security guards, Pope Michael escorted these leaders to a terrace
overlooking Kayin's beautiful rose gardens. As they approached the
center of the garden, the two Witnesses were waiting. The Beast and
his prophet stopped dead in their tracks.

One guard whispered to another, "They've come like the Bible
said they would."

"Remove these intruders!" shouted the head of security.

"Wait," ordered Kayin. "Let's hear what these two beautifully
dressed prophets have to say."

His words burning with righteous indignation, the shorter
Witness announced, "We are aware of the lie you've used to deceive
the people of this world."

Winking at his delegation, Kayin mocked, "What is this lie you
say the people have no knowledge of?"

"You're not God." Walking toward the deceiver, the prophet
pronounced, "There is only one true God: the Father, the Word, and
the Holy Spirit." 1

The closer he got, the more panicked Kayin became.

"Satan has created an unholy trinity consisting of himself, the
Beast, and his false prophet. 2 The counterfeit miracles you both have
used to deceive billions of people are just for a season. You two will
be the first humans cast into the lake of fire." 3

The glory of God burst forth from the prophet's face. The flabbergasted delegates shielded their eyes as the Antichrist was forced to look away.

"Don't be deceived, these two beasts have been given power to rule until God's Word is accomplished." 4

Kayin decided to make a hasty retreat.

"The sign of the end of the age is coming," thundered the other Witness. "John prophesied, 'I looked when He opened the sixth seal, and behold, there was a great earthquake; and the sun became black as sackcloth of hair, and the moon became like blood. And the stars of heaven fell to the earth, as a fig tree drops its late figs when it is shaken by a mighty wind. Then the sky receded as a scroll when it is rolled up, and every mountain and island was moved out of its place.' 5 Remember this truth the elect seeing the sign of the end of the age will be delivered out of the Great Tribulation. 6 They will not experience the day of the Lord, God's wrath against the wicked."

During a break at a camp checkpoint, Billy B was asked by some of the teenagers to teach about the day of the Lord. The word spread quickly. Soon three hundred kids surrounded the former trucker.

A curious high school senior asked, "Billy B is it true another war needs to happen before the day of the Lord can begin?"

"The Word highlights three wars in the last days, Jerusalem, Jehoshaphat, and finally Armageddon. Jesus warned us of the Jerusalem war in Luke 21:20. After forty- two months of peace, the Jewish people were completely lulled to sleep. Then the Abomination of Desolation broke the peace. How many remember when Joshua Kayin and his armies attacked Jerusalem?"

Every hand went up. It was an event still fresh in everyone's mind; an evil massacre of an unsuspecting people the world would never forget. 7

"The next war will take place in the Valley of Jehoshaphat, which is located near Bethlehem. 8 Muslim nations are going to attack the Jewish people just before the day of the Lord." 9

"Gee, Billy B," asked a teenager from Montgomery, "if the Jehoshaphat war takes place before the day of the Lord, then when does the Battle of Armageddon take place?"

"Armageddon is the last event of the day of the Lord. It follows the pouring out of the seventh bowl. Whereas Armageddon takes place after the 70th week, the Jehoshaphat attack will erupt sometime in the second half, just before Jesus opens the sixth seal."

"I see it," yelled a new convert. "This war will take place right before the resurrection, when we are caught up to be with our Lord."

Shaking his head, Billy B shared, "This is a critical prophecy many refused to acknowledge. The return of the Lord for His saints from the wrath to come will be imminent only after surrounding nations attack the Jewish people in the Valley of Jehoshaphat."

"Yes, Pastor... Most arrived about ten minutes ago... They're waiting for you in the fellowship hall... That's right, they look frightened... I'm afraid so... No, we are still printing them... Yes, I'll get right on it."

As J.W. Brown entered the fellowship hall, the pastor could hear the murmuring. Every eye followed his uneasy stride as he walked toward the podium. He could also sense their urgency. He knew how easily it could get out of hand.

"Hello everyone, for those coming for answers this morning let me assure you I too have been seeking the Lord. We all need His wisdom to help us overcome the confusion that has affected so many Christian families in our city."

"Pastor, what should I tell my wife? When my son told me he was going to join the underground resistance I just couldn't believe it. You know my Ray. He was only fourteen when his sign up date expired. And now my wife blames me."

Without any emotion the pastor replied, "I'm so sorry, Mr. Largent. It's regrettable this cult has targeted so many of our children. In view of this tragedy, I've written a new doctrinal guide. Its focus is to strengthen our young people with biblical truths I've taught for many years."

"What biblical truths?" asked Ray's father.

"It seems those deceived weren't grounded enough in the doctrines of the Bible."

"You mean my son will lose his salvation if he follows the teachings of this cult?"

His anger could not be discerned with the human eye. Nothing was more important to J. W. Brown than the biblical legacy passed down from his great grandfather. A theology his grandfather preached to thousands. A doctrine his own father taught him as a young boy. Nothing was more important to J. W. than the religious heritage of the Brown family.

After gaining everyone's attention, J.W. boldly shared, "I need you all to hear this. The lie you can lose your salvation through disobedience to God has been sown by the devil for thousands of years. Jesus said, 'Not everyone who says to me, "Lord, Lord," shall enter the kingdom of heaven, but he who does the will of my Father in heaven.'" 10

"So how do we do His will?" asked a worried mother.

Looking into her fearful eyes, he couldn't remember how many times he had taught on this passage.

"By professing Jesus as your Savior through baptism. Jesus warned, 'Many will say to Me in that day, "Lord, Lord, have we not prophesied in Your name, cast out demons in Your name, and done many wonders in Your name?" And then I will declare to them, "I never knew you; depart from Me, you who practice lawlessness."' 11

"What is he trying to say?" whispered a grandmother who had just lost two nephews to the underground resistance.

"Don't you see the connection between the warning of this passage by our Lord and this Watchman cult?"

While J. W. paused, the spirit of the antichrist moved off the podium toward a couple sitting in the first row. The demons could move about freely since this pastor never discerned their presence.

"Trust me; the prophecies of these Watchmen are false. They teach demons can actually control the actions of a believer. Add their so called miracles of healing, and you come up with a perfect picture of the false teachers Jesus warned us of."

"Pastor, are you saying my Ray was never a Christian because he was deceived by these teachers?"

"Mr. Largent, God chose who would be saved before the foundation of the world. He predestined those who were chosen for salvation. Nothing can change that. The blood of Jesus will atone for the sins of only those chosen. Jesus said He will not lose one of his own. Salvation is not about measuring up to a specific standard, it's about believing in the death, burial, and resurrection of Jesus Christ. If your son truly is a believer, God will never allow him to be deceived. Let's remember salvation is by grace alone."

Hands of desperate parents covered the fellowship hall. J.W.

knew he would never be able to answer all their questions.

"Saints, we must protect our families by exposing the manipulations of this cult. Are you aware of how many underage children they have targeted? These evil Watchmen are encouraging children to disobey their parents and reject the biblical teachings they have always believed in. Believe me, the cornerstone of the doctrine of Christ is predestination and the imminent return of Jesus Christ."

To J.W. Brown, this was just another attempt to put out a fire spread by false teaching.

"Pastor, I have heard both Pastor Bishop and Evangelist Corbin teach. I don't believe they are false..."

"My friends, I personally have damaging evidence concerning these false teachers. Bethany's own Thomas Bray and Gerald Pierce have produced evidence these so called evangelical ministers are leading a cult."

"Pastor, I seriously doubt..."

"Excuse me. If you desire to defend the false teachings of these men, please do it after our meeting. For those of you who have not been able to find your children; I'm afraid you have no other choice but to report them to the local NWC branch office. I'm painfully aware of how agonizing this must be for you. The fact remains, we cannot change our fundamental doctrines even if those we love have been deceived. Our Lord died for those who were chosen for salvation before they were born. The grace given to His chosen is irresistible; in other words, every believer picked by God for salvation will persevere. Those not chosen will go to hell. His Word can be trusted, no matter what we supposedly see or feel."

Stepping off the platform, the weary pastor left for his office. After a short prayer, his associate dismissed the meeting, completely unaware most were leaving just as confused as when they arrived.

Darkness covered the Middle East as armored units advanced toward the Valley of Jehoshaphat. For years, Israel had friends who would stand with them. That day was long gone. The United States, Israel's most valued ally, remained silent as neighboring nations positioned themselves for another all out attack.

The abandoned Bethany Assembly was a strange sight to the widow. Lee Ryan still had many wonderful memories of this sanctuary. She never dreamed her life would take such a cruel turn.

"Oh, Lord, where could Jason be?"

The peace of God was strangely absent.

"Father, please strengthen me or I'll never make it."

In her mind she heard, "Do you love Me, Lee?"

"You know I do."

"Do you trust Me?"

"I trust You with my life."

"Will you obey Me?"

"Yes, my obedience will further the kingdom of God."

"Then peace be with you, My child, as you forgive Damien for his betrayal of your beloved Lance."

The release of anger came deep from within her soul. Lee knelt before God; her tears of repentance soaking the carpet floor. Bent over, she confessed her bitterness toward the teenage Judas responsible for her husband's death.

"Wherever you are, Damien," cried Lee, "I forgive you. If it is still possible, Lord, I ask You to save his soul."

Outside, in the church parking lot, Commander Doyle Mercer and another agent were engaged in a conversation with Jason Wylie, the town's most respected lawyer.

"So, Chief; how's the new ID Security Station going?"

"Practically empty Jason. Our ID system will be assimilated throughout the country by the end of the year. The resistance movement is history."

As the Mole stalled, a truck quietly rolled to a stop on the other side of the church. The driver got out and ran toward a broken sanctuary window. Lee watched as the stranger squeezed through; carefully dropping from the ledge to the sanctuary floor. Ducking behind the large podium she held her breath.

Outside, Doyle Mercer waved goodbye.

"Nice talking with ya, Jason, but we gotta go. We've got four more churches to check out before dark. You know these resisters; they're like cockroaches."

The lawyer shouted a hearty goodbye. Hurrying back to his van, he softly prayed, "Please, Lord, only You can warn Lee."

The stranger cautiously edged toward the podium.

"Is anyone there?" he whispered.

"Damien?"

"Is that you, Lee?"

"What are you doing here?"

"I was praying and the Holy Spirit led me to come to this church. Are you aware there are ID agents in the parking lot talking with Jason Wylie?"

Reaching the window, Lee could see the approaching agents.

"Let's get out of here," pleaded Damien.

"Why should I trust you?"

"Please, forgive me, Lee. I was in bondage to the devil when I sold Lance out. But because of you, Lance, Lamar, and Carl, I asked God to forgive me. You gotta believe me. There are no words to express how sorry I am."

Opening the door to the activity center, the agents could hear talking in the sanctuary.

"We got visitors, Doyle."

The dark green van jumped the curb onto the lawn of the church. Skidding to a halt, the driver's door flew open.

"It's Jason," whispered Lee. "C'mon, you can make it."

Bursting through the sanctuary doors, they pointed their guns at a man climbing through an open window.

"Don't move!"

"You go, they've already got me."

Grabbing Damien's arm, she pleaded, "Not without you."

The two bullets tore through his left lung. From the ledge of the window, he tumbled to the sanctuary floor.

Glancing up to make sure his escape route was clear, Jason yelled, "It's time, Lee!"

Whirling around she ran and jumped into the waiting van. Accelerating down Vaughn Road the van took a quick left onto Hillsborough Avenue.

Dropping down from the ledge Doyle was not pleased. This wasn't the first underage resister he had to kill.

"What do you think Chief?" asked the other agent.

"Whoever was with the kid, got away in a green van identical to Jason Wylie's."

"You think Wylie is mixed up with the resistance?"

"Have you ever scanned him for an ID?"

"Not personally. But somebody must have checked his registration file."

"I know that!" snapped an annoyed Doyle. "I checked his file during last month's inspection of city employees."

"So was everything in order? Did he have an ID?"

"He had a number, alright. Let me ask you something. Have you ever caught anyone attempting to falsify registration files?"

"Sure. Remember the three sisters who refused to register last month?"

"Refresh my memory."

"It was during a shift change. Day shift had a hard time punching up the girls' files and turned the problem over to the swing shift. Swing shift checked again. The computers showed all three girls having valid ID numbers. So they let them go."

"Why didn't they just scan them?"

"They didn't bother to."

"What a bunch of idiots."

"Yeah, a total screw up. It took us a while, but we finally discovered the hacker's hideout. The guy who created the girls' fake IDs was a real genius."

"So, what ever happened to this computer hack?"

"He was killed trying to escape. What a mess. We are still looking for his older brother who got away. Get this; their old man is Thomas Bray, the famous Bible prophecy teacher."

"I just wonder," reflected Doyle. "You know what? I think it's time we pay Mr. Jason Wylie an official visit."

Scanning the dead body the other agent cursed.

"This is Damien Haley. He used to be one of our best informants."

While Doyle filled out the resister's death report, the other agent phoned the morgue for a pickup. Through it all, no one cared the blood of another martyr had stained the carpet of Bethany Assembly.

It was a while before either spoke.

"Are you okay, Lee?"

"I suppose so. What happens now?"

"I know a family leaving for a Watchmen Camp. It's hidden deep inside the Florida Caverns State Park. It would be good for you to join them."

"Did you see the man I was trying to help?"

"Wasn't it Damien Haley?"

"How did you know?"

"This may be difficult for you, Lee, but Damien was picked up a few hours after Lance's arrest. A Watchman named Carl Russell found him hiding in a burned out warehouse. It's pretty amazing how God protected the boy. When the NWC used him as an informant, they purposely didn't register him. Don't you see, Lee? Believers never would have trusted Damien if he had the mark."

"Why wasn't I told?"

"It was for your own protection."

Lance's final goodbye surfaced in her mind.

"Damien told me God led him to the church. As soon as I saw his face, I knew he was saved. Just moments before, the Lord convicted me of my bitterness. After Lance was martyred, I thought I could never forgive Damien. But when it came right down to it, it wasn't that hard at all."

"And how is that?"

"There isn't anyone I can't forgive after what Jesus has done for me." 12

"Our God is faithful," praised a relieved Jason.

A family of four was waiting when they arrived at the gas station. The Mole discreetly signaled for the father to meet with him. Lee could barely make out their discussion.

"Good news," beamed Jason. "You'll be inside the Florida camp by midnight."

With tears running down her face, she asked for a final hug. Lee had lots to say but the words just wouldn't come.

With her head resting upon his massive chest, he whispered, "It will be all over very soon, my dear friend. We are going to see our Blessed Hope coming in the clouds."

She would never forget the Mole. His love for the body of Christ was a gift from above. As the RV pulled out of the parking lot, Lee Ryan waved a final goodbye.

In her mind she heard, "'Greater love has no one than this, than to lay down one's life for his friends.'" 13

SIXTH SEAL : SUN, MOON, AND STARS

"I looked when He opened the sixth seal,
and behold, there was a great earthquake;
and the sun became black as sackcloth of hair,
the moon became like blood.
And the stars of heaven fell to the earth..."
Revelation 6:12-13

His face was majestic as He stepped before the Throne. Raising the scroll for all to see, Jesus opened the sixth seal. The cheers from the heavenly host were glorious. The time had come for the sign of the end of the age.

It was near one o'clock in the afternoon when the bottom rim of the sun turned black. The rumbling beneath their feet needed no explanation for those in cell block C.

In his cell David Cowley was praying. The passage in his mind was from the Holy Spirit. The evangelist knew it by heart. He was ready. "I looked when He opened the sixth seal, and behold, there was a great earthquake; and the sun became black as sackcloth of hair, and the moon became like blood. And the stars of heaven fell to the earth, as a fig tree drops its late figs when it is shaken by a mighty wind." 1

Within minutes, threats from Doubt, Fear, and Death, produced a panic in cell blocks A and B. The frantic prisoners were begging the guards to set them free.

A nineteen-year-old boy convicted of selling crack started screaming, "I'm too young to die. Let me out."

The intersession by the saints could easily be heard. The

bombardment of threats toward them by prisoners in cell block B was expected. The evil spewing forth was a reflection of the demonic bondage of those who had the mark. The guard on duty deserted his post just after the earthquake hit.

"Everybody ready?" barked the worried producer. "C'mon, guys, it's now or never. 5... 4... 3... 2... 1..."

"Afternoon everyone, this is Natalie Roberts, reporting live from our News Office in Chicago. We interrupt all TV coverage to announce the outbreak of an earthquake throughout the world. Immediately following this initial eruption, news agencies in Munich, Rome, and London, reported the moon turning red on its outer edges. We now switch to Ross Griffith in Washington, DC for a detailed update."

Clutching his notes, an animated Griffith looked frightened.

"Thank you, Natalie. As the sun started to turn black in our country, almost simultaneously, the moon was turning red on the other side of the world. Astronomers are studying both eclipses which began several minutes ago. Scientists are at a loss to explain such a rare phenomenon."

"Ross, at this moment Congress is discussing the implementation of the New World Coalition Emergency System. Of course, only Joshua Kayin has the power to activate this disaster alert worldwide. All member countries are expected to abide by any decisions set forth by the NWC. The United States has..."

"Excuse me, Natalie; we have just received a news story from the U.S. Seismological Bureau highlighting a shift in the earth's core. This appears to be the cause of the massive earthquakes occurring throughout the earth. Several experts have assured us this scenario was going to happen sooner rather than later. We expect to have updated reports every five minutes along with a complete evaluation of these cosmic eruptions. Please stay tuned."

As mankind anxiously awaited some sort of news, Carl continued to make his rounds in his yellow Chevy. He had just received a final list of underage resisters still at large. Most had been on the run for over a year.

"Not pretty, parents turning in their own kids," he moaned.

At first, store owners were making jokes while chatting with customers outside their shops. Once the earthquake hit, most abandoned their businesses. Even though looters were not far away, most owners didn't even bother to lock up.

Stopping at Sluman's Garage, he saw a teenager duck behind a pile of garbage. The boy knew he was in trouble. Jumping up he started to run. Carl hit the gas. Cutting through Sluman's parking lot he closed in. There was something familiar about the youngster but Carl couldn't quite place him.

"Hey, wait!" yelled the Watchman.

The boy never hesitated until he heard these words in his spirit, "Trust Me, my child. There's nothing to fear."

Slowing down, he turned and faced the yellow Chevy.

"Carl, Carl, it's me, Simon Colson."

"Well glory to God."

As both brothers in the Lord joyfully gave each other a high five, devastating earthquakes continued to pound the earth. Every nation would soon be engulfed with the fire of God's wrath. The day of the Lord was coming like a thief in the night for those who refused to repent and watch. 2

The office of Wylie and Wesson was a perfect front for the Mole. By God's grace, Jason had done a brilliant job in directing resisters to camps throughout the Southeast. He had just finished sending a final memo to all Watchmen in Bethany. Only moments ago, another Watchman inadvertently injured an agent during a successful escape. This only escalated the hostility. Bethany agents had just been given the authority to shoot anyone resisting arrest.

Suddenly, the Mole heard these words in his mind, "Mayday, mayday, you must leave now."

After locking the front door, he rushed out the back entrance. Jason couldn't resist making one final search before heading to the Birmingham Camp. Guiding his dark green van down a narrow alley, the lawyer knew that the risk he was taking for just one more look.

It was only a minute before three squad cars converged on his office. Doyle Mercer wasted no time.

"You two check the back, you two the alley and you two come with me."

After an agent attached a small device; the front door was blown to pieces.

"We're in, Chief."

"What'cha ya got?"

"This is so strange. Wylie disconnected the surveillance equipment but left his computer on standby."

"So the little coward fled the coop," laughed Doyle. "He didn't even take the time to dispose of his evidence. Punch up the screen and let's see how much he knows about the Christian resistance."

As soon as the agent touched the keyboard, a small puff of smoke emerged from the back of the computer.

As the inside of the computer melted, Doyle screamed, "Turn it off, turn it off, it's a set up, you idiot! He must have known we were coming. He was tipped off. But who is the rat?"

"Do you want us to issue a warrant for his..."

"This is top priority, guys. I think we've got a major player in the resistance right under our noses."

"Hey, Chief," hollered an agent from one of the squad cars. "We just received a positive ID on Wylie's green van. He's on the Eastside, close to Lakeview High."

"Let's go. This is the last time Wylie slips through our hands. He can join his buddy Corbin for all I care."

By late afternoon, half of the sun was blacked out. Mountains around the world were trembling. No nation was untouched. The mass panic, especially in the major cities, was spreading. The mourning for the dead and those missing was heartbreaking. An hysterical world looked to its leader, Joshua Kayin, for a miracle.

Death had once again invaded Israel's borders. Lifeless bodies lay scattered throughout the Valley of Jehoshaphat. It was a major earthquake that finally forced their tanks to sputter to a halt. Miraculously, thousands of Arab soldiers decided to withdraw.

"Hashem has delivered us!" screamed an overjoyed Rabbi. "He

will fight for His children."

Most knew nothing of Joel's frightening end time prophecy. 'Let the nations be awakened, and come up to the Valley of Jehoshaphat; for there I will sit to judge all the surrounding nations. Put in the sickle, for the harvest is ripe...Multitudes, multitudes in the valley of decision. For the day of the Lord is near in the valley of decision. The sun and moon will grow dark, and the stars will diminish their brightness.' 3

As the Jewish people rejoiced, stars were losing their light. The day of the Lord was near.

Both boys woke up from their nap at the same time.

"Did you feel that?" gasped Ray. "It's an earthquake. Hey, wake up girls, the sun is turning black."

"It's the sixth seal." yelped Jay. "We gotta get out of here. We need to find a spot that's safe from these aftershocks."

Making it through the deserted train yard was easy enough. Arriving downtown, they caught a quick glimpse of ID agents scanning people on Main Street.

Crouched behind a Bethany Herald truck, Ray whispered, "Rapture Man, are you sure the Holy Spirit is leading us? Right now our boxcar is looking a lot better."

"Agents coming our way," whispered Cindy.

Just then, a driver rushed out of the Bethany Herald Distribution Center and jumped into his truck. Starting the engine, he pulled away from the curb.

"So where are they?" cursed his partner.

As the truck drove away he mumbled back, "I know I saw two."

Guards watched from across the street as the ground under the old jail rolled and heaved. A large sink hole abruptly separated the exercise yard from the cafeteria. The prison guards pulled back from the street to the parking lot when the ground spilt under the power poles. The screaming only increased as jagged cracks spread up the walls of the cell blocks. Amazingly, some prisoners never let up mocking the overcomers who were on their knees praying.

The cave-in of cell block A could be heard a block away. With the sixty-year-old facility disintegrating, the head guard decided to free the prisoners. In cell block B, the metal bars were already twisted out of place. Most were pushing on their cell doors trying to get out. Rushing down the corridor, a guard yelled for everyone to step back. Another guard started shooting his revolver into the air. At first, his shots didn't even faze the crazed prisoners.

"Get back. We can't unlock your cells unless you stop pushing."

Smoke from a broken generator was seeping through the walls. It would take only a few minutes for all the cells to be engulfed. Punching in an emergency code, only the doors of cell block B opened. The prisoners frantically surged down the smoky corridor.

Across from the jail, families of prisoners were arriving. Most couldn't even watch. The ground under cell block A was opening.

"They're not going to make it."

They could hear the prisoners' shrieks. A swelling hole was swallowing the cell block. Those trapped cried out one final time before plummeting to their death. Cellblock C was relatively unharmed. The prisoners mocking the overcomers were dead.

Looters were systemically robbing the most expensive downtown stores. The gas pumps at Sluman's Garage were already empty. The desertion by police and firemen was expected; they were searching for their families. Suddenly, the door to the security booth swung open. In ran the guard who was tackled earlier by David's cell mate.

"You're free to go. Once you get outside, you're on your own. I'm warning you, the National Guard has been ordered to execute anyone refusing to register. It's a war zone, guys. I pray your God will be with you."

The last cell he opened was David's. As the guard turned the key the Watchman asked, "Why did you come back for us?"

"Aw, I was just showing off. I don't like Kayin either. That's why I never registered. I guess no one ever bothered me because of my loud talking. It was strange the day I mouthed off about you. There was something inside me pushing me to harass you. I'm Lester Beasley. The other day I saw you pray with a prisoner."

"Lester, he gave his heart to Jesus. Have you seen the change in his life?"

"Yep, a downright miracle. You better get going before they catch you."

"Only, if you let me pray with you first."

As the resisters fled, David prayed with the young guard. For the first time in Lester's life, he believed in the death, burial, and resurrection, of Jesus Christ. Confessing his sins and asking for forgiveness seemed so natural. By the time they'd finished praying, Jesus Christ was Lester's Savior. The Holy Spirit was now indwelling his human spirit.

"Wow, what a wonderful peace."

"Let's go, bro!" shouted an anxious David.

Reaching the front door, they heard footsteps.

"What now?"

"God will provide, Lester."

"Well, He'd better hurry."

Backtracking toward cell block C they hid behind a broken wall.

David prayed, "Lord, can You provide us with a way to escape?"

The agents rushing toward the front door stopped as the ground shifted. The sound of grating stone pierced the air. They hesitated while the building shook. As soon as things quieted down, they entered cell block C.

"Are you all right, Lester?"

"I'm okay. Man! God sure works fast, doesn't He?"

David grinned as the new convert slipped through the exposed crack on the rear wall. After reaching the street, they both began to praise the Lord for His faithfulness.

"Hold it right there; you're not going anywhere."

His right hand was shaking as he cocked his revolver. The young agent was just a boy, really; trying to do a man's job.

Slowly moving toward the rookie agent, David paused.

"We haven't done anything wrong."

Never looking down, he removed a mini-scanner from his belt.

"Let me see your ID."

In the time it took to turn the scanner on, Lester stepped in front of David.

"You're no killer."

"Stop right there or I'll shoot."

Lunging forward, Lester knocked the gun out of his trembling hand. Jerking away, the young agent took off running.

"No wait!" yelled David.

Norman's black truck had just left the parking lot. Hitting the brakes, he hollered, "C'mon, David, get in. Everything's breaking loose on Main Street. Do you hear me? Half of the sun is black."

Stephen Corbin's face flashed in his mind.

"I've got some unfinished business to take care of."

"Are you crazy? These agents have permission to shoot any resister on sight. They know your face. This is downright suicide. We've got to get out of Bethany right now."

"What do You want me to do, Lord?" David whispered.

Adjusting his CB radio, Norman just shook his head.

"Listen to this. The National Guard just executed three underage resisters near Lakeview High School."

"Any details?"

"Here it is; two boys and a girl. Wait a second. The boys were Tanner Harrison and Reggie Lincoln. The girl is, uh, Phillips. Amy Phillips. Did you know these kids?"

"Yeah, just babes in Christ."

Amidst the looting of stores, agents shooting resisters, and the panic overwhelming downtown, these words came in David's mind.

"There is another who needs someone to care."

The believers inside the truck refused to interfere as they prayed. Their next stop would be the safe confines of the Birmingham Watchmen Camp.

Waving for them to move on, David shouted, "God bless you and be safe in Jesus."

They waited until Norman's truck was out of sight.

"Let's go, Lester."

Running toward the jail, they rushed up the stairs, opened the front door, and disappeared into a wall of gray smoke.

After safely making it through downtown Bethany, a grateful Jason Wylie turned onto I-65 toward Birmingham.

"Praise the Lord. Thank You for making it possible for my wife and son to make it safely to the Watchmen Camp. Through the entire Great Tribulation, You have supernaturally protected us. 4 And now You've made it possible for me to share the coming of the Son of Man with those I love."

Setting the cruise control on fifty-five, he leaned back and turned on the news. But something wasn't right. The peace of God, something Jason had always trusted in, was absent. Exiting the highway onto an access road, he heard these words in his mind.

"Go back. There are four young ones who need help."

He was struggling with what he was hearing. God wanted the Mole to reflect back. There were many times when he trusted the Lord, even when it meant others would be arrested if he was wrong. Then Jason remembered a Friday night prayer meeting when the Holy Spirit gave him a unique word of knowledge. A group of law students were praying for the salvation of Muslims living in Sudan. The powerful anointing touching these students was the result of their heartfelt intercession for a people they never met. Jason was not convinced the word in his mind was from God.

"Oh, Lord," pleaded the young law student, "I can't interfere with such a mighty presence of your peace."

After two more promptings, Jason Wylie decided not to speak. Within seconds of his third refusal, the Holy Spirit led another student to sing the exact word Jason was supposed to speak. As the students rejoiced over this word of encouragement, the young law student fell to his knees and asked God to forgive him for his stubborn self will. He vividly remembered the Lord's response.

"My son, I'm not angry with you. I will just use somebody else who is willing."

The Watchman spun the van around and headed back toward Bethany. The prayer he had made that night in a little chapel in Chapel Hill, North Carolina changed his life forever. It was a moment in which he committed himself to God's will; no matter what the consequences.

Driving down Main Street the alert lawyer could hear gunshots up ahead. The looters didn't even bother to look as two agents chased down four teenagers.

Very softly he heard, "Go to Vaughn Road."

His tires squealing past Max's BBQ, Jason saw them rounding the corner. Skidding to a stop, he opened the side door of his van.

"My code name is..."

"Who cares!" screamed Ray as all four teenagers piled in.

Hitting the gas, the van lunged forward. Everyone hugged the floor as one bullet struck a speaker in the backseat. Another punctured the driver's door, narrowly missing Jason's leg. Gunning the engine, he sped down an alley between some apartments.

"Praise God, we've lost them."

The Mole glanced back at the exhausted teenagers. He smiled after recognizing Cindy Johnson from Bible studies at Lakeview High.

Paul Bortolazzo

"Hey Jason, what's up?"

"Nice drop in, Cindy," he playfully teased. "Who are your friends?"

"This is Ray Largent, Jay Wilson, and Faye Braun."

"Excellent, you're all on our final list."

The trip to the Watchmen camp would not be easy. The intensity of the aftershocks was rising. Turning onto I-65, he began dodging the cracks in the highway.

"This is crazy; I've heard rumors about a resistance leader called the Mole."

"Me too, Ray," added Jay. "But no one knows his real name."

Before Jason could answer, Cindy asked, "I don't suppose my parents could be inside the Birmingham camp?"

After thumbing through the J's on his list, Jason paused.

"Cindy, according to my files, your parents never reached this camp."

Bowing her head, she prayed, "Father, I come to You with a thankful heart for the miracles You have done for us. I give You my folks and place them in Your loving arms."

Her hands covering her mouth, she gently began to weep.

Grabbing another printout, a smiling Jason shared, "If your parents are Warren and Joyce Johnson, they checked into a camp outside of Jackson, Mississippi, over a year ago."

"They sure are!" squealed Cindy.

FOR I AM YOUR GOD

'Fear not, for I am with you; be not dismayed, for I am your God. I will strengthen you, yes, I will help you, I will uphold you with My righteous right hand.'
Isaiah 41:10

"What about Lakeview High?" asked an uneasy Simon.

Leaning against his yellow Chevy clipping his fingernails, Carl never looked up. He was waiting to see if the young Watchman had any fight left in him.

"Too dangerous, you hear about Stephen's execution?"

"I know all about it. So what are our chances?"

"Of finding, Josh? Not the best odds, I guess."

"Where could he be? We've looked everywhere."

Lowering his nail clipper, he mumbled back, "Maybe we should look in a place where he would never go."

"Why would Josh do something like that?"

"Kinda makes you think, doesn't it?"

"You can't mean the downtown ID Security Office?"

Entering the smoky solitary confinement, they desperately searched for the abandoned guard post.

"You think he's okay?"

Shrugging his shoulders, Lester said, "You find his cell; I'll try and locate the key cabinet.

Each cell was six by six, padded, with no windows. David jogged through the smoky corridor that had broken the spirits of so many.

After finding the key Lester raced toward the cell.

"David, you'd better brace yourself, he may be dead."

The guard inserted the key into the lock, activating the release. The heavy metal door swung open; flooding the cell with smoke.

Shielding his eyes, the prisoner whispered, "Praise the Lord."

"Are you okay?" asked his former cell mate.

"No time David," insisted Lester.

Grabbing hold of the prisoner's left arm, he slung him over his shoulder. The rumbling only grew louder as they reached the front door of the jail. Cautiously David peaked out. Several National Guard soldiers were setting up temporary headquarters on the front steps.

"Let's try the rear exit," offered a nervous Lester.

Locking the front door, they took off. The backdoor was buried under concrete and dirt.

"Did you hear that? They're coming through the front door?"

Lester was blanking out.

"In Jesus' name," commanded David, "be gone you foul spirit of Confusion."

Opening the door to the underground parking lot, Lester hollered, "Follow me."

Rushing down the stairs, they could hear shouts from behind. The garage housed six police cars, one swat truck, and a jail bus. Lester's squad car was the only one left. Jumping in, he hit the button to the entrance door.

"How long will it take?"

"A couple of seconds."

The agents hit the basement floor running.

"Pray," whispered the ex-guard. "4... 3... 2... 1..."

The souped-up squad car took off like a rocket. Hitting the ramp, the closest agent sprayed it with bullets. Leapfrogging onto the main road they never bothered to look back.

Lester Beasley knew Bethany like the back of his hand, so their chances of escaping were looking pretty good.

"The quickest route is by the ID Security Station."

"That's insane, Lester, there has to be another way."

"If we don't, they could easily trap us at the river before we reach the interstate. Trust me, it's worth the risk."

Driving toward the ID Security Station in his yellow Chevy, Carl was reviewing their options.

"We can position ourselves at a high lookout and wait to see if Joshua is hiding near the station."

"What's our second option?"

"We can drive up and check to see if they got our boy. If not, at least we still got our wheels under us."

"You know, Carl, I never did think you were an everyday normal Christian."

"Huh?"

"What's our third option?"

"Let's park my Chevy behind Amos's Barber Shop and search for Joshua on foot."

Softly, the Spirit of Christ whispered to Simon, "'Fear not, for I am with you; be not dismayed, for I am your God. I will strengthen you, Yes, I will help you, I will uphold you with My righteous right hand'" 1

Glancing out the window, the sun was almost black. Everything in his life had changed. Nothing else mattered anymore—school, fun times, his friends' approval, even getting married someday. All Simon wanted now was to please Jesus. He wanted to stand before the Christ at the judgment seat and say he gave it everything he had.

"Carl, whatever the Lord gives you, I'm up for it."

Slowing his yellow Chevy down to five mph, the flabbergasted Watchman asked, "You are?"

"Let's just do this for our Jesus."

An excited Carl said, "Okay, check it out, there's another option."

Wondering what he was thinking the boy leaned over.

"I'm going to walk into the Security Station and ask them if they know where Joshua is."

"Say what?" choked Simon.

"Agents will never suspect a Watchman cruising into their station. It's a lock."

Simon had never met a Christian who didn't fear anybody or anything. Carl had learned to trust in the Lord, no matter what the consequences. As they drew closer, the younger Watchman received a word of knowledge.

"Carl, I think Joshua is in the main lobby. In fact, in just a little while, he will be standing handcuffed near the main counter."

"Okay, when I go in, you need to be ready..."

"You're the driver. The Lord wants me to get Joshua."

"Simon, I understand Josh risked his life for you. But we're facing some high stakes, if you know what I mean. It's one thing to give a word of knowledge on a Sunday morning. It's quite another when three lives depend on it being from the Holy Spirit."

"I admit, Carl, hearing from the Holy Spirit is new to me. But I can sense He is leading me to do it."

"How?"

"When I ask for Joshua, God is going to provide a diversion."

The Watchman looked up and shouted, "This is so God."

Across the street, the angel Mordecai smiled at the foul spirit.

"You have no right to interfere, Mordecai," hissed Fear. "I have permission to..."

Instantly the angel delivered a blow sending the demon reeling backward.

"You want some more you lying little imp?"

Realizing it was no match for this angelic warrior, the spirit of Fear departed for a more opportune time.

As Carl edged by the ID station, Simon tried to get a look inside the main lobby.

"Remember, you need to exit through the back door."

"What if you're wrong?" whispered Doubt. "What if Joshua isn't there?"

"Carl, what if I'm wrong? What if Josh isn't there?"

"He will be. This isn't about you, it's about trusting God."

"I'm ready, bro."

Turning into the back lot, the Watchman parked near the rear entrance.

Glancing over, Carl grinned and whispered, "See ya around."

Simon got out and walked down the cluttered sidewalk. Turning right, he headed for the main entrance. His heart was pounding nails as he approached the receptionist.

Relieved to see anybody out and about, the bleached blonde smiled.

"May I help you?"

Trying to look as grown up as possible Simon nodded.

"I'm looking for my brother, Joshua Hirsh."

Before she could answer, the door to the interrogation room swung open. Sandwiched between two agents was a handcuffed Joshua. The hope of seeing their parents again was rekindled when the Watchman from the Westside signaled to the Watchman from the

Eastside he was okay.

With bullets raining down on his brown squad car, Lester took the last possible turnoff before reaching the ID station.

An all out police alert was tripping alarms in every ID station in Bethany. Hastily, one agent pushed Joshua back into the interrogation room and shut the door. Simon barely had time to get out of the way as the two remaining agents bolted for the entrance.

With the receptionist hiding under the counter, Simon tried the door to the interrogation room. It was locked. Bending down under the counter, he pleaded, "Can you help me?"

The frightened blonde pushed a button automatically opening the door.

"Come on, Josh, let's go."

Both boys sprinted toward the rear entrance. Looking through the bulletproof Plexiglas window in the back door, they could see the yellow Chevy was ready to roll.

"It's locked!" shouted Josh.

Turning around they made a hasty retreat.

Stopping dead in his tracks Simon whispered, "Wait."

They could hear someone coming down the hall.

"Yes, Lord, I do trust you."

Grabbing Joshua, he pulled him into a storeroom.

As the seconds ticked by, Joshua asked, "How'd ya find me?"

"The Holy Spirit."

"What now, Simon?"

The boys tensed up as the footsteps grew louder.

"Whoever comes through the door, you take him high, and I'll go low. Then let's try for the front door."

Their pursuer was hesitating. When the door opened, Simon lunged forward. The long-legged receptionist screamed, as she jumped back with one shoe in her hand.

"Boy, these heels are killers," she griped. Pulling a key from her purse, she grinned, "Here it is."

Leading them to the back door, she took a quick peek before unlocking it. After Joshua escaped, Simon paused.

"Why would you help us? Do we know each other?"

"Get going, kid. And if you see my little brother, tell him how much I love him. His name is..."

While holding the front door shut, Mordecai just smiled as two perplexed agents struggled to get back in.

The receptionist closed the double plated reinforced backdoor, securing the locks. Stuffing the key in her purse, an agent running down the hall spotted her.

"Hey, Jeri, you're not allowed back here."

The bleached blonde didn't even try to hide her tears.

"I heard something. None of you were here, so I checked it out. Actually, it's the best thing I've done in a long time."

By the time the agent opened the backdoor, the yellow Chevy was long gone.

"Frank, we've got an in-coming signal."

"Glory to God, Billy B, it's the Mole's van. We thought we might have lost him."

"He's got some overcomers with him."

"Incoming," announced Frank over the camp loudspeaker.

As the teens poured out of the van, parents with missing children held their breath.

"Great to see you, Cindy," greeted a radiant Hope Bishop.

"Praise God, Hope. I want you to know your obedience to the Holy Spirit played a big part in my being here today."

"We've got some great news from Mississippi. Your folks love you and are super proud of you."

After giving her classmate a hug, Cindy turned toward the waiting crowd.

"Everybody, I want you to meet some kids who saved my life. This is Ray, Jay, and Faye. We thank the Lord for ya'll. We never would've made it without your prayers."

A mother couldn't help but ask about their parents. There was an awkward silence before Ray Largent volunteered to speak.

"Thanks for your concern but my family received the mark last year."

Jay Wilson could relate. He shared how his folks assured him they were Christians. Despite his passionate warnings, they refused to believe the President of the United States was an evil Antichrist taking over the world. They registered a week before their due date.

Deep within cavern #2, Ben and Ida Hirsh were counseling kids overwhelmed with losing their families.

"Hey, Pastor Hirsh," asked a checkpoint guard, "have you heard about the teenagers who just arrived?"

"Did you catch their names?"

"Sure did. There was Cindy, Ray, Jay, and Faye."

"Faye!" cried Ida.

All eyes turned to Faye Braun, who wasn't handling it as well as the boys. When she accepted the Lord as a teenager, she thought for sure her whole family would become Christians. She bought everyone a small leather New Testament to celebrate her first Christmas as a believer.

Her younger brother sarcastically whined, "Oh goody, look what Jesus is giving me for being such a good little boy."

Such sarcasm didn't stop Faye. As the years went by, she saw many families put their trust in Jesus as their Savior. This loving teenager would write testimony letters about how great it was to be a Christian. She would give her family CDs, hoping their hearts would be touched through Christian music. She just knew Jesus would save her family. Fighting back the tears, she was clearly struggling.

"I'll always love my family. Fourteen months ago my folks and my brother each received the number of his name." 2

From among the crowd, Pastor Mark Bishop and his wife Julie silently watched this heartbreaking scene. The courageous sacrifice of these four overcomers was sobering. They had risked everything for Jesus. In these last days, God supernaturally raised up an army of young people who refused to deny their Lord. Remarkably, from the most criticized generation America ever had.

The possibility of seeing their precious Faye again ignited the Hirshes' faith. After reaching the entrance, they could see the crowd milling around the new arrivals. As they ran, it seemed like they were moving in slow motion.

"Faye! Faye!"

"Ida, Pastor Ben, it's a miracle."

Prayers of gratitude erupted through the crowd.

Tears running down her cheeks, the exhausted blonde fell into the arms of her spiritual parents.

"It's so great to be with ya'll. Hey, where's Josh? I've got some stories…"

THE END OF THE AGE

'Lo, I am with you always, even to the end of the age.'
Matthew 28:20

David Crowley's arrest by ID agents spread quickly among the intercessors. Martyrdom was the next step. Last week, the youth held a prayer vigil in honor of the man of God who risked his life for so many. Those rescued by this Watchman formed a circle to pray. In their hearts, he would never be forgotten.

The bullet-riddled squad car could barely make it up the long dirt road leading to the final checkpoint. Those on duty quickly waved them through.

"Cowley's alive!" shouted a lookout. "David's alive."

Believers could be seen pouring out of the caverns as they reached the picnic area.

For many overcomers, seeing the evangelist alive was one in a million. Easing out of the police car, the Watchman received a big hug from Mark Bishop.

"Praise God, David, you made it."

A relieved Julie Bishop added, "We heard so many rumors but we refused to give up."

"We've got someone here who needs some help."

Mark grabbed the right arm of the frail looking man.

"Okay, David, I've got him..."

The pastor froze. He could hardly recognize the man who had just spent five days in the black hole.

"Jimmy, is that you?"

"It's me alright. Other than that, I don't know how I feel."

"Hey, everybody, meet Jimmy Curtis from Sluman's Garage. Jimmy, are you a Christian?"

"Well, Pastor, it kinda goes like this," confessed the skinny mechanic. "When you're all alone and have nothing left to hang onto, the hand of the Lord looks mighty inviting."

As two nurses took care of Jimmy, Mark muttered, "Amazing, simply amazing."

A grateful David joyfully acknowledged, "I want you all to meet Lester Beasley. God used this man to free more than sixty overcomers facing execution at the county jail."

"You're an answer to prayer, sonny boy," praised an eighty-year-old grandmother.

"Thank you so much. To see so many of you here is a real miracle."

Prompted by the Holy Spirit, Mark shared, "Jesus said, 'I am the vine, you are the branches, if a man remains in me and I in him, he will bear much fruit. Apart from me you can do nothing. If anyone does not remain in me, he is like a branch that is thrown away and withers. Such branches are picked up, thrown into the fire and burned. If you remain in me and my words remain in you, ask whatever you wish and it will be given you. This is to my Father's glory that you bear much fruit, showing yourselves to be my disciples.' 1 We give you glory, Jesus, for those who remain in You and bear much fruit.'"

Amidst their praise, Lester pointed at his bullet ridden squad car.

"I think we should also thank the Bethany Police Department for providing us with such well ventilated transportation."

Joining the celebration, Jason Wylie motioned to Mark. Within the hour, all Watchmen would be joining their perspective camps. The coming of the Son of Man was near, right at the door. 2

While the crowd moved toward the safety of the caverns, Mark talked with Jimmy.

"So have you heard from your sister, Jeri?"

Choking up, he sadly confessed, "Afraid not. You see Jeri works as a receptionist at the downtown ID Security Station. She didn't think she had much of a choice. Jeri received her ID in the first month of registration. Pastor, it's so strange the way things have worked out. When we got into trouble as kids, Jeri would always be the one to do the right thing, even when it really hurt."

Jimmy glanced up. The moon was almost all red.

"Wherever you are, Jeri, I will always love you."

As the overcomers returned to the caves, the main topic was

David's miraculous escape from jail. Near the entrance to the main cavern, David asked Mark if they could take a walk.

"Is it true about Stephen? I heard he gave his life so others could go free."

"He fulfilled the calling the Lord gave him." 3

To his left, David could see families hugging one another. Then he saw her. She was walking alone.

"What about Michelle? How did she take it?"

"Julie and I were with her when she was told of his execution. After a long cry, she shared about their wedding day. Stephen told her he wanted their lives to count for something. For him, it was not enough to go to college, get a job, get married, buy a house before you're thirty, have some children, and then die at eighty. This man of God wanted so much more out of life. He always prayed to be about his Father's business."

Near cavern #2 Michelle Corbin was praying.

"Praise you, Father, for Your divine love and grace You have showered on us. You are so faithful. And to my precious Jesus, who died in my place that I might have eternal life. Forgive me, Lord, for the times I doubted Your love for me. And to the Comforter who indwells us. Words cannot express how grateful Stephen and I are to You for leading us through this evil world. All praise and honor and glory to the only true God: the Father, the Son, and the Holy Spirit."

With a bright red moon overhead, she looked up and smiled.

"I love you, Stephen. See ya at the judgment seat of Christ." 4

"You're on, Mole," challenged a playful David as he tackled his friend.

An excited crowd of kids cheered as they rolled in the dirt each going for a pin.

"These two deserve each other," laughed Hope Bishop.

The body of Christ had a deep appreciation for Watchmen.

They both had a good laugh while dusting themselves off.

"David, did you see any Watchmen in the last eight hours?"

"No, Jason, we may have been the last ones out alive."

Standing nearby were the Hirshes and the Colsons. David's answer brought a piercing to their hearts. They had prayed that no matter what trials their sons would face each would remain faithful.

Turning toward Marsha, a bewildered Ida was on edge.

"I felt so sure God would bring them back. The Holy Spirit even gave me a verse this morning. 'See, I have set before you an open door, and no one can shut it; for you have a little strength, have kept My word and have not denied My name.' 5 This is for Joshua and Simon. God promised me He would open a door for them to come back to us; a door no man or demon can shut."

"What are their chances, Ben?" asked a shaken Allen.

"I refuse to believe our sons will take the mark. Hey, Jason, are there any Watchmen still out on rescue?"

"The only one I know for sure is Carl Russell. And we've had no contact with him since the National Guard jammed all communications inside the city. Sorry, Ben, but by now, Carl is probably with the Lord."

The emotion coming from so many people was almost too much for the exhausted lawyer. Moving through the crowd, he joined his wife and son.

Hugging him from behind, the young man shouted, "Jason, you made it."

"Praise the Lord, Matt, our Jesus is faithful."

"I want my parents to meet you. Dad, Mom, this is the Mole, Jason Wylie."

"We can't thank you enough for what you've done," responded an indebted Tom Bray. "You have saved so many by putting your life on the line."

"I thank God for it all. It was an honor to work side by side with Matt and Sam. Your sons rescued hundreds of underage resisters."

"Praise Jesus!" yelped Ashley while hugging Jason's wife, Jackie.

Picking up his four-year-old son, Noah, Jason remembered, "Didn't Sam do a number on those agents? You know I received a fax from the three sisters he gave his life for. Trust me; Samuel Hosea Bray will always be their hero."

Slipping an arm around his mom and dad, a proud Matt reflected, "It was worth it, little bro. No price is too high. We're going to see you soon."

Pastor Mark Bishop joyfully declared, "Brothers and sisters in Christ, we can praise God for allowing us to come together to witness the events preceding His coming. The apostle Paul warned us the day of the Lord would come like a thief in the night to those not watching. As sons of the light, we are not in darkness so that this day should surprise us like a thief. So, my dear saints, let us be found spotless, blameless, and at peace with our Lord, for surely, the Son of Man can now come at any moment."

"Someone's coming," Billy B shouted from the tower. "Jason, is the checkpoint manned?"

"No, everyone's come in. There aren't any more scheduled arrivals. Any idea whose car it is?"

Billy B watched intently as it crept up the steep hill.

"It's Carl. It's Carl!"

Spinning around Jason hollered over the crowd, "It's Carl Russell. It's Carl Russell."

As soon as the old yellow Chevy came to a stop, it was mobbed with believers.

Sticking his head out the driver's window, Carl just grinned.

"Anyone up for a special delivery?"

Jumping out, a giddy Simon announced, "Look who the Lord found."

Joshua's words were lost over the cheers as Ida grabbed her son's handcuffed hands.

"God's never late!" yelled Jay Wilson, the official Rapture Man. "Josh made it for the big snatch."

"Son, what happened to you?"

"Well, Mom, as you may have guessed I hitched a ride in the back of a camp supply truck. When the truck arrived in Bethany, I decided to begin my search for Simon. So when the driver stopped at a light just off Main Street, I jumped off."

"And then what happened?"

"You won't believe this, Dad. Two agents were eating burgers and fries on the corner where I landed. One asked to see my ID. After scanning me, they took me to the downtown ID Security Station. The rest is history."

"But why didn't they execute you?"

"It sounds crazy but something always distracted them. It was like there was somebody behind the scenes protecting me."

Mordecai smiled. His assignment was over. As he lifted off, the warrior angel relished the idea of being created in the image and likeness of God. Within seconds, he joined the heavenly host lined up behind the Son of Man. All eyes were focused on the Father; it was almost time.

"But how did they rescue you out of the ID station?"

"Well, when Simon walked into the station..."

"Simon did what?"

"That's right, Dad, the Lord led us to be bold and not lean on our own understanding. Carl, Josh, and I, are here today because you all petitioned the Lord for our safety. Believe me, there were times my faith was almost gone."

"So, what kept you going?"

"I once heard a believer at my high school comfort someone with something her father taught her. It goes like this, if you stand for the truth, God will always be on your side. Where are you, Hope?"

With her parents at her side, a thrilled Hope Bishop jumped up and shouted, "For the glory of God, Simon, for the glory of God."

THE COMING OF THE SON OF MAN

'Then the sign of the Son of Man will appear in heaven, and then all
the tribes of the earth will mourn, and they will see the Son of Man
coming on the clouds of heaven with power and great glory.'
Matthew 24:30

As the moon turned a deep red, overcomers could only marvel at the
faithfulness of His eternal Word.

Opening his Bible, Pastor Mark read, "And there will be signs in
the sun, in the moon, and in the stars; with perplexity, the sea and the
waves roaring; men's hearts failing them from fear and the expectation
of those things which are coming on the earth, for the powers of the
heavens will be shaken. At that time, then they will see the Son of
Man coming in a cloud with power and great glory. Now when these
things begin to happen, look up and lift up your heads, because your
redemption draws near." 1

Their praise was electrifying. His Word had become a guiding
light to all who trusted in the Son of Man.

"Listen up, saints. Jesus said, 'When you see these things
happening, know that the kingdom of God is near. Assuredly, I say to
you, this generation (people) will by no means pass away 'til all things
take place... Watch, therefore, and pray always that you may be
counted worthy to escape all these things that will come to pass, and
to stand before the Son of Man.'" 2

From the entrance of cavern #1, Lindsey Bishop called out,
"Look up everybody, the Little Dipper is going out."

The deceived inhabitants of the earth began to curse God and all those who followed Him. As earthquakes rocked every nation, the miraculous signs and wonders of the Beast and his false prophet didn't matter much anymore. Those living in Jerusalem, Munich, Rome, and Moscow, would wake up to a black sun. Those on the other side of the world anxiously watched as stars surrounding a blood red moon lost their light. As the sky turned pitch black, a multitude of souls who never worshipped the Beast, prayed and received Jesus as their Savior.

In the midst of total darkness, with mankind paralyzed with fear, a faint light could be seen far off in space. Many covered their eyes as lightening swept across the sky from the east. 3 The Son of Man was coming on the clouds in the glory of His Father. A host of angels, girded with golden bands around their chests, were at His side. 4

Many were crying in anguish when Jesus shouted, prompting the heavenly host to encircle the earth. Then God blew His final trumpet. In the twinkling of an eye, the dead in Christ (Old and New Testament saints) received their resurrection bodies. 5 Then angels gathered His elect from the face of the earth. All who were ever saved were gathered before the judgment seat of Christ. 6

The words of the apostle John could not be denied. A deep sense of shame was overwhelming those who had worshiped the Beast. 7 He wrote of the coming of the Son of Man, "'And now, little children, abide in Him, that when He appears, we may have confidence and not be ashamed before Him at His coming.'" 8

Standing before His Throne saints roared, "Our God reigns."

Those who anticipated the sacrificial death of their Messiah were worshipping side by side. Isaiah foretold of the resurrection of Old Testament believers. "Your dead shall live... Awake and sing, you who dwell in dust... And the earth shall cast out the dead." 9

A multitude of believers from every nation would never hunger or thirst again. The Blessed Hope had just delivered them out of the Great Tribulation of Satan's wrath. 10 'For the Lamb who is in the midst of the throne will shepherd them and lead them to living fountains of waters. And God will wipe away every tear from their eyes.' 11

An angel ascending from the east, having the seal of the living God, called out with a loud voice to the four angels standing on the four corners of the earth.

"'Do not harm the earth, the sea, or the trees 'til we have sealed the servants of our God on their foreheads.'" 12

As the saints worshipped, the angelic host looked on in sheer admiration.

A gleaming Mordecai declared, "The Father sent his Son so they may have everlasting life."

"It's the plan of the ages," rejoiced Amad.

"Yes, I see some of our assignments," affirmed Ian. "What a sight to behold."

A curious Mordecai asked, "Ian, what was it like to see so many reject your message and receive the deceiver's mark?"

"I could only think of one thing."

"What was that?"

"The Father's desire has always been to spend eternity with His creation. His will was that none perish but all should come to repentance. 13 Think of it, to be created in the image and likeness of God and then allow habitual sin to rob you of everlasting life." 14

Heavy sorrow struck Mordecai as he wondered aloud, "What could be so important to humans that would make them reject the everlasting love of the Father?" 15

Ian said, "Peter warned believers, 'For if, after they have escaped the pollutions of the world through the knowledge of the Lord and Savior Jesus Christ, they are again entangled in them and overcome, the latter end is worse for them than the beginning. For it would have been better for them not to have known the way of righteousness, than having known it, to turn from the holy commandment delivered to them. But it has happened to them according to the true proverb: "A dog returns to his own vomit," and, "a sow, having washed, to her wallowing in the mire.'"

BLOW THE TRUMPET IN ZION

'Blow the trumpet in Zion, and sound an alarm in My holy mountain.
Let the inhabitants of the land tremble; for the day of the Lord is
coming, for it is at hand.'
Joel 2:1

The Lamb of God stood before His Father's Throne. As the Ancient of Days gazed upon His beloved Son, the saints erupted in glorious praises. The scroll, containing the wrath of God, lay before His nail scarred feet. Six of the seven seals on the outside of the scroll were open. The day of the Lord was at hand. 1

It was a surreal setting as former members of Bethany Assembly reluctantly returned to the abandoned church on Vaughn Road.

"Will you all just listen to me," pleaded Jolene, a former choir member. "Jesus said, 'Then the sign of the Son of Man will appear in heaven, and then all the tribes of the earth will mourn, and they will see the Son of Man coming on the clouds of heaven with power and great glory. And He will send His angels with the great sound of a trumpet, and they will gather together His elect from the four winds, from one end of heaven to the other.'" 2 Burying her face in her hands, she cried, "Don't you see what's happened? Jesus has gathered His elect. We've missed the rapture."

"That's rubbish," scoffed a rebellious Harriett Jones. "No one really knows."

"We'll know in a very short time."

Seated next to the frightened pastor was a disorientated teen that had just lost his family.

"What are you babbling about, old man?"

Never bothering to get eye contact, the dazed pastor shared, "The coming of the Son of Man was like the days of Noah and Lot. The same day Noah stepped into the ark, the flood came. The same day Lot left Sodom and Gomorrah, the wrath of God destroyed both cities. Jesus said it will be just like that the day the Son of Man is revealed. Deliverance then wrath, on the same day." 3

"The Bible doesn't say that," sneered Harriett.

"Revelation 8:1 says there will be thirty minutes of silence in heaven after Jesus opens the seventh seal. Then seven angels will sound trumpets in successive order. Soon our earth is going to be burned up by His fire. In II Peter 3:10 Peter prophesied the day of the Lord will come like a thief in the night and the earth will be burned up."

They had no words; they could only listen.

"The first trumpet will burn one-third of the earth's vegetation. 4 The second trumpet will kill one-third of the sea's living creatures. 5 The third trumpet will infect our water and many will die from..." 6

"This can't be happening!" screamed Jolene. "It's like we're trapped in some evil nightmare."

"Why are you still here, Pastor?" Harriett suspiciously asked. "Why aren't you over at your church trying to help explain this mystery to your congregation? Shouldn't they be preparing for these so called trumpet judgments?"

"I already have. Their denial is like yours. Goodbye, I need to continue my search."

"C'mon, Rev," mocked another teenager, "Who are you searching for?"

"For anyone who hasn't worshiped the Beast, his image, or received his mark."

Not waiting for a reply, he walked out into the cold night air.

"Oh, he's a fool," cursed Harriett. "I'm sick of hearing this type of gloom and doom preaching. I think we're going to be just fine. If you ask me, trying to interpret the Book of Revelation is just guesswork. Look at how many famous Bible teachers have been wrong. Everyone has their own interpretation of the end times for God's sake."

As some got up to leave, the evil spirit of Religion continued to speak through the Sunday school teacher to anyone who would listen.

Members from Bethany Presbyterian Church could hear his heavy sobbing as they entered the sanctuary. Taking seats around their respected leader, a staff worker named Rhonda spoke first.

"Pastor Brown, are you okay?"

His bottom lip quivering, he blurted out, "No, I'm not. His visitation couldn't have been more devastating."

"What does this all mean, Pastor?"

"How many of you saw Jesus coming in the clouds?"

Most sat motionless. The shock was emptying them of any strength.

While subconsciously rubbing her right wrist, a shaken Rhonda whimpered, "I don't understand. I've been a Christian all my life. I haven't hurt anybody. My faithfulness to my church has been excellent. What has happened to us?"

Looking away, her pastor confessed, "The Beast has deceived us with his mark."

"Deceived who?" interrupted his stunned associate pastor. "That's impossible. Salvation is a gift. Once a person is saved, they can never be deceived. Registering for an ID microchip can't take away one's salvation."

"There are no words to express how wrong I've been."

"What do you mean wrong?" challenged Ray Largent's father.

"I can now see critical errors..."

"Errors, what errors are you talking about?"

"I've taught for years the entire seven year tribulation period was God's wrath. I never saw the difference between the Great Tribulation, which is Satan's wrath, and the day of the Lord, which is God's wrath."

"What difference?"

"The Great Tribulation began when Jesus opened the fourth seal of the heavenly scroll. The day of the Lord begins when the seventh seal is opened." Clutching his lecture notes, he sobbed, "Why couldn't I see this truth?"

In a fit of rage, several members started to curse.

"I trusted you, Pastor!" screamed a member of the worship team. "You assured my family Joshua Kayin wasn't the Beast. You insisted our ID numbers had nothing to do with the mark of the beast."

"Yes, I believed..."

An irate board member interrupted, "You even labeled Mark Bishop and Stephen Corbin as instruments of the devil. These were the very teachers trying to warn us. Remember, you taught Jesus would never allow His bride to be deceived by the Antichrist."

"I never thought the timing of the rapture was..."

"You stinking liar; now we're all doomed to the lake of fire."

A hysterical mother hollered, "We trusted your knowledge of the Bible and you deceived us. My daughters are waiting for me to come home and assure them that everything is okay. What am I going to tell them? You're just a wolf in sheep's clothing and we fell for it."

"What a lie," moaned Ray's father. "Almost thirty Sundays a year, he taught us how eternally secure we are. In the end, we trusted his teaching rather than God's Word."

The once popular J. W. Brown had nothing more to say. Sliding his chair back, he got up and walked out the side entrance of the sanctuary.

Minutes after the coming of the Son of Man, Jessie Hyatt and Jake Jamison met at the lunch tables behind the Industrial Arts building at Lakeview High. The tall brunette was in deep thought.

"I'm scared, Jake. It's happening just like Luke said it would."

"I know. Last night I had a creepy nightmare about Ned and Drew Henley. They were begging for me to cross over this enormous ravine separating us. I kept trying to find a way, but I wasn't able to."

"Anything else?"

"I heard a voice say, 'You'll never be allowed to cross over for eternity.'"

They both could hear loud laughing coming from the football stadium.

"Why, it's J and J," greeted a giddy Rachel Pressley. "How ya'll doing?"

"I suppose you saw Jesus coming with His angels?"

"Naw, Jake, we missed it. During the eclipse, Annie and I were partying with some of our friends. The weed we smoked was so awesome."

"What's up with that, Rachel? You were never into drugs."

"Lighten up, Jessie," teased an out of control Anna. "Trust me; the pills I took can make all your problems go away."

"Cool it, girls. We are in serious trouble. Now is not the time to be loaded. We need to seek the truth about what has just happened. We need some answers."

Rolling her eyes, an irritated Rachel mocked, "What answers? Jessie, you don't get it, do you?"

"Get what?"

"Let me spell it out for you. No, better yet, let me name some names: Cindy Johnson, Ricky Jackson, Drew Henley, Luke Appleby, and Hope Bishop. Where are they Jessica? Can you tell me where a single one of them are?"

"They didn't tell anybody where they were going..."

"Oh, give me a break. You couldn't possibly be this stupid, could you? Cindy Johnson ran like hell when they tried to give her the mark of the beast. Ricky Jackson has been convincing kids for over a year not to register. They're all resisters, Jessie."

"Yeah, I know about the resistance movement. Jake and I were hoping the Ryans could take us to one of the camps."

"A lot of good that will do you now."

"What are you saying, Rachel?"

"Hello, is anyone at home?"

"Jessie, have you ever compared the events of Matthew 24 with the events of the seals in Revelation 6? You know the heavenly scroll sealed on the outside by seven seals. The events of the first three seals were the beginning of sorrows. The fourth and fifth seals were the Great Tribulation. 7 The sixth seal was the sign of the end of the age."

"Luke shared these events with me a couple times, Anna."

"Oh, this is sweet," snickered Rachel, "real sweet." "Well, I hate to break it to you but we just experienced the opening of the sixth seal. As good ole' Luke Appleby used to preach, the days of the Great Tribulation will be cut short by coming of the Son of Man." 8

"You mean when Jesus came a little while ago..."

"Hallelujah, sister. C'mon, don't you remember the twins preaching their end times show at lunch time. First, we see the sign of the end of the age, the sun, moon, and stars, losing their light. Then we see the Son of Man coming in the glory of His Father with His angels. When the trump of God sounds His angels will gather the dead in Christ before catching up believers from the earth. Next up is the day of the Lord. 9 Back to back signs of back to back events. How am I doing?"

"So if we missed His coming, what do we do now?"

"Do? There's absolutely nothing we can do. The day of the Lord will erupt thirty minutes after Jesus opens the seventh seal. Talk about seeing some heavy duty fireworks."

"You're not making any sense."

"Fire, Jessie. God's wrath is going to be poured out on this earth and there's nothing anybody can do to stop it."

"Oh, my God, there must be something we can do?"

Glancing at her watch, Rachel whispered under her breath, "I'm afraid that question is a little too late."

An atmosphere of depression was engulfing the room as the false prophet cautiously entered Kayin's inner chamber. The recent visitation had completely paralyzed the Lawless One. 10

"Yes," said the Pontiff, "I have seen the recent reports concerning the disturbance... We'll have final count of the dead from the Jehoshaphat assault in... That is correct, there are still over two million Jews left... Yes, I am aware of the powerful impact the two Witnesses are having on..."

A beleaguered Joshua Kayin turned away from the window and picked up a plaque from his gold plated desk. It was a collage of pictures depicting the day his armies overwhelmed Jerusalem. To the two beasts, the slaughter of millions of Jews was a tribute to the Wicked One.

"Excellent image of our enemies being destroyed," bragged the prophet. "Think of it, before you are finished, you will kill more Jews than in the Holocaust."

Both leaders were rejoicing at such an achievement. Who would have ever dreamed it could happen again? Even so, the next crisis facing them was far more critical. At the sounding of the seventh trumpet, the Lord will strip Satan of his power over the earth and begin to reign spiritually. 11

With his wife sobbing in their bedroom, Pastor John Ryals sat listless in his den. The lights were off, the blinds drawn; updated reports coming from the radio could be heard faintly in the background. On their new coffee table, a bottle of pills lay open next to a spilled glass of water.

The flashback of memories was tormenting the disorientated shepherd. What could he say to his congregation? He'd already left a prerecorded message at his church.

The lonely figure used the side gate to their backyard. He wasn't even sure they were home. Even so, it was worth a chance. The pounding on the kitchen door awakened the pastor from his depressed stupor. Slowly rising from his favorite chair, he walked over to the blinds and peered out.

"Go away."

"Pastor Ryals, I've got to talk with you."

"Why? What could I say that could make any difference?"

"Please let me in."

Reluctantly, he unlocked the door and walked back to his chair.

"Pastor, are you okay?"

His listless stare, the garbled tone of his words, total despondency was near.

"What do you think?"

"It's insane out there. You won't believe what's happened to the downtown WFM office. Some religious fanatics have set it on fire. I think there's going to..."

"Tell me, Dwayne, where's your family?"

"Rachel and Anna are out with some of their friends. Gloria is visiting her parents who live over on Vaughn..."

Interrupting again, he mumbled, "So, what's your story?"

"Our people are really hurting. I've been praying..."

"This is too funny; I don't remember you ever praying."

Until this moment, the dejected preacher had never discerned how evil Dwayne Pressley really was. The deacon sat back and smiled.

"A lot of people are ready to give up but not me. I must have been a fool to come to you for counsel. Tell me, when are you going to meet with the members of our church? Remember, you're our pastor."

"Don't you know...?"

"Know what? Now listen up, old man, stop this nonsense. There are some very frightened people who want some answers."

Walking over to the kitchen, he muttered, "Is that so?"

"They're asking for you. Now what are you planning to do?"

Returning from the kitchen with a cloth, the weary pastor knelt down and wiped up the spilled water off his brand new coffee table.

After the Pressley girls left to party, the quietness of the moment helped Jake and Jessie collect their thoughts.

"Jess, we've got to seek God before it's too late."

"You mean ask Jesus to forgive us of our sins?"

"Why not? I haven't told you, but I've been hearing voices in my mind. One voice keeps telling me God will never forgive me."

"Sounds familiar," sighed Jessie.

"The other voice always speaks of Jesus."

"That's strange, I always thought..."

As the two teenagers shared, a slim man in his late fifties approached the lunch tables from their blind side.

"Hello, do you mind if I join you?"

"Sure, why not. I don't know what you believe, mister, but my friend Jessie and I have been discussing how Satan has been playing with our minds."

"You mean spiritual warfare?"

Both just stared at this stranger they had never met.

"Yeah," answered a wary Jessie, "that's what Hope used to call it."

"You mean Hope Bishop?"

"Do you know her?"

"Actually, I knew her father."

"It's strange to think we'll never see them again."

"Oh, I wouldn't say that."

Up until now, with their emotions raging, Jessie and Jake weren't really listening. Suddenly this mysterious man had their full attention.

"What do you mean?" asked Jake.

"It's really pretty simple. Even though you missed the coming of the Son of Man, the Holy Spirit is still saving those who have not worshipped the Beast."

"Who are you?"

"What really matters, my friends, is not the messenger but the message. You don't have much time. Have either of you ever worshipped Kayin, his image, or taken his mark?"

"No sir, they tried to make us but we escaped."

"That's great to hear."

In the next ten minutes, the stranger shared the plan of salvation in such a way a seven-year-old could understand.

"Jessie, Jake, you must now decide whom you're going to follow. We are just minutes away before God begins to demolish this earth and all who followed the Beast."

"Sir, I want to trust Jesus with all of my heart."

"Me, too," added Jake. "We want to be forgiven of our sins, so we both can be with Jesus for eternity."

The conviction from the Holy Spirit drew the teens to their knees as they fervently prayed for Jesus to save their souls.

Afterward, Jessie whispered, "I can just sense His forgiveness."

"It's like feeling really clean all over," grinned Jake.

"Goodbye, my friends, I must continue my search."

Before they could answer, the stranger turned to leave.

"Wait, sir. We can't thank you enough for sharing the gospel with us."

"What is your name?" called out a radiant Jessie.

Not missing a step, he yelled back, "My name is Elmer... Pastor Elmer Dyer."

With tears streaming down her face, she cried, "God bless you, we will never forget you."

"That's right, Elmer," hollered a grateful Jake. "We will see you in heaven someday."

Tears of regret filled his eyes as he walked away. Glancing down at the mark on his right hand, Pastor Elmer Dyer knew that day would never come. 12

The End

Scripture References

Chapter 1
1. Revelation 13:1, 17:7
2. Rev 17:12, Ezekiel 38:1-14
3. Matthew 24:15, Daniel 9:27
4. Revelation 5:1
5. Revelation 5:2
6. Revelation 1:14-15, 10:1-2
7. Revelation 6:1
8. Revelation 6:2, 13:7
9. Revelation 13:1-7, Dan 7:24-25
10. Matthew 24:4-5
11. Rev 12:11, 13:2 Matt 24:15
12. I John 2:18
13. Daniel 9:27, Isaiah 28:15
14. Isaiah 2:2-4
15. Isaiah 62:6
16. Rev 3:2-9, Matt 24:4-31, Rev 6:1-17
17. II John 2:26-28
18. Matthew 24:21-31, Rev 7:9-14
19. Matthew 24:33
20. Isa 28:15-18, Zechariah 13:8-9
21. Luke 21:20, Ezekiel 38:11-16
22. Revelation 6:1-2

Chapter 2
1. Matthew 24:36
2. II Thessalonians 2:1-4
3. Ezekiel 38:1-16, Luke 21:20
4. Daniel 9:27, Matthew 24:15
5. Daniel 9:25-26
6. Dan 9:24, Rom 11:25-27, Rev 10:1-7
7. Daniel 9:24
8. Nehemiah 2:1-8
9. Daniel 9:27
10. Mark 13:3
11. Matthew 20:18-19
12. Matthew 24:3
13. Matthew 24:4-29, Rev 6:1-17
14. Matthew 24:33
15. Ezekiel 3:17-21
16. II Timothy 3:5
17. Mark 16:17-18

Chapter 3
1. Hebrews 13:6
2. I Thess 1:10, Rev 11:15, 19:11-21
3. Revelation 5:1
4. Revelation 6:2, Matthew 24:5
5. Daniel 9:27, Luke 21:20
6. Rev 17:12-13, Eze 38:1-14
7. II Thess 2:1-4, Revelation 13:7
8. Revelation 3:3, 1 Thes. 5:4-7

9. Matt 24:21-22, Rev 6:8, Rev 13:5-7
10. Revelation 13:7, 14:9-10
11. Revelation 3:5, 12:11
12. Rev 13:16-18,14:9-10, Mat 24:21-22
13. Rev 3:3, Matthew 24:4-29, 33

Chapter 4
1. Titus 2:13
2. Galatians 1:10
3. Luke 17:30
4. II Peter 3:10
5. I Thessalonians 5:4
6. II Thessalonians 2:1, 3

Chapter 5
1. Matt 24:30-31, I Thess 4:15, II Thess 2:1
2. Matthew 24:40-41
3. Acts 4:12
4. Titus 2:13-14

Chapter 6
1. Mark 13:27
2. Matthew 24:40-41
3. Matthew 24:8
4. Matthew 24:21
5. Matthew 24:10
6. Matt 24:12, 10:34-39, II Tim3:1-5
7. Dan 9:27, Matt 24:15, II Thess 2:3-4
8. Matthew 24:22
9. Matthew 24:13
10. Matthew 24:33
11. Matt 24:29, Rev 6:12-14, Joel 2:30-31
12. Matthew 24:27
13. Matthew 24:30
14. Mark 13:27
15. Matthew 16:27
16. John 5:28-29, Matt24:30-31
17. I Thessalonians 5:9
18. Revelation 12:12
19. Revelation 6:16
20. Matt 24:29-31, Rev 6:12, 7:9-14, 8:1

Chapter 7
1. Daniel 9:27
2. Rev 16:14-16, 19:11-21, Dan 12:11
3. II Thessalonians 2:1-3
4. Revelation 7:9-14; 15:2
5. Revelation 6:17
6. Mark 14:41
7. Matthew 9:37-38
8. Matthew 24:21-22
9. Daniel 7:7-8; 20-25

10. Daniel 9:27
11. Revelation 13:3-4
12. Revelation 13:7
13. Matthew 24:6
14. I Timothy 4:1
15. Matthew 24:13, I Thess1:10
16. II Timothy 3:1-5
17. Hebrews 3:12, 14
18. Matthew 5:28
19. James 5:16
20. John 14:30

Chapter 8
1. Daniel 7:24-25
2. Revelation 6:4
3. Matthew 24:6-7
4. Revelation 2:1-3:22
5. Revelation 3:14-19
6. Luke 21:36
7. Revelation 12:11
8. I Timothy 4:1-2
9. Ezekiel 33:1-11

Chapter 9
1. Luke 21:6
2. I Corinthians 15:51-52
3. I Thessalonians 4:16-18
4. Revelation 6:1, 8:1, 15:1
5. Revelation 19:20
6. Galatians 1:10
7. Matthew 24:3
8. Matthew 24:9
9. Revelation 21:9-10
10. Matthew 28:19-20

Chapter 10
1. Revelation 17:1-15
2. Jeremiah 7:18
3. Jeremiah 44:18
4. Ezekiel 8:14-15
5. Jeremiah 44:19
6. Revelation 17:9, 18
7. Revelation 17:16
8. Revelation 13:11-12

Chapter 11
1. Revelation 17:13
2. Luke 14:26-33
3. Matt 24:21-22, 30-31, Mark 13:27
4. Romans 8:31
5. Daniel 7:7-8, 20-25
6. Daniel 9:27
7. Genesis 26:35

Chapter 12
1. Jeremiah 44:17-25
2. Exodus 20:45
3. Revelation 17:3, Rev 13:5-7
4. Luke 14:27
5. Matthew 24:21-22
6. Matthew 24:33
7. Matthew 24:6
8. Mark 13:37, Revelation 3:3
9. Matthew 24:24
10. Revelation 3:3
11. Matthew 24:13
12. Revelation 20:4
13. II Timothy 1:7
14. Revelation 3:21-22
15. I Corinthians 12:8-10
16. Hebrews 13:2
17. Luke 10:27

Chapter 13
1. Revelation 6:5-6
2. Mark 13:7-8
3. Revelation 13:4
4. Revelation 13:7
5. Revelation 14:12
6. Revelation 13:16-18
7. Matthew 13:39, 24:13, 28:20

Chapter 14
1. Revelation 3:19-22
2. I Corinthians 6:9-11
3. Revelation 3:15-18
4. Romans 3:23, I John 1:10
5. Revelation 22:18-19, 3:5
6. II John 9
7. Matthew 24:29-31, Rev 7:14
8. II Thessalonians 2:1-4
9. Joel 2:30-31, Matt 24:29, Rev 6:12-14
10. Luke 21:28
11. Revelation 12:7
12. II Thessalonians 2:7
13. Revelation 6:7-8
14. Revelation 6:7-8, 13:1-18
15. I Peter 4:17-19
16. Revelation 12:12
17. II Peter 3:10, Joel 2:30-31
18. Galatians 5:19-21
19. Revelation 17:4

Chapter 15
1. Revelation 13:16-18
2. Daniel 11:31-32
3. Daniel 11:30-32
4. II Peter 2:20

5. Matt 24:4-5, 10-11, II Thess 2:3
6. Daniel 9:27
7. Revelation 13:16-17
8. Revelation 13:18
9. II Peter 2:20-22
10. Hebrews 10:26
11. Hebrews 10:29
12. Jude 1:1
13. John 6:40
14. John 8:31
15. II Thessalonians 2:11-12
16. Acts 13:52
17. Ephesians 2:8

Chapter 16
1. Revelation 3:5
2. Revelation 20:4
3. Revelation 3:5, 22:18-19
4. Revelation 13:7, Rev 6:7-11
5. John 9:4
6. Matthew 24:14, Revelation 14:6
7. II John 1:9-11
8. John 14:21, 15:23
9. I Timothy 4:16
10. II Timothy 2:19

Chapter 17
1. John 3:16
2. John 14:2-3
3. Revelation 1:7
4. Revelation 19:13
5. Revelation 13:8
6. Revelation 4:1
7. Isaiah 2:17
8. II Timothy 4:3-4
9. Matthew 24:40
10. Mark 13:26-27
11. Luke 17:26-30, Matt 24:30-39
12. Matthew 24:15
13. Matthew 24:15, 30-31
14. II Thessalonians 2:1-4
15. Luke 18:8
16. Luke 21:20, Ezek. 38:1-14

Chapter 18
1. Ephesians 6:12
2. John 3:16
3. Mat 24:29, Joel 2:30-31, Rev 6:12-14
4. Matthew 24:27
5. Matthew 24:31
6. I Thess 1:10, Matthew 24:29-31
7. Revelation 13:7
8. Matthew 24:15, Daniel 9:27

9. Revelation 3:10, 6:7-8
10. Revelation 10:1-7
11. Revelation 13:8
12. Colossians 1:13

Chapter 19
1. Revelation 8:1
2. Revelation 6:7-8
3. Rev 12:6-7, Daniel 12:12, 10:21
4. II Thess 2:34, Matthew 24:15
5. Revelation 13:15-18, 14:9-12
6. Joel 2:30-31
7. Isaiah 13:6-13
8. Luke 17:26-30
9. Revelation 12:12
10. Matthew 24:36
11. Matthew 24:15, 30-31
12. II Thessalonians 2:1-4
13. John 10:27-29
14. Matthew 24:10
15. Revelation 3:12
16. Revelation 3:5
17. Ezekiel 3:20-21
18. Matthew 7:15
19. Revelation 14:11
20. Daniel 7:7-8, 24-25
21. Daniel 9:27
22. Revelation 12:10, Job 1:7-12

Chapter 20
1. Mark 13:26-27
2. Revelation 13:7
3. Galatians 4:16
4. Revelation 17:16
5. Daniel 7:24
6. Daniel 11:11, 43
7. Revelation 14:6-7
8. Matthew 24:14
9. John 14:6
10. II Corinthians 5:17

Chapter 21
1. Rev 7:9-14, 10:1-7, 19:11-21, 21:9-10
2. Matt 24:30-31, I Thess4:15, II Thess 2:1
3. Revelation 21:9-10
4. Revelation 3:10-11
5. John 17:15
6. Matthew 24:13
7. I Thessalonians 5:9
8. Revelation 3:11
9. Revelation 3:5, 22:18-19
10. Hebrews 10:35-36
11. Ephesians 6:10-18
12. II Thessalonians 3:3

The Coming

Chapter 22
1. Samuel 4:21
2. II Thessalonians 2:1-3
3. II Thess 2:4, Matt 24:15, Dan9:27
4. II Thessalonians 2:7
5. Ezekiel 38:1-12, Matthew 24:15
6. Revelation 12:1-6
7. Revelation 12:1
8. I John 2:28
9. Matthew 10:32-33
10. II Timothy 3:15, I Timothy 4:1
11. Revelation 3:3, II Peter 3:10-14
12. Revelation 12:11
13. I John 4:4
14. II Peter 3:4

Chapter 23
1. Revelation 13:2
2. II Thessalonians 2:3
3. Revelation 13:1, 17:7
4. Revelation 17:12
5. Revelation 17:10
6. Daniel 2:40-42
7. Revelation 13:3-4
8. Revelation 9:20
9. Revelation 19:20
10. Revelation 12:7-14, 13:1-2
11. Matthew 10:37-39
12. John 3:16
13. Luke 18:27

Chapter 24
1. Titus 2:11-13
2. I John 4:20
3. Hebrews 10:25

Chapter 25
1. Revelation 7:4-8, 14:1-4
2. Revelation 12:1
3. Revelation 12:2-5
4. Revelation 12:6
5. Ezekiel 20:34-35, 37
6. Revelation 10:7, 11:15
7. Revelation 12:9
8. Revelation 12:12
9. Revelation 12:4
10. Revelation 15:6
11. Revelation 14:6-7
12. Revelation 14:8
13. Revelation 14:9-10
14. Revelation 12:7
15. II Thessalonians 2:7
16. John 14:30, Revelation 13:2
17. Matt 24:15, Dan 9:27, Eze 38:1-14

18. Revelation 13:11-17
19. Revelation 13:14
20. II Thessalonians 2:11
21. Revelation 13:16-18, 14:9-10
22. Matthew 24:25
23. Revelation 11:5-6
24. Revelation 11:7
25. Revelation 11:7-8
26. Isaiah 55:6-7
27. Isaiah 55:8-9, 11
28. Ezekiel 38:11-14
29. Matthew 24:16-20
30. Isaiah 28:15
31. Zechariah 13:8

Chapter 26
1. Ezekiel 38:10-12
2. II Thess 2:4, Matthew 24:15
3. Revelation 14:6-7
4. Matthew 24:14
5. I Thessalonians 5:3
6. Rev 13:6-7, II Thess 2:3-4
7. II Thessalonians 2:11-12
8. Matthew 5:10-12
9. Jeremiah 30:7-9
10. Isaiah 55:11
11. Revelation 11:5
12. Revelation 14:9-11
13. Revelation 17:16
14. Revelation 13:8
15. Revelation 17:6
16. Revelation 17:16

Chapter 27
1. Revelation 14:9
2. Galatians 5:19-21
3. Revelation 3:16, Gal 5:19-21
4. Revelation 3:5, 22:18-19
5. Galatians 5:7-8

Chapter 28
1. Joel 2:28
2. Joel 3:14
3. Joel 3:15
4. Revelation 6:9-11
5. Revelation 13:3-4
6. Revelation 13:16-18, 14:9-11

Chapter 29
1. Matthew 24:25
2. Ezekiel 38:10-12
3. Matthew 24:38-39
4. John 14:1

Chapter 30
1. John 17:17-21
2. I Thessalonians 5:3
3. II Corinthians 5:17
4. John 14:15-16

Chapter 31
1. Revelation 14:12
2. Revelation 3:5, 14:11, 22:19

Chapter 32
1. Revelation 6:9-11
2. Revelation 9:20
3. Daniel 7:7-8, 24-25
4. Daniel 11:39
5. Daniel 9:27
6. Revelation 3:5, 12, 21
7. Matthew 7:13-14

Chapter 33
1. Mark 13:11
2. Revelation 14:9-10
3. Matthew 24:33
4. Luke 21:16
5. I Corinthians 3:18
6. Matthew 24:4-5
7. Matt 25:13, I Thess 5:4-6, Rev 3:3

Chapter 34
1. Matthew 10:32-36
2. Matthew 24:45-46
3. Matthew 24:47-51
4. Hebrews 3:12-14
5. Galatians 5:19-21
6. Revelation 14:6, Matthew 24:14
7. II Thessalonians 2:9
8. Matthew 18:12

Chapter 35
1. Hebrews 11:5-13
2. Matthew 7:21-23
3. Hebrews 12:5-6
4. I John 1:10
5. I John 3:9
6. Hebrews 6:4-6
7. Proverbs 11:30
8. Revelation 3:10
9. Luke 22:31-32
10. Acts 6:8, 7:57-59
11. II Timothy 2:3-5, 7
12. Psalm 91:11-12

Chapter 36
1. Hebrews 3:7

2. Mark 16:17-18
3. Matthew 24:33
4. II Thess 2:3, Matthew 24:9-12
5. I John 2:26-27
6. Romans 1:20, Revelation 14:9-12

Chapter 37
1. Matthew 16:27
2. II Corinthians 5:10
3. I Corinthians 3:7-15
4. I Corinthians 3:15
5. John 5:28-29
6. Daniel 12:1-2
7. John 5:24
8. Matt 13:42, 22:13, 24:51, 25:30
9. Joel 2:30-31, Isaiah 13:9-11
10. Revelation 21:9-10
11. Revelation 20:11-15
12. Revelation 21:2-11
13. Matthew 24:50-51
14. Matthew 7:21
15. Matthew 22:12-13
16. Revelation 11:18, 19:7
17. II Corinthians 5:11
18. Hebrews 3:12, 14
19. Matthew 13:39
20. Matthew 13:43
21. Matthew 13:41-42
22. Matthew 7:21-23
23. I Corinthians 8:3
24. Matthew 7:21-22
25. John 4:14
26. Matthew 26:15
27. I Thessalonians 5:2-3
28. Hebrews 13:5
29. Matthew 10:32-33

Chapter 38
1. I John 5:7, John 1:1-11
2. Revelation 16:13
3. Revelation 19:20
4. Revelation 17:17
5. Revelation 6:12-14
6. Matthew 24:13, 21-22, 29-31
7. Matthew 24:15, Ezekiel 38:11
8. Joel 3:12-15, 2:28-32
9. Zechariah 14:2
10. Matthew 7:21
11. Matthew 7:22-23
12. Mark 11:25
13. John 15:13

Chapter 39
1. Revelation 6:12-13

2. Revelation 3:3, II Peter 3:10
3. Joel 3:12-15
4. Luke 21:36

Chapter 40
1. Isaiah 41:10
2. Revelation 13:17

Chapter 41
1. John 15:5-8
2. Matt 24:33, Mark 13:29, Luke 21:31
3. Romans 1:5-6
4. Matt 16:27, 2 Cor 5:10-11
5. Revelation 3:8

Chapter 42
1. Luke 21:25-28
2. Luke 21:31-32, 36
3. Matthew 24:27
4. Matthew 24:31, I Thess 3:12-13
5. I Corinthians 15:52
6. Jn 5:28-29, Dan 12:1-2, Mk 13:26-27
7. Revelation 14:11

8. I John 2:28
9. Isaiah 26:19
10. Revelation 7:14
11. Revelation 7:16-17
12. Revelation 7:2-3
13. II Peter 3:9
14. Galatians 5:19-21
15. I Samuel 15:22-23
16. II Peter 2:20-22

Chapter 43
1. Revelation 8:1
2. Matt 24:30-31, I Thess4:15-17
3. Luke 17:26-30, Gen 7:13, 19:22-25
4. Revelation 8:7
5. Revelation 8:8
6. Revelation 8:10
7. Matthew 24:21
8. Matthew 24:21-22, 29-31
9. Joel 2:1, II Peter 3:10-11
10. II Thessalonians 2:8
11. Revelation 11:15, 14:1-4
12. Revelation 13:16-18, 14:9-11

AUTHOR PROFILE

Paul Bortolazzo is devoted to teaching God's truth concerning the coming of the Lord Jesus Christ. This ministry offers a variety of outreaches including 'Til Eternity Conferences, End Time Seminars, College and Youth Presentations, and Bible Prophecy classes. If you would like more information about this prophetic ministry, please contact us. It would be a privilege to work with you by helping bring an end-times presentation to your church or area.

Paul Bortolazzo Ministries
PO Box 241915
Montgomery, Alabama 36124-1915

email:bortjenny@juno.com

www.paulbortolazzo.com

Please check out my website. This site was created to help empower the saints to overcome in these last days. It contains my books, teachings, radio shows, and YouTube's on the coming of the Lord.

.

'TIL ETERNITY

FACING THE CONSEQUENCES OF THE SECOND COMING

By Paul Bortolazzo

A non-fiction, student-friendly, chronological listing of the 70 Events coming before, during, and after the Coming of the Lord.

In this late hour, the love for the world is at an all time high. False teachers are turning many Christians away from the truth. Church leaders are refusing to judge between the righteous and the wicked; between those serving God and those who aren't. Such compromise will usher in the greatest persecution believers will ever experience. The only way to overcome will be through obedience to the Holy Spirit (Rev. 3:21-22).

'Til Eternity highlights the events coming before, during, and after the Second Coming of Christ. We will begin with the next event on God's end time calendar. After studying the last seventy events in order you will discover:
- *What events will warn His Coming is near?*
- *Who are the teachers deceiving so many?*
- *Where will His Coming end?*
- *When will the Great Tribulation be shortened?*
- *Why will the Beast overcome so many saints?*

Purchase online at Amazon, Barnes & Noble, and the author's website, in paperback, Kindle and eBook. Visit www.paulbortolazzo.com for links, prices, and more details.

Made in the USA
Charleston, SC
20 January 2012